and she called him

ROMEO

a paradise cove story

SANTANA BLAIR

Dedication

To dreams.
And to the young girl who loved words and often lost herself
in her own imaginary world.
She had a dream that one day she would share her stories
with the world.
This is for her...

Whatever our souls are made of,
his and mine are the same.
~ Emily Brontë

Prologue

September

He watched as she drew little flowers around her notes, her bottom lip drawn between her teeth, clenched in concentration. Ever since she walked into his class freshman year, he hadn't been able to keep his eyes off her. She had been a new student then, content to stay in the background of all the preexisting friendships among classmates who'd grown up in the close knit community of Paradise Cove.

He'd been captivated by her, and it had grown every day since.

In his eyes, Brooke Thomas was perfect. She always had been. She was so beautiful, it had begun to make him heartsick to know he hadn't been able to tell her so. But Brooke was far more than a pretty face. He'd fallen for a girl who was the epitome of beauty and brains—a complete package that tied his tongue into impossible knots. She stood out in her classes for all the right reasons. She was one of the most intelligent kids at Paradise Cove High, but never once did he see her make anyone else feel inferior. Yet, he still did. His grades were all right and he had enough self-awareness to know he looked pretty good. He felt like an okay guy. But being "all right," "decent," and "okay" wasn't enough—not for a girl like her.

If he ever got a chance with Brooke, he'd be so proud to show her off to any and every one. But he wanted to make sure she felt the same about him. He was going to earn this girl by showing her he could be amazing too. Basketball gave him an opportunity to do just that. On the court, the doubts and reservations faded into the background. He'd built himself a reputation. The media predictions calling him the next big thing came after every game, and the cheers grew louder with each passing season. He succeeded in catching the eye of every college with a top basketball program, but still hadn't managed to catch the interest of the girl he wanted more than anything.

He realized his miscalculation lay in thinking if Brooke saw him as a rising star, it would persuade her to give him a chance. If anything, it'd had the exact opposite effect. He had never seen Brooke at a pep rally, let alone a game. She didn't go to any of the parties his friends organized. He sat through too many school dances hoping to work up the courage to ask her to dance, only to leave disappointed when she didn't even make an appearance.

Quiet and reserved, Brooke was friendly enough to speak to everyone, but she didn't cross paths with the people in his circle. She spent most of her free periods in the art wing or designing sets for school plays. In class and the hallways were his only windows of opportunity to catch her eye, and those began to turn into daily reminders that his game plan was no match for Brooke.

Most people wouldn't understand why he panicked at the idea of failing to talk to her. His feelings for Brooke had gone unnoticed, probably because no one else in the school would expect the two of them to end up together. They wouldn't understand it, at least not at first. Truth be told, he didn't even know if Brooke would understand. But he couldn't worry about explaining it to anyone other than her, not when he was running out of time to get the girl of his dreams to even notice him.

This year was going to be the year that set the course for his future. He'd be under the microscopes of scouts and nearly everyone else. The entire school and community would be waiting for him to give them another winning season, adding to the trophy case serving as the pride and joy of the community.

Crazy as it may have seemed, none of that mattered more than the knowledge that this year would be the year he'd have to find the courage to make a bigger, bolder move. He didn't know if he'd ever get the chance he wanted with her, but he at least needed to have a real conversation with her.

When the first bell of the school year rang, the shot clock started. It was the fourth quarter—time to play the hardest. If he did, he might be able to get the win he so desperately wanted.

He just had to take the shot...

Because he would never forgive himself if he let her disappear from his life without at least trying.

Act I

SENIOR YEAR

~ Paradise Cove ~

Chapter 1

JAYSON

Jayson decided someone in the scheduling office this year must have been his guardian angel. For once, Brooke was in more than just one of his classes. He was going to take it as a sign.

Glancing to his right, he caught sight of her as she released her bottom lip from between her teeth. Reddened from the harsh attention, it sent a familiar stirring urge coursing through his system, causing him to wonder what that lip would feel like against his. In an instant, he was busy getting lost in his daydream watching her concentrated movements as she shaded the petals of the flowers she'd drawn on the pages of her ever-present sketchbook. He was so entranced, he hadn't noticed she'd turned her attention on him.

Caught, he had two options: he could look away and pretend he hadn't been checking her out, or he could smile at her. Scratch that, he only had one option. He smiled. Instead of the sweet smile he hoped for, the sweet smile she gave freely to everyone but him, he got the annoyed look she'd been giving him a lot recently. She turned back to her notebook, angling it purposefully away from his gaze.

If she thought that was going to stop him from looking, she was sorely mistaken. He was going to look until he figured out how to talk to her. Until then, he would enjoy the view...

Her creamy brown skin was practically flawless, only

spotted by flecks of paint or smudges of charcoal on her fingers from her incessant drawing. He wasn't sure if she knew about her rainbow beauty marks, but he loved spotting them on her.

She crossed her legs, drawing his attention further. Her jeans were torn at the knees, not in the overpriced designer way, but like a favorite pair of jeans worn into a comfortable state of disrepair. Paired with a simple white tee and a black blazer, she made them look effortlessly sophisticated.

She wasn't like the other girls some of his friends went for. She never wore makeup, and her brown hair was always pulled into a ponytail or some kind of bun. And if she was the kind of girl who went crazy in a shoe store, he wouldn't know because she always wore black Dr. Martens. She was amazing. He just needed to figure out how to tell her so.

As the bell rang and the class quickly packed up their things and rushed out, Jayson made sure he stayed far enough behind Brooke to remain unnoticed. He was very aware of the fact that he was becoming that creepy guy, but decided it was a fair trade-off to get as much information as he could so he could figure out what a girl like Brooke liked to talk about. His plan to be a silent observer disappeared when his best friend, Brian Moreau, caught up with him.

Brian and he had been best friends since the second day of kindergarten. They'd been teammates ever since they were old enough to join the youth league. When Jayson fell off the jungle gym in second grade and ended up needing stitches, Brian was in the exam room next to him because he'd promptly jumped off the same metal bars and broken his wrist. Over the years, situations may have changed, but the message was always the same: they'd catch each other, fall together, or break each other's fall. Up until Brooke, Jayson had always told Brian everything without exception.

Nowadays, Jayson told Brian *almost* everything.

He wasn't embarrassed by Brooke. That thought was the furthest thing from his mind. Maybe it was because if he kept it to himself, Brooke remained something special, only for him to think about. Maybe it was because he was embarrassed he'd been failing epically at getting to know her for the past three years. Whatever the reason, his best friend remained oblivious. As they walked the halls, Jayson only partially listened to Brian talk; the other part of his attention span was zoned in on the girl who had no idea how gorgeous she was. Brooke kept her head tucked down as she weaved through the hallway, eventually stopping at her locker where her friend Valerie waited for her.

Jayson only looked back once as he continued walking.

Brooke

Brooke could feel him watching her.

She could easily conjure up the image of that intense gaze since she was beginning to know it well, but she fought the urge to look back at him. Instead, she focused on her steps, clutching her books to her chest. She didn't know what Jayson Williams was trying to do, but she didn't want any part of it. He wasn't just Jayson, he was *Jayson, the school's golden boy and star varsity athlete,* all kinds of gorgeous and popular. She was just Brooke, and being just Brooke was completely okay with her.

Whatever Jayson wanted, she didn't care to know. She was too smart to be fooled into accepting the smiles he gave her. She had promised herself she wouldn't be distracted by his tall, athletic build, soft, intoxicating green eyes against his coffee and milk complexion, his dimpled smile, or the charming personality that won everyone over—everyone except her.

She wanted nothing to do with him.

This year, she was going to remain focused on maintaining her grade point average at any and all cost. Boys would be a distraction. She didn't date. She was too busy to become one of those girls consumed by boyfriend drama. The same drama that loudly dominated the school hallways and fed the rumor mill. She was happy with being who she was, with going unnoticed. Most of their grade didn't really bother her, minus the occasional bribe to do their last-minute assignments. That they all called her "the smart girl" more than they used her actual name didn't bother her. Or that she stayed off their invite list for weekend plans.

But then Jayson had to go and change that.

She still caught herself pondering his motives. *Why did he look at her like that? Why did he smile at her when the rest of his friends didn't even pay attention to her?* The one question she wondered that most was the one that made her stomach churn with nervousness. *What did he see when he looked at her?* She thought of her own image. Her brown skin was usually makeup free with the exception of the slight lip balm addiction she had. She kept her thick brown hair pulled back into a bun away from her face. She dressed her average five-foot six-inch frame nicely, but casually. She never gave her body too much over thought. It was something she never really saw the point in doing.

She was plain old Brooke Thomas—and that was just fine by her.

As Brooke opened her locker, Valerie mentioned Jayson had been following her again.

Brooke shrugged, hoping her nonchalance would put a quick end to the conversation.

"What's your point?"

Valerie rolled her eyes. "My point is he likes you!"

"Yeah, right. I don't know what his agenda is, but I do know Jayson doesn't like me. He could have any girl in this school—actually, let's amend that, he could have any girl he wanted period, I seriously doubt he'd be chasing me when Marisa Coates is probably throwing herself at him as we speak."

Valerie shook her head. "He could have any girl, huh? Well... how come Jayson hasn't had any of them? He's notoriously single and nobody knows why... except me. He likes you. He could barely take his eyes off of you when he passed by. I don't have to remind you he does this *every day*."

"Maybe he's checking you out, Val."

"Don't deflect. He likes you. I know these things. I'm Asian. My people have a reputation for being geniuses."

Brooke couldn't suppress her smirk. "So we're reinforcing a stereotype today? Should I point out you're only half Asian."

"So I'm at least half-genius."

"Maybe you're just half-insane."

Val blew a stray lock of black hair out of her eyes. "You don't have to admit it if you don't want to, but it's the truth. I'm your best friend. I wouldn't make something like this up."

Brooke paused and drew in a breath. Val had just said the one thing Brooke was afraid to think about, let alone admit. *What if he did?*

"And, for the record, you blow Marisa out of the water on your worst day!"

Brooke shut her locker and found her smile again. "Now I know you're fully crazy! I'm going to be late. I'll meet up with you later."

Valerie gave her a knowing look and yelled after her, "I'm Asian!"

Brooke couldn't stop the laughter that bubbled forth as she turned toward the stairwell. Valerie. Best Friend. Soul Mate. *Sister from another mister.* The girl had been a godsend to Brooke's life. Always a bit too quiet and happily independent, she had never quite mastered the art of making friends. When her mother's job moved them to Paradise Cove, a smallish but incredibly beautiful Oceanside town in Southern California, she hadn't expected to make any friends right away. She'd kept to herself the first few weeks, until her name had been called to pair up with the girl with the bright pink stripes in her otherwise jet black hair, better known as Valerie Lee. Valerie's mother was Puerto Rican and her father was Chinese Filipino, but Valerie was one hundred percent her own unique, authentic self, and Brooke loved her for it.

Their friendship naturally developed into something

Brooke truly cherished. At times, they couldn't have been more different, while other times, they were practically one soul. Where Brooke was quiet, Valerie was loud. When Val was daring the world, Brooke kept her grounded. If Brooke tried to hide in her comfort zone, Val redrew the lines.

Three years ago, Valerie Lee had swooped into her life and changed it for the better.

She breezed through the doorway of her favorite room in the school and quickly grabbed her materials as she headed to her corner spot by the window. The view of the courtyard and the sparkling waters just beyond it always help to ignite her creative spark. She was already pulling out the well-worn, oversized, button-down dress shirt she used as her art smock when Ms. Cullen strolled into the classroom with a smile.

Since Brooke had transferred over to PCH, Ms. Cullen had helped transform her art hobby into her passion, constantly challenging Brooke's talent and ability to create without restraint.

It was proving easier said than done.

"Use your emotions," Ms. Cullen had said. "Paint with your heart, not your head."

Brooke knew she was right. Truthfully, she had known all along. She just had no clue how to fix it. It was good she had the next few months to figure it out. Brooke had been handed a syllabus at the start of the semester and given free rein in hopes to create an impressive portfolio. While other students worked on more basic projects, Ms. Cullen had told her to use the class time to work freely, handing in the projects assigned when completed. Brooke had been given a goal, time, and the materials to accomplish it. As she set up her easel, she attempted to quiet her mind, trying to determine just how she was supposed to let go.

JAYSON

Jayson usually looked forward to lunch knowing he would get to see Brooke again, but when he showed up in the cafeteria today, she didn't. Disappointed, he took his usual seat with his teammates and listened to them talk about the same things they talked about every day: girls and basketball. Fortunately, at the moment, they were all content to talk about the upcoming season.

"I heard Coach is going to try out Griffin on Varsity," Hendricks said around the large bite of burger in his mouth.

Jayson nodded. "Wouldn't surprise me. Griffin's paid his dues on JV the last three years. He's definitely improved. I played a few pick-up games with him over the summer. He's a hustler on the court, real fast and makes smart, on-the-spot decisions. He'd be a great sixth man. I'd like to see how he works with us."

"All I know is this season needs to be even better than last season, and that means we are going to have to put in a lot more work in practice and on our own." Brian pointed his water bottle at all of them. "I want to graduate with another state trophy and go out as the best."

"You and me both." He bumped fists with his friend.

A grin overtook Brian's face. "Since we have a few weeks until it gets serious, I say we party hard in the meantime."

"Um... no."

"Um... yes. Come on, Jayson! It's senior year. This year was made for us to have some fun!"

Jayson shook his head. "You said the same thing last year. Besides, I'm pretty sure partying every weekend would erase the line between fun and trouble. I need to focus this year."

"Whatever, bro. You say that every year, and every year you go out there and dominate. I'll tell you what, come to my house this Saturday. We'll throw some food on the grill... get some girls in the pool... you can focus on that."

"I'm in!" Hendricks enthusiastically offered.

"I'm out." Jayson stood, collecting his things. "I'll catch up with you later, B."

He hurried off to see if he could make it to English class early, leaving his friends grumbling about his lack of party animal spirit. Just as he had suspected he would, he spotted Brooke sitting in the empty room, hunched over her sketchpad, ear buds in her ears. Her forehead was wrinkled in concentration as she elaborated on the drawing. He leaned over to get a better view. It was a letter B intertwined with vines full of beautiful blossoms and thorns. It was intricate and a transformation that could only be described as...

"Beautiful..." His heart flipped when he realized he'd actually spoken to her.

She quickly turned and looked at him, pulling her ear buds out of her ears in one furious tug. Her chocolate brown eyes were as wide as saucers. "Excuse me?"

"The picture. It's beautiful. You're really good."

Brooke stared for a moment, then turned away, muttering a quick and quiet thanks just before she turned to a fresh page in her journal.

He racked his brain, trying to find something great to say—anything that would keep them talking—but he couldn't think fast enough before their English teacher, Mr. Phillips, walked in and asked to speak with him after school. He already knew what was coming, and it was the worst possible timing with Brooke in the room. For the first time in years, he wished she hadn't been in his class.

It was as if his thought conjured up her attention. Brooke looked up at him, her eyes narrowing into something akin to curiosity. He couldn't bear to imagine what she may have either overheard or assumed. Her gaze was too much for him. He averted his face and slipped into his seat, keeping his eyes fixed on his notebook for the rest of class.

Unable to prolong the meeting any longer, he waited a few minutes after the last bell rang before making his way back down to the English wing. When he walked through the open doorway to Mr. Phillips' room, he came face to solemn face with not only his teacher, but his guidance counselor, Mr. Rhoades, and basketball coach, Coach Beckett.

This was getting really serious, really fast.

"Have a seat, Jayson," Coach Beckett said warmly, yet the concern was visible in his eyes.

Jayson slid into the first desk he came to. *Brooke's.*

"We called you in because we need to talk. It's still early into the school year, but after adding in last week's test, your grades are dangerously low. If it continues it would put you at risk for academic probation before basketball season even starts."

"In addition, we need you to raise your SAT scores. This is a big year for you. We've planned on it happening the past three years with your eligibility to play for the division one schools. Now is the time to make sure everything is set up for you to have the best choices available for you," Mr. Rhoades added.

He didn't need to hear anymore. Academic probation would mean his position on the team would be jeopardized. If he couldn't play, scouts wouldn't see him and his college plans would be ruined.

"What do I have to do?"

"Look, we know you, we know your situation, and we'll do anything we can to help you and your mom." Coach Beckett placed a hand on Jayson's shoulder. He had been a father figure to Jayson, the last thing he wanted was to disappoint him.

"The ideal would be to have you maintain no less than a B average in all your classes."

Mr. Phillips cleared his throat. "If you can bring up your test scores for English to the A range, that should help your GPA phenomenally. Let's all work together to help you get out of this danger zone."

"We're catching the trouble early so you can have the best senior year possible," Mr. Rhoades added.

Jayson nodded. "I'll fix it. You have my word."

"I know you will. You give any of us a call if you need help or guidance. We're all on your team, Jayson."

"I know, Coach."

For the rest of the day, Jayson was distracted and moody. But it was only after he had repeatedly snapped at his younger brother, Jayden, as they played a game of ball in their driveway that Brian called him out on it.

"Jay, what's up with you today?"

"Nothing." He shook his head and took a drink of water before tossing the bottle across the driveway into the recycling bin.

"I'm your best friend. I know something is going on with you. You've been way too distracted. Is it a girl?"

"Yes. No."

"Ha! I knew it. It's Marisa, right? She's been telling everyone she likes you—"

Jayson cut him off. "Definitely not."

Brian seemed to be searching his mind before a slow grin overtook his face. "So, are you finally ready to talk about Brooke?"

He felt the full weight of the simple question settle in as his best friend stood there doing his best impersonation of the Cheshire Cat. "How long have you known?"

"A while… I should be insulted you didn't tell me yourself. You must not think much of my role as best friend if you believed I wouldn't pick up on it. Instead of calling you out, I decided to have some fun with you until you broke down and came clean."

"Do you think everyone knows?"

"Can't say for sure. It could just mean my best friend skills are slightly above average," he teased.

"It was a little surprising at first. But now I can see the appeal. She's real cute and has a nice body too. A sexy, smart type. I wonder if she wears glasses."

Jayson pressed the heels of his palms into his eyes. "Please shut up or I may be forced to injure you."

Brian laughed. "Calm down! I'm messing with you. I guess this crush is a bit strong, huh?"

Jayson had already come this far, he supposed it was time for some full disclosure.

"She's everything I want in one really nice package, Bri. But she doesn't even take me seriously. If I asked her the time, she'd probably look at me like I was the dumbest guy in the world. Maybe she's right. Maybe I'm just a dumb jock. I'm on the verge of failing English already. She's too good for me."

"What are you talking about? You're far from dumb. Your grades slipped. It happens. Just do whatever it takes to bring them back up and enjoy thinking about college next year."

With a friendly shove, Brian left him to mull over things as he rejoined the game.

For hours, he couldn't seem to quiet his racing mind. He didn't know how to tell his mom about his lackluster school performance. She'd always worked hard to make their lives easier, he didn't need to go and make it harder for her. The way their lives were scheduled meant whatever time he had after school, games, and practices, he was usually on little brother duty. He had no other choice but to figure something out. After Jayson washed the dishes and got his three youngest brothers into bed, he made sure Jayden was doing his homework and not talking to some girl on the phone before he went downstairs.

Coming up with a plan he hoped was brilliant, he decided to throw out a prayer. He would need all the help he could summon if he was going to pull this one off. He refused to be a failure, especially at this. Holding his breath, he picked up his cell phone to send an email to his coach, Mr. Phillips, and Mr. Rhodes. They all seemed to love his solution, and he felt half of his anxiety leave. Now, he just had to work out all the details so the rest could go away.

Brooke

Valerie followed Brooke into the kitchen. They were supposed to be studying for their chemistry test, but needed a break. Brooke opened the pantry and pulled out a new bag of tortilla chips. Her mother kept them stocked with all their favorite study foods, and Val clasped her hands over her chest in a playful prayer of thanksgiving.

"Salsa or queso?" Brooke held up a jar of each.

"Um... is that seriously a question?"

Brooke laughed as she placed both on the counter, leaving Val to open them as she went to find them bowls. Trying her best to casually clear her throat, she used the search to avoid her friend's eyes. "So... Jayson told me my sketch was beautiful today..."

"Stop, drop, repeat, and elaborate!"

"Nothing to elaborate. Before English class, he happened to see my sketchbook and told me the sketch was beautiful."

Valerie reacted the way Brooke had expected. She abandoned the jars as she hopped off the counter to do her signature happy dance—a funky mix of something resembling an Irish jig, tap dancing, and a few pelvic thrusts thrown in for good measure.

"I told you so!"

"What exactly did you tell me?"

"That he is so into you! Come on, Brooke. He notices you for a reason. Do you need me to tell you the reasons? Sometimes when a boy becomes a man, his body goes through very special changes..."

"Val. Stop. Maybe he just has good taste in art?"

"Mark my words, Brookie Boo, the boy has good taste in women. He, without a doubt, likes you."

Val did a happy little skip past her as she grabbed them two bottles of water.

"Good googly moogly, he's so freakin' hot too. I'm proud of you. My bestie went and got herself a boo."

"I did not. Stop saying that." Brooke filled the bowls, hoping her friend wouldn't notice she was flustered beyond belief just hearing the words "Jayson" and "boo" being in the same sentence as her name.

Val tossed her a bottle of water. "At least you didn't deny he's cute."

Because I'm not blind.

Brooke raised an eyebrow in frustration. "Why do I let you come over here, eat all my food, and drive me crazy?"

"Because I am the greatest best friend in the history of all best friends, you love me, and I'm going to babysit all the gorgeous bambinos you'll make with Jayson 'hottie with the body' Williams."

Valerie punctuated her assertions with a series of jerky pelvic thrusts.

"Valerie!" Brooke tossed the bag of chips into her friend's arms and grabbed the tray as she herded them back up the stairs.

Chapter 2

Brooke

Jayson made absolutely no effort to look away from her despite her giving him her best annoyed glare. With Val's singsong taunts playing on a constant loop in her mind, everything about class that day was unnerving her. She had never wished for the power of invisibility as much as she did now. But alas, she was stuck in her simple black t-shirt and jeans, watching the clock, diligently waiting for the bell to ring and give her the permission to run and hide from his green eyes.

"Hey, Brooke."

Great. Now he was talking to her. Her plan for him to give up on seeking her attention was fading into the background. If she were a rude person, she could have ignored him. But she wasn't rude... just perturbed by his attention. She gave him a quizzical glance and murmured a quiet hello before packing up her bag to head to the door, thankful for the ability to tuck away in the art room and recollect her wits before their next class together.

Brooke's mind was still on art when she arrived to English ten minutes early as usual. She'd skipped the cafeteria opting to eat in the art room while she began to paint one of her recent sketches. She'd hoped painting anything would re-inspire her to create something new and fresh. Artist's block sucked.

She shook her head in frustration as she pulled open the door to class, only to freeze when she realized Jayson was already there with Mr. Phillips and Mr. Rhoades. She stammered over an apology and began to back out.

"Wait, Ms. Thomas. We were actually just discussing you."

Brooke's eyes widened as she shot Jayson a look before stepping back into the classroom.

"As one of the school's best students, I was wondering if you'd be willing to help Mr. Williams out."

"How so?" She hoped her nerves weren't showing. She could be aloof as long as she didn't have to actually interact with him.

"As a peer tutor. I'd try to arrange some class time for you both, but much of the work will have to be arranged between the two of you and your own personal schedules. You can count any time toward your senior year community service requirement," Mr. Phillips explained.

"In addition to helping Jayson with English, if you'd be willing to help him with any other common classes you have and SAT prep that would be great." Mr. Rhoades added.

Brooke had already started chewing on her bottom lip at the mention of tutoring. She desperately needed to fill those service hours, but the thought of spending them alone with Jayson made her nervous. Against her better judgment, she looked over at him.

"I'd really appreciate any help you can provide. I'm a hard worker. Please help me?"

A quick nod of her head later, Brooke couldn't believe what she had agreed to.

Why couldn't she just say no to his dimpled smile and sparkling green eyes?

Jayson Williams and his stupid dimples.

Valerie was going to have a field day with this. She sat at her desk and squeezed her eyelids shut. It didn't help. She could feel his ever-watching eyes. Jayson hadn't stopped smiling since Brooke said yes, and now she had to speak to him before the rest of the class filled in, bringing on an audience.

"When do you want to get started?"

Jayson shrugged. "Whenever. The sooner, the better."

"Well... you tell me. I'm sure basketball ties up your schedule a bit..."

She was sure he had heard the sarcasm in her voice, but his smile was proof he ignored it. "The season hasn't actually started yet. How about tonight?"

"Fine. Where?"

"Uh, the library downtown is open evenings, or we could meet at my house."

She held up a hand. "Let's just stick to the library."

A small smile played on his lips. "Whatever you say, Brooke. I'll see you around five then?"

"That's fine."

"Brooke?"

"What?" She failed to keep the edge out of her tone.

"You have some red paint on your nose."

With a groan, she dropped her head to her arms on her desk. This was going to be awful.

JAYSON

Jayson paced by the front door. He couldn't believe this was happening to him. Today, of all days, the babysitter was late. Worse yet, he didn't even have Brooke's number to call her to let her know, and she struck him as the type who would not wait around if she felt like he was blowing her off. She needed to know he was taking this seriously. Jayson kicked his backpack in frustration. He couldn't blow this opportunity. He needed her help, and he needed her to get to know him.

She looked beautifully furious with her arms crossed as he sprinted toward her. The clock read half past six, and she had started packing up her stuff.

"Brooke, please don't leave."

"You have wasted an hour and a half of my time. Just because I'm not a jock or a queen bee social wannabe doesn't mean I don't have a life!"

He reached out to touch her arm, stopping himself when she stepped away and side-eyed the gesture.

"Brooke, I'm truly sorry. I didn't have your number to call you and explain. I ran full speed all the way here. Please stay."

Her face remained stoic, but she silently lowered herself back to sit in her chair. Jayson sat quickly as well. He didn't want to waste anymore time or risk pissing her off again. He pulled out his books right away as she opened her notebook.

First, she helped him work through that night's general assignment before she moved onto the bigger reading assignment.

"So, Romeo and Juliet. We read the first scene in class today, do you have any questions about it so far?"

"All I have are questions. I still have no idea what's going on."

"We have a few minutes left. Why don't we reread it quickly and break it down? Before we start, what do you know about them?"

"They were teenagers who fell in love and then they died."

"Well, yeah, but there's a bit more to it than that."

"It's the way they speak! I can barely figure out what they're talking about half the time."

"Let's break it down. Shakespeare didn't come up with this original concept. Before Romeo and Juliet, there was the story of two ill-fated lovers named Pyramus and Thisbe written by Ovid. In Shakespeare's story, the lovers are in Verona, Italy, and both are young members of feuding families. The feud's gotten so bad, the prince forbade them to fight in public. Anyone who does will be killed."

"Sounds intense."

"Juliet is thirteen. There's this guy, Paris, who wants to marry her, but she doesn't want to..."

"That's understandable. She's only thirteen. I wasn't ready for a lifetime commitment until I was fourteen and a half."

She pursed her lips, fighting her smile. "Meanwhile, Romeo is infatuated with a girl named Rosaline. He decides to sneak into a rival family's party to see her. The party was hosted by a Capulet..."

"Juliet's family?"

"Right! So, Romeo sneaks into this party for Rosaline, but once he sees Juliet..."

"Bye, Rosaline. Hell-o, Juliet."

"Let's reread the beginning now."

He'd managed to get through the first few scenes with actual comprehension of what was going on. Even more than that, he was surprised to realize he was looking forward to reading what happened next.

Together, they packed up and walked out.

"My mom's over there." Brooke pointed to the waiting car along the curb.

"Oh, good. Well... I'll see you tomorrow. Thanks for everything."

She handed him a piece of paper. "Here's my cell number and email, just in case. Do you want a ride home?"

He'd love to be near her a bit longer, but shook his head. "I'll walk. I need the exercise."

Her mouth opened quickly before she snapped it shut and gave him a quick nod. As she turned and walked away, he wondered what she'd stopped herself from saying. The thought was only forgotten when he remembered something far more important.

He finally had Brooke's phone number.

Chapter 3

Brooke

"I don't like Tybalt."

Brooke whipped around to find Jayson leaning on the locker across the hallway from her, his brow furrowed.

"I'm sorry?" She couldn't help but tilt her head in amusement.

"Seriously, what's the dude's deal?"

"He's defending his family's honor."

"He has issues. I mean, who picks on Benvolio?"

"Um, Tybalt?" He'd been reading ahead of their sessions. The surprise tied her tongue in knots. She sat there doing her best impression of a goldfish while he ranted on.

"Tybalt does! Then he puts himself all in Juliet's business."

Brooke decided to try to reason with him. "She's his younger cousin and Romeo is a romantic flip-flop. He could be protecting her honor and her heart."

"I'm sorry, but if Juliet is old enough to marry Paris, then she's old enough to decide who she wants to dance with at a party."

Her mouth opened and closed several times before he let out a long exhale.

"I have to head to class now, but I had to get that off my chest. I'll see you later, Brooke."

"See ya, Jayson."

She watched him walk away, leaving her baffled by what had just transpired.

Unknown: I've been thinking about what you said.

Brooke: Who is this?

Unknown: Jayson Williams.

Holy mother of... he was actually texting her! Sure, she'd given him her phone number, but that had been almost two weeks ago. Pulling the ear bud out of her ear, she sat up in her bed and checked the time. It was almost midnight. *Did this constitute as booty call hours? Was this a booty call... err, text? How dare he!* Her phone buzzed again.

Jayson: Did I wake you up?

It was nearly midnight and she was on his mind. The heat spread from her face to the rest of her body. She shook her head as if the action would clear her mind from the swarming thoughts threatening to turn her into a character from a primetime teen melodrama. Still, the very idea of a text from Jayson gave her an undeniable thrill of excitement. Or maybe it was giddiness? She'd have to figure that out later. First up, she needed to know why he was texting her near midnight.

Brooke: No, I was up. Just listening to music. So, what did I say?

Jayson: When we first started reading Romeo and Juliet, you said Romeo was a typical guy. That he was so in love with Rosaline, then saw Juliet and completely changed his mind and moved on.

Brooke: "Young men's love lies not truly in their hearts, but in their eyes."

Brooke: Romeo was vapid and noncommittal. Totally thinking with his "little Romeo."

Really, Brooke! She face-palmed herself and let out a chagrined groan at sending the message before she could edit out her lame penis reference.

> *Jayson:* You see, that's where I disagree. What if he thought what he felt for Rosaline was the real deal, but when he laid eyes on Juliet, he realized he didn't have a clue before her?

> *Brooke:* So, you're saying it was love at first sight? Is that even possible?

> *Jayson:* Maybe it's destiny. Maybe it's happenstance. But it's something...

> *Brooke:* I'm listening...

> *Jayson:* I mean, what if he had never even seen Rosaline? If there was no Rosaline, there would be no Romeo and Juliet. If he didn't show up at that party, he might have missed out on meeting the love of his life. I don't know about love at first sight, but I think if you saw the person you thought could possibly be THE ONE, you're going to have some type of feeling. At least he acted on it and told her how he felt.

She sat up in bed. This guy...

> *Brooke:* Hmmm... interesting perspective.

> *Jayson:* Sure, he forgot about Rosaline pretty fast, but when you find THE ONE, everyone else doesn't matter anymore. All you see is her, whether she's standing in front of you, across a room at a party, on a balcony, or walking into a classroom. Even when she's not there, she's still the only one who matters.

Stunned, she stared at her phone until it buzzed again.

Jayson: That's all I wanted to say. Sleep tight, Brooke.

Brooke: Night, Jayson.

Brooke arrived at the coffee house first. They had made plans to study at the small café instead of the library this time, and if she was being honest, it made her feel a bit more nervous. Studying at the library allowed her to keep their interaction as strictly business. Meeting at the café felt a lot more intimate. It was something she would do with Val or a date... The thought alone made her blush with embarrassment.

She picked out a small table in the corner to provide them with enough space to spread out their books. She was just opening up to the review points she had written in preparation for this afternoon when he stepped through the door. His green baseball cap was easily recognizable above the heads of everyone else in the shop, his beaming smile directed her way.

"Am I late?" He gave her a teasing wink.

Her eyes were rolling before she could stop herself. "No. I just got here a few minutes ago."

"Good. I'll grab us some drinks before we get started. Do you want a coffee?" He dropped his backpack on his chair and spun his cap backwards on his head. It was a habit of his that gave her an unobstructed view of his eyes. The green was unlike any other pair she had seen, captivating soft portals to his soul that fascinated her more and more each time she saw them. She forced herself to look away and actually respond.

"I'm not much of a coffee drinker. I'll take a chai tea latte, though—no whip." She was pulling out her wallet when he waved it away.

"Keep your wallet in your bag. It's my treat."

He left no room for argument as he walked away. When he returned, he had not only their drinks, but a plate full of brownies.

"I came straight from working out, so I'm famished. I brought some extra brownies so we could share."

"Thanks for the thought, but I'm good."

"Are you really passing up brownies? Are you not much of a chocolate eater either?"

She felt a smile slip through. "Hardly. I'm very much a chocolate lover, but when it comes to brownies, I'm pretty particular. I've had the best, and now all the others just won't do."

"The best? That sounds like something I need to experience."

"I know a girl. Maybe I can work something out for you," she teased back.

He leaned forward in his seat, the beautiful natural tan skin of his forearms catching her eye as the muscles shifted and rippled just below the skin. Everything about him was throwing her off her game and she was struggling to keep a firm grip on reality. Clearing her throat, she opened her notebook and put them back into business mode.

No more dimpled deviations.

JAYSON

"Have you started working on the Romeo and Juliet paper yet? If you need an extra help on the theme or outline, we can squeeze in a few extra sessions."

Brooke stretched her fingers as she dropped her pen onto the notebook.

It was a habit he'd come to notice the more he spent up-close and personal time with her. Every time she did it, he had to fight the urge to reach out and take hold of her. He wanted to intertwine their fingers, feel her palm against his, fill each other's empty spaces in the subtle yet intimate gesture.

"I'm just about finished with it, but maybe I'll email it over before I hand it in."

"Look at you over achieving. I haven't even started yet." She gave him a flash of a teasing smile before she turned back to pack her books into her bag.

They had been meeting at least three times a week for the last month, and Jayson had started seeing a positive effect on his grades almost immediately. Tonight, they had just finished a late study session for a big test the next day. If he had thought texting her would get her to open up to him, he had been wrong. No matter what he tried, he still hadn't gotten her to drop her guard around him. Every time he'd get her to be a little friendly or even joke around with him, she'd catch herself, forcing their study sessions to remain business transaction. Aside from a couple of times she'd slip into a smile, she didn't deviate from the topic at hand and every offer to socialize outside their study sessions was turned down swiftly.

This particular night, as they both walked out of the library together, he decided to ask her again anyway.

"I borrowed some film and play versions of Romeo and Juliet, I was wondering if you'd want to come over on Saturday and watch them with me?"

"I can't, but I hope you enjoy them."

Jayson stopped her.

"Why don't you like me, Brooke?"

She shook her head. "I don't even know you. Not really anyway."

"Get to know me then."

"What are you trying to pull here?" Brooke shot back defensively.

"Nothing! I'm being serious. I just want you to give me a chance. Please?"

"Look, Jayson, it's late. I have to walk home tonight."

He nodded. "Yeah, I know. Maybe I could walk you home? I can make sure you get there safe and you can start to get to know me. That's like a two-for-one packaged deal."

He could see the moment her resistance cracked.

She smiled. "You are persistent."

"My mom would've chosen the word stubborn. I like to think of myself as dedicated..."

"Or exasperating." Brooke laughed.

"Unyielding, relentless, adamant, or even tenacious, but usually only when I want something badly." He fixed his eyes on her, and she instantly looked away.

"Someone has been practicing SAT vocabulary."

"I follow my tutor's orders. So, am I walking you home or walking behind you? Either way, I have to make sure you get home safely."

Brooke went to work on her bottom lip, which Jayson now realized meant she was nervous.

"Yes. You can walk me home, but only because I don't want to get kidnapped."

"Smart decision." Jayson nodded, and they began their walk in silence. After all his work to convince her, he suddenly felt panicked. He had no clue what to talk about, so he was grateful when Brooke broke the silence.

"So, I hear basketball season is officially in effect."

"Yeah, I'm excited. We started practices and had our JV-Varsity scrimmage."

She tucked her hands into her jacket pockets and looked up at him, her brown eyes fixing on his. "Ah, okay. I heard something of the sort. When did you start playing basketball?"

"My dad put a ball in my hand when I was about two or three years old, and I didn't stand a chance. I fell in love with the sport, and it turned out I was pretty good at it too. I'm not the most confident person, contrary to what people may think about me." He swallowed around the lump of nerves bundled in his throat. Brooke's eyes widened in awareness, but her lips stayed shut, almost in silent encouragement to keep going. "No matter how I feel off the court, the moment I step out on the hard maple floors, I'm free of any insecurity. For those four quarters, I'm the most confident version of myself. Sometimes, especially lately, I wonder if I do it well because I love it, or if I love it because I do it well."

Her lips curled into a small smile. "That's a pretty deep question. Will you let me know when you figure it out?"

He returned her smile with a nod. "When I figure it out, I

promise you'll be the first to know."

They held each other's gazes for a long moment. Jayson felt the electricity passing between them, and for the first time since he'd began his quest to get to know her, he felt a strong sense of hope—hope she was feeling the same thing he was. Brooke looked away first and cleared her throat before steering the conversation back into safer waters.

"You're the team captain, right?"

He nodded. "I haven't seen you at any games."

"There's actually a really great reason for that."

"What would that be?"

"I've never been to any of the games."

He clutched his heart. "You're killing me, Brooke."

"I don't know much about the game, and I'm not really a rah-rah type of girl."

He laughed. "You should come to a game anyway. You might not be the rah-rah type, but you might find you enjoy it."

She shrugged. "Maybe."

"So, you know how I started with basketball, but what about you? How long have you been into art?"

She shrugged again. "I guess it's always been there as an outlet, but I only got serious a few years back. When we moved here, my art was my only friend for a while. Then it became so much more. Now it's just about all I ever want to do when I'm awake."

"You're really good."

"I lack passion or emotion in my art. At least... that's what I keep hearing. But I can't seem to get past this block to let me get my emotions on paper or canvas."

"You will. You just need inspiration."

"If it were only that easy."

Acting on instinct, Jayson put his hand on her hip and steered her clear of the approaching passersby.

She felt perfect under his touch. It was everything, yet wasn't nearly enough. If he was able to, he would have paused time to keep them in the moment. He wanted more time to memorize the curve of her waist against the palm of his hand. He wanted more time to pull her into him farther to see what it would be like to wrap his arms around her and just hold her. Remembering he couldn't, he quickly pulled his hand away, leaving them to walk on in silence as he pretended he didn't see her lip caught tightly between her teeth.

Coming to a stop in front of the small, two-story, colonial-style house with a gable roof and swing on the front porch she called home, she finally let her lip free and looked up into his eyes again.

"Well... this is my stop."

Already? He should have walked slower... or faked a leg cramp.

"Thanks for walking me home, Jayson. I appreciate it." She offered him a tentative, warm smile.

"Anytime. Thanks for the help as always."

Brooke dipped her head as she turned to walk up the porch steps just before whirling back around to face him. "Hey, Jayson?"

Her mouth opened and closed several times. Her apparent struggle to find the right words was telling. He desperately wanted to hear what it was that had her so worried, watching as she replaced the fear with a smile.

"Get home safely."

He focused his eyes on hers. "I will. Goodnight, Brooke."

Brooke

The next morning, she awoke with a fresh determination and a vision. Pulling her hair up into a messy bun she hit the power button on her IPod dock and let the music fill the air before she put her brush to the canvas. For hours, she painted and painted, feeling more driven and focused than she had been in months. The smile on her face was almost a constant even as she concentrated on blending life into the color splashed creation.

> *Jayson:* Just in case you haven't watched the Romeo and Juliet movie with DiCaprio... don't.

She laughed. Putting down her brush for the first time since she started, she took a seat on the paint-splattered floor of her small art room. She'd wondered if she'd hear from him over the weekend, and seeing his name pop up on her screen sent her mind into overdrive as she turned over all the details from their conversation on the walk home.

> *Brooke:* That bad, huh?

> *Jayson:* I'm not a fan. I still have one more to go. Sure you don't want to join me? I have a lot of popcorn, soda, and free critical commentary.

She thought about it for longer than she'd ever considered any of his offers. He was surprising her with his enthusiasm for Romeo and Juliet. A big part of her wanted to see him enjoying it; a bigger part worried about spending even more time with him.

> *Brooke:* Can't. Thanks for the offer.

> *Jayson:* Oh, okay. I understand.

For some reason, she had a moment of fear that something... whatever it was... was going to be ruined between them. Before she could stop herself, she sent another message.

> *Brooke:* I just need to do some painting today. Let me know how you like the last one, though!

> *Jayson:* Of course.

Brooke spent all weekend in that small room, only leaving to eat and use the bathroom. By the time Sunday night fell, she collapsed into bed, satisfied with the nearly-done canvas drying in the other room, but even as her tired body begged for sleep, she still lay there thinking of Jayson. It wasn't the first time he had occupied her thoughts since their tutoring sessions began, and ever since he walked her home, it seemed as if her brain had three thought processes: Jayson, art, painting Jayson. It was like he had worked his way under her skin and she couldn't manage to do anything without him creeping into her thoughts and sketches.

When he had told her the reason behind playing basketball, it had surprised her. He had come across as vulnerable and genuine. Even more surprising, she had known exactly what he meant. He had put words to some of her most recent thoughts, and by doing so, he had dominated every thought she'd had since. She kept telling herself she couldn't like him, that it wouldn't be good. That was all fine in theory, but in reality, not so much. The problem was, the more she told herself she couldn't, the more butterflies she felt every time she thought about what would happen if she did.

Chapter 4

JAYSON

When Brooke had texted to invite him to her house for the day's SATs' cram session, he had done his best not to fist pump in the middle of the hallway. Instead, he kept his composure until he made it into the gym's locker room that afternoon. He was counting every little bit of positive interaction with Brooke as a giant leap of progress. He'd been slowly chipping away at her exterior, determined to see the secret person of her heart. Every pure glimpse of her smile made him want to know all the things that put that smile on her face so he could keep it there. He was hoping spending time with her in her home would allow her to be her most comfortable with him.

He had stopped by the coffee shop on the way over and picked up drinks, but still arrived on her doorstep fifteen minutes early. More eager to see her than embarrassed, he knocked heartily. The woman who answered the door had a warm, welcoming smile.

"You must be Jayson. I'm Evelyn, Brooke's mom."

"It's nice to meet you Mrs. Thomas. I hope it's okay that I'm a bit early. I'm sure Brooke wasn't expecting me quite yet."

"Nonsense. Come on in and put your stuff down." She ushered him into the house and took the tray of drinks from him as he put his bag down. "Aren't you sweet?! I'll just put these in the kitchen for you both. Brooke is in her art room. Just head up the stairs and it's the second door on your left. She always has the music going loud when she's working on a piece, so I'm sure she didn't hear you come in."

Jayson smiled his appreciation as he made his way to the second floor. Step after step, he followed the bass of the familiar classic rap song, halting only when he realized she was rapping along. He bit back a smile as he stepped into the doorway. She was rapping into her paintbrush as she sashayed with the rhythm. Her hair pulled up, her shoulders were mostly bare as she stood in front of the canvas in a pair of paint-splattered denim overalls over a white tank top. He was sure to die watching the most beautiful girl he'd ever seen in his life look more stunning than ever completely in her own element. She was just gorgeous...

He cleared his throat. "Brooke?"

Her palette was in the air before the scream left her mouth as she spun around and leapt backwards. "Geez, Jayson! How long were you standing there?"

"Not that long." He couldn't tamp down the smile that gave him away.

"Yeah, right. If you say anything to anyone—" She balled up her fist and shook it at him in a silent threat as she turned off her playlist. "I'm assuming my mother let you in."

"Yeah, she sent me up here. This room is incredible. Are all of these yours?" He stepped into the center of the room, admiring the color splashed walls and easels displaying works in progress. If only he had the time to properly look at each one. He was sure there were stories in her art that revealed a lot about that heart of hers he so desperately wanted to win.

"Yeah." She smiled softly as she seemed to step out of herself and try to envision the room from his perspective.

"This is amazing. It really is. It must feel great to have your own space to create at home."

She chuckled as she moved to put her paints away. "It was the third bedroom becoming my own space that sold me on the idea of us moving to this house. I could call it a perk of being an only child, but it's probably more parental guilt. Either way, I have this all to myself."

"It's just you and your parents then?"

"Nope. Just me and my mom. I never knew my dad. Turns out, he wasn't too keen on meeting me. So my mom did the job for him."

He felt his smile fall as the pain flashed in her eyes. If he could have one wish in that moment, it would have been to wrap her in his arms. "I'm sorry. I didn't know."

"How could you have? Besides, there's nothing to be sorry about. I'm pretty sure he did me a favor by bailing. He doesn't worry about me, so why should I waste my thoughts on him?" She ran a hand across her neck, leaving a bright streak of purple behind. The tension and conflict radiated from her body with a palpable presence. Her bottom lip caught between her teeth as she turned away from him.

He stepped closer, wanting her to know he was there with her and whatever she was feeling was no cause for her to turn away. What caught him by surprise was when she leaned into his touch.

"Do you know what sucks most about being the only child of a single parent?" Her voice rasped, thick with heavy emotion.

"Tell me."

"The fear of being lonely for the rest of my life. If something happens to my mom, that's it. I won't have any family anymore. I have Val, she's like my best friend and sister wrapped into one, but it's different. I live with the knowledge that I won't have any genetic connection to anyone anymore. It would really suck to be lonely for the rest of my life."

"You won't be." He gave her shoulder a gentle squeeze. "You're an incredible person, Brooke, and that alone tells me you'll always have people who love you and will show up for you."

If he had his way, he was going to be one of those people.

She turned to face him, tilting her head up to study his face, looking for traces of dishonesty. He wasn't worried. She wouldn't find anything but pure, unadulterated adoration for her. He left his hand on her shoulder as he stroked her warm skin with his thumb. He wanted this girl. The more he saw her, the more he learned, the more he realized how much he wanted her to be his.

Jayson felt his eyes move from her face down her graceful neck, along the curve of her shoulders. Her deep cleavage was visible and alluring. He forcibly pulled his eyes away to avoid gawking at her. Barefoot and paint-splattered, Brooke Thomas was not only gorgeous, she was sexy.

Feeling the heavy moment between them grow heavier, Brooke gave a wobbly smile. "We should get out of this room. We have some SAT prep to do."

"Yeah, you're right... we should." But he didn't want to, especially when he got the strong feeling she didn't want to either.

"Jayson, I'm sorry if I blurted out a bunch of my sperm donor issues... I usually don't talk like that with others. I don't want the rest of the day to be awkward or anything."

"No apologies necessary."

"Thanks. I guess you're easy to talk to."

He winked as his heart soared. "I'm available whenever you need a set of ears."

"Let's get downstairs. You can help me decide what kind of pizza to order. We're going to need some brain food."

Brooke

"Are those what I think they are?"

Brooke snickered and gave her best friend the most knowing of looks as she shooed her away from the cooling pan on the counter. "Maybe, but don't even think about it. They still have to cool."

"Excuse me? You can't make your brownies, parade them in front of me, and then tell me to forget about it. I'm pretty sure that's a violation of the Thomas-Lee Chocolate Treaty Pact initiated after the nearly fatal battle of the pillows last year. Do you really want to risk the innocent lives of your pillows?"

Brooke laughed. "I'll have to risk it. These are for someone else."

Val's indignant pout dissolved as her eyes grew wide and mischievous. "By someone, you wouldn't happen to mean that gorgeous, green-eyed study buddy of yours, would you?"

Brooke wasn't sure she had the ability to play coy this afternoon. "They are for Jayson. It's a bit of a bribe, like hush money. The other day when he came by to study, we ended up getting on the topic of my sperm donor and I might have gone a bit over the emotional deep end."

She gave her best attempt at a smile, hoping Val's perceptive gaze wouldn't incite another breakdown. "It's not that big of a deal."

"It's a very big deal. I know you don't talk about your dad very often."

"He's not my dad, Val." Brooke shut off the oven as she resumed cleaning up her baking supplies from the kitchen counter. "I don't need to talk about someone who doesn't matter. It's not some recent development in my life either. He's never been here. I can't miss something I never had, can I?"

"I know you're smart enough to know the answer to that, Brooke. I'm just surprised you talked to him about it. I thought you weren't a fan."

"I'm not..." Her voice wavered in betrayal of her assertiveness. "We spend a lot of time together, he's a nice enough guy and he's easy to talk to. Plus, he caught me off guard. And I was stressed about college again. So... yeah, like I said, it wasn't a big deal."

"Are you trying to convince me or yourself?" Val snorted in amusement.

Brooke narrowed her eyes in annoyance. "I'm never making you brownies again."

Walking through the hallways of PCH on Monday, Brooke was still trying to figure out all the feelings. Now that lunchtime had arrived, whether she was ready or not, it was go time. She focused her attention on the steps her cherry red Dr. Martens as she drew closer and closer to him. Pulling in a heap of oxygen, she looked up just in time to see his friend Brian nudge him purposely, trying to alert him of her presence. It wasn't necessary, though. Jayson's eyes were already fixed on her, full of happiness, hope, and something more.

"Hello, Jayson." *Cringe.* She was supposed to say hi. It was supposed to be fun and casual, like she spoke to him every day, because she did speak to him every day—multiple times a day. She was failing horribly.

"Hey, Brooke!"

"I like your hair." *Face palm.* Abort mission. She was beginning to doubt her own IQ as she fumbled for words and any sense of sophistication. It wasn't without reason, though. Jayson most often wore one of his baseball caps when he was around her, but today, his dark curls were uncovered. The texture caught her artist eyes, her hand itching for her pencils and sketchbook to draw him. "Your haircut. I meant, I like your haircut."

"Thanks." His smile was genuine, even though his eyes shone with a chuckle. She returned the smile, feeling herself relax a bit. "Would you like to sit with us?"

"No! I mean, no thanks. I only came over here to give you these." She held out the plastic container full of brownies. "I figured you might like to give these a try, especially now that you've officially kicked butt on the SATs."

He gave her an even deeper smile. "I don't know about that. We'll see when the scores come in."

"We'll see that I'm right. Anyway, here you go. I hope you enjoy them."

Jayson gratefully accepted the treats, immediately popping the lid off and taking a hearty bite of one of the squares. "Oh my..." His eyes fluttered closed as his words faded into mumbles of pleasure. His reaction was so genuinely pleasing, she forgot all her fears of awkwardness and laughed happily. "Didn't I tell you these would ruin you forever?"

"I am ruined. What have you done to me, woman?" He quickly polished off the square.

"I have to try one of these." One of his teammates reached for the open container, only to be left in want as Jayson swung the container out of reach and snapped the lid back on with a growl.

"I won't be sharing, sorry."

"There's plenty in there," Brooke explained, but Jayson's nearly murderous look at his tablemates confirmed he wouldn't be sharing, no matter the quantity.

"I'm glad you like them. I have to get going, but seriously... I'm proud of you."

Jayson's eyes grew softer. "Thanks, Brooke."

She went through the rest of her day with a mind that refused to shut up. The thoughts were so distracting, when Jayson walked up behind her in the hallway and touched her arm, she actually screamed and dropped all her books, embarrassingly drawing the attention of everyone around her.

"I'm sorry. I didn't mean to scare you. I was calling your name, but you didn't answer."

Brooke knelt to gather her stuff. "Didn't hear you. I have a lot on my mind."

"Oh. Do you want to talk about it?"

Her cheeks warmed at the thought of telling him he was the thing on her mind. "Uh... no, it's not that important. What can I help you with?"

Well... that had sounded a bit harsh. How did she go from the bumbling, blushing girl to *that* in less than a second? This was why she didn't do this with boys—especially boys like Jayson Williams. She was constantly reaffirming she had neither the skills nor the savvy to even pretend like she knew what she was doing.

Jayson handed her the last two books. "I was wondering what you were doing on Friday?"

Brooke froze. "I don't know. Why?"

"Well... I was thinking... and hoping... maybe we can hang out. I have a game here at six. It's the very first of the season. Maybe you could come watch me play, and we could go grab some food after. I know a great burger place."

Brooke hesitated.

"I don't know. I've never been to a game."

"All the more reason to come. I promise it'll be a good game. Besides, we could celebrate the A I'm going to get on the English test today."

Brooke smiled. "If you get an A, I'll come on Friday... deal?"

"Absolutely."

By the time the last bell rang on Friday, Brooke was a ball of nerves. Ever since Jayson found out he'd gotten a ninety-four on the test, he'd been smiling from ear to ear. Although Jayson had invited her to "hang out," Brooke felt more like this would be a date, and seeing how she had never been on a date before, she was really wondering if she could actually go through with it. It wasn't helping that her best friend wouldn't stop gloating about her "non-date."

"You know, you kind of suck for making me go alone tonight."

"Sweet Brooke, you know I love you, but my mother would kill me if I ditched this family dinner to be the third wheel on your date."

"I'm not going on a date with him, Val!"

"You're going to a special event with him, then you're going out to eat afterward alone... together. Sounds like a date to me."

Brooke groaned aloud. "This is going to be a disaster."

"You mean to tell me there's not even a tiny bit of you that's super excited for tonight."

"No," she lied, grateful they were only on the phone and Val couldn't see the way she was fighting a smile.

"You lie! It's totally a date, and you're a lot excited about it."

Brooke gave her phone an annoyed glare.

"Okay, fine, but I'm only looking forward to it because it will be nice to see him in his own element, not because I like him or anything."

"All those muscles... all sweaty..."

"Valerie Lee!"

"I'm sorry, did I upset you by talking about your *date?*"

"You're the worst, you know that, right? Jayson and I... we're not dating. I'm not even sure we're really friends. We're just... friendly."

Val snorted. "Maybe you're just friendly with him, but he sure doesn't want to be your friend. I see the way he looks at you, the way he treats you—or should I say tries to treat you because you shoot him down all the time? He texts you about books!"

"We're friends. I helped him with his grade and he wants to thank me with dinner. Completely platonic."

"Platonic, huh? When's the last time it's taken you three hours to choose an outfit when we go out to eat?"

"Bye, Val!"

Val ignored her. "Seriously, Brooke, why is it such a big deal to admit maybe you were wrong about him? That maybe you like him after all?"

"Because even if I did *hypothetically* enjoy his company, I'm smart enough to know I need to be realistic about the situation."

"What situation is that?"

47

"He's who he is, and I'm who I am. It's like the plot line to any teen rom-com movie out there. I'm not interested in being the punchline to someone else's joke."

"What if he's not joking?"

All the way there, she wondered if she should have just stayed home, but her pride and integrity to keep her promise kept her from turning around and going home. Even now as she stood in the gymnasium, she questioned if it was too late to just turn around. But she couldn't. In her heart she knew why, and that answer, while true, scared her to death.

She looked down at her outfit self-consciously before walking away from the safety of the door. She had paired a floral printed skirt with trouser knee-socks, a soft pink tank top, a black cardigan, and her favorite black Dr. Martens. She took a deep breath as she stepped forward and felt his eyes fall on her.

Those green eyes that always seemed to seek her out were now what she sought out whenever he was near. In his maroon and white jersey and shorts, there was nothing to keep her from admiring the muscles in his arms. She bit down on her lip to stop herself from gaping at the sight of him.

From the moment she'd laid eyes on Jayson, she'd known he was pretty incredible to look at it. However, there was something captivating about watching him in that number twelve jersey among his teammates. Standing at about six-foot-four, he wasn't the only tall one on the court, but he was the one that drew the attention. He carried himself confidently as he listened to what their coach was saying and spoke to his team before he broke away from their bench and headed right toward her.

JAYSON

Jayson couldn't remember a time when he'd been so nervous before a game. He had arrived to the gymnasium earlier than early to make sure he would be there to greet her when she arrived. At the seats had begun to fill, he'd had to fight the distracting worry she wasn't going to show up. If that hadn't been distracting enough, he also had to avoid Marisa, a cheerleader who was having a hard time accepting his disinterest in her.

With only a few minutes before the game was set to begin, she walked through the gymnasium doors.

He thought he had been distracted before she arrived, but now he knew what real distraction was. Everything about Brooke's body was just *right*. His eyes were drawn to the small expanse of uncovered skin on her legs, and his blood heated. He wasn't sure he would be able to keep his eyes off her during the game. Brooke wasn't just cute; she was drop-dead beautiful. If he had his way, he would have rushed toward her and told her everything he felt right then and there. But he couldn't—not yet. She tucked a stray piece of hair that escaped her otherwise neat ponytail behind her ear as Jayson moved through the gaggle of giggling cheerleaders.

"Hey! You made it!"

"Yeah... a deal is a deal, right?"

She was nervous, but she was here. Before she could say anything more, Jayson pulled her in for a warm, lingering hug.

"I'm glad you're here."

She felt so amazing in his arms. Just the way he'd imagined she would. And her hair... what was that amazing smell? He wanted to breathe in the scent of her shampoo, but knew it would thoroughly freak her out, so he quickly committed the scent to memory and released her from his embrace.

"You promised me a great first game experience, so here I

49

am. It's pretty crowded, though. I'm going to go see if I can find a seat."

She was officially freaking out. Jayson could tell from her guarded stance and worried eyes scanning the bleachers. Her lip pulled tight between her teeth. He wanted to put her at ease so she would want to come to a second game.

"Okay. Don't leave after the game. I owe you that burger. It will take me about fifteen minutes to shower and change."

She nodded once before hurrying over to find the nearest available seat. While Jayson hustled onto the court to finish warm-ups, he shook the nerves out of his limbs. It was a new and strange feeling. He'd never been nervous before a game, but he was getting the chance to show Brooke he was good at something.

"Your girl is here, huh?" Brian gave him a lopsided grin.

"She's not my girl yet, but yeah... I convinced her to check out the game. Let's make it a good one, okay?"

It wasn't really a question, and Brian understood. "Let's get it done."

They bumped fists as they jogged over to the center of the court for tipoff.

Tonight, they were facing one of the best of the division and their arch-rival team, the Falcons. It would be good to be a spectator today. Neither team would give up a win easily. They both wanted a win to start of the season, and they both wanted those bragging rights. The last time they had played each other was for the state title. Jayson and the rest of the Pirates had secured that win. His eyes met with those of Drew Wilkins, captain of the Falcons. It was a look of mutual respect and disdain. The ref dropped the ball.

Game time.

Brooke

Brooke settled into an empty seat not too far from the team. She was relieved not to have to awkwardly search through the crowded stands for a seat, but her relief soon faded into discomfort. She felt eyes on her, watching—and they didn't belong to Jayson. Looking first to her left, then her right, she quickly spotted the source of the unwanted attention. Several girls and a good amount of the cheerleaders seemed to find her attendance particularly intriguing. Now, more than before, she wished Valerie had been able to come along with her. Val would know how to handle these girls. Brooke knew how to ignore them. She was determined not to be intimidated, or at least not look like she was.

She made it through the first two quarters and was actually enjoying herself a little bit. She didn't know all the rules of the game, but after a quick Google search and watching the first quarter, she was able to figure out enough to follow the basics. One thing was evident: Jayson's abilities were without question. It was clear he was the leader of his team. She admired his skills almost as much as the way he gave every guy on the court their opportunity to shine. Her mind was pulled back to the floor as the buzzer sounded for halftime. Jayson smiled and waved at her as he and the rest of the team filed past to the locker room. After he disappeared, she pulled out her phone to find waiting messages from Val.

> *Val:* Have you shaken your pom-poms for your man yet?

> *Val:* And by pom-poms, I mean your boobies.

> *Brooke:* Do you realize our team initials are PCP? As in you must be high on PCP right now.

Val: Oh, come on, Brooke. I know one particular Paradise Cove Pirate who sure love to capture your booty...

Val: BOOTY! Get it!

Brooke: I got it!

Val: That was golden and you know it! But seriously, how's the game going?

Brooke: Surprisingly okay. The team is winni-

She couldn't finish typing the message before she was approached by Marisa and her ever-present clique. For the last three years, Marisa had never paid much attention to Brooke. She'd never had much reason to, but tonight, Marisa had Brooke set dead center in her sight. She dug her fingernails into her palms to redirect the nervous energy coursing through her veins.

"Well, if it isn't little Miss Betty Crocker. What are you doing here?"

Brooke focused her eyes straight ahead, trying to ignore the girls surrounding her. It was like they were a pack of wolves and she was fresh meat.

"I'm watching the game. I was invited..."

"By Jayson, right?" Marisa's raised a perfectly arched eyebrow. "You think that's supposed to mean something?"

Brooke clenched her jaw, but felt her eyes blink at the sting of her words.

"Listen to me, Brooke." She narrowed her eyes, and Brooke bristled with anger and embarrassment. "Whatever you imagine is going on with you and Jayson is a joke. You don't belong here. You're a nobody. Do yourself a favor and disappear. Leave Jayson to me."

Normally, Brooke would have a dozen comebacks on the tip of her tongue, each one sharper than the last and all ready to be unleashed. Tonight felt anything but normal, though. Under the judgmental eyes of Marisa and her loyal league of

lemmings, the embarrassment she felt overtook the anger and her retorts fizzled. Her skin burned hot as she scanned the packed gymnasium.

She never felt more like an outsider than she did right then.

This was not her world.

Brooke was gone before Jayson returned to the court.

Chapter 5

Brooke

Brooke stood in front of the bathroom mirror, growing angrier the longer she stared at her reflection. The furious cry had left her eyes puffy and her skin blotchy. Pulling her hair free of the band that kept it tidy, she ran her fingers through in a frustrated pass. She was pissed off she had let them get to her like that. Up until now, she had managed to ignore them, to let their insults roll off of her back, but tonight, they had done some damage.

Alone in her home, grateful her mother had gone over to a coworker's that night, she was free to deal with her thoughts and feelings without having to put on a pretense. As she replayed the past weeks over and over in her mind, she questioned all the whats, hows, and whys between the start of the year right up until then. *Why had she let them break her? Why did what was said tonight hurt more than their usual jibes?*

She had mulled around the answers as she made her way through a pint of espresso chip ice cream before resigning herself to bed.

Val: So, how'd it go?!!!

Brooke: It didn't. I remember why I haven't gone to any games before now. I hate cheerleaders. I hate high school. I'll fill you in tomorrow.

Jayson: Brooke? What happened? Where'd you go?

That had been the last message she read before she powered off her phone and put it in her nightstand drawer.

Saturday morning came too fast, and Brooke was woken by the sounds of her mother getting ready to go into work. She lay in bed until she heard the car back down their driveway. No sooner had she sat up in bed did she hear a knock at the door. Swinging it open, she was surprised to see Jayson standing there. Remembering she was in her pajama shorts and black tank top, her hair falling around her shoulders in a sleep-styled frenzy, she grimaced. He, on the other hand, looked heartachingly handsome.

Of course he would. His green fitted cap was turned backwards on his head, and his gray Henley hugged his muscled torso, leaving him looking deliciously formidable. His green eyes were sharp, focused on her face with such an intensity, her arms broke out in goosebumps. She had to fight the urge to shiver.

"Jayson? Why are you here?"

She ran a harried hand over her face, trying to make sure she didn't have anything embarrassing on it from her sleep.

"You left yesterday and didn't answer any of my calls or messages last night. Did I do something to upset you? If I did, I'm so sorry."

She had run out on his game, ditching their plans without so much as a text message, and here he was on her porch, apologizing. Brooke was positive her face changed from surprise to a mix of emotions he wouldn't understand. She barely had the grasp needed on understanding them herself. She heaved a sigh heavy with emotion and let her body lean against the door, crossing her arms over her chest.

"No, you didn't upset me. Not on purpose anyway."

"What does that mean?" Jayson's eyes were dark with hurt and confusion.

"It means I don't know why you invited me to the game!"

Jayson grabbed her hand. "I invited you because I wanted you there...*for me.* You have to know that by now."

Brooke's heart raced at the unexpected declaration and

the even more surprising intimate gesture of holding his hand. She didn't pull away. "Well, I was vaguely threatened and informed, quite clearly, I wasn't wanted there and anything more than a tutoring relationship would be a joke at my expense."

"That's not true!"

"Maybe it's partially true..."

Jayson's eyes flashed, his voice rising. "No! It's not true at all! Brooke, come on. I've had a crush on you for years. That's a lot of time to invest in a practical joke, don't you think? I remember the exact moment it started. It was when I saw you walk into class on your first day at PCH. You wore a pink plaid button-down shirt over a white tank top with those khaki shorts and flip flops. I couldn't take my eyes off of you, and I haven't since. I had never gone on a date before, and once I saw you, I knew I wanted you to be my first date. I wanted you to be my first kiss, my first girlfriend. I wasn't going to waste my time on anyone else... and I haven't. The first time we read Romeo and Juliet, I told you I was ready to make a lifelong commitment when I was fourteen and a half. I wasn't joking when I said it. From the time we were freshman I've wanted this! Whatever is growing between us, you mean to tell me you don't feel it?"

Brooke swallowed hard. She didn't even know Jayson had noticed her before this year. "I'm not like Marisa..."

"Exactly. That's why I'm falling for you. And it's the same reason she's crazy jealous. She can never be you, Brooke, and you're the one I want. Maybe I am stupid—stupid for hoping you'd ever want to be with someone like me."

He let go of her hand as he turned and headed down her porch stairs. Brooke found herself standing on her porch with tears in her eyes and a lump in her throat as she watched him walk away.

Brooke knew she had screwed up.

She knew it even before he walked off her porch. Now, it was left up to her. She needed to do something. She rushed through her shower, then scoured her closet for a floral dress she paired with her well-worn denim jacket. She pulled on a pair of knee-socks and Dr. Martens before capturing her hair into her usual bun. Grabbing her phone and bag, she left her house, heading to find him.

She stopped on the sidewalk in front of a large craftsman home. The color was soul-soothing gray, and the plants along the walkway added bright pops of color that pleased her artist eyes. Walking along the stone pathway, she tried to even out her breaths. She had rehearsed what she'd say the entire walk over, but as she climbed the wide steps, it all fizzled away under the waves of nerves threatening to pull her under. Brooke smoothed her dress and hair once more before ringing Jayson's doorbell. She fought the urge to pace the length of the large front porch, only to be startled back to reality when a small boy with striking green eyes similar to Jayson's appeared behind the glass door.

"Hi!" Her voice chirped octaves higher than usual.

"Hello." Those green eyes took her in as they danced happily with amusement.

"I'm looking for Jayson…"

"I'm not supposed to talk to strangers."

Right. "You're pretty smart. You should never talk to strangers, but I'm a friend of Jayson's. I really need to talk to him."

"Okay!"

Brooke smiled. "Is he here?"

"Yes."

"May I talk to him?"

"Yes." He stood there, unmoving. She was beginning to second guess her decision to come when Jayson appeared in the door. Clearly surprised, he moved the little boy aside to open the door.

"Brooke!"

Maybe it was her imagination, but he was ten times more handsome when he was saying her name. She swallowed her lusty thoughts along with the last bunch of nerves holding her ability to verbally communicate hostage. She could tell she was blushing, but she couldn't help it. Or maybe she just didn't care.

"Jayson... hi."

"What are you doing here?" Jayson stepped out onto the porch.

"I'm here for you." She spoke each word purposefully, keeping her eyes fixed on him. He'd gotten real with her that morning, and it was her turn. He deserved that much from her. "I wanted to maybe go for a walk... or I could take you to lunch... my treat. I want to talk to you about yesterday... and today."

And the last three years. She left that part unsaid. His eyes flashed with regret, and she felt like an idiot. As if he could read her thoughts, he stepped a bit closer and captured her gaze again.

"I'd love nothing more than to go for a walk with you or take you to lunch—*my* treat—but I can't. I told my mom I'd watch my brothers today. Then I found out the twins have a science fair project they've barely started, so now it needs a lot of work."

"Oh... okay. Maybe another time..."

Brooke offered a faint smile. She gave a small wave and turned to head down the porch stairs. He grabbed her hand, halting her, and her whole body reacted.

"Wait! I'd love it if you stayed and helped me out. I'll make sure we find some time alone so we can talk too."

With a flash of that dimpled smile, there was no way she could say no. He led her through the front doors and almost immediately she came face to face with four pairs of amazing green eyes. They made no attempt to cover their eavesdropping, flashing her four charming smiles. Jayson let out a knowing chuckle.

"Brooke, these are my brothers. This is Jayden, who you may have seen around the hallways this year. The twins are Jaylin and Jordan. They're ten. Don't worry if you can't tell them apart. It took me almost a year to figure it out myself. And our smallest brother is..."

"I'm Justin and I'm six. You smell good!"

All the brothers were equipped with good looks and swoon-worthy eyes, but she was certain Justin was the true charmer in the bunch. The laugh burst through her lips before she could pretend to hide it. She dropped down to her knees and extended a hand.

"Hello, Justin. It's very nice to meet you."

From that very moment onward, they all made her feel very welcome. While Brooke helped Jayden with his weekend homework, the twins were busy building their volcano and display. Jayson juggled playing hide and seek with Justin, doing the laundry, and supervising the volcano construction. She couldn't help but watch him, though she tried to do it undetected.

Jayson Williams was apparently so much more than she would have ever assumed about him. As she sat in his house watching him, all the warm and fuzzy feelings that she had smothered down came rushing to the surface. The more she got to know Jayson, the more she wanted to know. And now?

Now, she wanted the whole story.

He looked up from where he sat on the floor with Justin and gave her a smile that held the look of a guy who wanted her.

JAYSON

From time to time, he would feel her eyes on him and he'd turn to meet her gaze. Today, it was different. She didn't look away or scowl. Instead, she held his gaze, making it clear she was no longer trying to hide the unsaid things in her eyes. With a quick glance and small smile, volumes of unspoken words passed between them. His heart thumped in his chest, and he forced himself not to rush over and ask her what she was thinking. He had laid a lot of his feelings out on her porch that morning, and when he'd left, he'd been certain he wouldn't hear from her anymore. Then she showed up on his doorstep seeking him out.

He was almost positive he was dreaming.

The day had gone from bad to amazing when she agreed to hang out with him and his brothers. Here, smack dab in the middle of the craziness of his brothers laughing, playing, and inevitably arguing, she fit right in. His younger brothers vied for her attention, and he couldn't resist watching the clock, waiting for the moment he'd be able to send them off to their rooms so he could have all that attention for himself. Just as the thought of being alone with her settled in his mind, he was pulled back to the present at the sound of her laughter.

Hearing it had him convinced he had never heard her really laugh prior to today. He was now addicted to the sound. Brooke's laugh was pure heaven. He looked over at her smile lighting up the room. She looked over at him to gauge his reaction. He had missed the joke, but he joined the group's laughter anyway.

"Hey, guys, I'm about to order some pizzas for dinner..."

His brothers immediately began calling out their requested toppings as if he didn't order their pizzas on a regular basis.

"All right, I got it!" Jayson fixed his eyes on Brooke, who was cleaning up all the scrap paper she had used to help Jayden with his math.

"Brooke?"

She looked up, startled. "Yeah?"

"Any special requests for pizza toppings?"

Taking in all five expectant faces, she gave a quick shake of her head. "Oh, you don't have to... I mean, I'm not going to impose on your dinnertime... or take up anymore of your evening. I'm just going to clean this up and walk home."

He shook his head before she even finished talking. "You're staying here for dinner. It's not imposing, we're inviting you, right, guys?"

"Yeah, stay for dinner! Please!" Jaylin and Jordan chorused.

"You can sit next to me, Brooke!" Justin jumped up and

down before clasping onto her hand. Jayson tried his best not to join in on the begging. When she nodded her assent a moment later, it took the rest of his self-control not to fist bump his baby brother.

"Do you have any brothers, Brooke?" Justin asked around a mouthful of pizza.

"No, I don't. I don't have any sisters either."

"Do you have any pets?"

"Nope, no pets."

"Wow, you must be so lonely," Justin said with a solemn face.

Jayson looked to Brooke, who didn't bother to respond. Instead, she ran a hand over Justin's curly hair and smiled a smile equal parts sadness and adoration. It was a reminder of her feelings of loneliness and her fears of not having a family that made his heart squeeze. He was familiar with real loneliness, even with four brothers underfoot and a whole bunch of brothers on his team. Real loneliness crept into his heart the first time he knew his father wasn't going to be coming home.

She caught his eye again, and her smile deepened as she mouthed, "He's so adorable."

She was so adorable.

Tonight, he wasn't going to let her leave without telling her that. He couldn't stop thinking about how he felt the night before when he emerged from the locker room to find her seat on the bleachers empty. He avoided Brian's sympathetic looks and took out his frustrations on the Falcons, pushing his team to a punishing ninety-four to sixty-five victory. The rest of the team wanted to celebrate their win, but Jayson hurried off, finding himself walking by Brooke's house. Seeing the lone light on in the upstairs window practically beckoned him to knock on the door. Instead, he walked away, determined to be back first thing in the morning.

He had rehearsed what he was going to say all night long, but when she opened the door and stood in front of him, her hair tousled and curves fully on display, his brain short circuited. Next thing he knew, he was blurting out how long he'd been crushing on her. The fact that she was here, in his house, now, after all that, had him dying to know what she wanted to talk about.

Brooke

Dinner with five boys was a rowdy affair.

Brooke didn't know if it was because they were boys or brothers, but the jokes and gentle teasing were a constant as they ate more than she thought was even humanly possible. And she loved every minute of it.

After they finished eating, Jayson excused himself to get Justin ready for bed while the twins went to watch a movie in their room. Jayden had already said his goodbyes as he went to spend the night at his best friend's house. In the quiet of the kitchen, Brooke decided to finish clearing the table and start washing the glasses. When she came here, she had not anticipated spending the whole day with Jayson and his brothers, but she was so happy she had. It had been the best day she'd had in a long time, if she was being truly honest with herself.

Like Jayson, all the boys were so welcoming and absolute sweethearts. But more than anything, the highlight of the day had been watching Jayson. He was such a great older brother. He took care of them, played with them, and still made sure they were on track with their own academic work, even as he balanced housework to ease the load from his mother. She was certain Jayson was different than what she had him pegged for. In fact, he was rather remarkable. His physical appearance was stunning, the boy was drop-dead gorgeous, but what she saw from him that day stole her heart. It made him more than attractive; it made him beautiful.

Normally, she prided herself on not falling into the stereotype of the girls who got a crush on a boy and went all googly eyed. But even now, as she washed the dinner dishes, she found herself daydreaming about actually being with him, dreaming about being with him in a house similar to this one in the future... and she didn't even try to stop herself.

JAYSON

T hat was how Jayson found her, humming a song, washing dishes in his kitchen, wearing a wistful smile and a faraway look. He was pretty sure he fell completely in love with her at that moment.

"You didn't have to do that, Brooke. You already helped out a lot today."

She turned, startled by his voice, "Oh, I like to help. I really don't mind. Thanks for inviting me to stay—and for dinner."

"Thanks for staying. It was the best day we've all had in a while. Justin didn't stop talking about you until he passed out."

She smiled as she rinsed the last glass. "He's such an awesome kid. Can I ask you something?"

"Sure. Anything."

"The first night we met at the library and you were late, you were taking care of your brothers, weren't you?"

He nodded.

"And I was a jerk. Jayson, I'm really sorry."

"You don't need to apologize. I understood."

"No. I do need to apologize. I shouldn't have been so rude. Even before you asked for my help with school, I was rude and I was wrong. I'm so sorry."

He didn't doubt her sincerity. Her big brown eyes were wet with emotion. He wouldn't be able to tolerate it if she started crying over something that was already forgiven. Instead of dwelling on it, he handed her a kitchen towel to dry her hands. "Apology accepted. Follow me. I want to show you something."

Together, they exited the kitchen. Walking down a hallway, they passed a wall of framed pictures.

"Are they all of your family?" Brooke paused and studied the faces, her eyes drawn to one in particular. "Is that your dad?"

Jayson smiled slightly and looked at her, nodding. She squeezed his arm. "He's very handsome. You look just like him."

The familiar ache dulled the soaring happiness he felt at the realization she indirectly just called him handsome. Jayson dropped his gaze. "Yeah, my mom tells me that every day. I miss him a lot."

"May I ask what happened?"

Jayson hesitated, then nodded. "Let's talk on the back porch. I want to grab something to show you."

Moments later, they settled on the back porch, enjoying the cool night air. Brooke sitting on the step beside him, whispering about how she loved nights like this where she could listen close enough to hear both the ocean waves crashing in the distance and the crickets making their music. It was absolutely perfect.

Despite him being the one to invite her to sit with him and talk, they sat in a contented bit of quiet for a few minutes. Brooke didn't pressure him to start and he was grateful for the time to gather his thoughts.

"My dad's name was Joshua. He and my mom met when they were young. He used to say it was my mom who was his motivation to become a man. My mom's family is Dominican. My dad's father was Black, and his mom was Dominican. But they were both born and raised in the Dominican Republic. Their families were close friends, so it was inevitable my parents would meet. They fell in love and married as soon as they could, and I came along after that."

"What's your mom's name?"

"Jisela. My mom's a nurse. My dad was a carpenter. The smell of wood reminds me of him. He made furniture by hand to order and also built decks and porches. He built this porch we're sitting on and that treehouse. He was the best. Always worked his hardest, but always made sure he spent time with us. He coached my little brothers in little league and never missed a game of mine, no matter what. Sometimes, late at night if I couldn't sleep, I'd sneak out to his workshop in the garage and he'd let me help him sand a piece he was working on. He never made me feel like I was too little or young to help. Other nights, I'd find him and my mom dancing to some slow song on the radio. I watched the way they looked at each other and learned what love looked like. I just knew I had the greatest parents in the world. Then, one night, my dad was on his way home from a job and he stopped at a convenience store to get ice cream to bring home for dessert. He walked in on a robbery and the coward shot him. For no reason. My dad was dead at thirty-three. And I had to become the man of the house."

Brooke's forehead wrinkled in concern as tears fell from his eyes. He quickly dropped his head, trying to hide them. He hadn't cried in front of anyone since his father's funeral, but talking to her about him dropped all his usual pretense of emotional strength. He didn't want her to pity him or think he was weak. He was halted in that thought as she moved from her seat at his side and kneeled in front of him. She wedged her body between his legs as she placed her hands on his knees and squeezed them gently to get his attention.

"Look at me, Jayson. Your dad sounds like an incredible man. It's obvious he was so loved and he loved you all very much. He would be so proud of you. You help your brothers and mother with the best of your heart. I can see you are pretty incredible to do all you do with a smile."

"I do it because my mom has always worked hard, but now she has to raise us without him. She has to work even harder because I was so selfish. If I hadn't asked him for that ice cream, he would have been home with us. He would still be here."

Brooke shook her head. "You can't blame yourself. There's

only one person in the wrong, and that man will have to live with that judgment over his head. You are a good son, and I don't need to know your mom to know she would tell you the same thing. You are more considerate than any teenager I know. Most guys would not want to spend their Saturday with their little brothers and making sure their mother came home to a clean house."

"I know it's not easy for her, so I don't need to make it any harder. You know, she put every penny of the life insurance money into five trust funds for us. She hasn't spent a dime of it. She refused to uproot us from our home, and instead works harder than any woman I know. Watching my brothers makes it easier for her to pick up an extra shift when we need the money."

He unzipped the duffel bag he had carried out with him. Inside, she found tons of college brochures and pamphlets, letters and postcards.

"I started getting the brochures in ninth grade. That's when my name first showed up in the eligibility pool for college recruiters. They haven't stopped. I have two more bags of them in my room."

"Whoa…" She picked up five of them. East, west, Midwest, south—all the regions were covered. "They just keep sending things and calling?"

"There are rules. They couldn't call or email me until junior year. It's all regulated, but still, when you have more than one or two schools courting you, it gets overwhelming."

"One or two… hundred!" Brooke spotted several Ivy League brochures laying in the mix. "This is incredible, Jayson. You must be so proud of yourself."

He zipped the bag shut. "All of this was dependent on my grades. So thank you for helping me. My good grades help me help my mom."

"Of course. I'm glad I could help, but honestly, you were pretty much there, Jayson. It didn't take much work to help you pull your grades up." Brooke offered him a genuine smile of friendship.

"Would you keep studying with me? I know it wasn't part of the original plan, but studying with you gives me the confidence to pass the tests. Before I had you as a study buddy, I second guessed my way to bad grades. Please?"

When he finally stopped talking, he realized she was smiling at him. "I'd miss studying with you if it stopped now..."

She went to work on her bottom lip as he searched her eyes for what he longed to see. He had already put his feelings about her out in the open. Now, it was up to her to tell him she wanted to be his or how she truly felt, but the moment was interrupted when they heard a car pull into the garage.

"That's my mom. Come on, I'll introduce you to her, and then I'll walk you home."

Jisela Williams was a petite woman a bit shorter than Brooke. She had fierce jade green eyes, which explained where the Williams' brothers got them from. Her black hair was braided into a long French braid, and despite the printed scrubs she wore, she looked more like a model and Jayson's older sister than his mother.

"Mom, this is Brooke," he said, giving her a kiss on the cheek.

Jisela smiled brightly. "Ah, I've heard so much about you! It's so nice to meet you."

"Thank you. You have such a beautiful home, and your boys have been so welcoming to me today."

"My son tells me you're the smartest girl in his class, among other things." She gave Brooke a small smile and wink.

"I'm sure he exaggerated."

Jayson smiled slightly. "Mom, I'm going to walk Brooke home. She doesn't live too far from here. Justin is sleeping, Jayden is at Nathan's for the night, and I let the twins watch a movie in my room."

"Okay, the house looks wonderful. Thank you." She hugged Jayson, then hugged Brooke. "It was nice to meet you. We'll have to have you over for dinner soon. Some real, authentic Dominican food—no pizza this time."

"I would love that, Mrs. Williams."

Brooke

"Tell me some things I don't know about you," Jayson said as they rounded the first corner, walking slowly toward Brooke's home.

"Hmmm... anything?"

"Anything at all." He smiled and nudged her a bit.

"My middle name is Lynn."

Jayson broke out into a big dimpled grin. "Brooke Lynn. I like that. Brooke Lynn Thomas. Brookelynn Thomas."

She couldn't help but giggle a bit as well.

He turned around to face her as he walked backward a few paces. "My middle name is Mark. Tell me something else."

"My birthday is November second."

"No way! My birthday is November first."

"How weird."

"Not weird." He leaned in closer. "Destiny."

She blushed and tried to change the subject to disguise her nerves. "Tell me about Brian."

"Brian?" He raised an eyebrow curiously.

"Yeah, he's your best friend, right? A person's choice of best friend tells a lot about them."

"Something like birds of a feather, huh?" He traced his bottom lip in thought. "I met Brian in kindergarten and we were pretty inseparable from that day on. We've played every sport and every game together on the same team since I started playing. We're like brothers now. He's a bit more outgoing than I am, but we understand each other. Despite our differences, we never push each other to change... we just push each other to be the best versions of whoever it is we want to be."

"I totally get that. It's like that with me and Val. Sometimes we couldn't be more different if we tried. But we love each other unconditionally. She's always pushing me, and while I don't always appreciate it in the moment, I realize it's because she wants the best for me. She wants me to be happy."

"Being happy is a great thing to be." He offered her a wink, but the look behind it was what set her heart racing. The look was loaded with feeling... desire... determination. His words from the morning came rushing through her memory again. She folded her trembling hands together. She needed to talk about something... anything.

"Well... you already know I love art and reading, but I hate math. Don't really want to know what I want to do with my life, which makes college selection stressful. I'm afraid of snakes and I hate needles. Never been on a date. Never had a boyfriend. Never been kissed. But I'm the biggest romantic at heart. I love to watch old black and white romance movies."

Her mouth was going to be the death of her, she was sure of it.

Why did she have to go and say those things out of all the other things she could have said?

How was she going to face him now?

Her heart pounded in her chest. *Maybe he hadn't heard her fully?*

But then he stopped walking, and she knew he'd heard everything she'd said. There was no undoing it. He was looking at her; she could feel it.

"Brooke..." Jayson reached for her hand and placed it over his own beating heart. "That's what you do to me every time I'm around you. Even when you're not around me, I can't stop talking about you. That's why my mom said what she said back at the house. I've never been on a date, I've never had a girlfriend, and I have never kissed or been kissed. Do you know why?"

Her nervous energy had her ready to burst. "Maybe..."

"It's because I meant every word I said on your porch this morning. Since the first day I saw you, I wanted you to be my first everything. It's always been you. Always."

She forced herself to stop biting her lip. "I guess I just don't get it. You could have anyone, and we both know it. You're gorgeous—and I don't mean 'our little high school world cute.' I mean, you are the most gorgeous guy I have ever seen in my life. Why would someone like you ever bother looking at someone like me?"

Brooke shook her head in question.

Jayson took both her hands in his. His forehead wrinkled in confusion.

"Someone like you? You say that like it's a bad thing. Why you? You are everything. You're smart and funny. You don't take my crap. You're kind and a genuinely good person. Brooke Lynn, you're absolutely gorgeous. I mean it. In every possible way, you are so beautiful, it makes my heart ache. You are so unapologetically you, it's perfection. You're so sexy, and you don't even know it, so that makes you even sexier. Brooke Lynn..."

Oh, the way this boy said her name. With nothing between them but their unsteady breaths, Brooke couldn't help but to study his face with unrestrained admiration. The small scar in his eyebrow that gave his gorgeous face a touch of rugged appeal, the slight five o'clock shadow he had going on, proving he was more man than boy. She felt all the warmth in her heart spill out through her body as the last brick in the wall she had carefully built between them came tumbling down. The last thing she saw was the honesty in his green eyes as she stopped fighting and gave herself up to his kiss.

It was in the undeniable truth of their kiss she was forced to admit to herself she had fallen for him long ago. She reveled in allowing herself to feel the emotions she'd fought for what seemed like an eternity. If she thought their kiss would be tentative, she'd been wrong. Jayson kissed her with confidence and purpose. He reiterated all the spoken and unspoken sentiments in that kiss. His hand found its way to the small of her back, pulling her in as she came up on her tiptoes to meet his lips easier.

Eyes shut, she lost herself in the free fall as she got the first taste of him, the sweetness of the cola they'd drank earlier lingering behind. They stayed like that, wrapped in each other, neither of them wanting to see their first kiss come to an end. When Jayson pulled himself away, he placed a trio of kisses on her forehead and pulled her tightly against his side as he continued to walk her home.

Coming to a stop on the steps of her porch, he removed his arm from around her to allow his hand to cup her face in his hands. "You looked so beautiful today... I wanted to tell you so many times."

She smiled softly. "I have a confession. Lately, every time I get dressed, I'm hoping you think I look pretty."

"I've never seen anything prettier."

He kissed her cheeks, then the tip of her nose, and finally her lips again. As he did so, he slipped the hair band from her hair, letting it tumble down around her face beautifully. He tenderly brushed it back with his fingers.

"I have a confession too. I've been dying to do this. This morning, when you came to the door with your hair down... I swear, my heart stopped."

She made a mental note to leave her hair down more often for more of those touches. She leaned up on her toes and met his mouth for another desperate kiss before they reluctantly said their last goodbyes and Jayson left to go home.

"Hey, Jayson..."

He turned around and took half a step back toward her. "Yeah?"

"Text me so I know you made it home safely."

"I will. Sleep sweet, Brooke."

Chapter 6

Brooke

Waking up, Brooke could have believed everything that had happened in the last twenty-four hours was one really long dream. She almost did—until she saw the blinking light on her phone alerting her of the waiting message. She caught her bottom lip in between her teeth as she unlocked her screen, hoping it was from Jayson.

It was.

> *Jayson:* I heard this song a long time ago and it always made me think of you. I listen to it all the time, and after last night, I wanted to share it with you. Can't wait to see you again, Brooke Lynn.

Attached to the message was a link to a song. *"Beneath Your Beautiful"* by Labrinth featuring Emeli Sande. Just listening to it gave her goosebumps. She had never felt like a song was written for her until she heard the words to this song. She hopped out of bed and hooked her phone up to her speaker so she could turn it up as loud as possible. She listened to the song three times before she was able to pick up the phone and send a reply.

> *Brooke:* You know, you're some kind of surprising, Jayson Williams.

> *Jayson:* I hope that means you like the song.

Brooke: It means I love the song.

Jayson: Thank you for letting me see underneath…

Brooke: Thank you for climbing walls…

Her smile was fixed on her face as she listened to it on repeat for the rest of the day while painting non-stop.

Although they had messaged each other almost incessantly since their kiss and acknowledgment of their feelings, in none of their texts had they asked each other what the kiss and conversation had actually meant. Brooke's mind raced with questions. *Were they friends? More than friends? Friends who kissed?* He told her he liked her and they had kissed… but *did that mean they were dating now?* She wished she had the guts to just ask him, but she held onto the secret fear that maybe the kiss wouldn't mean that much after all. If she could prolong knowing, maybe she could prolong the heartbreak.

Now that it was Monday and they were going to face each other for the first time since that kiss under the streetlamp, she figured she was about to get the answers to all her questions. She just hoped they'd be the answers she wanted to hear. Brooke left her hair down with a small sweet thought about his compliment and rummaged through her closet. After a few tried and abandoned outfits, she decided to wear a simple white t-shirt with a new pair of skinny jeans that had been sitting in her closet for about two months. They fit her great, and after a few spins in the mirror, she concluded they did amazing things for her butt. For the first time in her life, she wanted to make sure her butt looked good in her jeans. Whether she was ready or not, it was time to face the hallways.

"So, he showed up on your porch and then what?"

Brooke couldn't answer. The sight of Jayson waiting at her locker took her breath away. It was a combination of nerves and relief that came over her. *Had he always been this handsome?* Yeah, he had. But today… there were brand new levels to his hotness. Today, he was absolutely drool-worthy. His gray hoodie covered all the muscles she knew lay beneath. Paired with jeans and Timberlands, his clothes were a simple accentuation of all his natural good looks. Those eyes that locked onto hers and that smile with those deliciously deep dimples. Those lips...

JAYSON

"Good morning, ladies." He smiled brightly as both girls came to a stop in front of Brooke's locker.

"Morning," they said in unison.

"You look amazing. You both do," he quickly added.

Brooke smiled her appreciation as she opened the locker, her eyes barely leaving his. Jayson's eyes, however, glanced down to give her butt the fully appreciative look it deserved. As he raised his gaze, he noticed several other guys apparently had the same thought. Jayson felt a primal urge to grab it and kiss her just so the others would know they were staring at his girl. But then she fixed her smile on him again, and that was just as satisfying.

Valerie cleared her throat and gave Brooke a nudge as she used the moment to exit. "Let me get out of here before one of you spontaneously combusts from all the heated looks going on right now. I'll see you in Chem class, Brooke. Bring those notes please!"

"Oh, you need my notes now? I thought you were Asian?" Brooke laughed.

Val let out a cross between a laugh and a snort. "I'm only half Asian, and I don't appreciate the stereotype. What kind of best friend are you anyway?"

Brooke chortled. "You're crazy."

"One hundred percent. Love you, B."

"Love you, V," Brooke called after her friend.

He laughed at their interaction. Brooke had always been quiet around him, but he could see Val had gotten to see

Brooke with her walls down long before he did. Their banter was silly and endearing, reminding him of his own friendship with Brian. He was suddenly happy Brooke had had someone in her corner all these years.

She turned her attention to him again and smiled softer. "Hey."

"Hey, beautiful." He reached for her hand, only to feel her stiffen. He followed her gaze to an approaching Marisa.

She sauntered up to his side, completely ignoring Brooke's presence. "Hi, Jayson. Great game Friday."

"Thanks."

"Anyway, I'm having a huge party after the game against Newport, you better be there. My parents are going to be out of town and I have the keys to the beach house."

Brooke bristled as she watched Marisa squeeze his arm flirtatiously. This wasn't going to happen, not with him standing right here. With Marisa, actions spoke louder than words, so Jayson pulled away, grabbed Brooke's hand, and bent his head to kiss her deeply. As they parted lips, Brooke shot Marisa a pointed stare as Jayson led her away.

"Word is you and the smart girl are hooking up." Hendricks grinned as he reached into his bag of donuts.

"Didn't you already eat breakfast?" Jayson warily eyed the bag of powdered baked goods.

"It's a snack. So, it's true then?"

Jayson slid into his seat. "First of all, her name is Brooke, and we're not just hooking up, we're a couple."

"Whoa! Mr. No-Hooking-Up-Ever has a girlfriend!" Vega enthusiastically jumped into the conversation.

"Guys, can you be normal about this?"

"Probably not." Hendricks reached for another donut. "But it comes from a place of love."

"Or in Hendricks' case, a place of sugar and glaze. So, now that you and the smart girl are a thing... I guess I'll be giving you an automatic plus one to all the party invitations."

"Dude, don't do that. Her name is Brooke. It wasn't cool before she was my girl, and it's definitely not going to be cool now that she is."

"I can't believe you didn't call me like immediately after!" Brian exclaimed as Jayson tried to move past him to get to his locker.

"I'm sorry, did you want to braid each other's hair and talk about what color tuxes we were going to wear at my wedding."

"Duh!"

Jayson laughed at his best friend's most serious face. "I'm sorry. I was a little distracted by the beautiful girl in my arms."

"But still, it was your first kiss. I've waited years for this conversation. You've got to give me something more than you spent the day with her, walked her home, and then kissed her."

"Sorry, buddy. I don't kiss and tell."

"Oh, don't give me that!"

"She's everything I expected and more. Spending the day with her was an absolute game changer... and kissing her... well, that was the best moment of my life up until now."

"That good?"

"That great. That girl is meant for me." Jayson shut his locker with a confident grin. "Now, let's get down to the cafeteria so I can see her again."

Brooke

By the time lunch came around, Brooke was pretty sure that the entire school was talking about her and Jayson—including the teachers. Several bold underclassmen had come straight up to her and asked her to her face if she was dating Jayson. The problem with this was Brooke still didn't know for sure what they were supposed to be now. She and Valerie took their usual spot in the cafeteria. As she unwrapped her sandwich, Val took the opportunity to get on her case again.

"Remember what I told you about Jayson?"

"Was that before or after we decided you're crazy?" Brooke's lips twisted into a knowing smirk.

"I'm just saying, you know you can tell me I was right and I won't even bring it up except once a year on you guys' wedding anniversary." Val shrugged.

"All right already. You were right, and I'm so very happy you were!"

Valerie smiled warmly. "I'm so happy I was too! Now all you have to do is name your firstborn after me and we'll call it even."

"My firstborn, eh?"

"Yup. I will accept nothing less. So, Brooke, tell me, how does he taste?"

"What kind of question is that!"

"He probably tastes like sexy looks."

Brooke snorted with laughter. She really wasn't going to argue that point because it was true. Jayson did taste as good as he looked, and he looked—

"Well, speaking of delicious!"

Valerie's eyes widened as they both spotted Jayson, Jayden, and Brian walking over. With them came three other guys from the basketball team if their height was any indication.

"Can we sit with you beautiful ladies?"

Val gave Jayson an approving grin. "You came bearing gifts of eye-candy. Smart man."

"Brooke and Val, these are my teammates. Brian Moreau, Adam Vega, and Corey Hendricks. Fair warning: watch your plates around Hendricks."

"Nice to meet you guys!" they chorused.

Valerie shot Brooke a secret smile, then became lost in

socializing with their new lunch buddies. When it seemed like they had a private moment, she decided to just ask him what she had been dying to know.

"Jayson, I have to ask, are we, like, together now, or kind of together? What I mean is, what is our status exactly?"

Jayson smiled quizzically, his dimples deep. "Brookelynn... you are one hundred percent, absolutely, most definitely my girlfriend. Sorry I didn't make it clear on Saturday night."

She couldn't fight the embarrassment creeping up into her face. "Without a doubt?"

"No doubt."

"I'm new at this." She let him take her hand.

His smile faded as he focused those green eyes on her brown ones. "I'm new at falling in love too."

Chapter 7

Brooke

 Jayson Williams **is in a relationship with** Brooke Thomas

𝕭 rooke's phone buzzed on the nightstand, alerting her to the notification before her alarm had even sounded. She stared at the bright screen for a long moment before she felt happiness bubble up inside her. Jayson had friended and followed her on every social media account she had when they first started their study sessions weeks ago, but now he had taken their relationship to the digital level. His assurance they were official at the start of the week continued to be reinforced every time he took her hand as they walked the hallway, with every tender kiss he placed on her lips when they parted ways. If the entire school hadn't already heard news, they would now have the proof sure to get the hallways buzzing even louder.

As she moved throughout the day, her smile dimmed. The stares fixed on her in the hallway could no longer be chalked up to her own paranoia. They were looking at her, scrutinizing her, and most definitely trying to figure out what Jayson saw in her. Her mind was torn between happy and anxious thoughts, and by the end of the day, she had turned off her phone so she didn't have to deal with the influx of friend and follow requests.

It had been a long day, but all the stress seemed to melt away as she rounded the corner, finding Jayson leaning against her locker, his attention was fixed on the pages of book he was reading, the corner of his mouth tugged upwards into the most adorable smile. Her heart flipped at the sight of her boyfriend waiting for her. "I believe this is the same way we started the day."

"Then there's no better way to finish it."

He pressed a soft kiss to her lips. "Practice was cancelled today, so I was hoping I could convince you to come over my house and work on some homework together."

"Oh, man! I actually have this afternoon booked to study with another really cute guy. You know, he claims he needs the help, but I just think he wants to ask me out on a date."

"You're *so* hilarious, Brooke."

His teasing was overpowered by the bright smile he couldn't mask. She was beginning to know the feeling well.

"Come over please. My mom will be there, and you'll get a chance to get to know her. She'll insist on feeding you, and you'll love it all."

"I was going to come before you bribed me with food."

Like Jayson had promised, his mother made them eat as they worked through their homework together. She filled their plates with moro, a delicious rice and bean combination, roasted pork, and tostones—something Jisela insisted she had just thrown together.

"This might possibly be the best meal I've ever had in my entire life."

Jisela smiled generously. "¡Gracias! I'm glad you enjoy it. ¡Come más! Eat more!"

Brooke opened her mouth to find some reason to object

when another full plate was put in front of her. Jisela whisked her empty plate back off to the kitchen just as quickly, leaving Jayson chuckling and Brooke with a slight case of whiplash.

"You might as well just get used to it right now."

"If she keeps this up, I'm going to have to roll home." She lifted another forkful of food into her mouth and closed her eyes in pleasure. "I really shouldn't be eating all this."

"If you enjoy it, why not?"

"Because..." She rolled the words around in her mouth, taking a moment before continuing. "Everyone's going to be looking at me more now, and I don't want to embarrass you."

Jayson paused mid-chew and kept his eyes focused on hers. "Embarrass me? Why would you—"

His eyes clouded over as he set his fork down. "Brooke, are you trying to tell me you think you're fat?"

"No. I just know I would probably be better off if I lost ten or twenty pounds."

Jayson shot up out of his chair. "Ten or twenty! Are you insane, girl!"

Pulling her to her feet, he looked into her eyes. "You really don't see yourself then. Close your eyes."

The breathy command sent a shiver over her skin, tingling in places she didn't know she could tingle. She did as he instructed.

Running his fingers through her hair, he drew in a breath. "I love your hair. Most people would just say it's brown, but it's not. You have all these different layers of colors... some red in there too. I wouldn't know, but I would guess it's natural, not created from any bottle or salon chair."

He was right. She drew in her bottom lip.

"I could go on all day about what I love about your face. I love everything about it. But for now... let's focus on your lips. You drive me crazy when you pull that lip in between your teeth like that. I know you do it when you're nervous or thinking things over, but every time you get going on that lip, I want to get going on that lip."

He leaned in closer, and before she could draw in any air,

his lips were on hers. Wrapping an arm around her lower back, he held her close to him as her knees went weak. The second her lips parted his tongue tangled with hers in a delicious movement that left her wanting as he pulled back.

"I'm not done yet, so we'll have to get back to that later."

His hand moved to cup her neck. His strong hands were gentle as his thumbs found a particularly sensitive spot near her ear. "Your neck... don't ask me why I'm fascinated with your neck. Maybe it's from the years of strategically picking seats behind you in any class I could try to match up with yours. I could always tell when you were in the art room because you'd have little speckles of paint on this neck, almost like rainbow freckles. I've spent a lot of time looking at this neck, thought about all the kisses I wanted to put there, all the little spots I wanted to taste. The first spot is going to be right here."

He tapped his finger twice on the spot where her neck met her collarbone.

"Now, the next things I say, I want you to remember, as your boyfriend, I'm saying this with the highest admiration and respect for you. Brookelynn, your breasts are possibly the most perfect breasts in the entire world. I want to touch you there... kiss you there... but I won't. Not yet. We aren't ready for that yet. We're both new to all this, and we're just getting started. I know I need way more self-control before we can get to that level. But trust me when I say, I frequently enjoy just thinking about getting to that level with you."

If she had breathed at all as she listened to him, she couldn't tell. Her chest was tight, and her body felt warm and loose.

How was he saying all the right things—no, all the perfect things?

"Your body is perfect. I could spend hours doing just this."

His hands moved down her ribcage and waist to her hips, his fingers just barely grazing the sides of her butt before he made the return trip back up. "Perfect. Don't ever feel like it's any different."

She barely managed a nod.

"Your butt... my God, Brooke. Your butt makes me feel like a caveman. I want to grab it all the time. You turn heads in the hallway, but you don't even notice because you are so not aware of how sexy your body is. It makes me proud and jealous all at the same time. Your butt is going into the level with the breasts. When we get there... please know I'll be very thorough."

She practically vibrated with anticipation. "Jayson?"

"Yeah?" His voice was throaty and rough, giving her another thrill. She was having just as much of an effect on him.

"Kiss me?"

"Broo—" Her name was lost in the deep kiss he gave her. She whimpered as he dipped his body to grab the back of her thighs, lifting her off the ground. It lasted only a moment before he returned her to feet.

"Open your eyes, beautiful."

She did as he said, looking at him through misty eyes. "Thank you."

"I wish I could finish, but I'm starting to forget we're not alone in the house. Just know you are the most beautiful girl in the world to me. Now, come on... let me feed you."

He didn't realize he had already fed her soul.

When the younger ones arrived home from school, they both helped them with their work as well. Brooke was in the middle of coloring with Justin when she smiled. She may have been falling for Jayson, but now she was also falling in love with his whole family. She had never experienced the kind of organized chaos that ensued with younger siblings, and she felt the love they all had between them.

"Brooke is the bestest colorer in the world!" Justin announced proudly as they were joined by the others in the living room.

"Is that so, mijo?" Jisela gave Brooke a playful wink. "Ever since your last visit, we've been hearing a lot about you Brooke. You stole the hearts of two boys that day."

Her heart swelled, happy the feeling of adoration was mutual. "I think there was a fair exchange of hearts that day, Mrs. Williams."

Jisela's eyes filled with a warmth as she gave Brooke's shoulder a gentle squeeze. "My boys have good taste."

When Brooke's mother arrived to pick her up after she got off work, she happily introduced Evelyn to Jayson's brothers and his mother. While their mothers talked inside the house, Jayson walked Brooke out to her mom's car.

"Text me when you're ready for bed." He played with a lock of her hair before tucking it behind her ear.

She nodded. "It all feels like a dream. My cheeks hurt from smiling."

"I would've never thought I could win your heart."

"Just don't go breaking it." Brooke looked at him seriously.

"I promise. I won't hurt you, Brookelynn."

He kissed her forehead and hugged her close until her mother exited the house. Though she was really enjoying being held by Jayson, she was excited to spend some quality time with her mother. She couldn't wait to tell her everything that had been building and developing between her and Jayson. She talked all the way through dinner excitedly with Evelyn gushing with her daughter at all the right points. Finally, she reached out and took Brooke's hand.

"Are you happy?"

Brooke eyes filled with tears. "I'm so very happy, Mom. But I'm so scared too."

Evelyn cupped her cheek. "Oh, Brooke, being scared to lose love once you have it... well that's just part being in love. Promise me you'll never scare yourself out of love."

Brooke nodded. Her mother was right. She would have to trust that Jayson would be there for her in the same way she wanted to be there for him. If that afternoon hadn't been enough proof, he had this special way of looking at her when he talked that offered so many silent assurances. If she was going to be good for him, if she wanted to have his love one day, she realized she needed to accept herself. She needed to recognize she was good enough for him to love, no matter what anyone else said.

Brooke's new resolve didn't remain untainted.

It only took twenty-four hours before it all started. Random comments from fake social media accounts began to trickle in to her feed daily. They accused her of paying Jayson to pretend to be her boyfriend. They called her names, told her to disappear from life, that once she was gone, Jayson would forget all about her. It didn't stay online. Notes being dropped into her locker became a common thing. In fact, that morning, Brooke found an anonymous letter in her locker reminding her she was a "nobody" and would be better off if she just disappeared. It shouldn't have bothered her, at least that's what she told herself, but it did. In that moment, she wished she could do just that: disappear.

She tucked the note into her notebook and tried to discreetly wipe the tears out of her eyes. She couldn't let them break her, not here where they could see they were tearing away at the strong façade she put on every morning. Instead of waiting for Jayson at her locker, she quickly shut it and headed down to the art room—her sanctuary.

Putting in her headphones, she let the rest of the noise fade away as she placed the brush on her canvas.

Chapter 8

JAYSON

Jayson had waited for Brooke to show up at her locker the same as he did every day. But today, he waited until he was almost late for first period. He wondered if she was sick, then thought against it since she had sounded fine when they'd talked on the phone the night before. Hurrying to his own first period class, he quickly messaged her.

> Hey Beautiful. Waited for you at your locker, are you here today?

He didn't get a reply until class was almost over.

> **Brookelynn:** Yeah. I'll probably see you later today.

That was all she had wrote. He could feel that something was wrong, and he wasn't going to leave it to chance on whether he'd see her. As soon as the bell rang, he hurried out of class and headed straight for the one place he knew she would be. Opening the door to Ms. Cullen's room, the smell of paint hit him, reminding him of his girl. This was her safe place. She was in here somewhere.

"Jayson? What can I help you with? I don't often see you down here."

Ms. Cullen's voice surprised him, but he gave her his best sheepish smile. "No, ma'am. I'm not usually in this wing, but I was looking for Brooke."

With a knowing glimmer in her eye, she smiled. "Ah, yes. Brooke is in the studio next door working on her piece for this weekend's art show."

"Is it okay if I go over?"

"Sure thing. She probably has headphones on, so she might not hear you knock. Just go on in."

Sure enough, when he opened the door, he found her transfixed to what was on the large canvas in front of her. Her hair was pulled up with no less than three pencils protruding from her bun. The large button-down shirt she wore was splattered in paint, and she had green paint smeared across her chin. His breath caught in his throat in awe of how serene she looked. When Jayson walked closer, her head shot up, eyes wide in surprise. Half a second later, she went to work on that bottom lip.

"Jayson? What are you doing here?"

"You act like the art wing is Siberia. I'm here to see you obviously. I missed you."

Wrapping her in his arms, he bent down to press a kiss to her lips. As he pulled back, his eyes moved over to look at what she was painting. There, underneath all the colors, his eyes were drawn into the center of the canvas. It was undeniably them. He was transported to that night under the streetlamp where they shared their first kiss. It was one of their very first intimate moments, one that meant the most to him because he'd finally gotten his beautiful girl to open up to him.

"You like it?" she asked tentatively.

"No, I love it. It's amazing, Brooke."

"I didn't know how you'd feel about me entering it in the art show. I originally intended for it to just be a sketch, but I couldn't help but to paint it. And once I started, I couldn't stop."

His heart seemed to swell four times its size in his chest. "I'd feel proud if you entered this in the art show. Can I have it when you're finished?"

"You really want it?"

He nodded, unable to pull his eyes away from the painting. "Absolutely. I need it."

"Okay." He could hear the smile come back into her voice. "The art show is Thursday evening. If it wins, it goes on display near the office, but after that, it's yours."

"What time on Thursday? I have practice, but I'd like to come after if you're okay with that."

"It's from six-thirty to eight-thirty."

"I'll be there around seven."

She exhaled a long, shaky breath. "Okay. I'd really like that."

"Brooke... is everything okay with us? Are you having second thoughts?"

He watched the emotions shift from happiness to that guarded expression he had seen countless times before. He stepped closer to tip her paint-streaked chin. He wanted her eyes on his during this conversation.

"Everything is okay." She pushed up on her toes and placed a kiss on his cheek. "No second thoughts."

"Hey, Jay, want to grab a burger after showers?"

"No can do. I have to get downtown. Brooke's in an art show and I told her I would stop by to support her."

"And it begins..." Brian made a sound strongly reminiscent of a whip cracking.

Jayson laughed as he pulled off his sweaty t-shirt. "Don't even start. We can grab burgers tomorrow after the game like we always do, but this relationship thing with Brooke... I have waited a long time for this girl, and it's new..."

"All right, I hear you, I hear you."

"Thanks, man. How about we do something this weekend?"

"Sure." Brian grinned. "If I don't have a hot date."

Chuckling to himself, Jayson tossed his sweaty t-shirt in the direction of his best friend. He hurried through his shower and dressed into a pair of his nicest dress pants and a button-down shirt. He wanted to make sure he looked like he fit in among the art gallery crowd. If Brooke was going to introduce him as her boyfriend, and he hoped she would, he wanted to make her proud. Brian had given him a ride into town, so he arrived a few minutes before seven. He walked around, halfway admiring the other pieces, but mainly looking for his girl. When he found her, he restrained himself from kissing her breathless. Her hair was braided into a loose braid. She wore a simple white sleeveless blouse with a black and white polka dot skirt that flared around her mid-thigh. Her black knee-socks were perfectly straight, and her feet were tucked into a pair of Dr. Martens shoes instead of her usual boots. Simple and sexy, and still completely unaware of that fact.

"You made it!"

"I told you I would. I wouldn't have missed it. You look beautiful, Brookelynn."

He placed a chaste kiss to her lips before giving his full attention to the completed painting on the wall.

"You're totally going to win."

"You're not biased or anything," she teased quietly.

"Biased or not, this is incredible. You are amazing. I mean, just looking at what you've done with a brush and some paint... how you captured every emotion I felt that night."

"Hey there, dimples!"

Jayson spun around... and looked down... to find Val had joined them. Last time he had seen her, he could have sworn her hair had been streaked with hot pink, but now, the top half of her hair was its natural rich black, while the bottom half was a vibrant turquoise. She had it pulled into a very sophisticated looking topknot. Her trouser shorts and suspenders over her simple black t-shirt and a pair of moccasins completed her look. If it was anyone else, the look wouldn't have worked, but on Val, it just did.

"How did your screening go?" Brooke grabbed her friend's hand eagerly.

"Seemed liked they enjoyed it. We'll see, though."

"You have a piece here too?" Jayson looked around the room, curious as to which piece belonged to her.

"Not in this room. In the adjacent building, there's a small community theater for a lot of indie films. I entered a small piece into the Short Film Festival. I just had my screening."

"Val is going to be bigger than any of those big name guys behind the camera. Her passion is documentary and film journalism."

"I'd like to see your stuff. I mean, if you're the sharing short."

"I like him, Brooke." She reached up and patted his cheek. "I like you, dimples."

He liked her too.

Jayson didn't even gloat when Brooke's painting was chosen for first prize. He had cheered like he was at a sporting event, and she giggled, telling him it made her heart proud that he refused to dull his enthusiasm. After the crowd began to thin, he carried the painting with the same amount of pride to the car with the promise to help her hang it in the main wing over the weekend.

On Monday morning, they decided to go see it before first period, only to find a crowd around it already. Her nerves kicked up, but he pressed a kiss to the hand he held.

"I told you it was incredible, babe. They all just want to see how…"

His words fell off as his eyes fixed to her painting, darkening with something she'd never seen before. She dropped his hand and pushed her way through the crowd, only to freeze. She had poured her heart and soul onto that canvas, and someone had covered it with ugly words in an angry red spray paint. She squeezed her eyes shut and drew in a breath. They were all watching her, waiting for her to break. Calmly, she took the painting off the wall and walked off. Jayson followed closely behind, assuring her he'd figure out who did it, muttering angry promises.

"Just forget it, Jayson."

"How can I? Someone did this to hurt you, I can't just forget it."

"Yeah, you can. It's not the first time, and it won't be the last—especially not while I am in this school, and definitely not while you're showing me any kind of attention."

He reeled at the information. "Why didn't you tell me what's been happening?"

"You think that would have helped? These girls... I won't let them know they got to me. I can't show them weakness. You trying to protect me... that's just going to make it worse. They ignored me before we started spending time together, now tormenting me is their favorite subject."

"Brookelynn, if you know who did this, you have to tell me. Please tell me."

She opened her locker door and stared at him as he watched the folded paper notes tumble to the ground. With a heavy sigh, she retrieved the notebook she needed for class, pulled out the original note, and pressed it into his palm. "Let's just say all of *this* is my friendly daily reminder I'm out of my league. I need to go check something in the art wing. I'll see you later."

Leaving him with the collection of notes and ruined painting, Brooke walked off to hide from everyone.

Jayson fumed as he read the notes. This was exactly the thing Brooke was so used to believing, and he wasn't fond of the knowledge anyone in the school was trying to bully her into leaving him. He tracked Marisa down fairly quickly. Surrounded by her usual group of friends, her eyes widened happily as he stalked toward her.

"Hi there, Jayson." She smiled innocently at him.

"Back off, Marisa. I mean it. Leave us alone."

Marisa smiled a bit, then said, "I have no idea what you're talking about."

"Yes, you do. I don't know if you wrote the note or ruined

the painting, but I know you know who did. Tell your friends to mind their own business. I don't want to date you. Never have. I only want her. I don't want to have to have this conversation again. Leave Brooke alone."

He stormed off down the hallway, not waiting to hear any reaction from her. Knowing Brooke, she was off writing a list of things that would convince her to push him away again and go back to hiding in the art room. He couldn't let that happen—not after all he'd worked through to get here in the first place.

"Did you really tell Queen of PC to back off?" Brian laughed as he swung into the seat next to him in their math class.

"You mean the Queen of Mean? Yeah, I did, and I'd do it again. Girl has a bad attitude and I'm sick of her and her friends bullying Brooke around, especially because of me."

He slid Brian the note that had been left for Brooke. "They ruined her painting, then I found out they've been filling her locker with these and messaging her online."

Brian sobered as he read it. "Is Brooke okay?"

He wanted to say yes, but the truth was, he didn't know. She was already cooling toward him. Every time he tried to hold her hand or kiss her, she'd stiffen and look around to see who was watching them. He hated it.

"We haven't even been official for that long and she's getting scared off because of them. I have to get her mind off the stupidity in the hallways."

"Do what I would do."

Jayson threw his best friend a warning look, and Brian laughed loudly.

"I am not that bad! I mean, take her out, wine and dine her."

Jayson smiled. "You know, that's not a bad idea. We haven't hung out without studying or my brothers in the way. Thanks, man. I'm going to text her about it."

He had a game schedule to work around, but he couldn't wait.

Jayson: Hey, Brookelynn... can you meet me down at the gym before you leave for the day?

Brooke: Yeah, sure. Everything okay?

Jayson: It will be.

Chapter 9

Brooke

After the day she had, Brooke was wary about walking into the gym during practice. Once she made it down to the large double doors, she hesitated, watching him through the glass window on the door until she made eye contact and he jogged over. She may have been used to seeing his face and all its gorgeousness, but watching Jayson Williams running over sweaty and shirtless? It was enough to make her grip the doorjamb to keep her body in check. She fought a strange desire to kiss every muscle, or maybe lick them to remind herself and everyone else he was indeed her boyfriend. She shivered from the thought.

"Hey. What's up?" she asked as he drew near. She willed her eyes to focus on his green ones instead of the deep lines defining his pectoral muscles and his one, two, three—eight pack of abdominal muscles... *seriously, eight?*

"Just wanted to tell you in person we're going out on a date Friday."

Her eyes widened in surprise. "I thought you had the big game against Newport?"

"I do. But it's a home game. Right after, I'm taking you out on a date. Our first official couple status date night."

She smiled happily for the first time all day. "Where are we going?"

"That's not how it works." He laughed. "Just prepare

yourself to be romanced."

"Okay, I can do that."

He pulled her in for a quick, but deep kiss. "Keep smiling, sweet girl. That smile makes my day."

Their moment was interrupted by the hollers and cheers of his team. Brooke's face burned with embarrassment as Jayson laughed.

"Hey, Williams, you plan on joining us for the rest of practice or are you studying the young lady's anatomy?"

"Can you blame me, Coach? My girl is freaking beautiful."

Coach Beckett tried to control his team, but still threw Brooke a small, teasing smile. "She'll still be beautiful after you run these suicides. Let's go, Captain."

"Yes, sir. I'll call you later, babe."

Babe.

With that simple term of endearment, she was able to float all the way home and through the rest of the school week without much more drama.

When Friday arrived, she was excited to be with Jayson. He had been so busy with intense two-a-day practices or workouts, their time had been limited lately. The team was prepping for an important game they would play before their date, so Brooke knew she'd really only be seeing Jayson between classes, lunch periods, and text messages before bed.

The day before, she had put her brave face on and told Jayson she wanted to go to the game to support him, but he insisted she enjoy getting ready for their date at home. He told her he wanted to give her all the first date treatment since it was her very first, and he wanted to pick her up at her house after the game.

Since Jayson was going to be picking her up around seven that evening, directly after school, Valerie and Brooke went to the nail salon to begin her preparation. Val helped her calm her nerves while simultaneously amping up her excitement. After their nails were manicured to perfection, Valerie bustled her home and helped Brooke curl her hair into beautiful ringlets. By the time her mom had arrived home, they were starting on her makeup.

"You may be talented with the paintbrush, my little Brookie boo, but I must say I know how to wield the makeup brush flawlessly. You look absolutely smashing, dahling."

"Oh, sweetheart! You are stunning," her mother said, tears ready to fall.

"Mom, don't cry!" Brooke giggled.

"I can't help it. You're my baby." Evelyn smiled warmly. "I stopped by the store and got you something to wear tonight. Something special. Come to my bedroom when you're all finished up here."

Brooke blew her mom a kiss. "I love you, Mom."

Brooke felt beautiful. More than that, she felt hot. As she admired her reflection for the second... or fourth time, she took note of everything. The spaghetti strap black dress her mother had bought fit amazing, like it was made for her and only her. Val's makeup job was simple and stunning, a dramatic smoky eye, but the rest kept to a minimal natural tone. She strapped on the black stiletto open-toed heels her mom had purchased as well before revealing herself to her mom and Val.

They both smiled brightly as she stepped in the room. Evelyn teared up while Val began applauding.

"You look amazing! Why have you been hiding that body?" Val cooed, coaxing her to spin around.

"You're so beautiful, Brooke." Her mom sniffed.

"Let's hope I get the same reaction from Jayson!" she laughed happily. She felt incredible and couldn't wait for him to see her.

JAYSON

> Thinking of you. Can't wait to see you. I'll text you when the game is over and I'm on my way.

Jayson had been excited for his date with Brooke all week. He had planned it meticulously and drew up a schedule for after the game so he could make sure everything ran smoothly. He even had an order of flowers scheduled to be delivered to her since he wouldn't make it to the florist on time. Storing his change of clothes into his locker for after the game, making sure the car keys he'd borrowed from his mother were stored safely into the pocket of his duffel bag, he sent Brooke a final text message before he ran off to join his team on the court and talk to his coach.

No sooner than stepped out on the court, he saw them sitting in the stands: college Scouts. He could spot them easily scattered throughout the crowd, eying each other competitively, waiting for the game to start. He felt his heart rate quicken.

Coach Beckett approached. "All right now, son, you know what this means. It's your time, Jayson. This is your season to solidify what they already think. The last three years, they've been drooling over you on the court... now it's time to make them really fight for you. You ready?"

"More than ever." Jayson nodded seriously.

He meant it. He had hoped for this for years. Now, it was happening, and he knew he had to show his ability and potential. Brooke had helped him stay eligible, but he had to put in the rest of the work to prove he was worth every penny of a full athletic scholarship. He shook the coach's outstretched hand before he ran over to join his brother and Brian.

He couldn't have asked for a better game. For the first two quarters, Jayson was a dominating force on the court. He was close to breaking his own personal best game record by halftime, and his team as a whole was performing flawlessly. By the start of the fourth quarter, his adrenaline was pumping. He had to bring the game to a close with a strong finish.

The ball rolled off the tips of his fingers, sailing through the air, a smooth three-point buzzer beater.

At the sound of the buzzer, Jayson was overwhelmed by his cheerful teammates. They were quickly joined by the animated fans from the stands. The air felt electric, pulsing with post-game endorphins and unbridled excitement. They were now three games into the season and undefeated. A win like this had them all invigorated with a renewed determination to make it to the championship playoff games undefeated once again. Then there was also the knowledge that he had just bested his own personal records in just three quarters. If he kept his focus and his game up to par, he'd have no issues with college recruitment. He looked up to see the recruiters as they stood. They all looked at him, smiling and giving a nod of the head before they began walking toward the doors.

Jayson felt like he was on top of the world.

Brooke

Brooke checked the time on her phone again. It was almost eight-thirty. She looked over at the bouquet of flowers that had been delivered in his name. She had already put them in water and read the card a dozen times. Jayson was an hour and a half late. He hadn't called, nor was he answering her calls or text messages. She was beginning to worry something terrible had happened, so she decided to give his home phone a try.

Jisela answered.

"Hi, Mrs. Williams, it's Brooke Thomas."

"Oh, yes. Hi, Brooke!"

"I'm sorry to interrupt your evening, but I was just trying to get a hold of Jayson. I was expecting him around seven and he hasn't answered his phone."

"Oh, dear. I spoke with him and Jayden right after the game. They were going to celebrate their big win. I thought you were with him."

"Oh, okay. No worries. I'll track him down. Maybe he lost track of time. Thanks, Mrs. Williams."

Within minutes, Brooke had phoned Valerie asking her to come pick her up. As soon as Val's car pulled up to the curb in front of her house, she grabbed her purse and sweater, then ran out before her mother could question why Val was picking her up instead of Jayson.

Val's face was somber as Brooke buckled her seatbelt.

"Thanks for giving me a ride."

"Of course. Are you sure you want to do this?"

"Yeah, I'm sure. I need to at least see for myself."

Val nodded once before pulling the car back onto the road. They were headed to the one place she thought he might be. Her heart was racing a mile a minute, and her stomach was in knots. She squeezed her hands together, hoping Jayson was anywhere but the one place she thought he might be. Tears stung at her eyes, but she blinked them away, refusing to let them fall, especially when she had no proof he had stood her up just yet.

"Please let me be wrong." Her voice was barely a whisper, but Val reached over and squeezed her hand reassuringly.

Brooke walked through the open front door, the smell of beer and teenage hormones assaulting her nose. *Was this what she was missing out on every weekend?* She passed an intense make-out session between two of her peers and almost crashed into a makeshift beer pong game happening on a table that probably cost more than some people's cars. She looked to Val in question just as a chanting crowd in the next room drew her attention.

MVP. MVP. MVP.

Something churning in her gut told her it was going to be bad. Her head told her to turn around and walk away, that she'd be able to forget this whole little interlude with Jayson. But her heart was a different story. Her heart demanded she walk into that room and find Jayson. Her heart demanded she ask him why he hadn't shown up for her, why he got her hopes up, only to let her down. Her heart needed to know.

Her heart was stupid.

It was like watching a bad car accident. Everything in you tells you to look away, but some twisted, morbid curiosity keeps your eyes stuck on the wreck. This time, the main casualty in the wreck was her heart. She wanted to look away. She didn't want to see Jayson betraying her trust on the dancefloor. But her eyes wouldn't listen to her brain. They wouldn't even blink. When Marisa decided to rub her body against his as they danced, Brooke saw it all. She started toward them, but once she saw Marisa lean in to kiss his neck, she was forced to stop. It felt like all the air had been sucked from her lungs, and all she wanted to do was get out of there before the tears came. She couldn't let them have the satisfaction. She turned around too fast and bumped into someone who caught her, but it was too late for the lamp she sent crashing to the floor.

"Brooke, are you okay?" Jayden's voice broke through the blood rushing in her ears just as Val took firm hold of her elbow.

They both looked over at Jayson.

"Jayson! What are you doing?" Jayden yelled, grabbing the attention of everyone else. She cringed knowing her hopes to escape unnoticed were fleeting fast.

JAYSON

J ayson had a specific plan. The same plan had fallen to pieces the moment he pulled the car to a stop in the empty parking space behind Brian's car. The celebratory mood from the victory had moved from the gymnasium to the Coates' beach house. As they all piled out of their respective cars, Jayson couldn't help but feel the word house was a bit understated for the property. The sprawling house was set on a private beach, and there seemed to be people in every direction. Jayden quickly spotted his best friend, and both boys headed off in the direction of the bonfire on the beach.

Brian bumped the side of his fist with his own. "Well, this looks like an epic night in the making."

Jayson shrugged and opened his mouth to reply when they were interrupted by the approach of a girl wearing Newport colors. Her smile was friendly enough, but her eyes were fixed on Brian, heavy with want. "Nice game number eleven."

"Well, thank you. I don't think we've met. I'm Brian."

"I know. You can call me Kat."

Jayson cleared his throat. Brian patted his shoulder absently. "Care to join me inside, Kat? I'll grab you a drink."

"It's too crowded in there. How about you join me? My car is back this way."

Her invitation was clear, and Brian moved forward before Jayson knew it.

"I'll be right back—"

"Oh, please don't hurry on my account. I'm leaving anyway. I've got to get to Brooke," Jayson replied wryly.

"Oh, right..." the rest of Brian's reply was lost as Kat's lips found his and they disappeared into the maze of cars lining the gravel. Jayson knew he'd be hearing about this tomorrow as soon as Brian had the chance.

Chuckling, he sent off a text message to his brother, reminding him to keep his head about him and check in.

Turning to open the door to the car, he froze at the sound of Hendricks' all too familiar booming voice.

"Captain Jay! Come on!"

"I can't. I'm going to be late."

"None of that. Just come in for an hour. Celebrate with the team!"

Checking his watch, he relented, agreeing to fifteen minutes max before he would absolutely have to leave. He reasoned his presence at the party was solely there to support his team, not hang out with Marisa and her friends. Fifteen minutes would be just fine.

The bass of the music pumped as Vega handed him a cup of his signature Jungle Juice. Jayson never drank alcohol, he rarely even partied, but by the time he emptied the cup, he was feeling way more loose and sociable. The second cup went down a lot faster, followed by two chugged beers someone put in his hands. Jayson had lost all sense of time when Marisa dragged him onto the dancefloor.

And he was completely unaware Brooke was watching him.

Jayson looked up at his brother's voice and saw Brooke. He'd never been drunk before that night, but the sight of her was enough to sober him to all the realities of how badly he had screwed things up with her. She was gorgeous and furious. The combination of the two gutted him at the full realization of all the ways the night had gone wrong. Just the sight of her set his heart soaring and crashing simultaneously. How could she be so devastatingly beautiful?

She had always been gorgeous, but that dress she wore put all the things he loved on display. It was simple, though her body was anything but. She was sexier than he ever imagined. Her cleavage was more alluring than ever before, and the curves of her hips and butt were now undeniable. Her hair and the makeup took her from beautiful to exotic and sexy. Brooke had stepped out of her comfort zone, and he knew she'd done it for him. She was always thinking about him, even now, her eyes glistening with hurt and anger.

He had done that to her, and the thought turned his stomach inside out. Without so much as speaking a word to him, she turned on her heels and hurried away from the party.

"Brooke! Wait! Please!"

Brooke

Brooke's vision was clouded with tears, and her balance was unstable as she ran in stilettos across the gravel driveway. Val did a great job of keeping up with her, only occasionally looking back as Jayson followed her unrelentingly.

"Brooke, I'm so sorry. Please, just let me try to explain."

"I don't care, Jayson!" she yelled, furiously wiping a tear away. *Not yet. Don't let them see you cry. Hold it...*

"Brooke, there were college scouts at the game and I played so good. I lost track of time celebrating..."

"Celebrating? Getting drunk and having some girl rub her butt on your crotch while you high-five your drunk teammates while your supposed girlfriend waits at home like a fool. Oh, well, excuse me then. Go celebrate some more! I get it. If you're embarrassed of me, you should have said something."

"I'm not! I would never be!"

Brooke snorted in a sarcastic chortle. "Please, Jayson, just save it. You wouldn't even let me come to the game."

"Brooke, I did that for you, not me. You were so uncomfortable last time, I thought you would feel more comfortable just waiting at home."

"I don't believe you. You didn't want me there, you didn't even bother to call me and say, 'Hey, Brooke, change of plans, I want to hang with my team so come to the party with me.' No, you couldn't do that because then you'd have to admit you wanted to party with all the people who've been leaving me nasty messages."

"Brooke—"

She let out a sardonic laugh. "You hurt me, Jayson. You promised you wouldn't, and you did it anyway. The ironic part is Marisa and all the rest of those people in there... they were right after all. Joke's on me! Good thing I'm a smart girl and I'll never let it happen again. Enjoy your victory."

"It was an accident!"

"*We* were an accident. You, Jayson, are exactly who I thought you were. And I'm glad I found out now rather than later."

She opened the car door, but he moved to block her way. "Brookelynn, you know that's not true. You know me better than this. I know you're angry, but please don't do this to me. Don't break my heart."

Brooke pushed past him and got into the car. "I can't break something I never even had. You can go tell Marisa she won. We're done, Jayson."

JAYSON

We're done, Jayson.

Tears burned Jayson's eyes as he watched her speed away out of sight. As the red lights turned off the road, his chest cracked open with emotion. He knew what it was like to lose someone you love, but the feeling of watching someone you love walk away from you... that was a whole other kind of pain. He had been certain he was falling in deep with Brooke before they were even officially a couple. Over the last few weeks, his feelings for her had gone far beyond a crush, but he knew she wasn't ready for those words yet. So, he held back from expressing the depth of his feelings for her. It had been weeks for her, but it had been years for him. Years... and he had blown it all in just a couple hours.

By the time Brian, Nathan, and Jayden reached him, he was trying his hardest not to break down and cry right there in the driveway.

"Jay, you okay? What happened? Where's Brooke?" Brian gripped his shoulder tightly, trying to get Jayson to look at him.

"I need to get out of here." He spoke roughly, shaking his head at nothing in particular but everything in general. Brooke was gone. *We're done, Jayson.*

Brian grabbed his keys. "Let's go. I haven't had anything to drink tonight."

As they walked toward the car, Marisa approached Jayson and handed him his cell phone. With a smile sweet as candy, she simply said, "Thanks for coming, guys."

She was so evil. She had manipulated him, bullied Brooke, and did it all with a smile. He wanted to yell at her to make her feel a fraction of the pain he felt, but he stopped himself from saying anything. Hurting her feelings wasn't going to change the fact that he screwed up. He had known all along Marisa was manipulative and jealous, but he'd still stupidly shown up at her house. Everything that happened was his fault. He'd failed Brooke.

The drive home was laced with silent tension. His brother had given up all mutterings about Brooke's feelings once he saw the tears that fell from Jayson's eyes as they drove. He was certain they all saw those tears, but he didn't care as long as they didn't try to talk to him about it. There was nothing they could say to make anything better. There was only one person he wanted to talk to. That person would be the only one who could make it all better. That same person had just told him she was never going to talk to him again.

Brooke

"I'm an idiot, Val."

"No you aren't." Val handed her a fresh batch of Kleenex.

Brooke laid back on her best friend's bed. "He played me. I should have known it was all one big joke. Marisa was right."

"I'm going to punch him in those dimples!" Val growled.

The memory of how that dimpled smile had made her knees week and her heart flutter washed over her and another sob rolled through her chest. "This is why I didn't want to do this with him. Now I'm one of those girls crying ugly black mascara tears over some pathetic high school crush. I'm going to be the laughing stock of the PCH for the rest of the year."

"Can I pull the honesty card here?"

Brooke let out a moan. The honesty card meant she was about to hear something she probably wasn't ready for.

"Can you pull the honesty card tomorrow? I need the best friend card for a little longer."

Val squeezed her hand. "I can do that. I have some ice cream in the freezer, I'll be right back."

Val let her vent out all her anger. And when she found more tears to cry, it was Val who held her and reassured her. Once Brooke had settled down a little, it was also Val who helped her clean up enough to go home. She slowly made her way back into the house, crept past the living room where her mother slept on the couch, and walked up the stairs to her bedroom. After she changed into her pajamas, she hung the dress in the back of her closet. She'd probably never wear it again. The thought made her even more angry when she remembered how great she'd felt about herself just hours earlier. Crawling into bed, she smothered a new batch of fresh tears into her pillows until she was ready to fall asleep, but not before she got back out of the bed and threw the flowers in the vase on her bedside table out of the window, shutting it firmly behind her.

Chapter 10

JAYSON

Not only was he chewed out and grounded by his mother for multiple things that evening, but he was brokenhearted and angry at himself for losing her. He couldn't stop calling her. He didn't want to let her go. It was not an option to him. He filled up her voicemail inbox to capacity. Eventually, she must have just turned her phone off because he began hearing the automated voice tell him right away the inbox was full. He knew what that really meant: you've screwed up the best thing that ever happened to you, the only thing you ever wanted, and you did it in less than a night. When he had practically memorized each one of the messages she had left for him on his phone, he moved on to rereading all the texts he had missed from her while Marisa had his phone. It killed him to know while she was excited for their first date, he was having his first drink. As she grew more concerned, he was dancing it up on the dancefloor.

How could he have forgotten something so important... the girl who had his heart?

She was wrong, he hadn't made a fool out of her, he'd made a fool of himself.

Maybe he was an optimistic idiot to think he could win her back. But he couldn't just give her up. If she wouldn't take his calls, he would just have to talk to her in person. She could hide at home, but she couldn't hide from school.

Come Monday morning that was where he'd have to take his chance.

Brooke

B rooke didn't want to go to school. Her mother had asked if she was sick, and she could have just said yes so she could buy some more time to hide under her covers, but her pride got the best of her.

Marisa may have gotten Jayson, but she did not want her to think she had broken her. She may have broken up with Jayson, but her vow to think the best of herself was one she intended to keep. She needed to go to school, to walk through the halls with her head held high. So, instead of staying home, she woke up even earlier. She wanted the time to get her thoughts together before she had to face everyone again. They would all be watching her, looking for red-rimmed eyes and every sign of her personal devastation so they could whisper about it through the halls. If they wanted to talk about her, she would give them something to talk about.

She scoured her closet for something that would do the trick. After showering off the smell of heartbreak and chocolate, she dressed into a tight-fitted, short-sleeved, cable knit sweater, a denim mini skirt, a pair of knee-socks, and Dr. Martens. She kept her hair down after straightening the remnants of her curls out, pushing it away from her face with a wide headband. She checked her reflection, pleased to see it was a meeting place between her personal style and pushing the boundaries of her comfort zone again. Despite how bad she felt on the inside, at least she looked good on the outside.

Walking through the halls with her eyes fixed straight ahead, she was almost to her locker when she noticed Jayson waiting for her. Her nerves zapping to life almost made her stumble, but she took a deep breath and steadied herself. Her jaw clenched to keep her emotions in check. *Stay strong.* That was the mantra for the day, and she repeated it over and over in her head.

At her locker, she ignored his presence and focused on entering her combination. She hoped he didn't notice her fingers shaking as she turned the dial. She fought the urge to look up into his sea green eyes, needing another moment of gathering her inner strength.

"Brooke, I really want to talk to you about everything."

JAYSON

For a moment, she froze, and he swallowed, preparing to repeat himself, to beg for her to look at him, for any sign she heard him. Slowly, she fixed her eyes on his, and his mouth went dry and he felt like his tongue went numb. Those brown, soulful eyes he'd longed to have look at him with affection for years, now looked at him with contempt. It broke his heart. She stood in front of him, giving him the chance to say the things he had been wanting to say to her since Friday night, and he was at a loss. He couldn't even explain how nervous he was, let alone talk about the thing that had torn them apart. She was waiting for him to go on, he had planned to go on… but he just stood there, lost. Things were not going according to his plan.

"You don't have to explain anything to me, Jayson," she finally said, her eyes flashing, then narrowing in anger. "It's not like I'm your girlfriend or anything."

There it was. The verbal gut punch. He wasn't giving up, though.

"I know I made a huge mistake. Several huge mistakes. I'm not denying that, but let's be honest with each other. We can't deny there's something bigger than that between us. And if you let me, I can make it right again."

"It doesn't matter what there was between us. I knew it

was going to happen. Eventually, I knew I would get hurt—knew I would lose you to someone else. If it wasn't Marisa, it would have been someone just like her. I had a lapse of judgment. I trusted my heart, not my head. No matter what could have happened between us, now more than ever, I realize us being together will always end badly. You belong with someone like Marisa, even if you don't realize it yet. We're not meant to be, Jayson. We're two different people from two different worlds. You're Romeo, and I'm Juliet. It's not a freaking love story, it's a tragedy waiting to happen."

"Maybe the tragedy is they let everyone who wanted to tear them apart win. The tragedy was they died because of a ridiculous miscommunication." He reached out, his fingers grasping the soft skin of her arms. "If you could ask them if they would do it over knowing what would happen, if they would still choose to love each other no matter how hard it would get, I bet they would choose love every single time. There's a reason for that. I don't want to lose you, Brooke—"

She closed her locker and pulled away from his touch. He watched her walk away before he could say anything more.

For the rest of the day, Jayson couldn't seem to get her alone. Valerie kept avoiding him and shooting him evil looks. The one time he'd been able to corner her to entreat her to help him win Brooke back, she threatened to punch him in his "pretty face." At lunchtime, she was nowhere to be seen. Jayson sat with his usual group of friends, having no appetite and feeling horribly ill.

The table's usual boisterous atmosphere was muted. They all knew nothing they could say would make Jayson feel any differently. Brian hadn't said much beyond apologizing for not being there to have his back, but Jayson didn't blame him for any of it. He wasn't supposed to be at the party. Brian had taken him at his word that he was leaving. Nope, the blame for this laid squarely on Jayson's shoulders, and his shoulders alone.

His brother, on the other hand, cared less about who was

to blame and more about what Jayson was going to do to fix it. He had been relentless all weekend, and it continued right into the lunchroom.

"You can't just give up, Jayson!"

"Don't you see I've been trying, JD? It took me years to even get the courage to talk to her. Weeks to get her to tolerate me, let alone get her guard down enough for her to fall for me—and I blew it."

"We were celebrating a great game. If you keep playing like you did that night, the championship is ours. Just try to keep your mind off all the bad stuff and focus on the game," Vega interjected.

"I don't care about the game!" Jayson snapped. "I never once in my life felt the way I felt with Brooke playing basketball. She's special. None of the games, fans, interviews, or parties could ever be worth the tradeoff. I'd undo every point I scored that night if I could."

His head was throbbing, and the pain in his stomach was growing worse. He just wanted to tell everyone to leave him alone, but he had a slim chance of that happening. Things were bad enough with his little brother looking over at him with that watchdog look every two seconds. Then everything got worse when Doug Hutchison approached him. Doug was on the football team. Although they had known each other since elementary school, they had never been close friends. Doug was usually a cool guy, despite the tendency to talk a little too much and try a bit too hard to be everyone's friend. However, Jayson wasn't in the mood to talk about sports and everyone knew he had limited patience—especially today.

"Hey, Jayson. Can you do me a favor?"

"What is it, Doug?" Jayson kept his eyes closed, trying to ignore the building headache.

"Could you put in a good word for me? I could use a date for the dance."

"What are you even talking about?" Jayson felt his patience cracking, knowing he couldn't be understanding Doug correctly.

"Brooke. She's been looking pretty good lately. I saw her at Marisa's party and she looked hot. I know a lot of people took notice, and I want to take my chance with her, hopefully to ask her out, you know?"

"What?" Jayson stammered for words as he stood up.

"Well... word is you two aren't together anymore. She's single now, and I want to ask her out before anyone else. You know how that goes. So, will you hook me up?"

"Do you want me to hurt you? Don't ever talk to me about Brooke ever again. Forget about her. Find another date."

It was official, he couldn't take anymore. For the first time in his high school career, he skipped out on the rest of the school day, spending the afternoon and evening locked away in his room.

When his mom came to bring him a sandwich at dinner time, he still couldn't force himself to eat. Instead, his mom sat on his bed and rubbed his back like she used to when he was sick as a little boy.

"You know you're making it hard for me to be upset with you, mijo. Coach called and told me you missed practice today."

"I didn't feel like going."

"Jayden told me what's been going on with Brooke."

Jayson rolled to his back, fixing his eyes on the ceiling. "He should mind his own business," Jayson growled.

"He cares about you, and he's worried about you. I am too. I know how strongly you felt about Brooke. I can imagine how badly you feel."

"I feel like someone took my heart, threw it in a meat grinder, and then stuck in back in my chest. It hurts so bad, Ma."

"Honey, I'm sure she'll forgive you eventually."

"You didn't see her eyes. I don't know if she'll ever look at me the same way again. She hates me. I hate me. How can I go to that school every day and see her knowing in my heart she hates me? It's like a reminder of how big of a failure I am..."

Jisela shushed him. "People make mistakes. You aren't

perfect, and most times, the path of love isn't as perfect as we assume it to be when we're young. It's rough and rocky, full of mistakes and misspoken words."

"Mom, you don't understand. I promised her. I promised her the mistakes I made weren't going to happen, and days later, I stupidly made the mistakes. I worked so hard to be better than what she expected me to be, better than those other guys who looked past her. I had her, and I made her hate me... her eyes, they were so disappointed in me. She'll regret me forever."

"No, she doesn't hate you. She's mad and hurt—and for good reason, I might add. But in my heart, I know she cares about you, despite the poor choices made. Brooke is a special girl. But you need to make the promise to yourself if you two do make it back together, you'll never do it again. You learned the lesson the hard way, but don't give up. Things weren't always so clear with your father and me either. There were times when I just knew we might not make it. But look what love gave us. It made us stronger."

"You think she'll forgive me?"

"I truly do. You're a special kind of guy, Jayson."

She gave him a loving hug and kiss on the cheek and left him alone to his thoughts.

Brooke

Heartache was apparently a good rejuvenation for her creativity. She hadn't worked on anything seriously since they trashed her art show piece, but now she was throwing her energy behind a new project, hopeful it would serve as a good distraction from missing Jayson. It was working for little blocks of time. Which was a start at least. She took her frustration out on the canvas, the dark colors and bold lines helping her find the things she wanted to say, but just couldn't seem to come out of her mouth.

The past few days had been rough. Every day, she ended up wishing she had just stayed home. Daily, she saw Jayson looking broken. The desire to hug him had become so overwhelming, she had to force herself to avoid him and his woeful gaze. No matter how he looked, she couldn't handle going there with him. It frustrated her that she was so angry with him, but her stomach still flipped and heart still fluttered anytime she caught him looking her way. *Why couldn't she just go back to ignoring him like she had for the last three and a half years? Why couldn't he just have left her alone?* Then none of this would have happened.

After what felt like the longest week of her life, she made her way to her locker just like every morning, still hearing the hushed whispers of underclassmen who treated her like a zoo exhibit. This one day of classes was the only thing separating her from the weekend, she just had to get there. For now, all she could do was wish for the ability to disappear as she pulled the hooded sweatshirt on to cover her face. She expected to see Jayson waiting at her locker like he had been every morning, so she was surprised to see Doug Hutchison there instead.

"Hey, Brooke. Can I talk to you for a minute?"

"Uh... sure. I guess."

Doug's family was one of the well-known wealthier families in town and Doug usually behaved accordingly. He played for the football team and tended to love being the center of attention. Now, here he was talking to her. Brooke tried to recall another time when Doug had spoken to her. She could only remember that one time he had once asked her for a pencil sophomore year, but since then, their conversations had been rather sparse. She hadn't even known he knew her name. She never did get that pencil back either...

"I know it's last minute, but if you don't have a date, would you go to the dance with me?"

Brooke felt like she'd been hit in the gut. She made a big production about putting her bag in her locker to buy herself time before she had to respond. "You mean like a date?"

"Yeah! If you're available that is." He smiled, his left eye doing this weird twitchy movement that was more spastic than an actual wink.

"Uh... no, I don't have a date, but I haven't decided if I'm going. Maybe I could think about it?"

Doug smiled. "Sure. No problem. No pressure. I'd really love to go with you, and it's senior year—we should go and live it up."

She smiled weakly. "Right. Well, I'll let you know. Oh, and thanks, you know, for the offer."

Doug gave her a hug... an awkward hug, but still a hug. Then, with a smile and a jaunty stroll, he disappeared down the hallway. That left Brooke standing at her locker wondering what the heck had just happened. Her mind had instantly begun swimming with thoughts. Doug, the homecoming dance, Jayson, her pencil... Jayson.

Brooke couldn't help but wonder what Jayson would think if he saw her with Doug. Honestly, she had thought about going to the dance, but she had thought she would be arriving on Jayson's arm, dancing with him, making the night special. She shook her head at the thought, chastising herself for once again allowing her thoughts to wander back to Jayson. She would never get over him if she couldn't stop thinking about him. She turned her attention back to her locker, grabbed her necessary textbooks and notebook, and tried to take a second to clear her mind and collect herself. Just when she looked up again, Jayson was approaching.

She blew out the breath she'd been holding as she braced herself for their next conversation. The last several attempts had gotten them nowhere. She didn't know why he kept trying. But deep down, she was happy to see him again, especially after Doug's invitation. She couldn't stop herself from thinking his persistence on clearing the air with her truly meant she wasn't just a stupid game piece he was playing with. Maybe he did care about her enough to fight to get her back...

"Brooke! Hey, before you say anything, yes, I'm trying again. I want to be with you and I'm not giving up. Just let me begin to make it up to you and let me take you to the dance this weekend. Matter of fact, why don't you let me take you out for a burger after school, then you can yell at me all you want."

He offered up one of his very best charmer smiles.

"I don't know, Jayson..." She felt her resistance cracking. She tried to remind herself of the hurt. "Doug Hutchison asked me to the dance."

Jayson eyes changed. "Doug? You don't really want to go out with him, do you?"

She didn't. Not really. Then again, she didn't know what she wanted anymore.

"I told him I would think about it."

She caught her bottom lip between her teeth as she watched the unsettled emotion clouding his eyes. The dark storm clouds rolling in. Jayson stepped away from her, the curtain of tension growing thick between them.

"Please, Brooke. He's not your type. You know it and I know it." He scoffed.

Brooke closed her locker and leaned against it. "No, I actually don't. Maybe I'd like to get to know him. Besides, just because we hung out a bit doesn't mean you know what my type is. Doesn't even mean you know me."

"Hung out? That's what you call what we had? All the time we spent together?"

"I don't call it anything anymore. You don't own me, Jayson. You can't have me, then forget about me, then pick me back up when you want me again."

"Is love a tender thing? It is too rough, too rude, too boisterous, and it pricks like a thorn."

He had stepped into her space as he recited the line from Romeo and Juliet, laying his cheek against hers. His whisper was for her ears only. She closed her eyes and tried to control herself from giving in. The smell of him was intoxicating. There wasn't even an inch between them, but his nearness still wasn't near enough. Jayson leaned in and kissed her. It was a soft kiss, full of emotion that gave her goosebumps and butterflies that reminded her of their first kiss under the streetlamp.

"I always want you. You own me, Brooke. Do you want me to stop?" He spoke with his lips still on hers.

Brooke struggled between the memories of him she cherished and the memory of him dancing with Marisa like that. It was seared into her brain, pushing emotions to the surface that brought tears to her eyes. "Yes, I do. I can't believe you would try to play with my heart like this."

She pushed him to the side, heading toward the stairs. She had made it part way before he caught her by the arm. She wished he would just go away. She was losing the battle to keep her tears in check and now a crowded hallway was giving them their full attention.

"C'mon, Brooke. Give me a break. I want to be with you, for you. Doug could care less."

Brooke bristled. "What? You think you're the only guy who would want to go out with me?"

"Doug didn't even know your name until he saw you with me. None of them did, then you showed up to a party in a tight dress and now everyone is talking about asking you out. You're smart, does that seem genuine to you? They only want you to make me jealous." Jayson rubbed his head in exasperation. "Why are you making this so hard?"

Brooke's anger made her whole body tremble.

"I'm making this hard? This whole thing is your fault. If you would have just left me alone, none of this would have happened. If you would have chosen me... if you would have showed up for me, you wouldn't be sitting here begging me to give you a second chance. You're the biggest mistake I ever made and I wish I never listened to you."

Brooke pushed him away and took off down the hallway, needing to get away from him as fast as possible.

"Forget it then! Forget everything I ever said! And forget you! I could have any girl I want, I don't need you," Jayson shouted after her.

JAYSON

Jayson had spent the last three days moping around, completely sure he was in the middle of a nervous breakdown. That was the only plausible reason behind his ridiculous behavior the last week.

Or maybe he was just that big of an idiot.

He hadn't meant to snap at Brooke. He'd meant to give her some time to be angry and then come back to him. Then his stupid jealousy got the better of him, and instead of doing all the right things he'd planned to, he had pushed her straight into the arms of Doug Hutchison. He couldn't forget how. As he screamed those ugly false words at her, the school hallway seemed to freeze, everyone staring at them. He couldn't forget how she froze and turned to face him with a look of pure humiliation and heartbreak. He knew then he had lost it. He'd hurried to her, trying to apologize profusely, beg for her forgiveness, but she didn't want anything to do with him. He didn't blame her at all.

An hour later, he found out Brooke had accepted Doug's invitation to the dance after all. It only took him another ten minutes to track Doug down and punch him until the fight was broken up and his fist hurt. Now, he was home, suspended from school and sick with a migraine and an upset stomach. He was sure the only reason his mother hadn't grounded him even further was because she felt so bad for him already.

He was completely losing it.

If he thought spending a few days out of school would hurt less since he wouldn't have to see Brooke ignoring him, he was wrong. He thought about her constantly. Trying to distract himself, he decided to focus on spending some time with his younger brothers, but it wasn't working out quite the way he hoped. Jayden, Jaylin, and Jordan all regarded him cautiously, like they were waiting for him to combust at any moment. He heard them in their own rooms talking about Brooke and how she helped them with their schoolwork, teaching them cool tricks on how to remember the complicated math problems they were learning. He was almost certain Jayden had called her for help with his homework over the phone a few times. But when they would catch sight of him, they would all fall silent.

Justin, on the other hand, couldn't—*wouldn't*—stop talking about Brooke. He pestered Jayson on when Brooke was coming over to play with him again. He wanted to know when Brooke would be picking him up from school. And when he didn't get the answers he wanted, he begged Jayson to take him to her house. Jayson knew he hadn't just broken his own heart, he'd broken his family's heart as well. They had fallen in love with Brooke from the first time they had met her.

He couldn't stop thinking about how he made everything worse. They couldn't be over, not when they had barely gotten the chance to start. He made a promise to himself. If he somehow got himself together and found a way to earn her back, he would spend all his life proving his love to her. He had lied. He did need her—he needed her more than he had ever needed anyone or anything. He couldn't let things with Brooke end up like this—he couldn't let them end at all. He needed her to see he was the guy she had fallen for and he would never make another stupid mistake or make her look foolish for giving him another chance. He didn't know how he was going to do it, but he knew he had to get it done.

He was going to get Brookelynn's heart back.

Chapter 11

Brooke

Under-the-wire dress shopping with her mom and Val resembled an Olympic event as all three hurried to try to find her the perfect ensemble. After a half dozen stores, she finally found something she felt good in. The dress was white, splashed with a soft watercolor floral pattern, pencil cut, and strapless, showing off her figure in the best possible ways. As much as she loved the dress, her heart wasn't into the shopping trip. Even so, she tried her best to put a smile on her face every time she caught her mother looking at her.

She knew her mom had been worried about her. Last night, as she went downstairs for a glass of water, she overheard her mom on the phone discussing how it hurt her to see her daughter hurting so badly. She only needed to listen for a few minutes longer before she was able to figure out the caller on the other line was none other than Jisela. She made her way quietly back upstairs, resolving to try harder at pretending to be happy again.

Now, as she stood in front of the mirror an hour before Doug was supposed to pick her up, she couldn't help but feel everything about this night was wrong. She felt the mistake in her heart; she saw the worry all over her mother's face. Brooke tried to offer a reassuring smile, but it wobbled at the corners. That just caused her mother and Val to look into her eyes with concern. But Evelyn said nothing. Brooke knew no matter what, her mother wouldn't press her to talk about Jayson anymore. She knew no matter what happened eventually, Brooke would find her way back to happiness again… whenever she was ready.

"So, can I have that honesty card conversation with you now?" Val sighed as Evelyn left them alone.

"Go ahead. You've waited long enough."

"I know Jayson screwed up, believe me, I know. I'm still pissed at him for you. But I'm just wondering how much longer you're going to keep up this 'you don't want him back' act. I mean, he obviously adores you. He has for a long time. I'm your best friend, I want you happy. Happy was what I saw the moment you let Jayson break down your walls. You going out with Doug… that's not going to lead to a happy you. I'm not even sure it's about making Jayson jealous anymore."

"How can I just act like it never happened?"

"The same way he acts like you never treated him badly." Val took her hand in hers. "Jayson made a mistake, but I bet you won't find a young guy out there who hasn't made one. He's owned up to it and has apologized publicly and privately every day since. He even beat up a guy because he cares for you so much. This is the guy who won't even trash talk on the court! Don't you think maybe a little part of you had him set up to fail?"

Brooke felt her defenses kick up. "Meaning what exactly?"

"You had him pegged for the bad guy long before you even had a conversation. Before you ever even talked to him, you wrote him off because of some stereotype. You expected him to do this even when he was doing all the right things. So, when he did mess up, you punished him even worse."

"So I'm wrong."

"No! Brooke, you have every right to feel hurt. But I also know, in your heart, you want it to be him you're going with tonight. And, Brooke… it's okay to want that still. It's okay to forgive the guy who makes your heart soar."

"Leaving so soon?"

Brooke whirled around at the sound of an unexpected voice. She had only lasted twenty minutes before she had to get out of there. She had excused herself to the bathroom and made a direct detour to the exit.

Apparently, someone noticed her escape plan because she came face to face with Brian.

"You scared me, Brian."

"You didn't answer my question."

His face remained somber, but there was a softness to his blue eyes that told her he wasn't looking to pick a fight.

"Turns out, this isn't where I want to be."

He stepped closer, his hands tucked deep in his pockets as he seemed to mull over the words that came next. "Maybe it's where you want to be with someone else?"

"Maybe." She shrugged, averting her eyes to hide the tears that instantly welled. As if her constant thinking about Jayson wasn't enough, now both their best friends seemed to have something to say about it all. He shrugged off his jacket and draped it over her shoulders.

"Look, I know we haven't really talked or gotten a chance to know each other, and I'm probably the last guy who could offer any relationship advice, but Jayson is my best friend and the best guy I've ever known. I decided a long time ago, no matter what, I'd always have his back, so here I am ditching my date and checking on his girl."

"I'm not his—"

"You are," Brian corrected. "I've been through a lot with Jayson. For most of our childhood, we were inseparable. He's always been so positive, the rock in our friendship, for sure. When his father died... things changed. There was a period of time I worried I had lost my best friend."

Brian cleared his throat roughly, emotion strangling his words. "Then I saw the shift start swinging back, and after a

127

while, I figured out it was because of you. These past couple months, I've seen my best friend smile for real again, and I know that was because of what you two have. I don't want to lose my friend again, Brooke. I know you have reasons, but I wouldn't be doing my job if I didn't tell you Jayson has the best heart and he's sorry. You have to know that by now. If your feelings for him are the reason you are out here, please give my boy another chance."

An hour after Doug had picked her up for the dance, Brooke found herself back home sitting on her front porch. She wrapped her shawl tightly around her shoulders to warm herself. It was a beautiful night, even with the cool air blowing in from the ocean.

The walk home had been the time she'd needed to think about everything buzzing around in her head. She wasn't surprised she ended up home early. She had known from the moment she saw him standing on her porch she couldn't go with him. In full honesty, she knew from the moment he asked her. Val had been right. While her pride convinced her to say yes to him to prove some point to Jayson, that quickly vanished and she'd felt stuck not wanting to hurt his feelings.

Loving the quiet of the night air around her, she wondered if Doug had stopped talking about himself enough to realize she was nowhere to be found. The thought made her giggle. It had been so long since she'd giggled. She didn't think she would be able to manage a full laugh, but she figured it was a start. Taking a deep breath of the night air, she felt her chest quiver with a stifled sob. She couldn't help but think of the evening walks she shared with Jayson. The evening walk that had given her her very first kiss. The evening walks where they talked and found their common interests. The walks where she realized Jayson was more than she ever imagined. The memories rolled in, and she felt a longing she'd been trying to bury. She could admit she missed Jayson terribly, but she remembered the pain and humiliation all too clearly.

Why couldn't she just forget him?

She wanted to forget it all. She wanted to go back to the days when nobody noticed her and she didn't have boys hurting her heart. Oh, her stupid heart! If she could have stuck to the plan and left her heart out of it, she wouldn't have been sitting on her porch crying over Jayson Williams.

Wiping away the tears, she stood to go into her house. Happy to be home alone since her mom had gone out to dinner with some friends and wasn't expecting Brooke home until much later, she wouldn't have to explain why she was home so early. She walked into the house, locking the door behind her, and went straight to her bedroom. She tossed her shoes into her closet before she even bothered to turn the light on. When she did, she was shocked to find a dozen roses laying across her bed.

As she cautiously moved toward the flowers with a bunch of questions flying through her mind, she heard pings of gravel hitting her window panes. She grabbed her cell phone, prepared to call the police, and slowly opened the curtain on her window. Brooke's breath caught in her lungs when her eyes fixed on him. It was Jayson... and he was in a tree.

JAYSON

Jayson had been prepared to wait in the tree outside Brooke's bedroom all night. After he saw Brooke's mom move the flowers from the front porch to her bedroom and leave, he quickly pulled on his hooded sweatshirt and climbed the tree. And that was where he had planned to stay for as long as it took.

He was surprised when he looked up to see the light in her bedroom flick on. It hadn't been nearly as long as he thought it would be. That knowledge made him excited that maybe there was a little hope for him yet. It also worried him. It was now or never. He reached into his pocket and threw...

She quickly unlocked the window and slid it open. "What do you think you're doing?"

"*But soft, what light through yonder window breaks? It is the east and Juliet is the sun! Arise fair sun, and kill the envious moon, who is already sick and pale with grief that thou her maid art far more fair than see...*"

"You are reciting Romeo and Juliet... in a tree? You are in a tree, Jayson!" she interrupted, trying to talk over him. He wouldn't be interrupted.

"*...It is my lady. O, it is my love! O that she knew she were...*"

"Do you want to break your neck and never play basketball again? Get down right now, Jayson!"

"I don't care about basketball. I need to talk to you, Brooke, and I'm not leaving this tree until you agree to hear me out. That's all I'm asking."

He could see the lip chewing begin.

Then, she spoke. "Did you give me these flowers too?"

He nodded.

She started to walk away from the window, then turned back halfway and called out, "I'll meet you at the front door."

Brooke was already waiting when he rounded the front of the house. She looked gorgeous. His heart was pounding, and although he was staring and probably drooling, he couldn't help it. He was jealous of Doug taking his Brooke out like that.

"You look spectacular."

She subconsciously crossed her arms, and Jayson immediately wished he could take her in his arms and make her feel the way she looked.

"You decided to climb a tree and recite Romeo and Juliet?"

"You didn't have a balcony." He smiled his best smile.

Brooke bit her lip.

"I have a lot to say, so please just let me say it all before you say anything. First off, I am so sorry. There's no excuse for my behavior. You are right, there's nothing I could say that would justify it. I promised you I wouldn't hurt your heart, and I hurt you twice. I'm sorry for that, and I will forever be sorry for that. But I will not give you up. I can't do that. You are the first girl I've ever loved, and yes, I said it. I do love you. I've loved you from afar for so long, now I just want to love you up close."

She met his piercing gaze with her own as her breath caught in her chest. "Jayson—"

Jayson stepped closer and ran his thumb along the side of her cheek. "Brooke, you are what I want. You are what I need. I've been going crazy without you. I can't eat or sleep. I say and do irrational things. I know I may not be many things, but I can be good for you. I can be better. I will earn the right to be called your boyfriend. I will make you proud to be my girlfriend every single day. I can promise you that because I mean it with every part of my heart. You are the only one I want. There's never been anyone else for me. Just you.

"You are a better person than most anyone I know, and I am counting on that to see if you can look beyond the stupid mistakes I made just this one time. Please, just look in your heart and remember what we had and what we still have. It's something greater than both of us. I'm not saying that to be assuming, I'm just saying it is. I can feel it in my bones. I am supposed to be your man, Brooke. I want to be that for you. That's what I'm here promising you right now. No more foolishness. No dumb mistakes. I won't promise you won't get mad at me from time to time, I actually will promise you more than likely will get mad at me sometimes. We might argue, but we'll always make up. I won't break your heart again. Ever."

She tried to look away from those soul-penetrating eyes.

"Brookelynn..."

"You humiliated me, Jayson!"

"I know. And it won't ever happen again." Jayson took her hands in his.

"You made me look like a fool in front of everyone. You hurt me, and you did it with the girls who hate me and make me hate myself."

Tears fell from her eyes, but she didn't look away from him.

"Don't you ever hate yourself, Brooke. You are the most amazing girl I've ever known or could even dream of. Everything about you makes that possible. I made a lot of stupid mistakes that night I never want to repeat again. But I heard you, Brooke. Now, hear me when I say I will always choose you. I thought about it long and hard, and I know I love you. I love you, my sweet Brookelynn. I know we're young, and I know this thing with us is new and scary to you, but, baby, it's the truth. I don't expect you to love me back, not right now, but I'm not going to water down my words, not anymore. I've been falling in love with you since the very first day I saw you. So, yeah, I'm telling you and anyone who cares to know I love you."

"Jay…"

"I love you, Brooke. I'm stubborn, so I'm pretty much determined to love you forever whether you love me back or not…"

With the tears flowing furiously, Brooke's walls crumbled as she wrapped her arms around Jayson. Jayson was crying too. He wasn't embarrassed. He was proud he was able to show his heart to the girl he loved so much. As he bent to kiss her tear-covered cheeks, he felt as if his heart was going to burst. And then, she looked at him and changed his world.

"I love you too, Jayson. I fell for you and everything that came along with you, and now I can't stop loving you."

Their kiss was electrifying. Jayson felt what was dead inside him come back to life. Brooke was perfect in his arms, and he didn't want to let her go.

Brooke

Brooke's toes curled with pleasure. They had kissed several times before, but something about this was both foreign and exhilarating. This kiss, long and deep, was filled with both love and forgiveness. She had missed him. Long before she was ready, Jayson pulled back from their kiss.

"What's wrong?"

"Nothing at all. I'd love to kiss you like this for hours, but I have to take you somewhere right now."

"Right now? Where?"

"You'll see. Just lock up the house and come with me."

Moments later, Jayson parked the car in front of his house.

"What are we doing here?"

He chuckled low. "Just be patient for a few more moments, love. I'll be right back to get you in a minute. Just stay here."

Jayson kissed her hand before running off into his house.

Several minutes later, he was back. He took her hand and led her to his backyard. Brooke froze in her tracks.

Jayson's backyard was filled with romance. The trees and fences were all decorated in the sparkling white tree lights that had been strung. Beautiful candles lined the railings of his patio. At the center, there was a romantic picnic set up for two.

"You did all this?"

He smiled warmly. "Of course. I owed you a great first date. I figured I should take you back to the beginning. This is where I first saw you look at me with the promise of more in your eyes."

She squeezed his hand. "It's beautiful, Jayson. So perfect."

"You're beautiful. And you're worth so much to me."

Music began playing, and they both turned to see Jisela peek out of the curtains and blow them a kiss before retreating away from the window.

"Your mom is awesome."

"I know I'm not dressed up very nicely or anything, but I'd love to have this dance with you."

She nodded. "You look amazing to me."

Jayson walked her to the middle of the backyard. Taking her in his arms again, he led her in a slow, sweet dance to the sounds of a love song filling the night air, the lyrics embracing them as they moved together. She pressed herself against him, laying her head on his chest, and closed her eyes, falling in love with the steady rhythm of his heart.

"Did my heart love till now? Forswear it, sight! For I ne'er saw true beauty till this night..."

Jayson's voice sent chills up her spine. Regardless of any fear she had before, she was going to throw herself into love with Jayson Williams. Val had been right. Brooke couldn't expect the worst out of someone who consistently went above and beyond to take care of her heart. She didn't want to go without him, and now that she was in his arms again, she was grateful she didn't have to. She pressed a kiss to his chest, right where his heart lay, and decided to give him the last bit of her heart, feeling no fear.

"My bounty is as boundless as the sea, my love as deep—the more I give to thee, the more I have, for both are infinite."

He drank the words from her lips, repeating them in reverence. *"My bounty is as boundless as the sea, my love as deep—the more I give to thee, the more I have, for both are infinite."*

They danced under the light of the moon until they collapsed onto the blankets and pillows laying on the grass nearby. Feeding on the treats he had brought, they whispered their reconciliation as they held hands under the stars. As the night wore on, Brooke found herself falling asleep in his arms under the warm blankets with a smile on her lips.

The rising sun woke Brooke. As she stirred in Jayson's arms, she realized they'd fallen asleep wrapped in each other's embrace beneath the cozy blankets. She pressed a small, intimate kiss to his neck.

"Jayson, wake up."

"Are you really in my arms again, or am I dreaming this? If I'm dreaming this, I'm not opening my eyes."

She laughed. "Open your eyes, Romeo. I'm here, and I'm not going anywhere."

He opened one eye and kissed her cheek. "Just checking, babe."

Jisela opened the door as they both sat up.

"Why don't you two come in and clean up for breakfast? I called your mom last night to let her know you were here and you were safe."

"Thank you, Mrs. Williams."

She smiled and disappeared inside.

"What are you doing after breakfast?" Jayson asked as she stood up and straightened her dress. She was barefoot and quickly spotted her shoes laying in the grass nearby.

"Um... I don't know. I didn't really have any plans before last night."

"I want to spend today with you, if that's okay..."

Brooke smiled brightly. "I like that plan."

She pulled him to his feet and looked up at him warmly. "I want to kiss you, but I feel like we're being watched."

"At my house? You better believe it. I guarantee at least two of my brothers are watching us right now."

Brooke giggled and turned, but Jayson stopped her. "Don't look!"

Before she could question him, his lips were on hers and he lifted her so her toes were no longer on the ground.

"You look so gorgeous, I couldn't help it."

Hand in hand, they walked toward the house barefoot.

Chapter 12

JAYSON

After Brooke had showered and slipped on an old sundress and cardigan Jisela had given to her, she joined the family at the table. Jisela had made them all a big breakfast. Jayson couldn't take his eyes off her as she entered the kitchen. She looked even more beautiful than the night before. She belonged here. He felt like it was all coming together. His father would have loved Brooke, and he had no question his mother did. Jisela had already begun to treat Brooke like a daughter, and he could see them falling even more in love with each other before his very own eyes.

She took a seat next to Justin, who'd saved the spot exclusively for Brooke. Justin excitedly chattered away about all the things he was learning in school and how he couldn't wait to show Brooke the picture he had drawn for her. He was in the middle of asking her to come to his class for show and tell when Jisela finally quieted him.

"Justin, mi amor, dejó comer!"

"Pero, Mom... I really want her to come!"

Brooke smiled warmly and kissed the top of his head. "I would love to come. If it's okay with your mom, I'd love to pick you up from school next week and you can show me all around your classroom."

"Mom, can she? Please!"

"Ay, Justin. Okay! Cálmate!"

Brooke smiled adoringly at his little brother before she leaned over and whispered something in his ear, which made him grin from ear to ear. Justin nodded excitedly and went back to eating. Just as she took a bite of French toast, the twins nudged each other conspiratorially and started singing.

"Jayson and Brooke sitting in a tree K-I-S-S-I-N-G..."

"Boys!" Jisela warned, but couldn't quite hide the smile that crept up on her lips.

Jayson shrugged and laughed while Brooke struggled between giggles and embarrassment. Jisela patted her hand. "It's so nice to have you back..."

"It's nice to be back." Brooke smiled gratefully as she and Jisela shared a knowing look.

After breakfast, Jayson walked Brooke home to bring her things back. He waited on the porch for her and couldn't stop from smiling to himself. It was a beautiful Saturday and he was going to spend it with the girl he loved. The girl who loved him. He was still smiling at the thought when she returned to the porch. Dressed in a pair of black jersey shorts and a t-shirt, she had traded in her usual choice of shoes for a pair of Nikes. It was something so simple, but he hadn't seen her in a pair of shorts in years, and it made his heart do some pretty spectacular things.

"Hey, pretty girl. So, what do you want to do? We can do anything you want."

"Anything?"

He nodded.

"Good. I want you to teach me how to play basketball!" She smiled brightly.

"Really?" He laughed.

"Yes, really. I figure I should learn some more about the game since my boyfriend is some hotshot basketball star... or so I hear."

He smiled deeply. "Now it's my turn to teach you

something."

Brooke returned his smile. "I'm excited to spend time with you. I missed you a lot, Jayson."

He reached out to touch her cheek. "I'm crazy about you, Brookelynn. I missed you more than you can imagine."

Hand in hand, they set off to the park to find a basketball court.

Jayson had never had so much fun. After she helped him through his usual workout, they played some basketball. The first thing he taught her was how to make a good jump shot, while she played some very interesting defense. When they had enough, Jayson suggested they walk downtown to get a milkshake and fries. While they ate, they discussed everything that came across their minds—likes, dislikes, serious topics, or just silly thoughts, both making the effort to reconnect again.

When they made it back to Brooke's where Evelyn had cooked them dinner, he enjoyed spending time with her mother and getting to know that part of Brooke's heart the most. They did the dishes together before making themselves comfortable in front of the television where they watched an old black and white love story with her mom. With his arms around her, he realized what happiness felt like.

Nothing else mattered except she was in his arms, they were together, and he was never going to lose her again.

Brooke

When Monday morning came, Brooke was actually prepared for the looks and whispers. For once, she felt comfortable in her own skin. She was well aware of what people may have been saying in whispered voices every time Jayson wrapped his arm around her or kissed her, but today, she did not care. Today, she was Brooke Thomas. Today, she was Jayson's girlfriend, and she was absolutely positive she wanted to wake up the same way tomorrow.

She couldn't help the wide, beaming smile as he put his English book in her locker.

"Aww, we're locker official now."

She pressed her clasped hands to her chest. He gave her a teasing eye-roll, but couldn't play it off as he bent down and kissed her forehead.

"Get used to it, cutie. You're stuck with my books and me all up in your space until graduation."

She shook her head. "I'm going to need more time than that."

"You're so freaking adorable, babe." He placed an exuberant kiss on her neck.

"Glad you think so."

"I know so. Hey, I was thinking, maybe this Saturday we could hang out with Brian and you could invite Val. We could do something as a group, grab dinner, then maybe go down to the beach. I know a great out of the way spot. We could set up a bonfire."

"That sounds fun. I'll ask Val when I get to chem."

"Great, I'll talk to Brian and we'll confirm everything at lunch."

Brooke laughed as she shut her locker. "Why does hanging out with your best friend make me more nervous than meeting your mom?"

"Don't be nervous. He's going to love you... almost as much as I do."

JAYSON

"Brian, I need you to be nice to her."

"I'm always nice." Brian raised an eyebrow in defense.

Jayson ignored him. "It's just... this girl is really special to me, and you're my best friend."

"I know how important she is to you. I get it. Everything

will be cool."

Jayson let the worry go as he spotted Brooke and Val walking over to them. His girl wore a soft pink sundress that flared around her thighs, her favorite denim jacket with the sleeves rolled up to her elbows, and those Dr. Martens boots she loved. With her arm intertwined with her best friend's, Brooke had a happy smile resting on her face.

"You jocks just had to pick mini golf!" Val called out as they came walking toward where they agreed to meet at the entrance.

"Mini golf is not a sport!" Brian looked hurt by the very idea.

"Close enough!" Val retorted.

Laughing, Brooke rose up on her tiptoes to meet Jayson's kiss. He kept it quick as possible, his mind already in overdrive as she let a little hum of pleasure escape.

"Let's play teams. Brian and me versus you and Val," Brooke said as they all approached the first hole.

"Ah, the lady wants to be on the winning team, I see," Brian teased, draping an arm around her shoulder.

"Oh, we're so going to win." Val pulled her dark hair streaked with bright purple into a messy bun. Jayson raised an eyebrow in amusement as she poked him in the chest.

"All right, dimples, I'm going to need you to get your head in the game. You're going down, Thomas."

Halfway through the course, the gloves officially came off. "You okay there, Val?"

Valerie shot Brian a menacing glare while a slew of Spanish and Chinese flew off her tongue in rapid succession.

"She said she loves me." Brian winked.

"Oh, for sure." Jayson laughed and let out a loud whistle. "Let's go, team!"

Brooke slipped under his arm, then wrapped her arms around his waist. Their eyes met, and Jayson was surprised to see Brooke's wet with tears.

"What's going on in that head of yours, beautiful?"

"I never thought I'd be doing this. Playing a silly game of

mini golf with friends, with my boyfriend... I'm just really happy right now."

"I want to make sure you stay happy."

Tucking her hair behind her ear, he captured her lips in the kiss he'd been dying to give her.

Val threw down her putter. "Hey! No kissing the enemy! I knew you were checking out her butt the last two holes!"

Brooke's laughter burst free as Jayson shrugged. "Have you seen it? It's safe to say I'm always checking out her butt."

Reaching up, Brooke covered his mouth with a free hand. "Can we go eat now?"

Deciding on pizza, the foursome abandoned their mini golf competition and made their way to a nearby pizza parlor, settling into one of the larger booths.

"So, Valerie, you speak Spanish and Chinese?" Jayson asked as they waited for their pizzas to arrive.

"Yeah. My mom is Puerto Rican and my dad is Chinese Filipino. They both wanted me to learn the language of my people."

"When she gets angry, it gets really interesting," Brooke teased with a smile. "What about you, Brian?"

"I can understand French, courtesy of both my parents. My dad is French and my mom is Haitian."

"Well, I'm the loser then, I guess." Brooke chuckled. "I only speak one language."

"But you're really good at it." Jayson winked.

"Thanks, babe."

"Really, you two..." Brian's words held no sting. He gave them a wink of his own just as the waitress carried over their food.

Brian added more wood the bonfire they had going before returning to his seat. After dinner, they had headed down to the isolated piece of beach Jayson often liked to come to when he wanted to have the privacy to think. It was a small hike to find it, so it remained free of tourists and mostly anyone else who didn't want to put in effort just to go to the beach.

"So, Val, Jayson told me you were into documentary film making. Are you working on anything right now?"

"Actually, I am. Well... I hope to be. I had an idea a while ago after a conversation with Brooke, and I was wondering if you guys would like to help me out?"

Jayson sat up, his interest fully piqued. "What did you have in mind?"

"I want to follow the journey of a high school athlete, especially with the amount of attention you guys have been getting with this undefeated season. I'd like to get the story from you guys, from your point of view. I think it would be telling to have the student talk about making that transition from high school sports to college sports and all the decisions and pressures in between."

"Well, that sounds great, but I'm not going to be a college athlete," Brian said before pursing his lips and focusing his gaze on the golden flames as they danced wildly.

"What do you mean?" Brooke dropped Jayson's hand and leaned forward in concern.

"It's not a painful decision for me, not totally. I played ball on a team since I could join the kids' league at the rec center. I've always played on a team with my very best friend." He paused and gave a small grin. "I had the best times of my life on the court, but it's time for me to move on. My passion is building and architecture—that's what I want to throw myself into now. I'll make this season the best because it's going to be my last wearing any school colors."

Brooke's eyes flew to Jayson's, as if she needed to gauge how he was dealing with this information. He gave her a small nod to let her know it wasn't news to him. Brian had told him last year he wasn't going to be making his college decisions with basketball in mind. Jayson understood. He would support his best friend no matter what, but that didn't mean he had the warm fuzzies knowing the time he had playing with his best friend was coming to a close.

"Well, maybe that's even better. I can focus the story on you two—two best friends on the same team choosing two very different paths. I know you guys are busy with practices, but I'd just have to film some interviews with you both and we could schedule those to be convenient. Everything else I can record like a fly on the wall. I want to do this right and tell your story. I know it's all fuzzy, it's still working its way out in my head, but I promise I'll lay out all the details with you before we get into filming. I'll run it by the coach too. What do you think?"

Jayson held back his smile for the sake of dramatic effect. "I think I'm ready for my close up."

"Okay, I seriously love him Brooke."

The look in Brooke's eyes told him the feeling was mutual.

By the end of their first real social outing as a group, it seemed like they had all been friends forever. Val teased him relentlessly. He already loved the girl and was happy she would get to be one of those he considered a friend. After they made sure to see the girls back to the car safely, they made their way to Jayson's. Brian shut the engine off and they sat in the quiet of the car. Jayson wanted to know how his friend felt and braced himself for any possibility.

"So?"

"She's all that you said she is. I totally get it. I'm really happy for you, dude."

"I'm so relieved to hear you say that. I knew you'd like her, but the chance that two of the people most important to me wouldn't get along made me nervous."

"No worries. She definitely gets the seal of approval."

Chapter 13

JAYSON

J ayson and Brooke thrived as their relationship progressed. Far from being a distraction, she was the best thing that ever happened to his athletic and student performance. As time passed, both his grades and game grew better.

Brooke had been the missing link in his life. Having his girlfriend be so supportive of everything had been key in him finding his confidence to be himself all the time. She was becoming the steady constant in his life and a major factor to his drive and future goals. She never failed to tell him how proud of him she was, and her actions showed it. During his final pep rally and senior night at PCH, his quiet girl stepped into the spotlight and stood up for him proudly as Coach Beckett read off his achievements as a player and captain. He loved her knowing smile as he ran over to the bleachers and kissed her. Just as he loved being in the front rows when she got all her academic achievement awards and local scholarships at the Senior Award night.

As the winter season finished and signs of spring became more prevalent, they found the perfect balance between their relationship and other activities. On that particular Saturday afternoon, Brooke was out shopping with Val while Jayson had gone to Brian's to spend some time with his best friend. After eating and playing some video games, they decided to go outside to play a friendly one-on-one game. After they were done, Brian got more quiet than normal.

"You okay?" Jayson asked, dribbling the ball between his legs. "You just played the most awful game."

Brian chuckled once at the good-natured ribbing, but the laugh quickly stopped as he stood up and sighed.

"We need to talk..."

Jayson looked up curiously. "What's up?"

They both sat down on the driveway. "Well, yesterday I got a letter in the mail. I got accepted into the summer volunteer building corps I applied to. I'm leaving the day after graduation for my assigned build location. It's New Orleans."

"So, after graduation, you're leaving until we all come home on college break in November?"

"Yeah, pretty much," Brian said solemnly. He attempted a weak smile. "I don't know why I'm making this such a big deal. We'll be okay. You'll always be my brother, no matter where we are or what happens."

Jayson nodded and did his best attempt at covering up his sadness with a smile. His friend needed his encouragement, he needed to hear Jayson say the words. "You're going to be great, Brian. And you're right, we'll be brothers for the rest of our lives. Just make sure you keep in touch."

"Of course. I'll keep you informed about all the new ladies I meet traveling as well. You know... since you're Mr. Committed now."

Brian shot him a teasing look, and Jayson couldn't help but to laugh.

"Yeah, yeah. You know there are certain benefits to being Mr. Committed."

"Oh really? Let me know when you think of some good ones..."

Jayson playfully shoved his best friend. He was going to miss this.

He would miss his brother.

♥

Brooke

Brooke was definitely enjoying her long overdue girls' day out with Val.

"We need to do this at least once a month before we go off to college."

"At least!" Brooke concurred. "Though, I don't want to think about you going off and leaving me."

"I could say the same thing to you."

"No you can't! I haven't even decided where I'm going yet and you've had your deposit sent in since November."

"What are you thinking about that anyway?"

Brooke sighed and took a sip of her latte as they settled into their seats at their favorite coffee shop. "I have no idea. Some days, I'm sure I want to teach. Other days, I'm sure I want to create art. Then there are days I'm certain I want to do something completely new. I've been working my butt off the past four years so I can hurry up and graduate, and now that it's closer, I have zero plans for my life. How is that?"

Val laughed. "I, for one, am glad to see you without a plan. Spontaneity is a good look for you, Brookie."

"I would hardly call this spontaneity, more like severe procrastination."

"Tomato, potato."

"That's not how it goes!" Brooke laughed loudly.

"So, what does the number one high school athlete in the country, also known as Jayson Williams, better known as your boyfriend and future baby daddy, have to say about this?"

"He has enough on his plate. I'm not piling on my indecision drama."

"I mean, are you two going to do the long distance thing? Are you going to schools nearby?"

"We haven't talked about it. Jayson hasn't made his

decision yet. He doesn't have to sign with any school until May, so he's still testing the waters. It's crazy. He has piles and piles of acceptance letters and offers, brochures and pamphlets. He could cover his walls, ceiling, and floor, and still have some to spare."

"You're not one to sneeze at, Brooke. You got into what? Ten schools?"

"Twelve. But now I wish I had only been accepted to one. They could have made this decision for me."

"Stop whining!" Val gave her a stern look. "You have a great life, an amazing boyfriend, the world's greatest best friend, and a dozen schools you loved that want you. You just have to make up your mind. No matter what you decide, you're going to do fine. And you'll visit me every other month no matter how far apart we end up, because the world's greatest best friend is high maintenance like that."

"Gah, how am I going to get through a crisis without you?"

"That's where video chat will come into play. You know, it can also come in handy with a lonely long-distance boyfriend."

"Valerie!"

Returning home to an empty house, Brooke changed into a pair of sweat shorts and her favorite PCH Basketball shirt Jayson had given her. She pulled her hair into a ponytail and made her way downstairs to start cooking herself some dinner.

She was browning the meat for tacos when she heard a knock on the door. She turned down the stove and ran to answer it. To her surprise, it was Jayson.

"Hey, I thought you were going to your Aunt's tonight."

"Change of plans. Can I come in?"

She laughed, "Of course. But let's go in the kitchen so I can finish cooking."

Once they stepped in to the kitchen, Jayson pulled out an envelope. "I got a letter in the mail today... and a phone call from Coach..."

Brooke's eyes widened with excitement. "Oh my goodness, Jayson! Tell me."

"It's official, I made All American! And they want me as All American Athlete of the Year. I get the cover of the magazine. They want to do an interview and photoshoot when I'm in New York."

Brooke jumped on him excitedly. "That's incredible!"

Jayson squeezed her to him tightly as she pulled her head back to look into his eyes.

"I am so proud of you, Jay." She leaned in to kiss him, but he pulled away.

"Wait one more second—the other half of my news. I got a call from the coach at Central. They want to come meet with me at the house, an official recruitment. Then, when I'm in New York, I have visits set up for campus tours as well. It's getting serious, babe. I have like two months to decide my future."

Brooke didn't even wait to hear anything else. She kissed him with all her love. She needed him to feel it even with the undercurrent of change happening.

"This is all great news, babe! You got this."

"Thanks for believing in me, Brookelynn."

An hour later, they were eating tacos together while watching ESPN on Brooke's couch. When they were finished, they cleaned the kitchen and went out to her back porch with a warm blanket to cuddle under the stars.

"Are you happy?" Brooke asked after moment of silence fell between them.

"I'm completely happy with you in my arms, especially right now with you in those booty shorts wearing my shirt."

She tried to work up a really good indignant face, but she couldn't hold it for more than a second before she felt herself blushing. He smiled knowingly. "I'm happy about my news, yes, but I guess I'm a little sad. Brian's leaving the day after graduation..."

"Wait, what?"

"Yeah, he applied for this summer volunteer build project he's been talking about for years. Tonight, he told me he's leaving the evening after grad day. I guess I thought I wouldn't have to think about saying goodbye to him until the end of the summer."

"I'm sorry, babe. I know how close you two are."

"Yeah, it's okay, I guess. I knew it was coming. I guess I wasn't as ready as I thought."

Brooke nodded and snuggled a little closer.

"What's going to happen to us after graduation, Brooke? I'm so scared college will change us."

She could hear the sadness and fear in his voice.

"You mean if we don't end up at the same school?"

"Well… yes, but even if we did, do you think college and all those college guys who are going to be chasing you will change our relationship?"

She sat up to face him, her expression earnest. "Not at all. I don't care who comes along. I know what I want, I know who I want… I haven't even decided where I'm going yet. Let's not worry over the worst case scenario yet."

Her voice quivered with emotion.

He smiled. "You want me, Brookelynn?"

"I want you every day for the rest of my life."

There was no quiver of uncertainty in her voice this time. Jayson felt his heart swell with love.

She kissed him softly. "Do you remember the first day I came over to your house and helped you out with the boys?"

"Of course. It was one of the best days of my life."

"Well… when I was in that kitchen washing dinner dishes, I found myself thinking all these thoughts, thoughts I had been too scared to even tell anyone. I'd spent hours with you and your brothers, we'd had dinner, then we cleaned up and I watched you handle household responsibilities. Then, when you'd gone to put Justin to bed… I stood in the kitchen imagining a life with you. A life where we'd have a house of our own, filled with some green-eyed boys of our own, doing school projects and eating pizza. My point is, when I think about you... when I think about us, I can't help but to think about the future. I have this feeling in my heart that tells me you are my forever, Jayson. I'm with you. I'm in this for the forever."

Her eyes glistened with tears, but they were strong, determined to make sure he knew his heart was safe with her.

It apparently worked. He kissed her then, her soft brown hair weaving itself around his fingers. She was pressed so close to him, he could easily feel the heat emanating off her skin. Her ears were on fire as he brought his lips to them.

"You are everything I want and need. Brookelynn, you are my rock, so reliable and strong. You make me feel safe, but anytime you touch me, especially when you kiss me, it's a connection that transcends everything else. You make me feel everything all at once. You don't even have to touch me, just fix those creamy brown eyes on me and tell me you don't feel the passion between us. It's intense and potent. It makes me feel limitless. Like I'm free falling into love all over again."

"Our love is incredible, and I'll always fight for it with everything I have." She promised him dropping a kiss to his lips before she settled back down in his arms.

"The coach from Central is coming next week. Will you come over for dinner while he's there?"

"Are you sure you want me there?"

"Positive."

"Then I'll be there. I'll even bring brownies for dessert."

"Seriously. Best. Girlfriend. Ever." He kissed her neck exuberantly, eliciting happy giggles from her.

The school was abuzz with the news Jayson had been named as Outstanding High School Athlete of the year. The school always was a little crazy for its athletes, but Brooke couldn't believe how crazy the energy had been. The student body, and even some teachers, were in a frenzy. She had even seen some underclassmen snapping photos of him with their cell phones and asking him to sign their copies of both the local paper and school's paper, which had him on the cover of each. He had been fielding off interviews, but emails still poured in. It seemed his scoring record had many people wondering when—not if—he was going to join the draft for the National League and play professionally.

The art room, however, was still her quiet haven away from the madness. She slipped her headphones in her ears and went into her zone as she started putting her feelings down on the fresh canvas. She quickly became so thoroughly engrossed in her art, she was startled to the point of screaming when Ms. Cullen tapped her on the shoulder.

"Sorry, Brooke. I thought you saw me walk up."

"It's my fault. I had my headphones on and I've been in the zone. What's going on, Ms. C?"

Brooke turned her music off and put her paintbrush down.

"Well, I took the liberty of sending a letter of recommendation and a digital portfolio of your recent work to the Seattle Arts Institute. I got this letter over the weekend."

Ms. Cullen handed a still stunned Brooke a thin envelope.

Brooke took the envelope and noticed her hands were shaking a little before she opened it and unfolded the letter. Ms. Cullen was eagerly waiting for Brooke to speak again, but she was having a hard time finding a voice.

Then, it finally came. "They want me…"

"I knew they would! Oh, Brooke, that's amazing! I'm so proud of you."

Ms. Cullen gathered her up into an excited hug.

"Thanks, Ms. Cullen, but I haven't decided where I want to go yet."

"Just think about it. It's an amazing opportunity, and if you want to take your art to the next level, they can help you. You deserve the chance. Your art has come such a long way, and you still have so much potential."

"I will think about it. I promise. Thank you so much for

this, Ms. Cullen."

Brooke tried to muster the most genuine smile she could.

The problem was, she couldn't stop thinking about it at all over the next few days. She and Jayson had gotten together to study for a test, but she couldn't concentrate enough to really contribute anything. Tonight was his big meeting with the coaches from Central University, and she had promised she would be there to support him. She scoured her closet before she chose a simple black sundress and ditched her Dr. Martens for a pair of ballet flats. She put her hair up, then let it down, then brushed it back up into a simple bun.

She shook the nerves out of her hands before pulling the pan of brownies out of the oven.

"Calm down," she told herself just as her phone sounded with a message.

> *Jayson:* Hey, Beautiful.

> *Brooke:* Hey!

> *Jayson:* You still coming tonight?

> *Brooke:* Of course I am. Just waiting for the brownies to cool.

> *Brooke:* You're amazing. Relax. They already want you, tonight is just about you making them prove they deserve you.

> *Jayson:* You're amazing. I don't know what I would do without you, Brookelynn.

> *Brooke:* xoxoxo

Brooke let out a breath before squeezing her eyes shut. A tear escaped anyway. She didn't have time to deal with emotions tonight. Jayson needed her, and she was going to show up for him. She would tell him tomorrow.

Or this weekend.

Soon.

She would tell him soon.

"Brooke, this is Coach MacManus. He's the head coach at Central University. Coach MacManus, this is my girlfriend, Brooke Thomas."

"It's a pleasure to meet you, sir." Brooke shook the hand he extended.

"No sirs please. You can call me Coach," the man said with a friendly smile.

"Coach," Brooke reaffirmed.

Jayson beamed a smile at her. She wanted so badly to forget about her own issues and share in his excitement. This was a big deal for him, so it was a big deal for her, and all she wanted to do was hide. Jisela ushered them all into the living room to sit. Brooke hung back as they all walked ahead of her, making her way into the kitchen to grab a drink of water.

She hadn't realized how long she'd been gone until Jisela showed up with a question on her face.

"Is everything all right, honey?"

"Oh! Yeah. I mean, yes. I'm all right."

"Are you sure?"

And just like that, she had to blink back the tears that rushed to the surface. Jisela's simple question laced with motherly concern had the same effect her own mom seemed to have on her. She loved this woman so much. She wrapped Jisela in an embrace.

"Yes, I'm sure. Probably just PMS or something."

Jisela's eyes filled with question, but she didn't say anything further since Jayson popped into the kitchen. "You plan on coming back in, babe?"

He looked so handsome in his shirt and tie, the excitement in his eyes was undeniable. This was his dream happening right in front of her. She needed to pull it together and find her backbone so she could support him properly. Clearing her throat free of emotion, Brooke gave him her best smile.

"Yeah, I'm coming right now. Sorry."

She didn't look back at Jisela as she took his hand and followed him back to their seats on the couch.

"Jayson, I'm not sure where we fall on your list of prospects, but we want to let you know you're our number one pick. We know we don't have as many trophies as some of those other schools that are courting you. I'll be real with you, since I came on board as the coach for Central, we have been very focused on building a team with national championship potential. We have some great upperclassmen players, and with you joining... well, it could be just what we need to make this year special. Frankly, I think this year will be the start of a brand new dynasty. You could be part of that dynasty, a starting point. There's no sitting on the bench to earn your spot. It's yours already, you just need to decide if you want it. As good as you are, I still think we could help you get better."

Jayson looked to her with a smile in his eyes. She gave his hand a reassuring squeeze.

"You'd get the full experience without being a plane ride from home. It's a bit of a drive or a train ride, but you'll still only be a couple hours from your family. I know your mother and brothers mean a lot to you."

"Yes, Coach, you'd be right about that."

He turned his attention to her. "What about you, Brooke? Have you considered Central?"

Brooke startled as all eyes in the room landed on her. She nodded. "I mean, I applied and they accepted me, but I haven't made any final decisions yet."

"Well, I hope you'll give the school a shot too. Jayson speaks very highly of you. He's frequently mentioned your support throughout this year. I'd like to think all my athletes had the same from their significant others."

"No matter what school or schools we end up at, I'll always support Jayson." *And dang it if her voice didn't sound like she was two seconds from bursting into tears.*

Jayson brought her hand up to his lips and kissed it before

interlacing their fingers. She saw the question in his eyes, but she pulled her gaze away and fixed her attention on the hemline of her dress.

Somehow, she made it through dinner and dessert without letting her emotions run to the surface. She helped Jisela pour everyone coffee before hiding out in the kitchen cleaning every possible thing she could find. Once that was done, she stole away upstairs into Justin's room and read him book after book until he fell asleep. She lost track of time until Jayson stood in the doorway.

"There you are. Everyone just left."

"Oh, I'm sorry I missed saying goodbye."

"Can we talk?"

She swallowed nervously as she nodded. She placed a soft kiss to Justin's head before she shifted out from under him.

Jayson took her hand and led her outside to sit on the porch. She wrapped her oversized cardigan around herself as they both took a seat on the wooden swing.

"What's going on in that head of yours tonight, beautiful?"

"Nothing. I'm just really tired," Brooke lied, keeping her eyes fixed on the curve of her thumbnail.

"Brookelynn, you've chewed on your bottom lip so much today, it's raw. You have been distant all week. I barely saw you tonight, and when you were in the room with everyone, your mind was a million miles away. I hope you know you can tell me anything. Are you upset with me? Did I do something wrong?"

"No, not at all." She took his hands in hers and squeezed them reassuringly. "It's nothing about you, it's me. It's just a stupid art thing bugging me. I'm sorry I've been so off lately."

"Is that all?" His eyes remained skeptical.

She nodded as she leaned in and kissed his cheek reassuringly. "I love you. I'm sorry if I didn't make a great impression with the coach tonight. I know tonight was important for you. I didn't mean to make you worry."

"Coach loved you. He had about three helpings of your brownies. But even if he didn't, I wouldn't care. I love you no matter what."

"So, you really like Central, huh?" She nudged him with his shoulder.

"Yeah, I really do. Coach was straightforward, and he was right. Central is an underdog, but they've been building a strong team with championship potential. Next year, if the season goes right, it could be an amazing breakout year."

"No matter what you decide, I meant what I said. I love you and will always support you, no matter what."

"Forever and always, you and me, right?" His thumb gently traced her sore bottom lip.

"You and me," she confirmed with a trembling smile.

She hated the fact that she lied to him. She knew she should talk to him about it, but she had seen his face after Brian told him he was leaving early. She didn't know how to tell him she was considering schools so far away from any of the ones on his list. Truth be told, she hadn't even thought a school like the Seattle Arts Institute would ever consider her for admission. Now, not only did she have to think about what school she wanted to go to, she needed to figure out what she really wanted to do with her life.

She needed to know the answers to those questions before she talked to Jayson. Maybe he wouldn't even have to worry about a long distance relationship, and until she made a clear decision, she hoped she could keep his mind doubt free. That's what a good girlfriend would do, right?

Chapter 14

JAYSON

Jayson joked with Jayden as they both headed toward the student parking lot. The hallway was nearly empty save for one familiar face. He jogged over to help a Ms. Cullen hang up the banner she was struggling with.

"Oh, Jayson, what great timing you have!"

"Hey, Ms. Cullen. How are you?"

"I'm great. I hear so much exciting news about you, congratulations!"

"Thanks. I'm still really absorbing it all. It's been a bit of a whirlwind."

"I could imagine, being in a magazine as big as American Athlete is a big deal. We're all proud of you. I'm proud of Brooke as well. I think she was in a bit of shock about being offered a spot at Seattle's Art Institute. Both of you have some major celebrating to do!"

Seattle! Jayson struggled to smile as the alarm wailed in his head. "Yeah, we definitely do! Well, I guess I should get going. Thanks again for the congrats!"

As they continued to walk, Jayden nudged him hard. "Why didn't you tell me Brooke was going to Seattle?"

"I didn't know, Jayden. She didn't tell me..."

"What's going to happen to you guys then? You aren't going to break up, right?"

"I don't want to talk about it anymore."

He didn't want to think about it either. Jayson struggled through his workout, distracted by the fact that his heart felt like it was breaking. Just a couple weeks ago, he couldn't wait to graduate. Now, graduation would bring a massive shift to his life. Brian would be leaving, and now his time with Brooke could be coming to an end.

During their many late night phone calls, they had often talked about their dreams of the future. Dreams that seemed to always count each other as a constant. Never in those conversations did they seem to talk about the time between now and then. They loved each other, but could they survive the next four years if they were so far apart?

He pulled a vibrating phone out of his pocket.

Brooke: Are you still in the gym?

Jayson: Yeah. About to call it a day, though. What's up?

Brooke: I'm outside in my mom's car. I just left Val's and I wanted to see you.

Jayson: Be right there...

"Hope you don't mind me showing up. I just needed to see you... kind of having a bad day."

He pressed a kiss to her lips before settling in the passenger seat. "I'm glad you came. We need to talk."

Brooke's smile faded. "Is it something bad?"

"Why didn't you tell me about Seattle?"

He fixed his green eyes on hers. They instantly filled with tears as she regarded his undisguised sadness.

"Who told you?"

"I think the real question is why didn't you tell me?"

She dropped her head, leaning her forehead against the steering wheel. "I wanted to tell you, I really did. I just don't know what to feel. I should be happy. This is something to be happy about, but ever since I read that letter, I just want to cry."

"The night the Central coaches came to my house... tell me the truth, did you know about Seattle then?"

She nodded, pulling her bottom lip between her teeth. "I thought I was doing you a favor by not adding my drama to all the stuff you're dealing with. I didn't know how to feel about any of it."

Jayson dug deep under his sadness and lifted her chin to turn her face toward him. He offered a warm smile. "You want to know how you should feel? Feel proud. Baby, feel happy. Your art is so amazing, a school that good wants you. You told me yourself how hard it was to get into that school. You worked hard."

"But it's in Seattle. That's a long way from Central. It's a long way from you."

"We'll make it work. If your dream is going to Seattle, then don't think about giving it up for anything."

"But what if you are part of my dream now?"

"Brooke, I honestly don't know. I've never done this before either. I've never been in love. I've never had to worry about missing someone like I know I'll miss you. I read love and distance can be compared to fire and air. If the fire is like that of a candle, a simple puff of ordinary air will extinguish it, but if it's a raging wildfire, the wind will only fuel it to grow stronger. I'm telling you, Brooke, the way I feel about you... what we have..."

"It's a wildfire."

He wiped a stray tear from her cheek. "Yeah, it is. I won't ever make you sacrifice your dream school for me. You've supported me so much this year, and I'll do the same for you always. If you decide to go to Seattle, I'll still be yours. We'll make it work no matter what. I waited years to have you, and I'm not letting you go, especially not over something temporary like distance. Whatever you decide, I'll support you, because I'm your guy and you're my girl. Follow your heart and make your decision for you and what you want. We'll figure out the rest when we need to. I promise."

Brooke nodded. "I will. I promise."

He kissed her forehead. "Please don't keep things like that from me. We are in this together, okay?"

"Okay."

Staying true to his word, Jayson didn't push her to see what decision she was thinking of making over the coming weeks. Rather, they engrossed themselves in planning for the prom and his trip to New York. He was flying out to play in the All American game and also for his magazine photoshoot and interview. He had asked her to join him, so Brooke had gotten permission from her mom to fly out with his family to be there cheering him on. Having Brooke come along with Brian and his family for his big game, Jayson felt incredibly excited. He was ready to show the country what he could do, and he couldn't wait to make Brooke proud of him.

The evening before the All Star game, Jayson did his last press meet and greet of the day before he hurried back to his room to get ready to meet Brooke down in the lobby. They had plans to go walk around the city together and grab a bite to eat. He had been so busy since they arrived, and with his family there, they hadn't had very much alone time to just sit and enjoy each other the way they were used to. Jayson had told Brian and his family he needed to have at least one evening where he could spend some much needed time with his girlfriend. Brooke had stepped up so much with his brothers, sometimes he felt like the only time they got with each other was between classes and when he brought her home. He didn't want her to get lost in the hustle and bustle of senior year basketball because she was much more important than that. He was determined to remind her how he felt about her so she would never forget how special she was to him.

"You look pretty nervous there, Jay. You do realize you and Brooke are already dating, right?" Brian teased from his place on one of the beds as Jayden's smile cracked. Jayson tossed a pillow in his friend's general direction.

"Shut up! You know I love this girl like crazy. We haven't had much time to do this lately, and now that we might be looking at a long distance relationship... I don't know. I can't let her think any of this will ever matter more than she does. I need some time with my girl."

"I get it, man. I'm just giving you a hard time because that's best friend code."

He knew Brian knew his fears. He'd spent the last few years of his life wanting Brooke. Now that he had her, he was faced with being separated from her. While he was positive he could commit himself to her no matter the distance, he hated the thought of not being near her. Just thinking about everything was beginning to make his chest ache with needing to see her. So when she walked off the elevator in her soft gray cashmere sweater paired with a black tulle skirt that fell to just above her knees and a pair of sexy black suede wedges, she took his breath away. Her chestnut brown hair fell around her shoulders in loose waves. His girlfriend was a classic beauty.

"You look amazing, Brookelynn. So incredibly beautiful. I'm so lucky."

She flashed a warm smile, her chocolate eyes melting with emotion. "Your mom helped me get ready. I wanted to look pretty for you tonight."

"You look perfect. I love when you wear your hair down. God, you are so sexy."

She still blushed happily when he told her such things. He pulled her gently into his kiss.

"Where are we going tonight?"

"I figured since you came all the way to New York with me, I needed to take my Brooke Lynn to Brooklyn."

She laughed happily. "That would be a fitting date."

"I thought so too. We're long overdue for a date night. Sometimes it makes me sad we don't get to have many actual dinner dates where I get to show you off as my girl."

"It's a busy time for you. I totally understand, Jay. Our

studying and watching movies in our sweats is just as special as dinner at any fancy restaurant. I'm in love with *you*, not the fancy dates."

"Best. Girlfriend. Ever," he growled amorously before pressing another kiss to her lips.

He led her outside where they caught a cab.

"I can't wait to watch you play tomorrow. I'm so excited."

"Yeah. I'm pretty pumped too. Thanks for coming. It really means a lot that you came all the way here for me."

"Of course. I wanted to be here to see you play. Not every girl has a super sexy, super talented boyfriend who does something this great."

"Not every guy has a girl like you supporting him and cheering him on. No matter what hype, they put on my game, I'm only as good as I am because of my family and you. But for the rest of tonight, no talk of basketball... just me and you."

She squeezed his arm as she snuggled closer into his side. They flirted their way through dinner and dessert. They kissed in the cold air as they walked along the Brooklyn Bridge before heading to the subway station.

"We took a cab here, so I thought we could attempt an underground adventure for the way back. Hopefully we don't get lost down here forever."

Brooke giggled excitedly as they swiped their purchased metro cards. "We're bonafide New Yorkers now, babe!"

"I'm pretty sure New Yorkers aren't this excited to get on the subway. It smells... interesting."

She buried her laugh into his arm as she clung closer to him. "Just protect me from the rats."

"Don't you mean the alligators and crocodiles that roam the tunnels down here?"

"Oh! And turtles with ninja abilities too!"

"This was way more romantic in my head." Laughing at their own jokes, they stepped onto the subway and Jayson quickly claimed a seat, pulling her onto his lap. She laid her head on his shoulder.

"I have something to tell you."

"Oh, really? Let me guess, you think I look sexy in my suit?"

"Well, duh!" She laughed. "But no, it's more serious than that."

Jayson held her closer. "You know you can tell me anything."

"I sent my deposit in for school before I left to come here."

"That's great, Brooke. What's the decision?"

"We just have to be prepared to travel whenever we possibly can to see each other."

"You know I will, babe. As much as I can, I'll be there to visit you." His eyes sparkled with sincerity.

"It might be a long walk from my dorm to yours."

She raised an eyebrow. He knew she was being vague on purpose.

Jayson smiled. "Are you saying what I think you're saying?"

"I know you didn't make your decision official. But I could see it in your eyes and hear it in your voice. I know you feel it in your heart, so I had to look at my own heart."

"But you made the decision for you, right? I told you I would never want you to hold yourself back from greatness for me. I'll be by your side no matter what."

"I know, and I know I made the right decision. I'm not holding myself back from anything. It's an amazing school, that's why I applied there in the first place. You happen to be a major added bonus. You and me together, Jay, that's greatness."

Jayson kissed her excitedly. "I swear you are the best girlfriend in the whole world. You'll never know how much love you make me feel. I am just so happy, Brookelynn. You're going to be my wife."

"Brooke Williams sounds about right to me," she said simply.

Jayson's eyes softened with love. "It sounds perfect."

Brooke

Brooke was too eager to wait patiently for the game to begin. She had been on the edge of her seat all day. Trying to keep busy, she had colored two dozen pictures and played numerous games of Uno with Justin in the hotel room. They went window shopping all together just after lunch, where she gave into temptation and brought a new pair of jeans and sneakers she planned to wear to the game later that night.

Once she got back to the room, she left the boys to their mother and decided to take a long hot shower before it was time to get ready. Pairing her new jeans with a sweatshirt that she had custom made back home in Paradise Cove, she felt like she was going to burst with pride. She left her hair down, the loose waves framing her face softly.

Jayson would be looking for her in the stands, and she wanted him to know she was there for him.

She wanted him to know she would always be there—*for him.*

The time was drawing closer. She looked around the arena in awe. She couldn't believe how many people were filling the stands and the amount of press lining the sidelines. They were all about to watch Jayson in his element, and her heart was about to burst with pride. Brian chuckled as she wrung her hands nervously.

"He's going to be great, Brooke. Stop worrying."

"I'm not worried."

He gave her a skeptical look as he imitated her nervous hand wringing. "Sure looks like you're worried."

"I'm not! I'm just..."

"Worried?"

"Oh, shut up, Brian."

With a gentle shove to his shoulder, she ignored his snickering and closed her eyes. Taking deep, calming breaths, she tried to ignore the urge to pace as the clock ticked closer to tipoff time. She really wished she was able to hug and kiss him before his big game, but he was about to show the nation what he could do...

And she wasn't worried at all.

JAYSON

Jayson sat in the locker room gathering his thoughts and finding his zone. Inside his left shoe, he'd slipped the last family photo they had taken with their father. He needed to carry his family close to him tonight. As for Brooke, he had taken to wearing the hairband he had stolen on the night of their first kiss on his wrist. Today, he wore it over the letters BLT he had written in black ink on the inside of his wrist.

Brooke Lynn Thomas.

She'd be there cheering him on regardless of anything that happened. At the start of the school year, she didn't know or even care to know anything about basketball. But now, here she was, with his colors on and his number written on her cheek. She would cheer him on and yell at the bad calls by the ref and be ready to hit someone if they dared to foul him. She loved the game because he loved the game. That just made him love her even more.

As he made his way onto the court, he scanned the crowds, quickly spotting her. She was standing on top of her seat, waving her arms wildly to grab his attention. The same girl who had so matter-of-factly informed him she wasn't a rah-rah type was now proudly wearing a sweatshirt that made him smile wider than he thought possible.

HE MAY OWN THE COURT, BUT I OWN HIS HEART. She beamed a smile his way before spinning around to show him the writing on the back, which read WILLIAMS and his number twelve.

This girl—*his* girl—wasn't just wearing his colors, she was wearing his name and number for everyone to see a fraction of her love for him. Her shirt was right; she owned his heart. She turned to face him and held up her hand. On her palm was a red heart she had drawn with a red marker. It had a bold J over its center. Then she folded her thumb down to form a number four.

He read her lips. "Love you forever. Love you for you."

He felt the tears stinging at the backs of his eyes. He held up a four in return and brought his fingers to his lips, then touched them to his wrist, over his BLT.

With that encouragement from his Brookelynn and the cheers from his family, he was more than ready. He played the best four quarters he had in him, and his teammates were right there with him. The game was beyond amazing, and the crowd was roaring with appreciation.

He walked out of the tunnel and saw the people who mattered most in his life waiting for him. His brothers all ran to him, pouncing on him to beg for the chance to be the first one to wear his game jersey. It felt good. They were his driving force in life, and he was happy he could make them all proud. Scooping Justin up into his arms, he closed the gap that remained so he could embrace his mother.

"I'm so proud of you, mijo. I'm always so proud of you." She reached up to hug his neck the best she could.

"I love you, Ma. Thank you for everything." He wrapped his arms around his mom. Brooke stood back, her smile of pride was telling as she silently took video for Val to use in her film, ignoring the tears that slid down her cheeks.

Brian clapped his back appreciatively. "You just put Paradise Cove in bold letters on the map."

"I wouldn't have gotten here if you hadn't been on the court with me all these years."

"Well, you had the talent, I just brought the good looks."

Brooke did burst into laughter then. Jayson's gaze flickered back over to her.

"Are you gonna get over here and hug me or what?"

She closed the camera, dropping it into her bag before she jumped up into his arms, hooking her legs around his waist.

"Oh no, they're going to smooch again!" Justin cried, horrified.

"C'mon, boys." Jisela ushered her younger sons toward the exit. "I'll leave you three to celebrate *responsibly*. Call me to check in."

"Yes, ma'am," Brooke chorused, along with Jayson and Brian.

The three of them alone, Jayson slid his hands from Brooke's thighs to her butt.

"Oh God, you two are going to smooch again, aren't you?" Brian teased.

"You better believe it," Jayson murmured.

After spending some time with his mother's brother and cousins in Washington Heights, he had to leave them early to head to his scheduled interview and photoshoot for American Athlete. He wasn't usually a fan of these interviews, but when they asked him about his motivation, it was an easy answer. He spoke of his family and talked about his dad. He allowed himself to get emotional. He made sure the world was going to know he was the son of Joshua and Jisela Williams, and it was their blood, sweat, and tears that made him the person he was.

He wasn't sure he was fully surprised when they asked about the moment he held up the number four just before tipoff and throughout the rest of the game. There was no way he could hide the happy smile the memory evoked. He was proud of his relationship, and so he eagerly showed the reporter the photos of them on his cell phone and the hairband on his wrist. He began to tell the world about his Brooke.

Brooke

ack in Paradise Cove, everyone immersed themselves in all the senior activities happening that spring. When Jayson's feature in the magazine came out, the town was abuzz about him landing the cover and such a huge article. Brooke still couldn't believe he had talked so much about them. They even printed Brooke's favorite picture of the two of them in the article. It was a picture Val had taken of them as they sat on the beach the day they had all hung out. In the light of the setting sun, the love between the two of them was obvious to anyone looking. She loved that he was so open about his family and their romance, and that he wasn't embarrassed to claim her as his girlfriend in front of a national audience. She was very aware most other eighteen-year-old guys in his position with such a big future ahead would easily keep a relationship out of the limelight—and that was only if they didn't dump their high school girlfriends. Jayson was so different than that, she knew she had the best kind of boyfriend there was.

That weekend, he was due to go on his formal recruiting trip to Central. Having stayed home from school sick for most of the week, she was happy to see him when he showed up at her house that afternoon. So happy, in fact, she almost forgot her bedhead probably looked crazy. She wore an oversized sweatshirt she had taken from his closet and never returned with a pair of pajama pants that had seen many better days. He, on the other hand, looked gorgeous. Her heart raced with the anxiety of knowing he'd be up at a college with a whole new league of girls while she'd be in her bed looking like she was two steps away from death.

"Hey, beautiful." He bent down and kissed her forehead.

"Hardly. I look horrible. If I didn't miss your face so much, I would order you not to look at me."

"I've missed you all week. How are you feeling?" He turned the royal blue cap he wore around backwards.

"I feel twice as bad as I look. Are you excited about your weekend at Central?" Her voice was raspy and her throat hurt, but she wasn't about to waste her time with him.

"A little. I'd be more excited if you were coming with me."

"I wish I could. They probably have all sorts of fun things planned for you."

She raised her eyebrow pointedly.

"What is that eyebrow for?"

"Oh, I know what happens on these recruitment trips. I Googled it!"

He laughed loudly. "I don't care what Google says, or what they may have planned. They don't have a germ-ridden, sickie-face babe like you for a girlfriend."

She threw the teddy bear that sat on the table next to her bed at him. "Don't tease me, babe! I'm serious, I've seen all those big-boobed cheerleaders... not to mention the rest of the female student body."

"What, you didn't Google their boobage too?" He couldn't resist teasing her more.

She pouted and pulled the blanket up over her face. His laughter filled the room before he leaned forward, pulled the blanket down, and kissed her pouting mouth slowly and gently. He leaned his forehead against hers and kept his lips touching hers as he whispered, "It kills me you still don't know how sexy you are, Brookelynn. I love you. I am in love with you."

"You kissed me, and I'm all germy sickie face."

That small kiss made her skin tingle with pleasure. She felt all warm and was certain it wasn't the fever this time.

"I know, that just proves how much I love you. Besides, seven days without kissing your lips is torture, I'll risk it."

He kissed her again, just as softly, then pulled away to look into her eyes.

"Oh, and, Brooke, for the record, I don't care about big-boobed cheerleaders. I never have. They aren't my type. I have a giant soft spot in my heart for this certain artistic book nerd who always cheers the loudest for only me. She also happens to have some really nice boobs herself and the sexiest butt I've ever seen."

"That's the sweetest thing I've ever heard!" She beamed happily and hugged him tightly.

JAYSON

Jayson couldn't believe it was all happening. Walking across the campus at Central, Jayson felt the surge of excitement flow through his veins. This could very well be his home away from home for the next few years. The prospect of playing there was just waiting on his final answer. He pulled open the doors to the athletic training center and found his weekend hosts waiting for him with a jersey and huge, hopeful grins.

"Glad you could make it, Williams! What do you say to running through a special practice workout with the guys?" Coach MacManus greeted him with a genuine smile.

"Absolutely."

By Saturday night, he already knew he wanted nothing more than to officially commit to Central. His student and team hosts had arranged a party that night either to lure him in further or as a reason to throw a party.

"You're going to have an epic time. This isn't like the high school parties you're used to, Williams." Vaughn suggestively arched an eyebrow. "The girls, for one. They don't play around. I'll hook you up with whatever your preference is. Blonde, brunette, or redhead? I even know a girl with green hair, would you believe it? Her body is bangin', though."

"What Vaughn was getting at, I think, is tonight, it's your choice. What's your poison?" an older future teammate, Cal, added.

Jayson shook his head with a small chuckle. "Thanks for the party. I'm sure I'll have a blast, but I'm good on girls. I

already have my girl, and it's more than a high school thing with us."

"Oh yeah, I remember reading something about that in your All American feature. She's hot, but are you sure you want to be that committed before you even start college? You could be missing out on a lot of fun."

"In all due respect, man, you don't know my girl. She's the best thing that ever happened to my life and my game. She's it for me—my forever girl. It doesn't get any better than her, so I plan on holding on to her for as long as I can."

They nodded, but he knew most of them wouldn't understand how he felt about his relationship. He didn't care. He wouldn't jeopardize what he had with Brooke for a stupid night of partying ever again. Whether they got it or not, they now knew where he stood before they all headed to the party. He looked down at the screen of his phone where one of his favorite pictures of Brooke was set as his screensaver. His mind wandered back to that bedroom in Paradise Cove. She was so wrong. Even sick with strep throat, she had looked just as amazing. He missed her.

Ignoring the drunken flirtations and red cups shoved his way, he made his way through the crowded room until he felt the cool night air hit his face. It was a strange realization that no matter how many deep breaths, he couldn't smell the ocean in the air. As right as Central felt to him, something was missing. Unlocking the screen of his phone, he fired off some emails to the coach, then went back to the dorm where he left a note thanking them for everything. Without a second thought, he packed his bags and caught a cab to the train station.

Sunday morning, he showed up at Brooke's with cartons of soup, tea, and a bunch of old black and white love movies he'd found on DVD. He'd even slipped in a Romeo and Juliet adaptation. When she instantly began crying, he took it as a

173

good sign, so he smiled as he popped in a movie and curled up with her in bed.

"You're back early!" she rasped.

"I saw what I needed to see. I told the coach I wanted in. Then I came back to be with you—where I needed to be."

She kissed his cheek lovingly. "I'm glad you're here."

Chapter 15

JAYSON

Prom had both arrived and passed in a flurry of excitement. They spent the night at a post-prom bonfire down at the beach with their friends, and Jayson knew he would never forget how happy he was. The way Brooke looked up into his eyes as he put his tux jacket over her shoulders shook his core. The love he felt for her was something he never imagined love would feel like. When she had given him that second chance, she had given him the world. More than ever, he was certain he needed her in his life for more than the now.

That night, after he had gotten Brooke home safely, he returned to his own home and found his mom in the kitchen drinking a cup of tea. He sat down with her and took the opportunity to have a talk he'd been wanting to have for a while. He knew she would understand everything he needed to talk about. Jisela loved Brooke, and most importantly, she loved the two of them together. She would hear everything he had to say and really listen to him as he poured his heart out. He told his mother how despite what anyone else said, his love for Brooke was beyond just the label of high school sweetheart. She was his soulmate, and when he thought about his future, Brooke was always there as his best friend, wife, and the mother of his kids. She wasn't just the one right now, she was the forever one.

Now that the excitement of prom had died away, graduation seemed to be instantly upon them. He couldn't believe he was graduating with high honors and the best GPA he had ever received. Excitement aside, he couldn't forget in a few hours, it would mark the end of an era. He would really have to say goodbye to his best friend. He did his best not to think too much about it and focused on the graduation party his mom, Evelyn, and Brian's parents were throwing for them after the ceremony.

He reached onto the top shelf of his closet to retrieve the wrapped packages he had hidden away. Tonight, he would give both Brooke and Brian graduation gifts he hoped would express everything he wanted them to know. He put them on top of his bed and checked his watch. It was time to get dressed for his final moments as a student at PCH.

Just as he reached for his white dress shirt, his brother Jayden poked his head in the door.

"Hey, you got a minute to talk?"

Jayson smiled. "I'll make a minute. What's up?"

"I just wanted to say thanks for being a good big brother. Next year is going to be hard not having you around as much, especially not playing on the same basketball court or team."

Jayson smiled, then motioned for Jayden to come over to him. He wrapped his arm around his biggest little brother.

"We had a great time on the court together. Now it's your time to shine. I'll be waiting for you over at Central. Maintain the family reputation, focus on grades, not girls, and I know you'll kill it."

"It's going to be different without you here. I mean, your room has always been next to mine. When I came over to PCH, we finally got to play together... I'll miss it. I'm going to miss you, Jayson."

"JD, we are brothers for life. We'll always be on the same team. I'll always be there whenever you need me. No matter what. I promise. I'm always a phone call or text away."

"We would like to introduce our class valedictorian, Brooke Thomas."

He clapped proudly and whistled as she stood and walked to the podium where their Principal shook her hand proudly, then stepped aside. Brooke hadn't let him hear her speech beforehand, so now he sat on the edge of his seat, waiting for her to begin.

"Life goes on. I'm sure we've all heard these simple words, or even uttered them in passing, but today, on the day we leave the safety net of Paradise Cove High, those simple words have more meaning than ever. Today, we officially enter the real world. For some, the last four years have been the best of their lives. For others... well, this day couldn't come fast enough. The successes and failures that seemed to define our high school career will not matter for much longer. My fellow graduates, what truly matters is the person we have grown to become thus far and the person we will strive to be in the next defining phase of life. It doesn't matter if we were the smartest kid in class, or the best athlete, or the prettiest cheerleader, or the artsy one, or the nerd, or the band kid... it doesn't matter! How we impact the world around us, how we make others feel, and how often we smile... that matters. That's what will define us as people, which is what will define our success. The person we will spend the most time in our lives with is ourselves, so please make sure you like the person you are.

"We've had so many teachers in our four years here, but my greatest teachers were you, my fellow graduates. I walk away from PCH today most proud of the relationships I have come to hold dear. In this school, I have found guidance, the best friendships, and I found love—all of which I will cherish forever. We walk away from this school today with a few tears in our eyes and a lot of pride in our accomplishments. Some of us will move away. Some of us may never come back.

But this will always be our home. Paradise Cove will forever be in our hearts. Today is the first day of the rest of our lives, so let's carpe diem and make sure to take lots of pictures along the way."

Jayson, Val, and Brian were on their feet, applauding loudly before she could even step back from the podium, and soon, each member of the graduating class—Marisa included—and the audience had joined them. Brooke smiled sweetly as she dipped her head in a grateful gesture, then she met his eyes.

He whistled loudly again, and she raised her eyebrows, silently telling him, *"Look what you've done."*

But it changed to a look of love as he yelled out "I love you, Brookelynn Thomas!"

She blew him a kiss before retreating from the stage.

That night, his backyard was full of music, laughter, tables of good food, and of course family and friends. Jayson smiled at the sight of it all. His mother was showing off his diploma to his Aunts Lina and Milagros, his father's sisters. Then there were his mom's brothers, Mateo, Fernando, and Hector, who were making sure people stayed on the dancefloor.

In the same moment, when he was so happy and surrounded by so much love, his heart reminded him of his father's absence. In the same instant, his heart began to ache and his smile waned. Brooke appeared in his vision. Her hair was down, and her perfect curves were enhanced in a soft pink sundress as she stood barefoot in the soft grass. She waved at him as she moved across the yard straight into his arms. Before he knew it, he was surrounded by his girlfriend, his best friend, and his family.

The night was one of the most memorable, he was certain. Brooke danced the whole night, rotating her dance time with him, Brian, and others in his family. Val had salsa danced with all his uncles and was doing a very impressive merengue while laughing with Brooke.

When the crowd started dying down, Jayson asked Brian to take a walk with him to the front of the house. Away from the yard, Jayson opened his mouth to talk, but immediately found it hard to get any words out from around the lump forming in his chest.

Brian smiled a little sadly. "It's been a heck of a ride, hasn't it?"

Jayson nodded. "Thank you for being the best friend I could've asked for. Through everything, you were there..."

Brian's eyes glistened, and he quickly looked away. "I'm going to miss it all. As much as we dreamed of the day when we'd leave this small town, now that it's happening, I can't imagine leaving."

"You're going to do great." Jayson nudged him. "But I'm going to miss you."

A moment of silence fell between them.

"I got you something. It's a bit mushy, but it's something I want you to have, especially this summer."

Jayson produced a small package wrapped in plain brown wrapping paper. Brian opened it and found a framed photo of the two of them when they were about seven years old. They were sitting on Jayson's porch with their arms wrapped around each other's shoulders, matching Band-Aids on their knees. He could remember that day vividly.

"Thanks, man. I needed this." He couldn't hold back the sob that escaped.

"Make sure you keep in touch. I mean it! And we will meet back at the shack for thanksgiving break for burgers and shakes."

"Most definitely. We're brothers, right?"

The two embraced heartily, and as they stepped away, Brian held on to his grip.

"Jay, I wanted to say something to you, for the record. I know I tease you about being so committed sometimes, but I want you to know what I really think. I've never seen you better than you have been this year. Brooke is a phenomenal girl. Any guy would love to have what you have. She's the one for you, and I won't share my best friend with anyone else. No matter what, don't lose her again."

"I know, and I promise."

The two exchanged another hug and a knowing smile.

They didn't have to verbalize much else.

After all the rest of the guests had gone and remnants were cleaned up, Jayson offered to drive Brooke home. He took the scenic route and drove them out to the beach, and the two of them took a stroll along the sand. With the moon full and bright, the stars twinkling above, Brooke looked like she belonged up there in the heavens instead of on the beach with him.

He brushed the sea windblown hair out of her face and bent down to kiss her.

"You are the sexiest valedictorian in history."

She smiled deeply. "You have to say that because you're my boyfriend."

"No. I'm proud to say that, as your boyfriend."

Brooke reached up and wrapped her arms around his neck. "This has been the most amazing night of my life."

Jayson swallowed. It was now that he had to tell her everything he had been thinking.

"This whole year has been a crazy ride. But I'm the happiest I've ever been. Babe, you have this amazing effect on my life, and in case you didn't know, I want to you to hear it from me right now. You are everything to me, Brookelynn. I love you more today than I loved you yesterday. I will love you more tomorrow than I do right now. You've helped me find my happiness, my confidence, not to mention my passion. I know without a doubt you will be my wife one day. I know we're still young and I don't have anything but promises and dreams to offer, but I want to make a deal with you."

Crying, Brooke managed a small nod. Jayson released her hands and knelt down on one knee.

"I want to start the next chapter of our lives together, and I want you to know how serious I am about us. I have this ring I want to give you, and I'm hoping you agree to be my wife. I promise you when we say 'I do,' *whenever* that day is, I will do everything to give you the life you deserve. I will be the best husband for you. I will love you forever. Will you marry me, Brooke Lynn Thomas?"

She got down on her knees and cupped his face lovingly. "You've got yourself a deal, Jayson Mark Williams."

Jayson kissed her deeply, until they fell over in the sand. They both laughed in each other's arms until Jayson kissed her again. He pulled the ring out of his pocket and slid its coolness down her left ring finger.

She sat up shocked.

"Jayson, this ring! How'd you afford this? It's amazing."

"I had some money coming to me anyways. I told you about the trust fund. Since I got the full scholarship, I asked my mom if I could get some money from the trust a little early because I needed to do this. She agreed."

Brooke couldn't take her eyes off the round solitaire diamond now sitting on her left finger. "I can't believe it."

"Believe it, baby." Jayson gazed at her. "I already asked your mom's permission too. I need you to hear me when I say we don't have to get married until you're ready, even if that's not until after we graduate college, but I wanted you to know I am serious about us. I want you to know everything you do for me, every sacrifice you've ever made or will have to make for me, it will not be in vain. I will do everything in my power to make sure your dreams come true."

"The moment you told me you loved me, my dreams started coming true. I love you forever, Jay."

The way she said his name like that. *Jay.* It was what she called him when they were able to be alone in their love expressions. Three letters, such a simple combination of sounds, but on her lips, they were anything but. Coming from her lips, they were an expression of love and lust, of desire and an intimacy he shared with no one else. When she called him Jay, in her own quiet, unspoken way, she was calling him hers.

Up to this moment, he was certain there wasn't a better sound in the world other than Brooke saying his name infused with all her love. But then, her soft brown eyes found his as she smiled.

She had called him Romeo. She had called him boyfriend. But nothing could have prepared him for the next moment when she kissed him with all her love, looked him in the eye...

And called him her always.

Act II

FRESHMAN YEAR
~ Central University ~

Chapter 16

Brooke

Summer passed by in a flurry of activity. One by one, friends left for school. It was harder than she expected to start packing up her things and sorting her life into boxes and suitcases, shifting things into mental columns of what she could leave behind and what was needed up at Central. Her mother hid her emotions behind shopping bags she seemed to bring home every day, no matter how much Brooke protested she didn't need any more stuff. Now that she was leaving, a part of her heart had filled with worry that her mother would be left all alone in the house. The only thing that eased her fretting was the budding friendship Evelyn had been developing with Jisela and Jayson's reminders their mothers would have each other to lean on.

Before Brooke was truly ready, she was packing her last suitcase. The very next morning, Evelyn was going to be dropping her off at Central University. Although she didn't have much of an appetite, she had plans to meet up with Val for lunch so they could say their "see you on breaks," both agreeing saying goodbye wasn't going to happen for them.

By the time Brooke got to the café, Val was already two tissues deep into her crying. Brooke sat down and joined her.

"How can you be leaving me?"

"It's not cool, I know. I have to leave for the airport in a couple hours and suddenly don't know what I was thinking going all the way to Massachusetts. I won't know anyone! Brooke... I had to buy a jacket!"

"I'm going to have roommates. What if they don't get my jokes? Or they smell? I don't want to make new friends!"

Brooke grabbed a fresh napkin as the waitress delivered their food.

"See! New friends won't know how to order my food. I wish things didn't have to change so much!"

"Oh, Brooke! You don't have to worry. You're so nice, you'll have plenty of friends. Plus, you'll have Jayson."

"Yeah, but he'll be in a different dorm, and I know he'll be so popular. I don't want to be the clingy girlfriend."

Val smiled. "That's your fiancé—cling away, honey!"

Brooke giggled as she looked down at her ring finger. Even though it'd been a couple months, the idea of being engaged still made her insides twist with happiness.

"How are Mama and Papa Lee handling the big move?"

Val snorted. "She was calling realtors near Boston the other day. The woman is crazy! If she tries to buy me one more lamp, I'm going to lose my mind."

"You too? I swear my mom has brought me enough school supplies for the entire four years. It's like I'm going to sleep away kindergarten."

"I'm gonna miss their kind of crazy."

Brooke nodded. "Me too."

"So, I wrote out some best friendship rules—a contract of sorts." Val unfolded a piece of paper she pulled from her pocket. "We video chat at least three times a week while retaining all rights to unlimited inappropriate text messages. We each retain the title of the others ultimate best friend no matter who we meet. I'll only share that title with Jayson for obvious reasons. And speaking of Jayson... when you decided to let him get some cookie, I must be notified within two hours..."

"Valerie!"

"Seriously, Brooke, I want to know. I'm impressed you've waited this long, but if your self-control snaps, one hundred and twenty minutes later, I better hear from you—text, call, sky write, send a carrier pigeon—"

"I hear your crazy loud and clear." Brooke shook her laughter away as she met her best friend's eyes. "I want you to promise me you'll take care of yourself, Val. Go to Boston and show them how brilliant you are. Never dull your shine. Not for anyone. Promise me."

"I promise." Val reached for her hand. "You have changed so much, Brooke. Your confidence just shines through, and finally you can see what I've been telling you all this time. You are a great person and an absolute knockout. Those college guys are going to chase you down."

"Oh, puh-lease!" Brooke playfully changed the subject. "Thank you for being my only friend since my first day at PCH. I love you, and you are my family for the rest of my life. I wanted you to know I will always be here for you. I promise what we have is forever."

Val's eyes overflowed again. "I love you too, Brooke!"

"Are you sure you don't need me to run to Target and get you another set of sheets?"

"Yes, Mom. I'm sure. I'll be fine, I promise."

"Have I told you how proud I am of you?"

"Not in the last twenty minutes." Brooke wrapped her arms around her mother and kissed her cheek. "I love you, Mom. Thank you for everything you've done to help me get to this point. I couldn't have asked for a better parent than you."

"Call me and check in every week."

"I will. I want you to have some fun too. Don't spend all your time worrying about me. I'm your daughter, I've totally got this."

"I know you do. When you see that boy of yours, tell him I expect him to take proper care of you."

They both knew Jayson would follow through with that without any prompting, but even so, Brooke agreed and walked her mom back to the now empty car.

After Evelyn said a tearful goodbye, Brooke was left to walk back to her dorm alone. Her brave face didn't really feel so brave anymore, and by the time she neared her dorm, she was nearly ready to call her mom to tell her to come back and get her. But instead she put a smile on her face and hoped eventually things would get easier.

Back in the dorm, she was pulled into a conversation by her roommate and two of the girls who lived in the room next to theirs. To her relief, her roommate was extremely friendly and something about her just seemed effervescent. Her name was Tracie, and she had massive dirty blonde curls that made her tan skin glow in comparison. She was bubbly sweet and made Brooke smile a little bit easier with joke after joke in her heavy southern belle twang.

"So, Brooke, I heard your boyfriend is Jayson Williams. Is that true?" the girl named Alyson asked.

"Kind of. How'd you hear that?"

"My dad kept going on and on about him, and he had that article from American Athlete. He talked about the first time he saw you and said you were his first kiss and only girlfriend. They printed a picture of the two of you in it."

"Oh yes, the magazine." She had almost forgotten about the interview that had given her a smidge of notoriety.

"So, I know I'm nosey, but what did you mean when you said he was kind of your boyfriend? Did y'all break up?" Tracie asked.

Brooke giggled at the thought and emphatically shook her head. "No, we are seriously still together. He's a fiancé now, not just a boyfriend."

She held up her left hand.

"Oh my word!" Tracie gasped and reached out to examine the ring. "Gorgeous and committed. Girl, you got a good one!"

Brooke laughed so freely, the wolfish looks of Alyson didn't even bother her so much.

JAYSON

H e was officially a college student. The feeling was definitely a layered one. He had felt odd saying goodbye to his mother and brothers the day before knowing he wasn't going to see them for a while. But he felt proud he'd gotten here.

And now, his girl was here. He hadn't seen her in almost a week, and just knowing she was somewhere on the same campus had set off his need to have her in his arms.

Jayson had already unpacked most of his things and was making up his bed when his phone vibrated with a text message from Brooke.

> *Brookelynn:* So, I may or may not be standing outside your place.
>
> *Jayson:* Oh, really? Well, I may or may not be running to meet you right now.
>
> *Brookelynn:* ;) Hurry up!

> *Sean:* Williams! There are hot freshman girls everywhere and I'm about to decide which one is going to be on my orientation week roster.
>
> *Jayson:* My hot freshman girl is out there—you better not even try it, Sean!

Jayson slipped his phone in his pocket and scrambled for the door.

Brooke

B rooke took the time walking over to Jayson's to think. Most of the girls she had met in her own residence hall seemed nice enough, but Brooke couldn't help but wonder what Val was doing. She couldn't wait to chat with her later. As she waited in front of the row of townhomes, she felt eyes on her as several guys lingered nearby. She realized she definitely wasn't in small little Paradise Cove High anymore. She moved a little farther from the group and took a seat on a small wall to wait for Jayson. She felt a tap on her shoulder and looked up to see a tall, fair-skinned guy with dirty blond hair and pale blue eyes smiling at her.

"Are you okay? You look a little lost."

Brooke smiled. "Oh, no. I'm fine! Just a little overwhelmed I guess."

"Understandable. I'm Alex... from Kentucky."

"Nice to meet you. I'm Brooke."

They both smiled.

"So, Brooke, what brings you to the neighborhood? You don't strike me as the groupie type."

"I'll take that as a compliment. I'm actually waiting for my—Jayson!"

She spotted her man the second he stepped out of the doorway a few feet away from where she sat. His plain white t-shirt and red basketball shorts somehow amplifying his good looks, she was in his arms before he even laid eyes on her. His arms quickly wrapped her up as her legs locked around his waist. All her feeling of homesickness vanished. Jayson was her home, and no matter where they were, as long as they were together, she got the feeling everything would be all right.

"I'm so happy to see you," he said between her happy kisses.

"Me too. You have no idea how happy I am to see you right now," Brooke murmured against his lips.

"What are you doing loitering in this lion's den?" Jayson only halfway joked as he looked around at his neighbors.

"I can handle myself." With one last smoldering kiss, Jayson set her on her feet and intertwined their hands.

"Let me show you around my new place."

"Your place is so nice!"

While Brooke had just moved into her traditional dorm in the freshman residence hall, Jayson had snagged a place in one of the new, near-campus townhome housing units. She followed him into the living room where a lone, comfy-looking tan couch sat, free weights lined the floor, and a big screen television was mounted on the wall with several gaming systems down below.

"I see you're going for the minimalist look when it comes to the decor."

He laughed at her raised eyebrow and pulled her down with him on the couch. "Oh, come on, babe. We're guys. All we need is the basics."

"I guess." She curled up against him. "I'm so glad you're here, Jay."

"Pretty rough seeing your mom drive away today?"

She nodded. "I don't know anyone, and the idea of starting over is a little daunting. I really miss Val already... and Brian, and your brothers. I felt so alone for a little bit today."

He lifted her chin to meet her eyes. "Hey, I'm here with you, and I'm here for you. Always. Whenever you need me, we're in this together."

She nodded and closed her eyes as she felt his gentle kiss.

"So, do you like anyone you've met in your dorm so far?"

Brooke shrugged. "They're nice, but..."

"But they're not Val."

"Exactly. Val was my friend way before I was ever Jayson's girlfriend. Now I kind of wonder how much of my new friendships will be genuine or wanting to get invited to parties and things because I'm attached to you."

"It's one of those things that will just have to clarify itself in time. Just get to know them. Keep an open mind."

"I will. I promise."

Just before he could give her the kiss she was already desperate for again, a door swung open.

"You must be the infamous Brooke!"

Brooke smiled as she took in the new face. He was an inch or two taller than Jayson with the look of an athlete evident by his muscled frame. His dark brown hair was just long enough to be styled into a casual mess. His gray-blue eyes were just as soft as his smile. His voice had a low timbre, his southern accent completely different from Tracie's.

"I'm definitely Brooke, not so sure about the infamous part." She stood to shake his hand, only to have him wrap her up in a bear hug.

"I'm from Virginia. We hug pretty girls."

Brooke smiled at the compliment as Jayson threw a pillow in their direction. "That pretty girl is already taken, Riley."

He released her with a playful wink. "The name is Sean Riley, and I have the pleasure of being your guy's roomie this year."

"Nice to meet you, Sean."

"Sean's also starting on the team this year, babe." Jayson kissed her cheek warmly, standing up beside her.

"Oh, how nice! I guess I'll be seeing a lot of you then."

"Definitely. Hey, I was going to order a pizza—you guys want something?"

Jayson reached in his pocket, pulled out cash, and handed it over to Sean. "Yeah, grab us a large."

"And a salad to counteract all the grease please," Brooke added.

"Will do. I'll be back in a bit. Nice to meet you, Brooke."

As Sean left the apartment, Jayson pulled Brooke into his bedroom, closing the door behind them.

"Sean seems awesome."

"He's a good guy. I think it's a great fit."

"We should hook him up with Val!"

Jayson's chuckle was so low, it made her spine tingle. "Val would eat him alive."

He couldn't fool her. Jayson was already protective of her best friend; he'd become the big brother Val never wanted. It made Brooke love him even more.

"Do you realize this is first time I could totally make out with you in your bed and not have to worry about being busted by one of your brothers?"

"You know that thought has crossed my mind... especially since you show up here wearing those cut-off shorts. You know how I feel about you wearing those cut-off shorts."

She giggled as he pulled her legs so she'd straddle his lap. She kissed his jawline, deliberately ignoring his lips.

"Sexiest legs ever."

"You say that about all my parts."

"I speak the truth. Kiss me, woman..." He playfully growled and nipped at her neck.

"You aren't even going to say please?" She teased him with a soft kiss below his earlobe.

"Please... kiss me, woman..."

"I love it when you beg for it," she grinned before leaning forward to kiss him deeply.

Chapter 17

JAYSON

He plopped down in an empty seat toward the middle of the room. Brooke wasn't here yet, so he dropped his bag in the seat next to him, ensuring she'd be right where he wanted her: by his side. The class begin to trickle in, filling many of the available seats up, which wasn't necessarily surprising since it was a required freshman course. He was wondering if he should text her when he saw her walk through the door. She wore her hair pulled up into a messy bun, her beautiful face completely bare. She nibbled her lip as she scanned the room, looking for him.

It gave him that caveman pride when she spotted him and gave him that beaming smile, completely oblivious to the lusty glares from several guys in the rows separating them. He could have hurt them for just looking at her like that, but he couldn't really blame them. Brooke wore a simple, curve-hugging white tank that highlighted her full breasts and waist. Then there were the yoga pants. If he could personally thank the creator of the yoga pant, he would do it every day for the rest of his life. The sight of his girl in yoga pants was the stuff his fantasies were made of.

She hurried over, bending to plant a kiss on his lips. "Morning, babe. I totally overslept. I look a mess, don't I?"

"A mess? How about you go back to the door, and this time you walk over here backwards? You know, so I can get the entire effect."

"Jayson Williams!"

"Brookelynn future-last-name-Williams, don't act shy on me now. You're drop-dead sexy, and you know how I feel about your body. I'm just showing my loving appreciation."

Her cheeks flushed, her eyes soft with that look of desire he had come to recognize well. "Jayson…"

She didn't hesitate to lean over and pull his face to hers, placing a tender kiss on his lips. "I love you for always."

The following weeks seemed to speed by as they got accustomed to college life. They had three classes together that semester, which was nice, and were bound to have more since Jayson decided to double major in English and Education, while Brooke was following all of her passions, double majoring in Art and Education as well as taking on the challenge of minoring in English. It would be hard work, but if anyone was up to the task, it was his Brookelynn. Jayson knew no one expected much from him academically, but he knew what he was capable of and he was going to surprise everyone, even himself, with his grades.

He made sure he put forth major effort to regularly chat with all his brothers back home. As promised, he and Brian video chatted about once a week. His friend had fallen in love over the summer in Louisiana. For weeks, all he had heard about was this amazing girl named Garcelle. Since school started, however, Jayson had noticed a major shift. Brian had stopped mentioning Garcelle altogether and seemed upset about something. Jayson didn't want to push him to talk about it, especially over the computer. If they were going to talk about it, it was best discussed in person. He planned on doing just that when they were all back home for Thanksgiving break.

He had just finished emailing his assignment to his professor when Sean came in with their mutual friend and teammate, Vaughn, who lived a few units down the road.

"You finish that paper yet?" Sean asked, tossing his bag on the floor near the door.

"Just sent it in. What's up?" Jayson spun his chair around to face him.

"The team got invites to the big rush party down on Frat Road. It's gonna be huge! You have to come, no excuses." Vaughn smiled.

"I don't know. I'm supposed to put some serious work in at the gym first thing in the morning. Plus, I want to see my girl tonight."

"Oh, come on, Williams! Tell your girl to come meet us there. Hey, tell her to bring some girls too—only cute ones, though. The gym isn't going anywhere. Matter of fact, if you come, I'll workout with you tomorrow. Deal?"

Jayson thought for a moment, then picked up his phone. "I'll text Brooke and see what she says about meeting us."

"Don't forget to tell her to bring the cute girls!"

"Brooke is not the one to cross, dude."

Brooke

Brooke and Tracie had decided to get in a Friday afternoon workout before the weekend officially began. Brooke was running on the treadmill and simultaneously listening to her roommate's hilarious stories. Tracie was in the middle of telling Brooke about her ex-boyfriend when Alex appeared in front of her treadmill.

"Hey, Brooke!"

"Hey, yourself!" She slowed the treadmill to a walk.

Tracie gave Brooke an eyebrow wiggle she had to ignore to keep her composure.

"You disappeared the other day before I could explain my running off to my fiancé."

"Well, when I realized you had a boyfriend, I realized my motives weren't exactly so pure. Oh well, the best ones are always taken, right?"

Brooke rolled her eyes. "Before Jayson saw me, I was invisible to the male population."

"I find that hard to believe. You could never be invisible. Maybe they were all just blind."

"Anyway..." she waved his comments off, "this is my roommate and friend, Tracie. Tracie, this is Alex. He's from Kentucky," she added with a chuckle.

They politely chatted for a few moments before Alex said his goodbyes and went to finish his workout.

"Good grief, he's cute!" Tracie breathed heavily.

"I mean, he's no Jayson. You want a hookup?" Brooke smiled.

"I can't compete. He couldn't take his eyes off you. He's smitten."

Brooke's mouth fell open. "He's not smitten. He's friendly. Plus, you'll never have to compete with me, you are gorgeous."

"Brooke, have you seen your body lately? I can't compete with those boobs and that booty, at least not without surgery and a trillion squats. I'm just trying to contain the effects of the freshman fifteen at this point, lest my mother have a coronary when I go home on break. I'm telling you, you haven't met crazy until you've spent some time with my crazy pageant mom."

Brooke laughed as her new friend launched into a humorous tale about her history on the child pageant circuit. She had definitely lucked out in the roommate department. She genuinely enjoyed spending time with Tracie. She was a sweet southern dynamo with a personality that seemed too large for her small body, but was a good-natured person who always seemed to light up the room. They always had a good time together, and Brooke was happy to make at least one new genuine friend so far.

Brooke's phone lit up with a text. She smiled as she read the message.

"We just got an invite to our first college party at the Kappa house. Are you in?"

"Oh yes! Mama needs a new boyfriend." Tracie increased the speed of the treadmill and left Brooke laughing loudly.

JAYSON

"Now this is a party..." Sean shouted over the reverberating bass of the speakers. He was talking to Jayson but eyeing a giggling sorority girl on the other side of the room. "I should see if the DJ will play my jam."

Jayson held up a hand. "No, you shouldn't. In the privacy of our dorm is one thing but if you try and perform a Vanilla Ice tribute right now, I'm going to have to reevaluate our friendship."

"Hey, I like that song."

"Hey, you're drunk!"

Jayson took the cup out of his roommate's hand and dumped the contents into the nearest trashcan.

"We just got here!" Sean protested.

"That's exactly the problem, Riley." Jayson swiped a bottle of water out of a metal bin. "Start chugging. We have an early workout tomorrow."

Jayson pulled out his phone to check the time. It was nearly ten, and the party was in full-force. Jayson continued dodging all the offers of alcohol he could and tried to make sure Sean didn't get himself into too much trouble, but he couldn't stop watching the door.

The two girls trying their best to keep Riley's attention had begun to drift his way, so he excused himself to avoid the unwanted drunken flirting and antics. He just wanted his girl. Every time he started feeling like he was missing home, he'd spend time with her, and that was all he needed to feel better. He moved toward the door, hoping to step away from the noise of the party so he could call her and make sure she was all right.

He had made it only halfway when he spotted her. Brooke walked into the room and effortlessly drew attention her way. Her hair was left down to fall between her shoulder blades. She wore a simple tight white tank under her denim jacket and a short ruffled floral skirt with her small feet slipped into a pair of black, peep-toe stilettos. Her makeup was typical Brooke, kept to just a little mascara and a touch of gloss. She was the most beautiful girl in the whole place.

Brooke's eyes searched for him immediately. When she spotted him, he watched her pull her bottom lip between her teeth. She knew what that did to him. Equal parts innocent and sexy, his girl was everything good wrapped in a beautifully package. Every time he saw her, his heart started pounding in his chest, much like it was doing now. He suspected it always would, that she was bound to have that effect on him for the rest of their lives.

Unable to wait another moment, he moved across the room toward her. When she was finally within reach, he grabbed her around her waist, pulling her into his body like they were meant to always be physically connected. His other hand cupped her neck, his fingers instinctively getting lost in the softness of her hair as he pulled her mouth to his, kissing her thoroughly and making his desires very clear. He felt her soft hum of pleasure through his lips, and it shot through his body like lightning. Everything in him felt like it was buzzing with their energy. She slipped her hand under his t-shirt, resting it on the muscled plane of his back. He followed suit, allowing his hands to move down her back, stopping just short of her grabbing hold of her butt like he wanted to.

♥

Brooke

Brooke savored the hungry kiss, and felt desperate for more when he pulled away.

"You look... phenomenal." He placed a tamer kiss on her forehead.

She smiled her love at him. "You look pretty hot yourself."

He wore his favorite green fitted cap backwards, so all she could see were those heart-stealing eyes sparkling in adoration as he looked at her. She felt the goosebumps break out along her skin. In his slim fit cargos and white tee that sculpted around his muscles paired with a pair of Air Jordans, his sexiness was oozing over the simplicity of his outfit. She leaned up and kissed his bottom lip again, letting her hands explore the warm skin under his shirt.

"You are so freaking sexy, Jay," she said breathlessly against his lips.

"I was just thinking the same thing about you, Brookelynn."

"Then why the frown?"

"I don't even know why I'm here baby. This is not my idea of fun." Jayson shook his head.

"Well, why don't we have some of our own kind of fun then?" She kissed him reassuringly. "Rumor has it you dance almost as well as you play..."

She reveled in watching his expression change as she tossed her jacket to the side. His eyes traveled from her face to the swell of her breasts in her tank top. "Show me what you've got, hoop star."

Taking her hand, he smiled brightly as he led her toward the improvised dancefloor. Closing the gap, he dipped his head to press a kiss on the tender spot right below her ear. "I want to see all your moves, Miss Brookelynn."

Brooke didn't bother with a reply as her body relaxed into

his, the gentle rock of her hips becoming one with the pulsing beat of the song. His hand found its place on the small of her back as they moved as one. Jayson's eyes were fixed on hers as she rolled her body purposefully just before she stole his hat for herself.

"Eyes on me."

"Always."

With his body pressed against hers, Brooke danced like he was the only one watching. She let her hips ease into the swaying rhythm their bodies quickly fell into. Jayson let her take control while matching her every movement, keeping them linked no matter what. His hand only left the curve of her bottom when she spun around and pressed herself against him. His fingers flexed, and she could feel his sharp intake of breath through the sudden tautness of his abs.

She challenged his control with each bump and grind. His hands on her body were sending her senses into overdrive. Jayson's voice in her ear came as his hand slid around to her front, pulling her closer.

"Play fair, baby."

They lost themselves in each other for song after song, until a cheer erupted from those around them, bringing them back to reality. Brooke didn't have a moment to contemplate whether she should have felt embarrassed before Jayson's lips captured hers as he tucked her under his arm to lead her away from their audience.

"C'mon, let's get a drink."

"Hey, Brooooooke's in the house!"

The loud slur of Sean Riley's voice boomed from behind her.

"Riley! Maybe we should switch to water now?" Brooke felt herself dip under the weight of his arm as he draped it around her shoulders.

"You think?"

"I do." She nodded as she took the cup out of his hand and placed it on a nearby shelf.

"Did you bring the girls?"

"What girls?"

"Riley, get your hands off my girl. She's not your booty call operator."

"Did someone say booty?" Tracie popped up between them, and Sean promptly placed his other arm around her shoulders.

"I'm not an arm rest."

"And yet, my arm is resting ever so comfortably."

Tracie smacked at his stomach, but left his arm where it lay.

Brooke snorted back a laugh as Jayson's arm came around her waist, pulling her into his lap comfortably. She bit back a sigh of relief. Her feet were killing her, but she refused to admit defeat, not when Jayson's eyes kept wandering to her legs in admiration. She leaned into him, watching as Tracie and Sean argued whether Tracie was too short or Sean was too tall. The amusement was almost enough to keep her attention focused.

Almost. She felt eyes on her.

It didn't take long to spot Alex's cool pale blue eyes fixed on her in a cool stare from across the room. She offered a polite smile as she shifted nervously. Wariness colored her thoughts as she remembered their last interaction, but they quickly evaporated when Jayson's hands moved from her knee, traveling over the warm skin of her thighs. The unease melted away under the flame of desire.

"What do you say, you want to get out of here?"

"Only if you'll take me back to your place..."

"Do you ever wish you could live the college life as a single girl and not worry about me?" Jayson asked her as they walked back to his dorm.

Brooke stopped walking, pulling him to a stop as well. "Of course not! Why on earth would you be wondering that?"

"Brooke, I see the way all these guys are looking at you.

Even though it drives me crazy, I get it. You are drop-dead gorgeous. Looking at you tonight, you put everyone to shame, and every single guy in there noticed it. You don't have to try. All you have to do is be you. Then I remember it's only freshman year. All these parties are going to come up, and I'm already over it. I don't want to drink and do stupid things. I just want to get good grades, play good ball, and spend time with my fiancée. It's fun to go out and have fun, but this whole drinking and mass party situation is not my style. I lost you once because of it, I don't want to lose you again. But I don't want to hold you back from whatever you want to experience either. I don't want to be something you regret."

Brooke intertwined her fingers with his.

"I could never regret you or us. I see girls every day who would pay someone to bump me off just to be able to get your attention. I hear them talking in my dorm, most of them don't even try to hide it. It's like Marisa, but ten times worse. But I don't care who looks or how they're looking, I decided that a long time ago. You're my man, *mine*. I choose you, always. I don't care about the parties. You know me, Jay, I'd rather be with you anywhere than at a party with a bunch of foolery. Tracie knows how I feel about it all too. If I tell her I'm not going to a party, she doesn't make me feel any kind of way or push the issue. I came to Central for us and this relationship, not for a few years of partying. I love you."

Jayson felt the weight on his heart evaporate into the night sky. She looked up at him with all the love and trust he could have ever hoped for. He wrapped his arms tight around her. "I love you, Brookelynn."

"You better love me, Jayson Williams. I already agreed to forever with you. This time around, I won't hesitate to beat a girl down if she touches you. Now, will you please carry me back to your dorm because these shoes are murderous."

"Absolutely."

Back in the quiet of his room, Brooke changed into one of Jayson's shirts before they curled up in his bed, kissing until they fell asleep in each other's arms.

Chapter 18

Brooke

$\mathcal{B}$ rooke hopped up the washing machine next to Tracie, pulling her sweat-pant-clad legs up, allowing her to sit cross-legged as the two girls waited for their laundry to finish.

"Wild Wednesday night, huh?" Tracie pulled out a package of chocolate cupcakes from the pocket of the hoodie she wore. "I brought laundry room sustenance."

Tracie handed Brooke one of the treats before holding hers up. "A toast! To girl time and clean underwear!"

"To clean underwear!" Brooke giggled, then took a healthy bite of her cupcake. "So... I never really asked, what made you come to Central? Georgia is a long ways away."

Tracie hummed as she seemed to mull around the words she was choosing. "I came to Central because Georgia is a long ways away."

Brooke could see the sadness well up in her roommate's eyes. She immediately reached out and gave Tracie's leg a gentle squeeze. "Hey, you know if you ever need to talk about anything, I'm here for you, right?"

Tracie wiped at the corner of her eye. "This is supposed to be fun girl time, not a sap fest."

"It could be both."

Tracie lips curled into a tiny smile. "No wonder why everyone loves you. You are an extremely likeable person,

Brooke Thomas. So, where's your guy tonight?"

"I think he said he was going to be in the gym for a bit, then they probably all went back to play that new football game."

"Ugh, you guys are so stinkin' cute, I can't deal. What's the secret?"

Brooke nibbled at the frosting on the remaining piece of cake. "There's no secret. I love Jayson. I trust him with every bit of my heart and love him with every bit of my soul. It may not always be easy, but there's no one I'd want to struggle with more."

"So, it's safe to say Jayson is the reason you came to Central?"

"I'd be lying if I said it didn't factor into my decision, but when I really thought about it, Central felt like the right place for me. I'm certain even if I went to school in the North Pole, I'd still have this ring on my finger and Jayson would take care of my heart."

Tracie rested her chin on her bent knee. "You make me believe in love and fairytales."

"I wasn't always a believer. I must admit, at first, I was pretty resistant to the whole thing. It took a while, but he won me over, and we've been writing our forever-after ever since. When he put this ring on my finger, it wasn't some little kid playing house moment. We knew it then, and we know it even more now. He's the man my heart is going to love forever. I have no doubt we were created for each other."

Tracie's blonde curls rippled as she shook her head. "Does he have a brother?"

"Not happening. I love you, but my future baby brothers-in-law are off limits!"

"Well, dang! I need love too."

Brooke gave her a sly smile. "Challenge accepted."

Over the next month and a half, they fell into a good schedule. They made as much time as possible for each other between classes and other responsibilities. Brooke was there as the basketball season started, in the stands cheering him on as always. She found her own passions too. She immersed herself in the art department, taking workshops when she could fit them in.

While she had begun to work out over the summer, she'd found herself falling in love with running. It had become a habit that helped to polish her confidence, and she was hooked. Joining Jayson in the gym when their schedules allowed had become some of her favorite "dates." Even when she couldn't work out with Jayson, she soon developed her own workout routine in between classes and tutoring.

"Fancy seeing you here."

Alex slowed his jog to a walk as she approached. She wished she could say it was a surprise to see him there in the gym, but it wasn't.

Brooke lifted one of her shoulders in a shrug. "I'm pretty sure you said that the last two times you've seen me here."

She pulled her hair up into a messy bun before stepping onto the only available treadmill, placing her next to Alex. Tomorrow, she would try the track instead.

"Touché." Alex's thin lips curled into an empty smile. "How's life treating you?"

"Better than ever." Brooke struggled to untangle her headphone cords. The sooner she could put her ear buds in, the sooner she could crank her music and lose herself in the run her body was craving.

"Your boyfriend is the buzz of campus. I hope he can perform this season and live up to the hype."

Her skin bristled, but she forced her smile to stretch even further. "The hype is there because the talent is there. Jayson will do what he always does, and I'll be cheering him on every second of every quarter."

"We'll see. This isn't high school basketball. In Division I ball, there's a separating of the men and the boys."

"Good to know my man won't have any problems then." Brooke bit down on her bottom lip just as a familiar arm draped around her shoulder, weighing her down.

Thank heavens for Sean Riley.

"Hey, Brooke, you want to come take a video of me lifting so I can post it on Instagram?"

Normally, she would have rolled her eyes at him and told him to go find one of his fangirls to be his camera person. But she was just grateful for the excuse to bolt from the cardio section of the gym. "See ya around, Alex."

Sean lifted a chin in acknowledgement of Alex's presence, but said nothing as he steered Brooke in the direction of the weight room.

"I'll take one video, Sean. I came to the gym to workout, not stand around watching you flex all day."

"Two videos and I'll load up the bar with plates for all your sets."

Brooke considered his offer for half a moment. "Two videos and a post workout protein shake. I can load plates on the bar by myself thank you very much."

"Deal!" Sean's shirt was on the floor before she could blink.

"You didn't say shirtless!" Brooke's outcry was tamped down by the hearty chuckle that followed. "God, you're such a peacock, Sean Riley."

"You just worry about recording me from my pretty side."

Despite all their new friends and activities, the time had come to Paradise Cove for Thanksgiving break, and they were both thrilled to be reunited with the home of their hearts. With Val and Brian returning home as well, they had all coordinated a reunion bonfire on the beach to see each other.

Brooke anxiously finished packing up her duffel bag waiting for Jayson to arrive. Wearing a pair of skinny jeans, a white tank top, and a black wrap sweater, she slipped her feet into a pair of floral printed Dr. Martens boots Jayson had gifted her for her birthday just as she heard his knock on her door. Tracie had left an hour ago to catch her flight back to

Georgia, so she greeted her guy with a warm kiss as he took her bags in one hand and the other found her waist as she locked up the room.

They were going home.

Brooke had spent the past two days with her mom. Shopping was done, movies were watched, and lots of catching up was had. Now, she was ready to see her old friends. Both Val and Brian were officially back in town. Val was coming over that evening, and she was bouncing with excitement to hug her best friend. She had spent the months away missing everything and everyone and couldn't wait to make the most of every moment until they all had to go their separate ways again.

She practically attacked Val on the porch when she arrived. Her friend had dyed her hair into a rainbow of blue hues, and in its current style of fishtail braid, it was an exotic collection of colors that made her look like a mystical beauty.

"Brooke! You are a sight for sore arms!"

Brooke laughed. "That's not how it goes..."

"Oh, tomato, potato!" Val squeezed her tighter.

"Gosh, I've missed you so much! I can't believe you really went and dyed your whole head this time. It's gorgeous! Did your mom have a fit?"

"She's been praying over me for the last twelve hours. Look at you, you hooker! You look amazing."

"Thanks, love. Come on, let's go eat so you can tell me all about Boston and catch me up on all things Valerie."

"Seriously, Brooke, I don't know how I'm gonna survive Boston in January. I've had a cold for like the entire first semester."

"I'm sure your grades are top of Dean's List, though."

"Well, naturally, but it's still cold... oh, but I wish you could see the leaves on the trees. It's the most beautiful thing, especially now. It's gorgeous with all the reds and golds."

"Hey, maybe that's the new hair color palette inspiration!"

"See, this is why we work so well. You are the peanut butter to my jelly, the bra to my boobs... speaking of your breasts, where is the mister?"

Brooke laughed loudly. "He's with Brian. We're going to meet up and bonfire later, all of us."

"Oh, yay! I haven't seen Frenchie since graduation. How is he?"

Brooke took a sip of water to mull over her words. "He talks to Jayson mostly. I think he's doing well, but it was rough after the summer. He fell in love and the girl broke his heart. My guess is he's going to be hurting for a long while underneath his smile. But I'm still glad he still reaches out to Jayson. It's good for them both."

"Gosh, that sucks... but I'm glad too. I'm glad he opened up his heart, I just wish it would've ended differently. He's a great guy."

"He really is. Jayson and I both lucked out in the best friend department."

"As did Brian and I."

JAYSON

Jayson was excited to be home, even if it was just for a few days. He knew he was fortunate to have a couple days off in the early season, so as soon as he arrived home, he threw himself into spending time with his brothers, catching up on all the things he missed, and hugging his mom a lot. When she sent him to the grocery store, he was thrilled to run into Coach Beckett and fill him in on how things were going on the team at Central thus far. He had missed everything. Even the smell of the ocean and town mingling in his nose seemed to welcome him home.

It seemed the visit was just what Jayson needed. Being

around his family gave him a refreshed spirit. Now, he was ready for a guys' night with Brian. They were going out to play some pool and have a burger before they met up with the girls and some other friends on the beach for a bonfire.

Jayson ordered a couple sodas as he waited for Brian to arrive. He hadn't seen his best friend in six months, and while they talked via video calls and text, it hadn't been the same.

Brian hurried through the door, and they embraced happily.

"How are you, man? I missed you, brother!" Jayson said excitedly.

"Good. Better now. It's good to see everyone again. Coming home reminds me why I love this place."

They smiled and took their seats. After their food arrived, they fell into easy conversation.

"So, how's college life for you? It's different than I expected," Jayson said.

"Yeah, it's a lot different. I have fun here and there, but this summer really changed me, I guess. It opened my eyes up a lot."

"You mean because of Garcelle."

Brian nodded tightly. "Garcelle… she changed me. Jay, I fell in love with her. She was amazing. I had never met anyone like her before. My last night in New Orleans, we spent it together, made all these plans, but when I woke up in the morning, she was gone. And she took my heart with her. Now, it's hard to find the desire to even want to talk to another girl, and I can't find her. It's like she disappeared. My mind's gone half-crazy over this whole thing."

"Ah, man, I didn't know that's how it all went down. Maybe she was afraid she'd never see you again so she left before she got left behind."

"Still doesn't make it hurt any less."

Jayson nodded. "I'm sure. I remember how bad it hurts. This whole love thing is not easy sometimes."

Brian attempted a weak smile, seeming to push around his hurt.

"So, you and Brooke, is everything good still?"

Jayson smiled. "Yeah, we're great. It has its challenges, though. She's oblivious to all the attention she gets. You know how they talk about going to college and gaining the freshman fifteen?"

Brian nodded and laughed.

"Well, Brooke has gone and gotten freshman fine! I mean, she has always been off the charts beautiful, but now, it's another level. Her body is insane, and she's still so humble and sweet, she doesn't really get how many guys want my position. You know, here in PC, most guys steered clear of her once I made my intentions known. But at CU, it's on another level. They don't care that she's my girl. If anything, they enjoy it because it gives them a challenge. She swears it doesn't happen, but I see it, and if I see it when she's right there with me, I worry what they try when I'm not around. I get worried about losing her sometimes, but she does a good job of making me feel better."

"Brooke is crazy about you, Jay. You don't need to worry about that. I've seen the way she looks at you."

"Her confidence is finally where it should have been all along. She doesn't dress to hide her beauty like before. These guys are coming out of the woodwork trying to get her attention and flirt with her. During the season, I'm not always around. I lost her once, and the thought of losing her again scares me every day."

Brian nodded emphatically. "I hear you, but remember, Brooke only loves you. You're the only one she's kissing and hugging—you're the only one she's claiming. As long as you do the same to her and reassure her, she never has reason to doubt your love has changed. Trust me, you chose a great girl. She's in it for the real deal. You guys have something really special. Not everyone gets that, especially so early in life."

Jayson nodded, truly knowing he was blessed. He could see the broken heart his best friend was still dealing with and knew the pain of that wouldn't just go away. They fell into easy conversation after that, catching each other up on all the other happenings in their academic and personal lives.

Jayson felt happy. Despite his fears of the distance straining their friendship, nothing had really changed. They were able to fall right back into step with one another, just as real brothers do.

They played a few rounds of pool before they headed down to the beach where they set up a bonfire as they waited for Brooke and Val to arrive. Jayson had just pulled his hoodie on when he saw the girls walking toward them with their shoes in hand. Even after all this time, watching Brooke approach him in the light of the sunset made his heart skip a beat. She looked refreshed and happy, her hair pulled into a loose ponytail and a sweater that fell off one shoulder, making it the sexiest shoulder he had ever seen.

"Hey, beautiful." He hugged her warmly before kissing her soft, full lips.

She smiled happily. "Missed you."

"All right, Romeo. Let me get my hugs in from this babe too!" Brian interrupted their moment.

Brooke quickly moved to hug Brian. "Mr. Brian Moreau! I've missed you so much."

"Hey, Brooke. You look fantastic!"

"You know, I know he's your best friend and all, but you can still text a girl and let her know how you're doing. I worry."

"My bad. I'll do better. I promise."

Jayson wrapped an arm around Val's shoulders. "Should I start calling you Smurfette?"

"Hey there, dimples." Val squeezed him in a hug.

"Gosh, I miss you, Val."

"Miss you guys too. You taking care of our girl?"

"I am." He gave her a squeeze. "Who's taking care of you?"

"Oh, dimples..." Instead of answering his question, Val reached up to pinch his cheeks, grinning like a Cheshire cat.

They spent a few hours talking and reminiscing. Jayson was happy they made time to get together like this, and hoped they would make it a tradition throughout the years to come. Jayson couldn't help but be content. He was home and sitting on a beautiful beach with his best friends. Brooke looked so purely happy laughing with everyone in the glow of the fire. He knew more than ever he would do anything to keep her that happy for the rest of her life.

Chapter 19

Brooke

Brooke's pencil moved across her sketchpad furiously as she brought the mental image of Jayson and herself to life on the paper in front of her. The simple lead sketch was teeming with sentiment and passion. *Jayson's hands holding her body close, their lips brushing one another's as they smiled, and whispered. His kiss had come softly just as her breaths slowed down with anticipation...*

Ever since she had awakened from the dream recounting their first kiss, she had been dying to have a moment alone to take the image in her head and transfer it to canvas so she could surprise him. The first time she had painted it, he had asked if he could keep it. When the painting was ruined, she wouldn't allow him to take it, unable to bear the thought of anyone else seeing it tarnished. She had vowed she was going to recapture the memory when the inspiration struck and planned to surprise him with it when she felt she'd gotten it right.

She couldn't get to the art room until after she got through tutoring two students that afternoon, so she settled for creating some renditions with pencil and paper while she waited.

"What are you drawing?"

Alex's voice came from behind, causing her to jump out of her seat with a start. She covered her own mouth to stifle her yelp of alarm. "What the—? Why are you creeping up on me like that!"

"Creeping?" Alex took a step back. "Maybe you weren't paying attention. I've been here the whole time. Just because you didn't see me doesn't mean I wasn't here."

"Yeah... well, maybe you should announce your presence before getting so close." Brooke closed her sketchbook and dropped it into her messenger bag before tucking her bag under the study cubicle she had reserved for the next two hours. "I have to go grab a book from the front desk."

Turning on her heel, she didn't look back as she walked toward the stairwell. This time, she didn't leave him with any kind of sugarcoated farewell message. Frankly, she was hoping he'd get the message that she was tired of seeing him around, period.

"Brooke, do you want to head down to the dining hall together? I'm starved." Tracie spun around in her desk chair. "What are you looking for again?"

"My sketchbook. I swear I had it in my bag at the library, but when I got to the studio, I couldn't find it anywhere." Brooke dumped out the contents of her bag for the fourth time, wondering how she could have misplaced something so special. She could kick herself.

"Do you think you left it in the library? Maybe it fell out of your bag?"

"Could be. I don't know." She pulled her lip between her teeth. "I feel so stupid getting so emotional, but that sketchbook has a lot of me on those pages. I've poured my heart into some of those sketches. They'll never be worth millions, but..."

"They're yours." Tracie stood and joined her on the search. "I get it, Brooke. There's no need to feel stupid."

Brooke wiped at her eyes with the corner of her sleeves. "Can we stop by the library on the way back from dinner?"

"No, we can stop by the library on our way to dinner. If it's there, you can fill your stomach with your heart at ease."

Brooke let out a heavy sigh. "It's probably in some garbage can already."

Tracie pulled her to her feet. "If it's not there, we'll go to the student union and load you up with chocolate so we can have a proper sobfest."

"Promise?"

Tracie's face shifted into a manufactured cheeky smile as she cupped her hand and waved. "Pageant girl's honor."

Despite the horrible pit in her stomach, Brooke laughed, once again truly grateful for her roommate.

JAYSON

Jayson shuffled into his apartment, followed by Sean and Vaughn. Just inside, they all froze as the smell of food hit them. Their practice had been brutal, and they had all planned on collapsing as soon as they could make it in the door, but now, the smell of food had livened their senses.

Sean pushed past him. "Please tell me this isn't a dream and the smell is really coming from our kitchen."

Brooke popped her head out of the kitchen, her hair pulled into a messy bun on the top of her head and her gorgeous happy smile overtaking her face. "Hey, guys! I hope you don't mind. Since I had to come over here to use Jayson's printer, I decided to cook you guys some dinner. I thought you might enjoy it after such a long practice."

"Are you kidding? Of course we don't mind!" Sean exclaimed, his eyes frantically searching the pots behind her.

"Good. It's almost done. Go take a shower and I'll finish up here. Vaughn, that means you too. There's plenty."

Sean ran off to the bathroom first, while Vaughn hurried back out the front door, calling over his shoulder he'd be back in five minutes.

Jayson, however, didn't move. His eyes were fixed on her.

219

"Are you upset? I didn't mean to just overtake your apartment, babe. I just wanted to do something nice for—"

He crushed his mouth to hers before she finished the unnecessary apology. His hands found their way under the Central U hooded sweatshirt she wore and gripped her warm flesh with need. Right as his self-control kicked in and he began to pull back, she arched into him, her hands tightening around the waistband of his shorts, pulling him closer.

"One of these days, we're not going to be able to stop, Brookelynn."

"One of these days, we won't have to." Her words were just as needy as he felt. Pressing a kiss to her neck, he finally found the strength to pull back.

"Don't you ever apologize for being here and doing things for me. I should be thanking you. This is incredible."

"When we went back on break I had your mom give me some lessons and pointers on cooking some of your favorite dishes. I hope I did a good job. It's my first time making Dominican food without an authentic hand to guide me."

"One of these days, I'm going to make you feel as special as you make me feel."

Slapping his butt, she grinned. "You already do. Go get cleaned up so you can eat."

"I don't think I can move at all," Sean groaned.

"That's because you ate four plates!" Brooke chuckled as she rejoined them in the living room carrying ice packs and muscle balm for their tired and sore calves and quads.

"Hey, if you don't want me to eat so much, you should start making mediocre food."

"Watch your mouth!"

Jayson stretched as he felt the food coma settling in. "That was amazing, babe. Seriously, it tasted just like my mom's and abuelita's."

"Thanks, guys. I'm glad you got a good meal in. It's my duty to the team."

Settling into her seat on the couch, she reached down, pulled Jayson's leg across her lap, and began massaging his fatigued, aching muscles. It didn't take long before she found a knot of tension in his quad and applied more pressure, eliciting a loud groan of pleasure from Jayson.

"Williams, remember what you told us during orientation?" Vaughn asked, his face somber.

Jayson nodded, knowing Brooke was trying to figure out what they were talking about, the question written all over her face.

"Well, I get it now. I really get it. You were right."

Sean nodded. "You're a really lucky guy, Williams."

He nodded. "I am."

Brooke

Brooke took a step back from the canvas, rolling her neck. She had spent the last few hours in one of the studios in the arts building. Checking her phone for the first time since she started, she wasn't exactly surprised to see she'd been there for over four hours. Once she started, it was hard to pull herself away from the piece until the all greens, blues, and purples evolved into what she had been aching to put on canvas. She quickly replied to Tracie checking up on her and made a note to return Jayson's call as soon as she got back to the dorm.

She took her time washing her brushes and packing her supplies away. She would have to leave her painting here to dry, but once it was done, she would ship it home for her mother to store it properly. She could imagine hanging it when she moved into her own place... maybe in the bedroom... Just the thought of decorating her future home made her stomach flip in girlish excitement. Brooke didn't know when or where that home would be, but she knew who it would be with. Jayson was her best friend, and she couldn't wait for him to get home the next day from his most recent road trip. She had made sure she had scheduled the night off from tutoring so she could meet the bus when it arrived on campus, then she was taking her man to dinner.

Shutting the light off in the studio, she tossed her bag over her shoulder and headed toward campus. Tracie would be waiting. They were having a girls' night complete with junk food and Netflix. She was more than grateful for the computer that paired her with Tracie as a roommate. The last few weeks had been hard, but made bearable by having such a good friend in Tracie—something she was going to remind her of as soon as she got back to their room.

"Well, hey there, stranger."

Alex jogged up beside her, flashing her a grin. She hadn't seen him around in a while, so she offered him a tentative smile.

"Alex, how's everything?"

"Good. You know, I'm glad I ran into you. I heard a rumor that you tutor in the Learning Center and need some extra help with my Lit class."

"You have to go to the Center and see what times are available."

"Yeah, I know that's the official way, but I was hoping maybe you'd help me out unofficially. My schedule's all kinds of crazy, so it would be easier."

The hairs on the back of her neck stood up in alarm. Tracie's warnings about Alex's intentions filled her ears and she remembered her own reservations.

"I'm already swamped myself. I'm double majoring, so the only time I have to tutor is what is available at the Center. My time slots are all booked. I could ask around for someone else who's available, though. I'm sure someone would jump at the chance."

"Just not you."

"I can't. I'm sorry."

"Maybe I should just come out with it instead of all the subtlety. I'd really like to hang out with you, Brooke."

"Alex—"

"I know you have a boyfriend."

"He's not just a boyfriend. He's my fiancé—the man I'm going to marry."

She moved to step around him, but he grabbed hold of her arm, squeezing it.

"That means you can't hang out and have a good time with me?"

Her gaze narrowed as she snatched her arm away from his grasp. "No, it means I don't want to. If you were genuinely interested in being my friend, maybe it would be different. But you're not. There are tons of girls on campus who'd probably love to hang out with you and go out, but I'm not one of them. I'm very happily taken, and that's not going to change."

"You really think he's not hooking up while he's out on the road? I'm an athlete too, Brooke. I know how easy it is. The line between fans and groupies gets blurry, and when they come knocking on his hotel door, you think he's really going to turn them down? Out of sight, out of mind."

"You don't know anything about the man Jayson is. I don't have to explain my relationship to anyone, least of all you. In fact, from now on, it would be best if we really didn't talk anymore. I hope you find someone who makes you feel like Jayson makes me feel."

"I could make you feel so much better." His hand stroked the side of her face, and her arm flew as she slapped him as hard as she could, the sound ringing in the air.

"Don't you ever touch me again."

Turning on her heel, she hurried away, leaving Alex and his ugly words hanging in the air behind her.

When she got back to her room, she let her bag fall to the floor beside her desk before throwing herself on the bed, muffling a frustrated scream into her pillow.

"Rough day?"

Tracie's voice came from the other side of the room, prompting Brooke to roll to her back.

"Def Con levels."

Brooke looked over and spotted her normally smiling roomie with a blotchy face and crumpled tissues scattered along her bed.

"Hey, what happened?" She scurried off her bed over to her friend's side.

"My mother... she has a terrific way with words. She just called to remind me of all the ways I disappoint her and how much she's looking forward to seeing me over spring break so she can criticize everything about me in person."

"She must be crazy. You're one of the best people I know. Just today, I was thinking how lucky I am that some computer put you into my life because I don't know how I would make it without you. You light up the entire room, and you make people feel awesome every day with your kind words and ready smile."

"You know, I picked Central because I thought it was far enough away from Georgia, she would finally leave me be. Wrong! I should have gone to Mars."

"I'm so sorry, Tracie. Things will be crazy during spring break with all the tournaments and such, but you're always welcome to stay around Cali for break. It's just me and my mom at my place back in PC. We'd love to have you."

"Thanks. I would love that, but my dad would probably send out the National Guard to bring me back. I need to be there for some fundraiser and do the 'good, respectable Senator's daughter act' for the cameras, because God forbid his daughter's in college and actually having age appropriate fun."

"Well, the offer is always there, whenever you need it."

"Thanks. Love you, roomie."

"Love you more, T."

"Wow, I can't believe the nerve of that creep! Who does he think he is?"

Brooke had just finished recounting the encounter with Alex as she sat pulling Tracie's hair into a beautiful thick braid. "It felt so good to slap him."

Both girls collapsed into laughter.

"Okay, but seriously, are you going to tell Jayson?"

"I am. I don't want us to keep any secrets from each other, but I'm going to wait until after our date night. I don't want anything to ruin tomorrow night. I've got the perfect dress and shoes. I'm going to be all dolled up and waiting for him the moment he steps off that bus."

"I swear, I'm in love with the way you two are in love."

"I'm just in love and missing him so much, especially today after the jerk who won't be named."

"Let's forget about him and focus on me and my on-screen boyfriend."

"Which one are we talking about now?"

Tracie wiggled her eyebrows as she reached over and grabbed her laptop. "It's Friday night! I don't have to choose, we can watch them all."

"That's what I'm talking about. Bring on the Twizzlers and eye-candy, girl!"

"I can't believe you're going to be wearing a sexy siren red dress and I'm not there in person to witness it."

Val's voice filled the room from the speaker on her phone.

"I'm wondering if I can go through with it. It's so fitted... and short... and red."

Brooke had prepared herself all day, and now that he was set to arrive in thirty minutes, she carefully pulled out the new dress she had dipped into her savings to buy. The little red dress was far past flirty. With the way it hugged her body, it was downright sexy. Her brown hair was softly curled, and she had spent far too long getting her make up just right. She checked herself out in Tracie's full-length mirror several times, allowing her mind to fill with thoughts of Jayson's reaction to seeing her tonight. Her imagination was making her tingle with anticipation.

"That's the trifecta of sexy. The both of you holding out this long is admirable and all, but if you aren't gonna give him any, then you wear that sexy, tight red dress, put a little extra wiggle in your strut, and let him touch the butt."

"I do let him—did you just drop a Nemo reference?"

"I did, and I heard you. Look at you over there letting him touch the butt!" Val cooed with equal parts pride and mischief.

"Bye, Val! Call you later."

"You better not. Enjoy your man's homecoming. I'll talk to you tomorrow and you can fill me in on all your deliciously scandalous behavior."

Her phone rang as she slipped her feet into the equally sexy shoes, pausing to see Jayson's name and face fill the screen.

"Hey, babe! I'm on my way out the door to meet you when you arrive."

"Brookelynn... there was an issue with the bus. We're stranded waiting on a new bus to arrive from the charter company."

She dropped down to her mattress as the full weight of his words sank into her chest. "So, you won't be here tonight."

"It looks that way. I am so sorry. I know you made plans for a date night, and I wanted nothing more than to be there with you tonight. I'm going to make it up to you, I promise."

Brooke bit her lip as the first tears fell. "It's okay. You can't control the buses. I get it."

"Brooke—"

"I'm fine, Jayson. Really, I am. We'll have other nights."

"We will. A lifetime of them. My battery's running low, so

I should probably go. I love you so much. I'll see you tomorrow?"

"Yeah. Tomorrow."

She ended the call and dropped her phone to the mattress. The tears fell without restraint. She knew what she'd signed up for, but it didn't mean it didn't drive her crazy to go without seeing Jayson in person. He always called and texted from the road, but it wasn't the same as having him in person when she just needed him to drive away all the other things in the world that made her crazy. She didn't feel like taking one for the team. Not tonight. Tonight, she was going to be selfish and cry about how much she wanted her man with her.

Her phone sounded with a text message she ignored. It was probably Val sending a stream of peach and eggplant emojis she wouldn't be able to muster up a response too. She didn't want to talk to anyone right now. She was going to change into her sweats, scrub her face clean, and eat her emotions in the form of carbs.

Another message sounded as the knocks at her door started. Apparently, it was too much to ask to be miserable without company.

"Who is it?"

"It's your lovable, spunky, forgetful roomie who left her room key on her desk." Tracie's voice sounded from the other side.

Heaving herself off the bed, she didn't bother to wipe away her tears as she unlocked the door. She froze at the smiling, suit-clad, handsome man filling her doorway—who was definitely not her roommate.

His smile dropped as he took in her tears. "Oh, babe, I didn't want to make you cry. It was supposed to be a happy surprise."

She launched herself into his arms, crushing her mouth to his in a desperate kiss of relief.

"I'll leave you two lovebirds alone. I'm crashing in Talia's room so you two have some privacy."

Brooke only halfway registered what she said as Jayson's hands made their way down to her thighs, gripping them and splaying them open wide so he could lift her and fit himself to her perfectly. In another moment, they were in the room with the door shut behind them. Her hands clung to him, fisting the lapels of his jacket, wanting more, demanding more. His tongue sweetly invaded her mouth, coaxing her to give him more of the same.

"I missed you, Jay."

"I missed you more than I ever thought possible, Brookelynn. We got in early, and I thought it would cute and romantic to surprise you. I didn't mean to make you upset. I'm sorry, babe. It kills me to see you crying."

He placed a sweet kiss to the tip of her nose as his thumb traced her bottom lip. "I dreamed of this face every night I was away. Missing these gorgeous lips of yours. Wanting to see you crinkle up your nose. Aching for those chocolate brown eyes that make my heart flip. I can't believe I get to marry you."

"I didn't think these road trips were going to be so hard."

He sat down, pulling her onto his lap, pressing a kiss to her shoulder. "I know. I'm so sorry."

"I don't want you to apologize. I know what I signed up for... it just got the better of me today because I feel like I haven't spent time with you in forever."

"I feel the same way. I know you sacrifice a lot for the sake of a relationship with me, but I want you to remember it's temporary. Once the tournament ends, I'm going to be around so much, you'll be sick of my face."

"Never that. You're my home, Jayson. It's hard to be away from home for too long."

Brooke brought her eyes to meet his. His hand moved into her hair, and he lightly fisted the soft curls before pulling her into a kiss that transcended all thoughts. With the reflexes of a phenomenal athlete, she was on her back on the bed with Jayson above her, never breaking his kiss.

"Welcome home, Brookelynn."

Chapter 20

JAYSON

His game and practice schedule only got heavier as they entered the tournament playoffs, which was the most difficult for Jayson to adjust to. The road trips felt endless, probably because his time alone with Brookelynn grew harder to come by. She came to as many of his games as she could to cheer him on, and while he thrived on that, he also longed for the summer where he could spend more than a few stolen moments alone with his fiancée. Her breakdown a couple weeks ago reminded him he wasn't alone in feeling this way. He missed their lazy days where they could lay in their sweats and binge-watch Netflix, or the Saturdays where they would take walks or go to the art gallery. He missed spending time with his family on Sunday for their big family dinners—something he loved bringing Brooke to, giving her a taste of the large family that would be hers too.

It wasn't unusual Brooke had been on his mind for the last few days of this trip. But now, he only had one more game before they would be heading back to campus, hopefully as national champions. As they boarded the bus to take them to the hotel, he settled into his seat and immediately pulled out his phone.

> *Jayson:* Flight went smooth. Just got on the bus. On the way to the hotel.

Brookelynn: Glad you made it safely. Down to the finals, Jay. I'm so proud of you!

Jayson: I miss you.

Brookelynn: I miss you too. So much, babe. I wish I could be there with you, but even though I'm watching from afar, I couldn't be any prouder to see you play. I'll be watching every second.

Jayson: I love you, Brookelynn.

Brookelynn: For always, babe.

"Checking in with your girl?" Sean asked, slipping into the seat next to him.

"Yeah."

Sean smiled. "One of these days, maybe I'll find a girl to settle down with. Maybe."

Jayson laughed. "It's not a bad thing, Riley."

"So you tell me. It doesn't ever scare you, being so young?"

Jayson shook his head. "I was barely fourteen when I first saw Brooke. Ever since then, she's the only girl I've ever wanted, and every day, I still want her more. So, no, it doesn't scare me. Brooke is the best thing that's ever happened to me. One day, I won't be able to run the court or break records, but I'll still have Brooke, and she'll look at me the same way she always does because she loves me for all the real stuff."

"Your girl is one of the great ones."

Jayson nodded. "Let's make sure we win this one so I can get back to her."

Another win clinched, securing their place in the final game.

One more win. That was all they needed.

Jayson sat in the locker room trying to get ready for the game. He'd checked his phone to see his mom and brother Jayden had arrived and were in the stands waiting. Brooke

had posted a picture to her Instagram account wearing her Central University jersey with his number twelve and blowing a kiss.

> **Good luck kisses for my Romeo**
> **@JayWilliams. Love you for**
> **always, Jay! You have my vote for**
> **MVP.**
> **#GOteamGO #CentralUniversity**
> **#thatsMYman #proudofmyboys**
> **#onemoregame**

He smiled. *Gosh, she was gorgeous.* More than that, his girl always seemed to know when he needed her kiss to calm his nerves. If only he could hold her in his arms. He could get lost in the sweet smell that always surrounded her. He reposted her picture and message to his social media accounts.

> **@brookelynn is the Best. Fiancée.**
> **Ever. You're my MVP everyday,**
> **beautiful. #thatsMYwoman**
> **#onemoregame #herkissesareMINE**

He hoped his nerves didn't show too badly as he tried to repeat his usual mantra. He barely slept the night before thinking about the moment rushing toward him. He never tried to invest too much emotion into a game. He lived by the words he repeated every time he got ready in a locker room, that it was just another game. But this game ran through his veins, and *sometimes*, it was more than a game. This was one of those times. He had come onto a collegiate team as a freshman and played in every game since. His team had found their strengths and worked on their weakness until they became a well-oiled machine that had powered through a season with no losses. It had all led to them being here walking into a national championship as a team nobody expected to see make it this far, let alone undefeated. All the years of hard work led up to this moment.

Win or lose, he'd still get to go home to Brookelynn. He'd get to focus on finishing the spring semester without grueling two-a-day practice. He'd get to go home and eat at his mother's kitchen table. But he was an athlete... he could still have all that if they won.

And he really wanted to win.

He let out a held breath as Vaughn sat down next to him. "You ready for this?"

Jayson nodded. "It's just another game."

"That's right. One more."

Jayson bumped fists with him, then slipped his headphones over his ears, dropped his head to focus on his feet, and hit play. He hadn't even gotten through a song when he saw a pair Timberland boots step in front of him. Too small to belong to any of the guys, he looked up into the beautiful brown eyes he'd been aching to see. She removed the headphones from his ears, letting them rest around his neck. He blinked once or seven times, wondering if his nerves were causing hallucinations.

"Please tell me you didn't really think I wasn't going to be here in person to watch you guys win the trophy?"

"Brookelynn..." He shot up and took her in his arms, lifting her off the ground. The rest of the guys hooted and hollered in jest and appreciation as he gripped her butt and she wrapped her legs around his waist. His eyes flickered all over her face. He couldn't decide where he wanted to kiss her first.

She bit down on her plump bottom lip, hiding her smile. "Gonna make me beg for it or something?"

Oh yeah. That's where he wanted to kiss her first. Her hands cupped the back of his neck as he took control of the kiss. The locker room erupted into another round of loud whistles and cheers, banging on the lockers in appreciation of their public display.

"Get it, freshman!"

"Now, that's a good luck kiss!"

"Share the love, Brooke!"

He heard his coach clear his throat. "Don't make me regret letting this persuasive young lady see you before the game, Williams!"

Brooke broke the kiss first, unable to stop her laughter.

Sean shook his head knowingly. "Give him a break, Coach. He actually plays better when she's in the building."

"I know that, hence the reason I let her in." Coach shot them a wink and held up a Tupperware case of brownies. "All right, everyone else, follow me. Jayson, I'll give you five minutes."

Jayson set Brooke back on her feet. "I was just wishing I could hold you in my arms before this game... and then you show up. I'm so glad you're here."

"I wouldn't have missed it for the world." She gave him a reassuring squeeze. "Win or lose, I'm so proud of you, Jay. I love you for always, no matter what."

Pulling her to the side, he dropped his voice. "I'm nervous, Brookelynn."

She rubbed his arms, as if she was transferring her confidence right into him. "I know, babe. But I know the second after tipoff, you are going to do what you do best."

"You think?"

She shook her head. "I know."

"You *are* pretty smart. If I win, will you wear that red dress again for me?"

Her happy smile overtook her face. "Deal."

"Um... Brooke, what happened to my big intro? You weren't just going to leave me in the hallway while you two make out were you?"

The familiar voice from the doorway pulled his attention away from Brooke. "Brian?"

"I might have found him wandering around some airport this morning..." Brooke winked and stepped aside.

Brian beamed him a smile before crossing the room and wrapping him up in a hug. "This is unreal, Jay. I had to be here to watch my best friend make history."

"I wish you were on the court with me, brother."

"Not me. I can't handle the pressure."

Brooke swatted Brian's arm. "Not helpful."

"I'm kidding!" Brian's smile faded as his voice turned somber. "Look, I know you're freaking out inside. But I know how long you've dreamed about this moment right here. It's just one more game, don't let the rest of the madness psych you out. Plus, if you lose, maybe your future wife over here will let you finally get some. Sympathy sex is still sex."

"Brian Moreau!" Brooke blushed furiously, but she couldn't hide her smile as she jabbed her finger into his chest. "No talk of the cookie out of you!"

Jayson laughed. He really laughed for the first time in a few days. "Gosh, I love you guys. I'm glad you're here."

"Go out there and shine, baby."

Social media erupted over the next four quarters. Videos captured the highlights of the game and snapshots of the gameplay. When it was all over, he would get back to his phone going crazy with notifications and messages from his family and friends. His Instagram feed would be photos and posts one after the other, celebrating the Central Lions' victory right along with him.

> @ValLEECali: I may be the only person in Boston proudly wearing a @CentralUniversity sweatshirt tonight, but I don't care. So freakin' proud of my friend @JayWilliams and his whole team for crushing it! #nationalchamps #CaliforniaLove

> @brookelynn: So proud of my boys! Congrats to @JayWilliams & the rest of @CentralUniversity men's basketball team! You did it, guys! #nationalchamps #number12isMINE

**@BMore: You just watched one of
the greats! #thatsmybestfriend
#undefeated #nationalchamps
@CentralUniversity**

Jayson still couldn't believe it. He kept looking over at the trophy as his teammates yelled and cheered loudly.

"First division championship win for us in ten years after an undefeated season!" Vaughn yelled loudly. "You did work this year, Williams!"

"*We* did work!" Jayson corrected as they embraced, slapping each other's backs enthusiastically.

Brooke broke through the crowds and flung herself at him. "You did it, babe! You did it!"

"I couldn't have done it without you!"

He took off his championship cap and placed it on her head. "You're my MVP, Juliet."

Uncaring about the waiting press, he kissed his fiancée for the world to see until they were surrounded by the rest of his cheering teammates.

Chapter 21

Brooke

She checked the time on her watch just as she slipped through the doors of the student union. She was due to meet up with Jayson for lunch, but her meeting with her professor ran way later than she anticipated. She grabbed her turkey burger and bottle of water before she scanned the room looking for him. She spotted the familiar green fitted cap turned backwards on his head and headed his way, only to stop short when she realized who else was sitting at the table with him.

Alex.

Her skin bristled with nerves and unease. Alex looked her way briefly, the coolness in his eyes evident before turning his attention back to something Jayson said, offering some false laughter. Brooke pulled her shoulders back, standing straighter to prove she wasn't going to be intimidated by him. Putting one foot in front of the other, she made her way to the table, placing her tray alongside Jayson's and slipping quietly into the seat next to him.

"There's my gorgeous girl."

"Hey, babe." Jayson pulled her in to kiss her as Alex looked on.

"Brooke, this is Alex. Alex, this is my fiancée, Brooke."

"Ah, yes, the stunning Brooke—"

"We've met." Brooke kept her voice even, but full of ice.

Jayson's hand fell to her thigh, and although his smile remained on his face, he squeezed it gently, the question in his eyes. She forced herself to look away from him, fixing her gaze on her sandwich, intentionally avoiding any further acknowledgment of Alex's presence or the stare burning into the side of her face.

When Jayson spoke again, there was a sharp edge to his voice, one that both thrilled and worried her.

"If you'll excuse us, Alex. I promised my girl some alone time over lunch."

"Oh, of course. I'll leave you two to it. It was nice chatting with you, and once again, congrats on the season. Brooke, it's always a pleasure."

She only looked to Jayson, watching him nod once as he leaned back in his chair, draping his arm around Brooke, sending an unmistakable message.

"Why am I just now hearing about this, Brookelynn?"

Jayson paced the width of his living room as she sat on the couch watching. "I told you I meant to! I planned on it, but then you were coming back in town and I didn't want to ruin it. Then I just forgot."

"Brooke, I needed to know this. I sat down with this guy, shook his hand, and you're telling me he's been making plays for you, telling you to cheat on me—"

"I shut him down. I would never betray you, just like I know you wouldn't betray me."

"If it was shutdown, why would the guy play friendly with me like that? He was messing with you, testing our relationship to see if you had told me. Believe me, if you had told me, he would have been laid out before he could have even thought about talking to me. Now, he walked away with a sense of satisfaction because he knows you didn't tell me. I shook his hand, Brooke!"

Her shoulders drooped in defeat. She realized the full

meaning of what he was saying. "Babe, I'm sorry. I swear I didn't keep it from you intentionally. I hadn't even seen him since that day."

He nodded, but his mind was elsewhere. Taking his hand, she pressed a kiss to his knuckles, trying to pull him out of his own stormy thoughts.

"I'm going to head out for a bit. I need the gym. I have to work some of this off."

"Will I see you before I have to go to work later? I'm tutoring in the library from five to ten, then I have some studying of my own to do."

"I don't know. I'll call you later."

Pressing a briefer-than-brief kiss to her forehead, he was out of the door grabbing his gym bag off the floor.

"I love you."

Her words bounced off the closed door. She was met with silence.

It was a strange feeling to have Jayson upset with her. For much of the past year, they'd been in a pretty solid streak of not arguing. Sure, they disagreed on small things from time to time, but they hadn't truly been upset with the other to this degree. For Jayson to walk out on her, he must have been really disappointed in her. The thought distracted her all evening.

Her stomach was in knots as she checked her phone repeatedly. She thought about calling or texting him, but put the phone down each time, determined to give him the space he seemed to need. Her phone battery was near dead, and in her emotional daze, she had left her charging cable in her dorm room. Since she still had one more tutoring session before she could leave, she would have to wait until later to talk to Jayson.

Brooke had decided it had been the longest day in history.

Finally heading home for the night, she replayed everything that had happened with Jayson with every step she took farther from the library. She thought about turning down the road to head to Jayson's dorm as the rain began to fall, cursing herself for forgetting her umbrella. She wrapped her thin cardigan around herself as she took the shortcut trail. That's when she felt it...

That cold eerie feeling when you feel someone watching or following you.

Her blood ran cold. It was dark, but she was almost back on the main walkway, just minutes away from getting back inside where she would be safe. She tried to walk quicker, but stumbled. A hand shot out and caught her before she fell to the ground.

"Alex."

JAYSON

Jayson: Brookelynn, can we talk? I know you're probably mad at me for leaving earlier and you're right. I'm sorry.

Jayson: I know it's late, but I can't go to bed without knowing my girl is smiling.

Jayson: Baby... I love you. I screwed up with how I handled things earlier, I know I did. I should have come to you earlier. If I could take it back, I would. Nothing is more important to me than you. You are my number one. I want to see you tonight, but I think maybe you fell asleep after work, so I won't wake you up. I'll be there in the morning with a chai latte and my best accept-my-apology-good-morning kiss before walking you to class. Sleep tight. I love you.

He was halfway to his place when he turned around to head to hers. Something didn't feel right. Maybe it was just the thought of Brooke being so mad at him she was ignoring him, but he needed to make it right before he went to bed. He pulled on his hood and jogged through the rain toward her dorm building. As he pulled open the door, he was surprised to see Tracie running toward him.

"Tracie? What happened?" His defenses rose.

"Have you talked to Brooke?" Her eyes brimmed with tears.

"Not in the last few hours. Why? What's wrong?" His voice was immediately overtaken by his rising panic.

"She's not answering her messages and she never came home this evening. I'm worried. She never stays out this late without letting me know she won't be back to the dorms. I thought maybe she was with you and her phone had died or something. I just had to check."

Brooke had been in the library earlier.

Jayson whipped out his phone and immediately began calling Brooke again.

Hey, it's me. I'm not available. Leave me a message and I'll call you back.

He hung up and dialed again.

Hey, it's me. I'm not available. Leave me a message and I'll call you back.

Hey, it's me. I'm not available. Leave me a message and I'll call you back.

Hey, it's me. I'm not available. Leave me a message and I'll call you back.

After each beep, he felt the knot in his stomach tighten in fear. Something was very wrong.

"Come on, Trace. Let's go check the library. They're open all night tonight. If she's not there, we'll go back to check your dorms."

At the library, he rushed to the front desk to inquire if they'd seen Brooke that evening. He showed them her picture on his phone.

"Oh, yes! She left already, close to an hour ago. She

dropped off a reference book on her way out, said it was too heavy to carry back to the dorm so she would just pick it up here at the desk tomorrow."

After offering the woman his thanks, Jayson turned on his heel and ran. He was halfway to Brooke and Tracie's dorm when his phone rang.

"What is it, Sean? I'm trying to find Brooke right now."

"She's here!" The panic in his voice was undisguised.

Jayson stopped and turned, pulling Tracie along with him. "Give it to me straight."

"Man, I don't know what happened. She just showed up a minute ago. She's all messed up. Someone did a number on her face. I think her legs are bleeding, but there's a lot of mud. She needs you."

"I'm on my way."

Never had he experienced a fury like he felt when he saw the love of his life beaten and broken. Her face was already swelling with bruises and mud covered what he couldn't see. She was wrapped in his blanket on the couch, but her exposed knees were bloodied and dirty as well. Her teeth chattered, and her eyes focused on her hands.

"She didn't have any shoes when she showed up."

"Call the cops, Sean."

Jayson sat in front of her, pressing a kiss to her wrist, hoping his presence would help her.

"Oh, baby... my sweet, sweet Brooke..."

"Jay... I want to go home." Her voice shook with fear.

"I know, baby. I'm going to call your mom. You're safe, my love. I'll keep you safe now, I promise."

"It was raining so hard, I thought I was going to drown. No one could hear me screaming. He wasn't going to stop—"

"Brookelynn—"

"He... he... must have been watching me. He had to have followed me from the library. I was hurrying 'cause of the rain. My phone was dead. When he grabbed me... I couldn't let him. I didn't want his hands on me, but he kept hitting me, punching me... my face... my stomach. I couldn't see through the pain. I thought he must want to kill me, so I tried to play dead."

Her eyes flashed with pain, then filled with tears.

"You're safe now, baby. I promise you are."

He felt helpless as he watched the tremors of shock rolled through her. Her eyes wide and panicked, she didn't seem to hear him as she continued on.

"He didn't want to just kill me. I must have blacked out because he had already taken my boots off and used the laces to tie my wrists together. He pulled my socks off and jammed them in my mouth. I knew..."

A sob came from behind him. Tracie.

A sound like rushing water filled his ears. Rage. White-hot, unfiltered rage.

She aimed for his nose and thrust her heel into his face as hard as she could. Curses and grunts. Another punch to her stomach made her draw her knees to her chest.

He wasn't going to give up. Another blow to her ribs. Her lungs seized up in pain as she tried to inhale.

She screamed despite the muddy woolen gag shoved between her teeth. Help. Please help me. She heard his low chuckle that came right before another string of muffled curses. She thrashed her head, avoiding the hand that attempted to brush the hair off her face.

Another punch to her temple, then everything was quiet.

Happy thoughts. Think happy thoughts.

She saw herself back in Paradise Cove... walking through one of her favorite parks to sit and draw. She would have taken off her shoes to feel the grass beneath her toes as she sketched. Val would be there, her hair a glorious lavender, and she'd chatter away about her new film project, making Brooke promise to be in the audience when she accepted all her future awards. She saw Justin running up to her, showing her his newest loose tooth, looking sweeter than ever in his tee-ball jersey. The twins would be causing mischief and stealing young girls' hearts, just like their older brothers. Jayden would be on the court challenging Jayson to a game of one-on-one, determined to be just like his older brother even if he didn't know it yet. Her mother and Jisela would fill the picnic tables with dish after dish of foods that made her mouth water. They would smile over at her as they called her over to help. Brian would eat too many plates, then proclaim he wouldn't be moving for the rest of the day.

Family surrounded the tables. Friends. New and old.

Tracie. Sean. Vaughn.

Laughter and chatter.

Strong arms enveloping her. A familiar scent that stirred a primal desire and made her feel at peace. His warm, rich voice in her ear.

"I love you."

This man was the love her life.

She wanted the dream...

She wanted their dream.

She wanted to marry this man and build a life with him.

She wanted to kiss him and hold him every day for the rest of her life.

She wanted to kiss him until she couldn't take it any longer.

She wanted more with this man.

She wanted to lay with him, become one with him, and make babies with him.

She wanted to make love.

She wanted to love.

She wanted to live.

She felt the rough pulling at her skirt, her shirt... his curses telling her to cooperate or else. This couldn't happen.

She didn't want to die.

She didn't want this.

She didn't want him.

*She wanted... **HIM**.*

She wanted to live.
She wanted to live...

She wanted Jayson.
The binding around her wrists had loosened. As she stretched her fingertips above her head, she felt the sharp rough edge of a rock protruding just enough for her to wrap her fingers around it. She swung it, hitting him in the face. His scream of pain was almost as melodious as the crunch of bone. The rock connected with the side of his face. She scurried free as he hit the ground beside her with a solid thud. He wasn't going to stop, and she wasn't ready to die. She scrambled through the wet dense foliage to step foot on the narrow brick walkway.

"I didn't want to die. I couldn't let him have me. I needed him to stop before he actually... I just wanted him to stop."

"I know, baby. You're safe now."

"My phone is broken. My art brushes are ruined and lost on that trail. My computer... I'm going to fail. I'll be kicked out of school, Jayson."

Her body trembled as the shockwaves of panic overtook her.

"We'll get you a new phone, new brushes... better brushes." He tried to keep his voice calm. He didn't want her to know he was freaking out. That the rage and sadness were almost blinding. He couldn't focus on that. He needed her to know he was in love with her, that he was going to make her feel better.

"They'll kick me out and we won't be together!"

"I'll get you a new computer. You won't fail. I promise. We will always be together. No one can ever stand in the way of that, Brooke."

Her fearful eyes met his as she spoke the next four words. "I killed him, Jayson."

"I know, and you're safe. I promise you everything is going to be okay."

"I had to... he wasn't going to stop."

Jayson gave his statement to the cops and sat by Brooke's side as she had to retell the entire event. Her body hadn't stopped trembling and seeing her in shock was killing him because he couldn't do anything to make it better. The ambulance ride to the hospital was an emotional whirlwind. The only thing that kept him grounded was Brooke's eyes pleading with him to stay with her as they waited for whatever came next.

The curtain shifted as a woman dressed in a plain black shirt and gray dress pants entered. She pointed to the badge that nested on her hip. "Brooke, I'm Detective Kelly. I spoke to the responding officers, but I have some questions I need you to answer."

Brooke's eyes narrowed in suspicion. "Are you going to arrest me?"

Jayson shifted his stance defensively. His hand found hers and linked them together. "Look at her. That piece of crap did that to her. She did what she needed to do."

The detective's somber face softened for a second with the hint of a sympathetic smile. "I just want to have a discussion with you."

"Can Jayson stay?"

The detective gave another small smile, this one meant to reassure. "Sure. Like I said, we just want to go over everything that happened tonight."

Brooke gave a single nod of her head.

"So, Alex Caine, have you ever seen him around before this evening?"

Brooke blinked as the tears pooled in her eyes. She nodded. "I met him the first day I arrived on campus. I was waiting for Jayson to come outside and he approached me."

"Were you friends?"

"Not even close." Brooke recounted each of her interactions with Alex. She told the detective about her apprehensions and ultimately their final run-in.

"Thank you for the information."

"What's going to happen to Brooke?"

Detective Kelly slipped her phone out of her pocket and began typing. "Nothing for the moment. The investigation is ongoing and I need to take this information back to my team. For now, Brooke is going to be treated for her injuries and follow the direction of the doctors. We'll be in touch."

When the doctor and nurse arrived to conduct their thorough examination and document all her injuries, he left her side knowing he had to call Evelyn and tell her. It was the hardest phone call he'd ever had to make. At the sound of her panicked voice answering the phone in the middle of the night, he immediately broke down into tears. He managed to get through the story, and Evelyn told him she was on her way through tears of her own. After, he made an identical call to his own mother. Jisela cried for Brooke and told Jayson she was coming and would be there as soon as she could.

All he could do was wait.

Brooke

B rooke felt safe in her mother's arms. She was able to be scared about everything that had happened and free to cry like a little girl. Evelyn lay in the bed with her, stroking her hair gently, soothing her daughter with calming words, reassuring her everything that happened wasn't her fault and she would be okay in time, but there was no rush for that. The cops had finally left, and all the examinations and tending of her wounds were over for the time being.

Brooke felt her heart heal a little more when the door opened and Jisela flew at her in the same maternal panic as Evelyn had. The two women embraced each other fiercely, leaving words unspoken, and then Jisela cried too. Jisela clucked over injuries, making sure her care was up to her own standards as both nurse and mother, then stroked the less swollen and battered side of Brooke's face with her soft hands. Once again, Brooke's tears came even though she kept trying to assure both her mothers the pain meds were sufficient, she was as comfortable as she was going to be, and she felt safe with them by her side. When Jisela's deep green eyes fixed with determination and strength searched hers, Brooke couldn't help but wonder where Jayson was.

JAYSON

J ayson paced the hall outside Brooke's hospital room. Once Evelyn arrived, he had to make more difficult phone calls. First to Valerie, then Brian. He felt their shock, rage, and worry coming through the phone lines. He was coming apart at the seams trying to keep all his emotions in check, but when his mother arrived at the hospital, he'd already had two meltdowns of his own.

His mother had been in there for an hour now. He told her he would be right in, but he found himself frozen in that hallway. He wanted to see her, to hold her, to kiss her, and more than anything, he wanted to make it all better for her. But he knew he couldn't do that.

He felt like he had let them all down.

He had promised both Evelyn and Jisela he would do right by Brooke, that he would protect her. He had reassured Brooke so many times he would always be there for her. But when she needed him most, he wasn't. He left her alone because he was upset. He hadn't kissed her with all of his love. He hadn't even told her he loved her before he left— something he'd always made sure to do since the night he won her back. If she hadn't been the fighter she was, if Alex had succeeded...

The thought made him die inside. He had failed her.

He sat down in the hallway and buried his face in his hands.

"Hey—"

Jayson looked up to see Evelyn standing next to where he sat.

"Why are you out here all alone?"

"Every time I see her... she looks so scared... I just don't know how to forgive myself for letting this happen. I am so sorry, Evelyn. I'm so sorry I wasn't there to protect your daughter."

"Hey now..." Evelyn reached down and pulled him to his feet, wrapping him up in her arms with love. "You didn't *let* this happen, Jayson. It just happened. Bad things happen to really good people sometimes. That's my baby in there. If I could have put her in a bubble for safe keeping the day she was born, I would have. But I know just like bad things can and will sometimes happen, so will really good things. She will get through this, but she'll need support. She's going to need you. You're her very best friend. You're the love of her life. Why do you think I gave you my permission to propose to her? I can see what you two have. So, trust me when I tell you don't need to know what to say, you just need to be there."

Jayson fiercely embraced Evelyn, allowing the tears he'd been holding in to escape. A moment later, the room door opened, and Jayson turned to see Brooke standing there in her hospital gown with his mom at her side for support.

"Hey..."

She held out her hand to him. "Can we talk alone?"

Her words were spoken slowly, each syllable more painful than the last, probably due to the stitches lining her inner cheek and lip.

Jayson nodded as he took her hand. Together, they walked back into the room, and Jisela left them alone, closing the door behind her.

"I was waiting for you," she said quietly as he helped her settle into bed.

"I know... I'm sorry. I was having a series of stupid moments."

She grabbed his hand and squeezed it. "You and me, right?"

Jayson smiled sadly. "Always and forever."

"Do you think you'll be able to stop looking at me so sadly?"

"I'm not..."

Her look silenced him. "You are. I know I look like a mess, and crazy things have happened tonight, but I need to know you can still love me like before. If your feelings have changed, let me know now..."

"Are you kidding me?" Jayson's voice crumbled with his own tears. "Brooke, I love you more than ever. My feelings for you cannot change. You are the most incredible girl. I don't deserve you. I'm so sorry I wasn't there to protect you. I should have been there to walk you home instead of working out and dealing with my stupid issues. I should have come to you and kissed you until you told me to stop. I promised you we were in this together, and I should have been there."

"I was so scared. I just wanted to feel safe. I wanted to get back into your arms and let you hold me forever. You make me feel better. I need you."

Jayson climbed onto the bed next to her and wrapped her up in his arms.

"I refuse to lose you, Brooke. I was so scared tonight, looking for you out there. When you didn't answer my texts and calls, I felt it in my heart. I knew something wasn't right. I am so in love with you. I need you. I will do anything to help you get through this."

She pressed her cheek, wet with tears, into his neck.

"I just need you. I need us. I was so afraid I wouldn't be able to see you again or you would never know how much I wanted you. I just need you and me, more than ever before."

He kissed the top of her head. "You've got me. Try to rest. I'm not going anywhere. I'm here."

She relaxed into him as much as she could, but he could hear her small hiss of pain as she did so.

"Close your eyes, Brookelynn. I'm going to tell you a story."

"Make it a good one."

"Once upon a time, there was this guy. His name was Romeo..."

The smell of coffee made him blink awake. The brightness of the room reminded him he was in a hospital and this wasn't a bad dream. Brooke slept, curled into him. The way his back and shoulder protested at sleeping in the too small bed was forgotten when he saw her face. The bruises were even worse this morning, a mix of colors that had no business marring her face. Her brown hair was all mussed, falling over her swollen eye and cheek. She was still his beautiful girl. His heart squeezed as he closed his eyes in a prayer of gratitude she was here with him.

He looked across the room to see their mothers asleep on reclining chairs. Their moms were watching over them, protecting them through the night. He was almost sure the coffee came from them, until he saw the message scrawled across the cup.

If you need anything, we're in the waiting room. – Riley

Pressing a gentle kiss to her forehead, Jayson eased himself off the bed. Quietly waking his mother, he made sure to tell her he wasn't leaving and to let Brooke know he'd be right back if she woke in his absence. Stretching his arms over his head as he stepped into the hallway, he caught the sympathetic smile of a nurse at a nearby station.

"Excuse me, but can you point me in the direction of the waiting room? I think my friend is there waiting for me."

"Sure thing, hon. You may be in for a bit of a surprise. They've been here all night."

They?

Following her simple directions, he pulled open the door to the waiting room to find it packed with his teammates. They were all in sweats and pajamas, as if they had rushed out without a second thought to their clothes. His tears came fast when he realized not one player was missing. His brothers on the court had all showed up for him and Brooke. It was a gesture that meant more to him than he could explain.

"Jayson?" Tracie blinked awake from where she lay tucked against Sean's looming frame. Sean's eyes quickly opened, and the both of them shot forward.

"How is she?"

"Did you hear anything?"

"Is she allowed to have visitors?"

"What can we do?"

The questions came at him fast, and he held up his hand. "She's been checked out. There was a lot of damage. She was beaten pretty savagely..."

He swallowed. "She's going to hurt for a while, but she's going to heal. There was no permanent damage, thank God."

Tracie let out an audible sigh. "The police aren't pressing charges, right?"

"We're still waiting for that info. They questioned her a few times, but it was clear self-defense. If she hadn't used force to stop him, he would have rape—"

Jayson's voice cracked as his eyes filled again. Sean pulled him into a fierce hug. "He didn't, though. Your girl is in there, and she's going to be okay."

Jayson nodded. "I want to thank you all. Being here for us... it means the world to me."

"You're a Central Lion. You're our brother, and she's our sister. This is what family does," Sean assured him, others joining in with nods of agreement.

"Is she awake yet?"

"No, she was sleeping when I left the room, but I'll let her know all of you came here for her."

"We're not going anywhere until you guys are released." Vaughn's gruff voice came from where he stood.

"They're all here? For me?"

"I'd say you're pretty well loved." Jayson gave her a small wink.

"Will you help me do something?"

He nodded. "Anything."

"I'm going to need a wheelchair."

He did as she asked, then made it his business to lift her into the chair before wheeling her out of the room and down the hallway. When they made it through the doorway and all eyes fell on her beaten body, Jayson felt her hand reach for his. He readily gave it to her.

"I just wanted to say thank you."

Again, her words were slightly muffled and clipped, but each one was spoken with such an undeniable strength.

"We love you, Brooke." Sean came forward and dropped to his knees to meet her eyes easier. "We want you to feel better soon. We might go hungry until you do."

Jayson's heart warmed to see the corner of her mouth tip up in the tiniest of smiles. "You only love me for the food."

Sean gave her one of his killer smiles before leaning forward and pressing a gentle kiss to her cheek. One by one, all the Lions came forward and followed suit until the only one left was Tracie.

"Hey, T."

Tracie took Brooke's hand. "You're my best friend, Brooke. Almost from the minute we met, you were my best friend. But now you're my hero too. Thanks for fighting. I couldn't begin to think about how I'd ever go on if anything ever happened to my best friend. I love you."

"Love you, T."

They gently embraced before Tracie kissed her cheek as well.

"I should get her back to bed, guys. She needs rest."

"Good morning, Brooke." Detective Kelly stepped through the open doorway, followed by another woman, both dressed similarly in their white shirts and black pants, the gold badge gleaming against the dark fabric. "This is my partner, Detective Carr. I know you've had a long night, but we just have one more question for you."

Jisela and Evelyn flanked the sides of Brooke's bed. Jayson made no effort to move out of the bed where Brooke had curled into his side. He felt less on edge today, but that didn't mean he was going to leave her side until he knew she wasn't in danger of more distress.

Detective Carr stepped forward, holding a large sealed plastic bag. "Do you recognize the contents of this bag?"

Brooke leaned in, taking more effort to see through the eye that wasn't swollen shut. Jayson knew the contents of the bag well. He recognized it almost immediately. He held his breath until her heard her shaky whisper.

"It's my sketchbook. I thought I lost it."

Detective Carr nodded once. "We found it among Alex Caine's personal property. We also found these..."

Brooke numbly shuffled through the stack of photos, each one more voyeuristic than the last. Pictures of her eating in the dining hall with friends. Snaps of her in the library. Others captured her in the art wing and gym. Her skin crawled with the undeniable realization he had been stalking her.

"We found a journal detailing his particular obsession with you. And if all that wasn't enough, campus security cameras caught him following you as you left the library. The path you took isn't monitored, though."

"So, what now?" Evelyn spoke as she rose to her feet. "Do I need to call a lawyer for my daughter?"

"I can't say anything officially, ma'am..."

"How about unofficially?" Jisela made her way to stand next to Evelyn, her arm wrapped around her in support.

Detective Kelly cleared her throat and reached out to give Brooke's hand a gentle squeeze. "Unofficially, it's a crystal clear case of self-defense. You had a stalker whose behaviors were growing more aggressive and erratic by the day. We have more than enough evidence. You were viciously attacked, and you did what you had to do. There's not a lawyer in the world who's going to argue any differently. Unofficially, the case is closed and the District Attorney will be making that official within the next hour or so."

Brooke closed her eyes, relaxing into Jayson further. "So, I can go home?"

Both Detectives smiled tenderly and gave her a nod.

Jayson pressed a soothing kiss to her forehead. "Yeah baby. You're going home."

Jayson stayed with Brooke until she was cleared to go home. Instead of going back to the dorms, Brooke went with Evelyn to a nearby hotel to sleep.

"I want you to try to rest, baby. Call me if you need me for anything."

"I will. You try to rest too."

"Promise you'll call me if you need anything?"

"I promise."

Jayson knew he had to let her go, no matter what his heart yearned for. He dipped his body and gave her a tender kiss before helping her into Evelyn's car. He kissed her once more, then stepped back to watch them pull away.

His mother opened her arms. Jayson smiled at her and hugged her with all the love he had in his heart for her.

"Thank you so much for being here, Mom."

She clucked her tongue at him. "I wouldn't have been anywhere else. When one of my sons need me, I will be there. I love you, Jayson. You make my heart so proud. Every day, I am so proud of the man you are."

"That's all I ever wanted—just to make you and dad proud of me. Now, I want Brooke to be proud of me too. I want to be a good man, a great husband, and an amazing father."

"You will be. I have no doubt."

She grabbed his face and kissed his cheek softly. "I love Brooke too. She's a strong girl, resilient. But even the strong have their moments of fear and weakness. Be there and love her through it."

Jayson nodded.

He walked his mom to her car and made sure she got there safely before he got into a taxi and headed home.

Home. It already felt foreign to him. It wasn't home anymore. Home was staying the night in a hotel with her mother.

Strange emotions churned at his gut.

"You want to talk about it?" Sean walked out of the room from the kitchen, handing Jayson a bottle of water.

"No. Yes. I don't know."

Jayson rolled his neck before collapsing onto the couch, in the same spot where Brooke had sat when he was giving her such a hard time about not telling him about Alex's previous advances.

"This really happened, didn't it? I keep hoping this is some nightmare I'll wake up from. That I'll find Brooke tucked in bed next to me completely fine and some psycho stalker didn't attack my girl."

"I think we're all right with you brother. It's like I can't believe it happened… and to Brooke. Your girl is probably the nicest person I've ever met. No one should ever have to go through what she did, but her heart, man… she's tough."

She was tough, but she was also a human with a heart of gold. The attack would forever leave a little tarnish on that beautiful heart, and as much as he wanted to erase it for her, there was nothing he could do to make it go away.

"You know, I wish I was the one who killed him."

Sean didn't say anything, only nodded once.

"Brooke is so dang sweet, I worry she's going to carry around some sense of guilt for giving that pissant exactly what he deserved. But me? I saw what he did to my girl… I know what he was trying to do. I would have no problem with my conscience for ending his life. I don't even care what that says about me."

"It says what we all know already. You love that girl to

death, and you'd do anything for her. If she ever starts trying to feel bad, you remind her she saved your wife's life. She saved all those babies you both are going to have one day. And even more than that? She saved the girl who would have been next on that creep's list. A guy as messed up as he was wasn't going to stop."

"Thanks, man. I mean it."

"Look, you're going to have to stop thanking me for things that don't need it. I meant every word I said in the hospital. This is more than a teammate thing. You're like my best friend and obnoxiously talented brother all rolled into one roommate package. I'm here for you, whether you want me to be or not."

Chapter 22

JAYSON

Jayson rapped his knuckles three times on the open doorframe. "You wanted to see me, Coach?"

"Yes. Please come in and shut the door behind you."

Setting his bag down, he took a seat opposite the older man. Coach MacManus stood and walked around the desk, rubbing a hand through his salt and pepper hair, coming to a stop right in front of Jayson.

"How are you doing, son?"

The term of endearment sent a signal straight to his tear ducts. Everything with Brooke had left him feeling raw. He hadn't been this emotional since the day they buried his father. "I'm... taking it moment to moment."

Coach nodded in understanding. "I heard about the team showing up for you and your fiancée at the hospital, but I wanted to reach out to you personally on behalf of myself and the coaching staff to let you know we have your back."

"That's definitely appreciated, sir. I thank you for that."

"How is Brooke?"

"She's back home resting. She's still dealing with a lot, but I think the rest and familiarity of home will go a long way in helping her recovery."

"I'm happy to hear that. You know, there's been some media buzz building about this. I'm not sure who leaked it, but there are some big names looking to see if you both want to do an interview, make a statement... you know how the circus is. For so long, you guys have been this darling couple. When word got out, it garnered more than the usual kind of attention. Now, I've been doing my best to keep them all at bay, but if you want to make a statement, I will help you do whatever it is you need to do."

"What Brooke went through... it was a nightmare. But no matter how much it was a nightmare to me, it was reality for Brooke. This is something she needs to decide. When or if she does, I'll support her. If she doesn't, I'll protect her privacy with all I have."

Coach's lips tipped up in a smile. "You're a good man, Williams. You let Brooke know I'm praying for her recovery and can't wait to have her back courtside next season."

"Will do, sir."

Jayson: How are you feeling today, baby?

Brooke: Ugh.

Jayson: That good, huh?

Brooke: I'll live. How are you? How's class? Have you seen Tracie?

Jayson. You better live, you owe me another eighty years at least. I'm okay. Missing you like crazy. Tracie's good. Haven't seen her out and about too much, but we check in with each other throughout the week.

Brooke: Miss you 2.

Brooke: I start counseling today.

Jayson: How are you feeling about that?

Brooke: I know I should... but I don't want to. I just want to stay in bed and sleep forever.

Jayson: Brooke...

Jayson deleted his last message before he sent it. *What was he supposed to say?*

What he wanted to say was she was scaring him and it only got worse when she said things like wanting to sleep forever. He wanted to tell her he missed her always. God, he missed the way she made him feel. She could tease him and still make him feel like he was the king of the whole universe. He missed her random daydream-inspired messages and the way her whole face would light up when she smiled at him. He missed the way she tasted. Her lips would be sweetly bruised and swollen if he could kiss her all day like he wanted.

> ***Brooke****: Hey, I have to shower before I head out to the session. TTYL.*
>
> ***Jayson****: Okay.*
>
> ***Jayson****: I love you, Brookelynn.*

He missed her telling him she loved him.

Brooke

Brooke set her phone to the side. She hadn't used it much lately, except for texting those who wouldn't allow her to be silent. She found herself in a weird predicament. She had a lot to say, but no desire to say it. It wouldn't change anything if she vocalized all the thoughts that had been plaguing her since she left that hospital.

In the two weeks since she left Central, she had laid in bed staring at the ceiling for most of her days. Now that she was entering her third week of convalescence, she was beginning to drag herself into the shower and put on clean clothes. Sweatpants and baggy t-shirts were becoming her uniform these days. She pretended she made her bed before booting up her computer and distracting herself with the coursework her professors had sent her. She was given a leave of absence due to her circumstances, and all her professors were allowing her to finish up the semester from home, but she'd have to go back to take the final exams.

It was a thought that made her queasy.

She hadn't been back on campus since the assault, and she wasn't sure she wanted to go back.

Her college career was on the line if she didn't, but so was her life. Jayson, the man she was engaged to, the man she loved, was there. A huge chunk of her friends were there. They were all moving on with their lives without her, and she hated it, so why wasn't that enough to make her want to go back?

That was probably the question she could bring up to the counselor. The one she'd been successfully avoiding for two weeks—until her mother realized she wasn't going to her appointments and put a stop to it. Brooke attempted to argue that she was an eighteen-year-old adult and no one could force her to go to counseling, but her mother had given her *that* look... and that had been the end of it.

Throwing her blanket to the side, Brooke forced her legs to get her out of the bed before she changed her mind. The large mirror on her wall froze her in her tracks as she moved toward her closet. Her hair was disheveled and badly in need of a wash and brush, but what was the point? She didn't care how she looked. The worse, the better. Her mood seemed to reflect her face, all mottled with healing bruises. The stitches were removed, and the swelling had gone down, but she felt like she was looking at a stranger. She lifted her tank top to see her pajama pants hanging low on her hips. She'd lost weight since she'd been home. Her appetite had left and had yet to come back. Her passion for running and exercise had dissipated as she lay in bed recovering from her injuries. Giving her reflection a mental shrug, she went to her closet and pulled out her old denim painting shirt splattered with every color imaginable. Slipping it on, she almost chuckled as she imagined what everyone would think of her appearance.

Paint-splattered shirt, baggy plaid pajama pants, her feet tucked into a pair of flip flops, messy, dirty hair.

She was going to counseling. Nobody said she had to actually put in any effort.

She looked at the plain building. There were no signs indicating she was where she was supposed to be. Just three numbers... nine zero one. She looked down at the business card her mother had tacked to her door—subtle, right?—and confirmed this was indeed the address. Pulling open the door, she stepped inside. There was no waiting room, no secretary, nothing but an empty room.

"Hello?"

Silence met her.

Wait... the sound of music in the distance beckoned her like a pied piper. She moved cautiously down the hallway, the music telling her she was moving in the right direction, leading her all the way to large double doors left wide open, revealing all the colors the rest of the building lacked. The familiar smell of paint beckoned her, and the easels scattered around the room held canvases of all sizes.

"Can I help you?"

A woman's voice came from the corner of the room she hadn't scanned yet. She was tall. Her salt and pepper hair was braided into a halo that wrapped around the crown of her head. Her features were undeniably Native American, and she carried herself almost regally as she moved toward Brooke.

"I have an appointment with Dr. Finch."

"Ah, you must be Brooke. Call me Suzanne."

"Look, Dr. Finch—"

"Suzanne." The doctor raised an eyebrow.

"Suzanne, I don't really want to be here. There's no need for me to sit on some couch and talk. Maybe you could just call my mom and let her know I'm fine."

Suzanne walked around Brooke in a perusing circle. Brooke shifted from one foot to another under her scrutiny.

"You don't want to talk?"

"There's nothing to talk about."

"Good. I didn't feel like talking anyway. Grab a brush and pick an easel."

Brooke's head whipped around. "I don't want to."

"Tough. We're either talking or painting."

"Where is your degree? Are you really a doctor?" Brooke was having serious doubts about this whole setup.

"Google me." Suzanne turned on her heel and went back to work on her own easel.

Brooke debated just walking out. Nothing was stopping her... except her feet. Her feet had a mind of their own apparently, because after ten minutes of just standing there being ignored by Suzanne, she was in front of an easel with a paintbrush in hand. Grabbing her pallet, she picked her colors, but paused before putting the brush to the blank space.

"I don't know what to paint," she called over the music.

"Thought we weren't talking today," Suzanne called back just as quickly.

Brooke's jaw snapped shut. For sixty minutes, she stood there, lips press together, paintbrush inches away from still clean canvas.

"Time's up. You're free to go."

"Seriously?" *This woman was certifiable.* How did her mother even find her?

"If you're trying to convince people you're fine, you might want to shower and wear real clothes next time."

There was not going to be a next time.

"See you tomorrow. Same time." Suzanne's voice was firm and final.

Brooke whirled around and sprinted from the room, then the building. If they thought she was coming back, they were all mistaken.

"Aren't you supposed to ask me how I'm feeling?"

Suzanne stirred a bit of honey into her tea before shrugging a shoulder. "I could ask, but I could also just wait until you're ready to tell me how you're feeling. So, what will it be today, painting or talking?"

Brooke didn't bother responding. She stalked back over to the same easel she'd stood in front of the last five sessions. She still had yet to paint anything, but standing there silent was more appealing than talking about anything. She was content to do just that when a familiar song filled the air.

Ditching her brush, she reached for a broken piece of charcoal and went to work.

Her lip pulled between her teeth. She couldn't tear her eyes away until she filled the space completely. Three hours had passed. The sun was setting, casting different shadows all around the studio. She hadn't even noticed.

"Is that your boyfriend?" Suzanne's voice came from behind her.

"My fiancée."

"He's good looking."

"He's gorgeous," Brooke corrected, not taking her eyes off what she had created.

"Interesting. Tomorrow, same time. And we're talking tomorrow."

"What if I don't feel like talking?"

"You already started talking on the canvas. Tomorrow, we continue the conversation."

"I was nineteen."

Brooke turned to face Suzanne in confusion. The older woman took her mug of tea and sat down on the couch. "I was nineteen when I was attacked. I was living in LA, had an internship with a phenomenal artist, my life was going according to my grand plan. I went out on a date with a guy I had met at a local gallery. On our first date, we went to an exhibit, then a coffee shop. We talked for hours. On our second date, he took me to a Thai restaurant, walked me home, forced his way into my apartment, and raped me. He's never been caught to my knowledge."

"I didn't know—"

"Of course you didn't. Just like no one will look at you and just know."

"How did you stop being afraid?"

"Because then he would win. If I cowered away from everyone and everything, all my life would be wasted on him. I got angry enough to fight to get my life back. Let me tell you, my life is good. I am happy way more than I am sad or mad."

And just like that, Brooke knew she would come back the next day and the next. Suzanne might have been unconventional in her approach, but she had made it clear if anyone could understand her feelings about the attack, it was going to be Suzanne.

Brooke had been seeing Suzanne daily for three weeks. Their sessions had started at an hour, but grew progressively longer. Now, Brooke was waking up at six, showering and heading over to Suzanne's place, and didn't return until nightfall most days. She hadn't been calling or texting anyone, but her mother left her to her own devices, probably grateful Brooke was actually going to counseling.

"You're going back to campus on Monday to take your finals."

Brooke neither confirmed nor denied. She was still mulling over the idea of just blowing them off. She'd still pass the course with a fail, but her scholarship would be thrown into jeopardy. She wasn't sure if that mattered, especially if she didn't go back to school.

"Hmmm... let's try another question instead. Are you finally going to talk to Jayson?"

"Who said I haven't been talking to Jayson?" Brooke heard the sharp, defensive edge in her voice.

"You haven't mentioned him since our first week together,

yet he keeps turning up in your art. Are you going to give him back the ring?"

Brooke's fist balled up. "Why would I?"

"You don't love him anymore..."

Brooke let the brush fall to the floor. Her rage boiled over, and she advanced on Suzanne. "I never said that!"

"You never said you love him either. Not to me. I'm sure you haven't said it to him either."

Brooke felt her rage evaporate in an instant, the sadness rushing in to fill its place. She hadn't said it to him since she left the hospital. He, on the other hand, still found a way to tell her every day. "Just because I haven't said it, doesn't mean I don't feel it."

"True, but everybody wants to hear it. You're not the only one who was affected by that night, Brooke. Talk to me."

Brooke felt the sadness creep up from her heart and wrap its claws around her throat. "I can't..."

"You can."

Suzanne's quiet strength encouraged her. She started from the beginning, from their very first encounter, and didn't stop until she was sobbing as she tried to explain what it sounded like when she cracked his skull with a rock.

"I killed him."

"You did what you had to do."

"It's not that simple, Suzanne!"

"Why not?"

"It was my fault. Maybe I was too nice and led him on... why didn't I have my phone charger? I could have called for an escort from the library instead of running out on my own. I was distracted by that stupid argument with Jayson. If I was invisible Brooke..."

Suzanne held up a hand. "Being nice to someone does not give them license to stalk and assault you, Brooke. He's the one who needed to stop. You have the right to wear whatever you want while you walk *wherever* you want *whenever* you want to walk and *no* person is allowed to touch your body without your consent. It is *not* your fault."

Brooke wiped her face free of tears.

"It's not Jayson's fault either."

"I know that." Brooke jumped to her feet in defense.

"I know you know... but does he know that?" Suzanne took her hand, urging her to sit. "You were the victim of a vicious attack. You are a survivor, make no mistake about it. But you need to open your eyes wider."

"What do you mean?"

"I mean, you aren't the only one who has to deal with the after effects. Your mother, your friends, Jayson, how do they feel?"

Brooke opened her mouth, but had no answer. She couldn't answer because she had never asked them.

"I want you to do something for me. Next time Jayson calls, answer the phone. Talk to him and let him tell you how he feels. Tell him how you feel. You've been pulling away because you don't want him to see you like this, and he's giving you space because that's what he thinks you need. He's just as afraid as you are."

Chapter 23

JAYSON

It had been weeks since he'd spoken to Brookelynn.

He still messaged her daily, but they often went unanswered. He called Evelyn to see how she was doing and to make sure she was okay. Evelyn told him she was spending more and more time at counseling, but even she hadn't really talked to Brooke in weeks. He was happy she was in counseling making progress, but there was a part of him—a huge part—that ached for not being part of the healing process. His sleep had been wretched since she left campus, but it had only grown worse in the last week.

Questions plagued his mind in the quiet of the night. He wondered how he'd ever be able to earn her trust back after he had left her unprotected... if he even could? Had he lost his Brookelynn for good this time?

Brian and Sean tried their best to lift his spirits, but it was no use. He didn't want to go out and act like the love of his life wasn't back home dealing with the pain all alone. She had always sacrificed for the sake of their relationship. She'd given up date nights and quality time for the sake of his sport. She'd chosen a school to keep them together. She'd dealt with a lot while he was off trying to win a trophy, and in the end, she'd fought with everything she had to keep her body to herself and ended up losing her peace of mind. He should have done a million different things to make it better for her, and now, it may have cost him the ultimate price.

He closed his math book and shoved it away. If he didn't know the information by now, he wasn't going to figure it out. His eyes burned with fatigue, and his body ached from spending hours hunched over the books. Picking up the phone, he scanned for any new messages from Brooke… none.

> *Jayson:* I miss my study buddy. I hope you had a good day today. I love you so freaking much, Brooke. Forever.

He moved to his bed and pulled his t-shirt off before laying back on his pillow. He hadn't washed it in weeks. If he closed his eyes, he could still smell the faint trace of Brooke in his pillowcase. The ringing phone pulled his attention. Sitting up, he wondered if he was hallucinating.

Brooke was calling him.

Brooke.

"Brookelynn?"

He heard her soft sigh, and his heart squeezed. "Hi, Jay."

"God, I missed your voice… baby, I miss you."

"I miss you too. I miss us."

It was music to his ears. He had to force his words around the huge lump in his throat. "I miss us too. How are you?"

"Some days, I'm not so sure, but some days, I'm starting to think it might be okay after all."

"Brooke…" Jayson stood up, pacing out his nervous energy.

"Jayson, I have a lot to say. Some of it might not be easy to hear, but I need to start talking."

"Okay, I can be a good listener. Just give me one minute and I'm all ears, okay?"

After hearing her agreement, he put the call on hold and ran out of his room into the living room where Sean and Vaughn sat playing on the Xbox.

"Well, Mr. Bookworm came out to play—"

"I need to borrow your car, Vaughn."

"What happened? Is it Brooke? Is she okay?"

"She called me."

Sean's eyes widened. "Good or bad?"

"I need to see her, Vaughn. Please. A car will get me there faster than a train. I'll be back by Sunday night, and I'll fill up your gas tank before I return it."

"Don't worry about it. Go see your girl... tell her we miss her."

Grabbing the keys mid-toss, Jayson returned to his room, pulled on his shirt, and grabbed his backpack and chargers. Picking the phone back up, he strolled out the living room, giving his friends a quick nod. He waited until he was in the car and had it started before he took his phone off mute.

"I'm sorry about that, baby. I'm back, and I'm listening..."

Connecting the phone to the car's speaker, he backed out of the parking space and headed toward home.

"How do you feel?"

He could feel her nerves through the phone. He could almost see her biting that bottom lip of hers, stirring the same desires it usually did.

"I feel happy you called... relieved to hear your voice and you say miss me. But usually, I'm just scared, Brookelynn. I've never been this scared in my life."

"Why are you scared?"

He cleared his throat. "I'm afraid I lost you. I didn't lose you physically that night, but since then, Brooke... I've worried you can't trust me anymore, that you don't want me anymore. I'm scared you can't look at me the same way because I let you down. I'm scared I lost the one thing that matters most. I'm scared of missing you for the rest of my life."

"Jay, I'm so sorry I haven't called. Not talking to other people is one thing, but I should have been talking to you."

"Will you tell me about you? How is counseling? How are

you doing? Anything. I just want to hear your voice. I need to fill up on your voice."

"I have this crazy counselor named Suzanne. Well... I thought she was crazy, but now I think she's probably a genius. It's just me and her, and we're in this huge warehouse that's her art studio. Its art therapy, but she's totally the tough love type. She called me out and made me realize I was so wrapped up in being viewed as a victim, I was missing the point that I was a survivor. She's been telling me to stop hiding. You were the first person on my list I had to stop hiding from."

"Were you worried I would look at you any differently?"

"Yes. Especially you."

"I could never, Brooke. I told you that in the hospital. You are my woman, the love of my life, and nothing is ever going to change that. I promise you."

"I am still madly in love with you, and I am always going to be."

Jayson's smiled overtook his face as he accelerated.

It was nearly midnight when he pulled Vaughn's car to a stop in front of Brooke's house.

"Hey, Brooke... you should come to the front door."

"Why? Are you here?"

Jayson didn't answer. Instead, he grabbed his bag and hurried to the front door with the phone still pressed to his ear. A moment later, the door was pulled open and his love was standing in front of him. To his relief, her face lit up with her smile and she was in his arms before he could say anything.

"You came."

"There's no place in the world I'd rather be."

"I love you, Jayson Williams."

"I love you, Brooke Thomas."

Brooke

It was incredible how just seeing Jayson standing in front of her eased every worry she had been carrying. Her body instantly felt lighter, and when he wrapped his arms around her, she just knew this was everything she needed. Pulling back to see his face again, she smiled.

"I'm kind of hoping you'll kiss me right about now."

"Give me those gorgeous lips."

Catching her face between his hands, he brought his lips to hers, giving her the most unrushed, toe-curling kiss. Brooke felt her body go pliant in his arms. She felt safe, loved, wanted.

"Will you stay with me?"

"Of course."

She pulled him into the house and locked the door behind them before she led him upstairs to her bedroom, never releasing his hand. In her room, she took the bag from his hand, dropped it near her closet, and locked her door.

"Are you tired? That drive must have been tough after class and studying all day."

"Doesn't matter. I'm not closing my eyes anytime soon. I need to look at you. My heart hasn't stopped racing since I saw your name and face on my phone screen."

He smiled at her, revealing his deep dimples that sent shivers down her spine. *Jayson Williams and those sexy dimples...*

"I'll have to thank Vaughn for letting you borrow his car to come see me."

"I'm sure he'll beg for a meal instead of any thanks."

Brooke laughed. "Maybe I'll send you back with some baked goods."

"I was thinking we could ride back together. Finals start on Monday. We could drive back Sunday night. You could stay with me and Riley for the week, and we'll all help you pack up your dorm before summer break."

School. It had been the one thing they hadn't really discussed over the phone earlier that evening. It was a discussion that needed to be had, and now was as good as time as any.

"About that... I haven't decided if I'm going back."

"For the term, or for good?"

"I just don't know if I can do it. It took a lot of strength to make it off that campus, Jayson. I don't know if I can go back."

Jayson pulled her down to sit on his lap. "I understand what you're saying. I hear you. But I think you're mistaken. You're so strong. You were strong before, but now, it's more of a fact than ever before. I'm so proud of you, no matter what you decide."

"You mean that?"

"Of course I do. If you can't go back, then we'll look at whatever you want to do. Maybe I'll stay with you."

"You can't give up school and ball. It's your dream!"

"You're my dream. I'll sacrifice anything for us. You've already made a lot of those sacrifices. I can do it too. I can move back here, and we can get our own place. I'll get a job. Or if you want to move, we can do that too. Anywhere you want to go. We can make a plan for our life."

"I couldn't ask you to do that for me."

"It's a good thing I'm deciding for myself."

"I don't want to argue—"

He pressed a kiss to her knuckles. "I don't want to either, so tell me more about Suzanne..."

Waking up with Jayson's arms wrapped around her was something she had missed tremendously. Feeling his kiss on the back of her neck made her hum in delight. Remembering Suzanne's words, she understood what she really meant about not letting a memory steal her future. For weeks, she had wondered if Jayson could ever look at her the same, if he would want her in all the same ways. Then he showed up on her doorstep and spent the rest of the night laying in her bed, kissing her fears away, assuring her with his loving gazes and hushed proclamations of love. As their eyes grew heavy, she felt him take the hand that held her engagement ring and kiss it. She said a prayer of thanks it was still on her hand. That her heart was still his.

Brooke hadn't thought he had been so affected, but she should have known better. Her man had the biggest heart of anyone she had ever known, and when it came to her, he had never attempted to hide it away. The way he loved her was enough motivation to fight through all the bad that would come their way, because their good was so much better than anything else she could imagine. She rolled over to face him.

"Hey, sleepyhead."

His eyelids didn't budge, but his lips curled up at the corners.

"I know you can hear me. My mom left for work. I'm going to go downstairs and make us some breakfast."

"Or you can stay here in my arms for the next forty-eight hours."

"We'll starve."

"Breakfast in bed? And don't you dare change out of that tank top and shorts. I'm still reacquainting myself with some of my favorite places in the world."

"Jayson Mark Williams!"

He rolled her beneath him, lips pressed against hers, stealing any desire she had to move. "Brookelynn... you are delicious."

"Maybe we can order in for lunch?"

"Tell Vaughn not to eat the whole pan of brownies in a day. Make it last."

"Are you sure you won't come back with me?"

They'd spent the weekend together. There was a lot of talking and reconnecting. There was a lot of kissing. More than ever, Brooke knew she was going to spend the rest of her life with Jayson. However, she hadn't decided anything further about school.

"I'm sure. You go on. We'll figure everything else out when you come home next week."

"It's going to be a long week."

"You just focus on kicking butt on your finals. I'll be here waiting."

Jayson tossed his bag in the car. "Remember, no matter what, I'm so honored to be your future husband."

"And my best friend."

"Especially that."

"Drive safe, okay?" She pulled on his shirt to bring him close, trying to distract herself with the loose thread on one of his sleeves so the building tears wouldn't come bursting forth until he left.

"Hey, now..." He lifted her chin. "I thought we decided no more hiding. If you're sad, it's okay. I'm sad too. The last thing I want to do is get in this car and drive away from you. When I get back, we are going to have so much time to really be with each other, we can get through this school thing together, no matter what."

She nodded. "I love you for always."

Wrapping her in his arms, he pressed a kiss to the top of her head. "Forever I love you."

JAYSON

Jayson couldn't believe his eyes.

Walking into the room for his final exam, he was stunned to see Brookelynn sitting there in her seat right next to his. Her hair fell around her face in soft curls, and she smiled so happily at his shocked expression.

"You're not the only one in this relationship who can

surprise someone."

"Get out of that seat and let me make you blush."

Brooke let out a light, happy laugh as she scooted out of her seat and threw her arms around his neck. "I'm done letting a memory steal my future. I want my life back."

"I am so proud of you."

"I am proud of me too."

He couldn't resist anymore. Burying his fingers into her hair, his lips were on hers, and then her tongue demanded his. Uncaring of any audience they had, Jayson dropped his hands to her lower back, pulling her into him even more. Brooke's soft moan of pleasure hummed against his lips, and he knew then he needed to pull back before he threw her over his shoulder and ran to his place, forgetting all about self-control.

"You ready to kick this final's butt?"

"Absolutely." He bumped her closed fist with his.

"Ms. Thomas..." Their professor cleared his throat to grab their attention. "It's so very nice to have you back."

"How do you think you did?"

"I totally bombed it. I'm probably looking at like an A minus."

"You're so modest!" Brooke shoved him playfully before he wrapped his arm around her.

"Where to? Are you going to your dorm or my place?"

"I want to go see Tracie... but if it's okay with you, I'd like to stay with you. Sometimes I have these nightmares, but I didn't have them when you held me while we slept."

"Babe, you don't have to have a reason to stay with me ever. I love when we're together. I love when I get to hold you. But as much as I hate that you have those nightmares, I'm happy I can make you feel safe."

Pressing a kiss to the tip of her nose, they walked on the familiar route to surprise her roommate.

"Brooke! I can't believe you're really here. I've missed you so much!"

"Tracie!"

The two girls embraced tightly as Jayson stood back and observed.

"You look so good!" Tracie thrust her away to get another look at her before pulling her back into her hug. "I'm so happy I got to see you!"

"Me too! I missed you. I'm sorry I haven't been calling or answering your messages."

"Don't apologize. I get it. I just wanted you to know you were missed. I missed my friend."

"I love you, Tracie."

"Love you right back."

Brooke finally released her friend and walked around the mostly packed room. "Wow, it feels like ages since I've been in here. Thanks for packing up most of my things, I owe you."

"Don't start with that... unless you mean you'll set me up with one of your man's delicious teammates."

Jayson guffawed while Brooke giggled. "How did I ever get through my days without you?"

"Are you back for the week?"

"Just about. I took one final and have two more to go. Two of them were papers I submitted last week. After that, I'm officially done with freshman year."

Tracie nodded as she took a seat on her bed, tucking her feet under her. "I have two tomorrow, and then I'm done. I'm leaving Wednesday morning."

"So soon?"

"You know my parents. I have some social obligation to fulfill and they wouldn't hear of letting me actually relax for a few days."

"Well, remember my offer. My door is always open if you can manage to sneak away for a break."

"Thanks." Tracie's smile didn't quite reach her eyes, and Jayson felt his own begin to fall. He didn't think he'd ever seen Tracie look so forlorn, with the exception of after what happened to Brooke.

"Hey, Brooke is staying with me and Riley for the week. You should come over tomorrow night and we'll have an end of the year bash. We'll keep it small and just relax."

Brooke smiled at him gratefully. "I'd like that."

"Sounds like a plan." Tracie nodded her confirmation.

They spent another hour talking with Tracie as Brooke packed up what was left. With a promise to see each other the next day, Jayson took her hand, and together, they made the journey back to his place. He held her hand a little tighter as they passed the turn for the shortcut path leading to the road where his townhouse was—the path Brooke had taken the night of her attack. She squeezed his hand in silent recognition of the moment.

They walked in silence until they climbed the steps to his front door.

Riley and Vaughn were on the couch with game controllers in hand and snacks spread out on the small coffee table.

"Hey, Williams, get over here and watch the total domination happening right now!" Vaughn shouted over his shoulder, keeping his eyes fixed on the screen.

Jayson opened his mouth to get their attention, but Brooke quickly shushed him. Dropping her bag, she quietly walked over to the couch and plopped down between them.

"Better step it up, Riley."

"Brooke!"

Both guys dropped their controllers and stood up, pulling her to her feet again.

"It's so good to see you!"

"You surprised Jay? Did he cry? He did, didn't he?"

"Oh, I missed you, girl. I lost five pounds!"

Brooke giggled and pointed to the near empty brownie pan. Vaughn shrugged. "I had to gain it back somehow."

"Gosh, I missed you guys."

Jayson picked up her bag to carry into his room. "Brooke's staying here for the week, Riley."

"Sweet!" Riley hugged her to him. "You look fantastic, Brooke. How are you?"

She nodded. "I'm okay. I appreciate all the love you guys gave and sent to me while I was home. It meant a lot to know I had friends who cared."

"Of course we care. We love you, girl."

Brooke smiled at each of them, tears glistening in her eyes. "Love you guys too."

Brooke

B rooke sat in the middle of Jayson's bed wearing one of his t-shirts. She really didn't have the time to just sit there because people were starting to arrive for their little end of the year get together but still she was stuck in thought as she wondered how everyone was going to look at her. It was easy with Tracie, Vaughn and Riley. They were in her circle and they were so happy to see her it was easy not to think about them looking at her as a statistic. But tonight would be different.

Jayson had tried to keep it as small as possible but inviting just a few members of the team quickly spiraled into the whole team and some of them were apparently bringing dates. She had messaged Suzanne a bit earlier to tell her about the party and to get her advice. When she got out of the shower there was a reply blinking in wait.

Suzanne: Have Fun

Have fun. That's all she said.

So now she sat on the bed playing out random conversation scenarios that would undoubtedly occur throughout the night. She was on the fourth one when Jayson slipped through the door. He looked just as scrumptious as ever. A new red baseball cap turned backwards on his head. He wore a gray thermal Henley, the sleeves pushed up to his elbows revealing his strong and sculpted forearms. His shorts hung low enough on his hips that if she lifted up his shirt to peek she would see that spectacular V that tempted her more and more every day.

"As amazing as you look on my bed in my shirt, some of the guys are asking to see you."

"You should lock the door and come over here." The words were off of her lips before she could think about what she was saying. Not that she regretted saying them, but maybe she could have used a little bit more finesse judging by the look of shock on Jayson's face.

"If I lock this door and come over there I wouldn't be able to control myself."

"So don't."

Brooke moved off his bed and approached him. She kept her eyes fixed on his with every step she took until she was nearly flush against his body. She deliberately reached around him and locked the door.

"Brooke-"

She dropped her hands to his waistband pulling at his button. "Jayson, I'm tired of waiting. We have been so good for all this time, what if we are just wasting time?"

He reached his hand up to cup her face in his hand. "Oh sweetheart. I would be lying to say that I didn't want to, to say I don't think about it, because I do… a lot. But I remember what we both told each other we wanted, what we promised each other, I don't want to let anyone, especially that coward, change our lives, or our futures."

"I know what I want Jayson! I want you. He could have stolen everything I've saved to share with you…"

"But he didn't baby. He's gone and he's never going to hurt you or anyone again. We'll share each other's body when it's our time, when we say so, just like we've always said."

Brooke eyes looked away, "I am making a fool out of myself, aren't I?"

Jayson shook his head and pulled her into his kiss. This time he didn't let her control anything and instead he picked her up off the ground wrapping her legs around his waist.

"Oh Brookelynn, you are so beautiful… so sexy. I am so in love with you. I want you Brookelynn, I want you so, so badly. If I believed for a moment that you didn't care about waiting until our wedding night, believe me I would put all of your sexy in a car and drive us to a nice hotel for the whole weekend. But I know you. And I know that you would regret it, even in some small way, because we weren't married. I couldn't live with myself knowing that you regretted something we did. I want to wait with you. Our first time should be that special, just what we always talked about…."

She kissed him gently, "So then marry me already. Let's just elope."

JAYSON

Her earnest pleas were killing his determination to be the strong one for them right now. But the woman he had spent years dreaming of was in his arms begging him for all the things he really wanted. He wanted to marry her, he wanted to sleep with her and to experience everything with her. She planted kisses along his jaw until she found the sensitive spot just below his ear. "I could be Mrs. Jayson Williams by morning if you say yes."

"Baby…"

He kissed her deeply. In that kiss his mind wondered if he could really do what she said, could they just run off and get married? He knew the answer and he knew that he had to be stronger for the both of them.

"You're making it hard to be bad Jayson."

She tried to work up a serious pout between his kisses.

"You're making it hard to be good. I would do anything for you Brookelynn. I would do anything to make you happy, and you know that. But we can't run off and marry like that right now, our mothers would kill us… Val would kill us!"

Brooke let out a snort of laughter even as she pouted. "It's our life not theirs."

"Exactly. It's *our* life. We made a plan and I love our plan. I know you love it too, even in the moments when it's hard to remember why we made the plan in the first place. Trust me. We're going to plan a beautiful wedding, the wedding of your dreams. We'll have all our friends and family there and you're going to be the most beautiful bride that ever existed. We'll have the best day ever and then I'll take you home and make love to you as your husband. We'll give each other the gift of each other in a romantic room where we'll be alone and not with a bunch of guys a few feet away. That's *our* plan baby..."

She let out a sigh mixed with contentment and a hint of sadness. "I do love that plan."

"I do love you."

Chapter 24

JAYSON

"What are you thinking about?"

Jayson was looking at her stretched out on the chaise lounge near the pool. They had been back home for two weeks and Brooke's peaceful smile was a good indication of how her demeanor had been for the last few weeks. It was joyous to see her finding herself again.

"That your body is an incredible, amazing, delicious distraction and that bikini is making it hard for me to think straight."

"Oh no, flattery is not going to work right now. What was going on in that mind of yours?"

Jayson smiled, "Well it's a multifaceted plan. The first one is tattoos."

"You want us to get tattooed?!"

Jayson chuckled, Brooke's fear of needles was still firmly intact.

"I want to get tattooed. And I want you to draw it for me."

She looked up at him. "You want my work on you?"

He kissed her worried mouth. "I want every part of you on me."

Brooke blushed happily. "Where do you want your tattoo?"

"On the inside of my wrist." He held up the wrist that held the hair band he had taken and worn since the night of their first kiss. He knew that she would already know what he wanted the tattoo to be.

> *My Bounty is as boundless as the sea,*
> *My Love as deep; the more I give to thee,*
> *The more I have, for both are infinite.*

It was his favorite quote from Romeo and Juliet, one he often recited when they were alone together. He'd often ask her to write the words out on his skin before his game, emboldening the letters that together spelled out 'My BLT'... BROOKE LYNN THOMAS.

"Are you sure? You don't have to prove your love to me anymore than you already have." She wiggled her engagement ring in his face. Then her face turned somber.

"You are my hero Brooke... and that's why I am sure. I want the tattoo."

"Well I will work on it..."

"Good then you can come with me when I get it done. In the meantime, if you're feeling up to it, I want you to pack a week's worth of clothes."

"Pack? For a vacation?"

He nodded slightly. "Only if you're sure you're up to traveling."

Brooke took his hands, "I know everyone is watching me waiting for me to crack. The truth is, I was waiting for myself to crack. But I guess I am pretty strong after all. I was one of the lucky ones. Am I mad? Yes. Do I have moments of fear? Yes. But I am not broken. He could never break me, he was the weak one, the coward. Being with you, being with the people who love me, that's where I am the best me, that's where I find my strength. So if you're asking me if I am okay to go away with you, my answer is absolutely yes. I have missed you so much this spring, the best thing I could ever do with my time is to spend it with you."

Jayson kissed her cheek gently, "Then that's what we're going to do. We leave in a couple of days. Pack things for the beach as well! I am going to go make some final arrangements, then later I'm taking my girl out to dinner."

She hugged him exuberantly. "You are the best fiancé I could have ever hoped for."

A few days later they were on their flight to the warm beaches of the Dominican Republic. Brooke couldn't stop smiling, it made his heart relieved to see her excitement. He was determined to make the most of every minute of the summer to make up for all the lost moments during the basketball season. During the plane ride she held his hand the whole time. Even when they weren't talking, she still held on to him as if he was her anchor, keeping her centered in their love.

A plane ride and shuttle ride later they arrived at their resort and Brooke was in shock with the natural beauty she kept seeing at every turn. She kept exclaiming that she wanted to paint all of it but she didn't know if her rendition would ever even come close to what she saw in front of her eyes.

"Oh Jayson! This is incredible. You do too much for me!"

He shook his head as he followed her into the doors of their suite. After tipping the bellboy and locking the door behind him, he found her standing on the balcony, with the tears falling freely.

"Hey..."

He wrapped her up in his arms and kissed the top of her head. He was sure that his worry was unmistakable in his eyes.

"I'm still okay Jayson." She gave him her sweet smile. "It's just the best place you could have brought me."

"I hoped so. I wanted a place where you can find comfort, where we could be us together with none of the mess. Just me and you... the way it should be."

"Always and forever."

He bent down to meet her lips with a kiss.

They spent the whole day on the beach and in the pool, stealing kisses and loving all the intimate talks that they had both missed in recent weeks. That night after a great dinner at a nearby restaurant, they returned to the room to get a good night sleep. The next morning, they had to be up early as Jayson arranged for them to have a surfing lesson. Jayson had just stripped down to his boxer briefs when he heard a knock on his door, before he could answer, the door opened and in slipped Brooke.

She stood before him in a bra and a pair of boxer shorts with her hair tossed carelessly. She was stunning.

Before he could say anything she held up a hand.

"I am not trying to be bad or anything... I was just wondering... or hoping, if I could sleep in here with you. I just want to be close to you. Things get rough sometimes at night, and I mean we've spent the night with each other before and we were okay... Jayson, I just need you close to me, I need you..."

He was next to her in a second. "I'm right here, Brookelynn. You can absolutely stay in here with me."

He kissed her neck and scooped her up in his strong arms and carried her to the bed. "Matter of fact, tomorrow move your stuff into this bedroom. I want you with me every night."

Her eyes sparkled with gratefulness.

They lay in bed cuddling and whispering their love for hours.

"Sometimes I wish I could sing just so I could sing you a love song."

She rolled to face him with a big beaming smile on her face.

"You could sing me one anyway... pretty please?"

He groaned with a chuckle then kissed her protruding bottom lip.

"That's no fair. You know I can't say no to you especially when you beg so sweetly."

"Spoiler alert, that's the idea." She winked and kissed his cheek happily. "Please sing me a love song Romeo."

Jayson smiled widely as his heart raced. She still had the ability to make him feel like he did the very first time he saw her. He kissed her soft lips gently once more for good measure before he began to sing in a low whisper.

He had heard her playing Christina Perri's *A Thousand Years* countless times as she sketched and one day he had realized it was the same song that he heard her humming the day he fell completely in love with her as she washed dishes in his kitchen. He had immediately downloaded it and added it to his own play list. The lyrics of the song reminded him of their relationship from the moment he had spotted her in the school hallways, through that moment right now as he held her in his arms engaged to be married, and the same lyrics would carry on into their future.

She never took her eyes away from his even when they filled with tears.

"I love you so much Jayson Mark Williams. That song... I love that song even more now."

"To me it's always been our song. I always heard you playing it so I looked it up. I can't help but see us when I close my eyes and listen."

"You're right. Maybe that's why I loved it so much. It's us... It's officially our song now."

They sealed their decision with a kiss.

With their lips still touching she softly began singing the second verse of the song. Her sweet voice coursed through his body and he felt his heart exploding with love for her yet. Together they sang the rest of the song, neither of them taking their eyes away from one another.

"I've been thinking a lot about our future and I decided that I really want to start planning our wedding Jayson." She spoke softly as she lay her head on his bare chest.

"Yeah?" Jayson hugged her closer. "When do you want to make this official?"

"Let's do it exactly one year from today, I initially thought we should do it right after graduation but now I don't want to wait that long. What do you think? Money might be tight with both of us still in school and married but I'll get a better paying job to help out. You'd have to move obviously but I have been doing research and emailing the Financial Aid office. There are grants we could apply for after we're married that could help cover expenses and we could try to get into family housing."

She sat up and looked down at him. He could see the hope pouring out of her eyes.

"Brooke I have thought about the day I could call you my wife since I proposed to you, honestly even before that. I am not going to need convincing. I told you we would do this whenever you were ready. If you want to get married next year, we're getting married. Don't worry about the money babe, we'll figure everything out together."

"Are you positive?"

He nodded happily. "Believe me I would much rather be living in our own place with you as my wife than a bunch of guys. Next year on this date we'll be in a bed together and you'll be my wife…"

He raised his eyebrows mischievously.

Brooke lay on top of him and kissed him slowly and deliberately.

"Let the countdown begin."

They spent the next day under the sun learning to surf and then having lunch on the beach.

Jayson made sure he got a picture of his girl in her bikini standing on the surfboard. With a purely happy smile lighting up her face and her wet hair piled on top of her head, she was reminiscent of a poster he'd love to have on his wall when he was teen. But better than that he got to have the real life woman in his bed. He posted the picture.

ROMEO
and she called him

One fairer than my love? The all-
seeing sun/ Ne'er saw her match
since first the world begun.–
Shakespeare.
Finally celebrating the past year
with the love of my life & future
wife @brookelynn.
She's the definition of true sexy
and she's all mine.
#thatsMYwoman #vacation
#besttripever #herbootythough
#curvesoncurves

Brooke pounced on him once she made it back to the sand. "Were you playing paparazzi over here on the sand?"

"Maybe. I couldn't help myself. We should move to some tropical island where you can wear bikinis all day every day."

She pressed a salty kiss to his lips. "This is the best vacation ever. I'm so happy right now. Thanks Jay."

"I would do anything to keep that smile on your face, Brookelynn."

"That's an easy fix, I just need to be with you."

"You've got me and this vacation is going to be the first of many special trips we take. Today is only the beginning. Come on, I've got a surprise for you back at the room."

Brooke screamed in happiness as soon as they opened the door and she spotted Val's pink hair. Brian's wide smile stood just behind her. Brooke and Val flew across the room and flung themselves at each other with laughter and tears. Jayson smiled warmly. He watched them while Brian and he exchanged a friendly hug.

"Thanks for coming man..."

"Absolutely brother. Thanks for the invite!"

Finally, the girls separated and Jayson squeezed Val in his own embrace.

"Dimples!"

"Strawberry Shortcake! Thanks for coming. Digging the hair."

"Thanks for the call! Missed you guys so much."

Brooke gave Brian a giant hug. "Brian! I am so glad to see you!"

Brian wrapped her up and lifted her off the ground a bit. "It's great to see you Brooke."

"Babe, you did this for me?" She looked back at him so adoringly he felt like his heart skipped a beat.

"We all needed it. Come on let's show them around."

> **@brookelynn: @JayWilliams
> surprised me and reunited me with
> my sis @ValLEECali and my bro
> @BMore here in the Dominican
> Republic. #besttripEVER
> #bestfriendsforever**

Together they all set about having the best vacation they could make it. Swimming in the amazing waters, embarking on great new adventures, they kept busy but they never stopped smiling. He had even planned to bring them all to meet his abuela and his family still on the island. One morning Jayson and Brian went out for a run together like they used to, stopping outside the hotel for a few moments when they finished to stretch. Jayson wanted the opportunity to thank his friend again.

"Thanks for jumping on a plane and coming out to hang with us. I knew that it would help Brooke to be around you two, you know people she loves and trusts. Truth be told, I needed this time away too."

"I always have your back. I love Brooke, I would do anything to help her as much as I can. I only wish I could have been there to beat that kid to death for her."

"Oh I wish I could have."

"I know you do."

Jayson nodded. "I was so scared, Brian. When I called you that night, I didn't know how to handle anything. I was so afraid that I had failed."

"But you didn't. You're both here, together. It didn't break you, it made you stronger. I see the way she looks at you; the same way she always has. You are everything to her, far from a failure. Remember the night of graduation? Remember what I told you?"

"I could never forget."

"I know you two will always make it, together. We can all see it. I hope to have a relationship like you two have one day."

"She made me want to become a man." Jayson could hear the emotion choking his words.

"Well you did all that and more. I am proud of you brother."

They exchanged a solid embrace.

Jayson cleared his throat as they stepped away. "We set the date for the wedding. It's going to be next year. I wanted to ask you formally, if you would be my best man. You have stood by my side all my life. I couldn't imagine standing up there without you there."

Brian grinned broadly. "Absolutely I will."

"Thanks! Just so you know I am planning on asking Justin as well."

"That's awesome man. So since I am the senior Best Man, I get to plan the Bachelor Party right?"

"Oh yeah! But I don't need to remind you about the woman I am marrying... she wouldn't hesitate to kick your butt, and I would be forced to let her."

"Oh I know you would! You would do anything you needed to do to make sure you survived for the wedding night!"

Jayson gave his best friend a knowing nod. "Three hundred and sixty-three more days, dude..."

They both laughed and made their way back into the suite.

Brooke

"Best friend confession time," Val stood behind her capturing her hair into a French braid.

"I promise you that I'm fine Val."

Val's face wrinkled in confusion. "Oh I know you're fine, I was going to ask if you did the deed finally!"

"VALERIE!"

"I'm just saying, you man is hot stuff. I know you've slept in the same bed since starting Central and now here in the gorgeous Dominican Republic, you two are sharing the same room... Seriously how do you do it?!"

"Sometimes I don't even know honestly." Brooke's smirk betrayed her. "I tried to seduce him a few weeks ago, so I won't even pretend to be a saint here."

"What do you mean you tried?! I need all the details! I can't believe you didn't tell me!"

Brooke chortled. "There was nothing to tell. He didn't take me up on the offer."

"How is that possible? I know Jayson and that man would do anything you ask him to."

"He would but he knew that my request was colored by things that shouldn't control us that way. We talked about having sex back when we first got together. Both of us had waited up until then, we decided that we could wait for marriage. He just reminded me of all the things I already know. He's the one for me so I can wait knowing that when I have him, he'll really be all mines, ya know?"

Val sighed. "Yeah I know... but I don't know how you lay in bed with him at night and never have an accidental slip?"

"Accidental?" Brooke laughed.

"Yeah, like oops his penis accidentally slips into your vagina."

"How do I ever survive my days without my crazy best friend?!"

"That's what I'm saying..."

Brooke turned around a grabbed Val's hands. "I need to ask you a serious question."

"Okay let's hear it."

"Jayson and I set our wedding date for next year, but I wanted to ask you to officially be my maid of honor."

For the first time since they'd been friends, Val sat there speechless with her eyes filling with tears. "Brooke, gosh I didn't expect to be so emotional, Brooke I would love to have such a special honor on your wedding day. I love you, girl!"

"Love you more than I could ever express V. Thanks for always being there especially after the attack. I know I wasn't the best at being a friend for a couple of weeks-"

"Don't you dare finish that statement Brooke! You are the very *best* friend I could ever ask for! And you better believe I'm gonna find you the best strippers money can buy for your bachelorette party!"

The two girls sat wrapped together in an embrace happily laughing through their tears.

"What's going on in here?"

Jayson's warm voice came from the doorway grabbing their attention.

"Oh you know we were just discussing Val's new role as my maid of honor for the wedding."

Val nodded happily. "I have some big ideas, keyword is big."

"I don't like that glint in your eye!" Jayson raised his eyebrow in mock sternness.

"Like Brian is going to have you spending your Bachelor party doing a puzzle and sipping on ice cold glasses of milk." Brooke teased him back.

"I happen to love milk!" Brian plopped down on the sofa next to them.

"And by milk you mean boobs!"

"Naturally."

Brooke tossed a pillow in his direction. Jayson's dimples came out to play as he settled in next to her and pulled her onto his lap.

"Why are you ganging up on me?!

Jayson's naturally in favor of boobs and butts just as much as I am, why do you think he can't keep his hands of ya?"

Val snorted in laughter.

"I'm not sure whether or not I should be offended."

"It's a compliment! You know it was hard for him to not give into you when you propositioned him."

Brooke's mouth dropped open. "Jayson Williams you told him?!"

Val snorted harder, "How *hard* it was for him…"

"Propositioned? You really said that." Jayson was trying to ignore Brooke's question.

"Of course he told me! You told Val right?"

Val's eyes cut to Brooke in mock disappointment. Brooke pursed her lips together holding in her laughter. "That's not the point. What did you tell him? Brian what did he say?!"

Brian laughter came loudly as Jayson grabbed her waist and pulled her even closer. "I told him the truth. That I'm love with you."

Brian chortled. "Yup, that's exactly what he said."

JAYSON

Just four kids from a small town…
Me @BMore @ValLEECali
@brookelynn #bestfriendsforever

Jayson posted the picture they had gotten a passerby to snap of them on the beach earlier as they got ready to spend their last night in their Dominican paradise. The four of them were heading to a family dinner hosted by his Tio Hector. He was excited to spend time with his extended family and get to introduce them all to his fiancée.

"Now your Tio Hector is your mother's brother right?"

"Yep he's the second born, my cousin Melanie is his daughter, she's about our age."

"Will your grandmother be there tonight?"

"Yes, she's excited to meet you. Her name is Juanita but we all call her Nanita."

"Nanita... I like that."

He pressed a kiss to her forehead. "I love that you're here with me, that I can share this with you."

"This has been the best week. I'm so grateful that you put all this together for us. I wouldn't want to be anywhere else but with you."

As they ate and laughed with his family, he couldn't help but steal looks at Brooke every second. Her laughter was almost constant as his family fussed over her and told her all of his embarrassing childhood stories. That laughter was music to his ears and her smile was a balm to his soul. In the twilight she looked divine. The white sundress she wore hugged her curves as her sun kissed skin seem to glow under the light of the setting sun. The flowers in her hair enhancing her natural gorgeousness.

He felt like the luckiest guy in the world that she was wearing his ring. He leaned over and kissed her bare shoulder.

"Hi." He whispered in her ear.

She smiled flirtatiously. "Hi"

"Has anyone ever told you how sexy you are?"

Her eyes filled with the fiery look of lust. The energy between them charged with their attraction. "Maybe."

A small growl rumbled from his throat as he leaned in and nipped at the sensitive spot below her ear. Her hand dropped to his thigh squeezing him tightly in response.

"Definitely." One breathy word and his hands were dying to get under her dress, his lips aching to be on her skin... he needed to taste her.

"I can't wait until you're my wife babe."

"Silly boy, I have been your wife since the night you were in that tree outside of my window. All the rest has just been technicalities love."

"Did you just out romance me?" He smiled.

"I had a sexy teacher." She kissed his dimples and then his lips slightly biting on his lower lip. She knew it drove him crazy and it took all his self-control not to sling her over his shoulder and run back to their hotel room. Instead, he watched as Brooke dragged Val up to join the rest of his family dancing. He watched her with his blood running hot with lust.

Brian looked over laughing deeply. "How you holding up over there brother?"

"You don't even want me to reply to that Bri."

Brian laughed deeply. "How are you going to last another year?"

"With a lot of cold showers."

He felt himself more relaxed than ever as he watched her face illuminated with the happiest of smiles. His eyes were constantly drawn to her as she and Val were educated in all the finer points of dancing bachata. The trip had been an experience that he would never forget and when her eyes called to him from across the yard, he knew the feeling was mutual.

Finding his way to her side, he pulled her into his frame and placed a kiss to her hands.

"May I have this dance?"

A vibrant smile overtook her face just before she placed her own kiss to his hands.

"Para siempre mi amor."

Forever my love.

And she called him Love.

ACT III

SOPHOMORE YEAR
~ Central University ~

Chapter 25

Brooke

Brooke had arrived back on campus to start her sophomore year of college much stronger and more confident than she had left it. It helped that she had Tracie for a roommate again. This year they had opted to find an apartment off campus to share together. Brooke was in love with the apartment and Tracie was just happy to be back on campus and away from her domineering parents.

With the expense of living off campus and determined to plan their wedding throughout the year, Brooke quickly found a job at a nearby bookstore. Tracie followed suit and took a job at the coffee shop next door to the book shop. This worked out perfectly for when they had to work late evenings. While things had gotten easier with time and she had continued her talks with Suzanne over the summer, Brooke still felt uneasy being out and about alone in the evenings. To help ease her worries she tried her best to coordinate her work schedule with Tracie so neither of them would have to walk back to the apartment alone at night. Jayson still wasn't comfortable with the two of them walking back together so he was usually there waiting to get them home safely and if he couldn't make it one of his most trusted friends would fill in.

Brooke had teased him lightly when he brought up the fact that he would make sure they had a safe escort home even when he had to be away but deep down it gave her the security and reassurance that she needed as she continued to take back her life. As she helped clean up the shop that night she saw him sitting on the bench that was in front of the store. He was hunched over a book and she had the chance to ogle him from afar. They had been together for two years and she still couldn't help the butterflies that came every time she saw him. She quickly finished up her work and said her goodbyes to her boss, hurrying out to meet him.

"Hey good lookin,' you come here often?"

Jayson's dimples made their appearance as he closed his book to take her in. "I do. Between you and me there's this girl who works here and I have the hots for her."

Brooke pulled him to his feet wrapping her arms around his waist. She drank in the sight of him. "Gosh you're delicious."

"Give me those lips Brookelynn."

They shared a deliciously long kiss in the light of moon before they turned to leave.

"Tracie didn't work today so it's just you and me."

"Ah well just you and me is my favorite combination of people."

"Is Brian still flying in tomorrow?"

"Yep but not until the afternoon and we'll go straight from the airport to the suit fitting. But I still want you to come and look at the car in the morning."

"Look at us being all domestic, going car shopping. I really don't know much about cars though babe."

"It doesn't matter, this is our first big couple purchase and I need to make sure my lady is going to be happy with *our* car."

Brooke sighed happily, "You know what all that sweet talk does to me Jay."

"I do, and I love it."

"Are you coming in tonight?"

Jayson shook his head quickly catching her pout in a smoldering kiss that made her toes curl inside her red converse sneakers. "Not tonight. I need to get back to my place and finish this paper before the busy weekend we have ahead of us."

"You can't finish it here?" She tried to keep her lust in check but it was a losing battle after a kiss like that.

"Not if I want to get an A on it. If I stay here I'm going to want to kiss you like that all night long."

"But I like that plan."

Jayson's chuckle was low and she caught her bottom lip between her teeth.

"You put those lips away, fiancée."

"One more kiss?"

"Always."

Jayson's thumb stroked her lip gently before capturing it with his own. He gave her everything in that kiss. His hand crept under her shirt gripping her waist as he pressed her into the door. He showed no sign of stopping until her moan slipped through her lips.

His smile was wide as he pulled back. "You see why I can't stay here tonight? But this weekend it's on girl. Now go inside so I can hear you lock the door for the night and I'll be back to pick you up in the morning."

"I love you."

"Love you more."

Brooke got through the door and closed it locking it securely before she heard Jayson knock four times to signal he was leaving.

"That sounded like it was a pretty amazing goodnight kiss."

Brooke dropped her bag at the door kicking off her shoes and practically floated over to the couch where Tracie sat on the couch watching television her notebooks long forgotten.

"It was."

"You're lucky you're my best friend, otherwise I'd be severely jealous."

"Hey I meant to ask you if you felt like going shopping next Thursday. I figured out Val's dress but I didn't want to wait too long to find your bridesmaid gown."

"You mean... like you want me in the wedding too?"

Brooke grabbed a piece of chocolate from the small pile on the table in front of them. "Well duh! You're my girl and I love you... we love you and we want you to be a part of our special day. So I'm sorry I've been rambling about this wedding for weeks now and I never officially asked you be part of my bridal party."

Tracie's eyes filled with tears. "I'd absolutely love to."

JAYSON

True to his word Jayson was at Brooke's place right after his workout. He had showered and changed and made sure to pick up one of Brooke's favorite chai lattes before he knocked on her door. A minute later the door swung open and she stood in front of him in a white tee shirt and her favorite pair of jeans that were torn at the knees.

"Gorgeous."

"Good Morning to you too."

She accepted the latte with a warm kiss.

"Come in, I made breakfast."

Jayson followed her into the kitchen his mind more on the way Brooke looked in her jeans than on pancakes. He gave her a playful appreciative swat on her butt as she walked past him.

"Mr. Williams!"

"Don't play coy, it just makes you even more irresistible."

With a deep smile she leaned down and rewarded him with a deep kiss that he felt in the depths of his soul. "Hurry up and eat so we can go find ourselves a car."

Jayson had worked every day that summer to save up enough money to help give them a cushion. When Brooke had told him that she was ready to get married and plan their wedding he knew that he was going to do everything he could to make sure it would be what she wanted. Neither of them wanted to ask their mothers for money and instead they threw themselves into planning a wedding within the budget they had set for themselves. Brooke had worked at a day camp as an art counselor all summer long to help save and now she was at the bookstore while they were in school. She didn't want the obligations of tutoring at the student center anymore but she still tutored for a few friends when she had the time. Buying them a car was a necessity in his mind though. Brooke wouldn't have to walk anywhere if she didn't feel comfortable in doing so. So he had worked and saved everything, making sure that he kept his promise to take care of her.

"I can't believe we own a car."

They were now the proud owners of a used Jeep Cherokee that was in excellent condition. Brooke hadn't stopped smiling since they signed the paperwork and handed over their money. Jayson was just happy to see her so excited.

"We need to hop in the backseat and christen it."

She kissed him softly. "You need to get to the airport and get Brian."

"He would understand."

"Go!" Her eyes shone happily. "I'll see you both later for dinner."

"Wear the red dress."

"Not happening, buddy."

Jayson was still smiling when he saw his best friend exiting the doors of the terminal.

"Have no fear your best man is here!"

Exchanging a hug and a few slaps on the back they quickly hustled back to the car before he got ticketed.

"Glad you could make it in for the weekend, Bri, Brooke is so excited to see you later. Toss your bags in the back."

"I wouldn't miss it. Is Val coming?"

Jayson shook his head, "She's buried in work and the flight

prices were just too much to swing right now. Brooke and her have been doing a lot of their coordination through video chat and text. But you'll get a chance to meet Brooke's roommate and the other bridesmaid, Tracie."

"Is she cute?"

Jayson gave his friend a knowing look.

"What?! It's just a simple question."

"It's not simple when you're asking if one of Brooke's best friends is cute. Brooke would not hesitate to hurt you."

"Relax. I'm not here for that anyway. I'm here to spend time with you and make sure we look good on the day you finally marry our girl."

Jayson's smile came fast and easy.

Chapter 26

Brooke

I t had become Sunday tradition that they hosted a "family dinner." In the beginning it was just a handful of them but soon it had become a much larger group, the majority of them coming from Jayson's team. A bunch of athletic guys, they all jumped at the chance for a home cooked meal. Tracie loved the weekly eye-candy, and Brooke loved being surrounded by the guys. She felt like she had another family here on campus this year, a bunch of large, hungry big brothers.

> @RileyCoyote: @brookelynn &
> @TeeRacie take good care of the
> CU team. Keeping us fed.
> #sundaydinner #fam

> @brookelynn: @RileyCoyote Just
> remember it's your turn to do the
> dishes Vanilla Ice

> @RileyCoyote: @brookelynn for
> the last time... it's a classic song!

"She looks good and she cooks? I'm so in love with you, Brooke, marry me!" Sean spoke loudly over his second plate of food.

"And now I'm going to have to kill him... shame, I really kind of like you, Sean."

"Hey, I can't help who I love!" Sean teased.

Jayson smiled as Brooke giggled and blew Sean a playful kiss. "I'm glad you both find it funny. I wonder if you would still love her if you realized that Brookelynn was the one that put up that video."

She gave Jayson a shocked look. "That was confidential pillow talk Jay!"

Jayson shrugged, that dimple playing a wicked game of hide and seek as he struggled to hold his laughter in check. It was true though. Brooke had compiled all of Sean's gym modeling into a slideshow set to the tune of the infamous *Ice Ice Baby*. It had taken a lot less effort once she enlisted the help of her film major best friend. It had become a viral hit.

"That was you, Brooke!?!"

The table erupted in laughter as Sean worked to swallow the mouthful of food he was in danger of choking on. "I plead the fifth."

She winked. Sean wiggled his eyebrows and Jayson sat up straighter. "Don't give my girl the eyebrows, dude."

Brooke laughed aloud and pressed an exuberant kiss to his cheek. "You know you're my guy, J."

"Yeah and so does the rest of the world!" Vaughn added.

"I swear you two have PDA encrypted into your DNA." Tracie teased.

"If your man had all of this going on, you wouldn't keep your hands off either, Trace." she ran her hands up and down Jayson's chest and abdomen, his muscles easily felt beneath his t-shirt.

"If I had a man, my hands would be the least of all of our concerns."

She laughed as Tracie sighed wistfully.

"I'll hook you up, T. Just say the word." Jayson smiled brightly as he pulled Brooke into his lap.

Just then Brian walked in with his second, or maybe it was his third, plate of food. Brooke looked on in amusement as

Tracie's eyes followed him hungrily.

"Hey, Jayson... the word... the word... the word... good gracious almighty the word!"

Jayson nearly spit out his soda all over Brooke in laughter.

An hour later Vaughn finally arrived, he had asked if he could bring a guest to dinner and Brooke had readily agreed. She had assumed that by guest Vaughn really meant that he wanted to bring a date, so when he walked in with a guy she'd never seem before it gave her reason to pause. The stranger was shorter than most of the guys in the room, granted he was surrounded by basketball players. Still he was considerably taller than Brooke, his mocha brown complexion was smooth and practically flawless save for a small scar near his hairline. His eyes were bright, chocolate brown drops that seemed to glow even brighter when he smiled.

"Brooke, this is my cousin, Max. Max, this is Brooke."

Brooke gave Max a warm smile. "It's nice to meet you, Max. Welcome, there's still food so you're lucky."

"I've heard a lot about this food I'd have been disappointed to miss out."

"Well please help yourself."

"Max please tell us something embarrassing about Vaughn." Tracie laughed mischievously.

Vaughn threw a playful look of warning at his cousin. "Max, please remember that I know where you're sleeping tonight."

"I'll plead the fifth." Max said with a cheeky grin.

Everyone laughed relaxing as the night came to a close. Her friends all chatted around her while Brooke was tucked into Jayson's side her feet tucked under her. She felt completely at peace, almost ready to fall asleep right then and there until she heard two words that shocked her system like a bucket of ice water.

"What did you just say?" She could feel all her muscles stiffen with tension, the loud thrum of her heartbeat building.

Vaughn's face froze, his laughter coming to a sudden halt.

"I was just joking around..."

"What did you just say to him?"

"Max's real name is Grant Tucker III but we call him Max. His dad is Grant Tucker. His dad is running for Governor in New York."

Grant Tucker. It was a familiar name but one she never spoke aloud. She looked from Vaughn's worried face to Max's look of bewilderment. There were billions of people on the planet, so there had to be more than one Grant Tucker out there. She took a deep breath.

"I'm sorry I thought I heard you differently. Excuse me I'm going to get a drink; I have a headache."

Her excuses were falling out of her mouth faster than she could move her limbs. They were all looking at her full of confusion but she couldn't look at them. If she did she wasn't sure she could trust her emotions.

"Brooke-"

She left them in the living room bypassing the kitchen and any source of water and headed straight to the sanctuary of her bedroom. Making a beeline for her computer she opened her search engine.

Grant Tucker New York Governor.

She must have been holding her breath because when Jayson knocked on the door calling out for her it all left her chest in a huge heaving sigh.

"Brooke? Can I come in?"

She couldn't talk so she found her way back to the door and opened it.

"Babe? Talk to me."

"My father... my sperm donor I mean... the guy who got my mom pregnant and left. Max's dad...."

Jayson's face paled, his eyes turning from worried to deathly serious. "Are you sure?"

"Positive. I looked him up and I saw him. I've always known what he looked like and his name but I never cared much, I still don't."

"But that means you have a brother."

"No, it doesn't. I don't know Max; I don't even know Grant. That was his choice not mine." She snapped.

"I'm on your side Brookelynn."

"Then tell everyone to go home. I want him to leave and not come back."

"I'll take care of it, why don't you call your mom?"

She shook her head, "I'm just going to bed. I'll be by in the morning to goodbye to Brian."

JAYSON

All eyes were on him as he returned to the living room. Vaughn's face was crumpled in worry. Brooke was in the process of actively shutting down.

Brian had stood up folding his arms across his chest, his formidable stance daring anyone else to bother Brooke. His friend relaxed his eyes only slightly as Jayson stepped to his side.

"Jayson... I don't know what I did but I'm sorry man."

"It's cool, she just feels a bit ill. We should give her some peace and quiet. We should all get out of here."

Vaughn opened his mouth to say something but quickly snapped it shut. He tapped his cousin's shoulder and they headed out after a quick goodbye. The others slowly trickled out in the same manner. Tracie waited until they were alone before she advanced on him.

"What happened?"

"I'm sure she'll tell you, T. I'm going to get Brian back to my place, I'll call in a bit to check on you ladies. Make sure you put the deadbolt on after us."

Tracie gave him a nod.

They had made it all the way back to his place before Brian spoke again. "Jay, you have to tell me what's going on? Brooke's face... I know something spooked her, and I know you know."

Jayson sighed as he shut the engine off. Taking a deep breath, he explained everything that Brooke had told him. Brian listened intently only letting a low whistle escape his lips.

"I need you to keep this between us. Brooke needs to handle this in her own way."

"You have my word I promise."

After Brian left, things were almost back to normal. Brooke didn't bring up the subject of Max or Grant but she seemed to like it that way. Together they continued to focus on school and wedding plans even with the tournament schedule about to begin. Brooke worked as much as she could in the weeks leading up to the games knowing that she wanted to be able to make it to as many games as she could. Making use of one of their last night's together Brooke insisted on coming over to make him dinner for a stay at home date night. And when she showed up in the red dress, he knew that it was going to be a great night, instantly grateful that Sean had went to Vaughn's place to hang for the night.

She tried to shoo him out of the kitchen but he informed her that he wasn't leaving her alone anytime soon. He waited patiently until the tray of lasagna was safely cooking in the oven before he scooped her up into his arms and carried her out into the living room. She sat on his lap, straddling him, her dress riding up her thighs and tempting him with every exposed centimeter of her creamy coffee skin.

"Baby, you're so beautiful."

"So are you." She took breath away with her kiss. Slow and sensual, her sweet little tongue teasing his own; his girl knew what she was doing as she drove him to the edge only to back away pulling her bottom lip between her teeth.

"Don't tease me girl, give me those lips."

His hands moved from her hips to grab hold of her curvy butt pulling her closer to where he really wanted her. Her eyes fluttered close in excitement, he wasn't even sure she was aware of the breathy moans that were leaving her throat. The sounds she made drove him wild...

"Let's elope... like right now."

Brooke shook her head in laughter. "Too late. You had your chance."

"Cruel woman."

"Ah, pobrecito." She kissed his knuckles once... then the inside of his wrist where the tattoo she had designed for him marked his skin.

"Even when you're mocking me you're sexy."

"Stop whining and take off your shirt..." Her voiced rasped with the lusty command.

He did as she asked loving the moment her eyes filled with fiery hunger. He was only halfway teasing when he suggested that they just elope. He leaned into her, the scent of her sending his senses into overdrive, his lips aching to taste her again when the front door opened and Sean, Vaughn and Max Tucker stepped through.

Brooke scrambled off his lap to readjust herself while Jayson counted to five to try and hold his frustration.

"Really, Riley?"

Sean held up his hands innocently. "Dude, I'm sorry! I had to come by and pick up my computer to finish this paper. I'll be out in a minute."

Brooke stood up. "Jay, I'm going to go to your room and freshen up. Keep an eye on the food."

She was trying to leave without talking to Vaughn or Max. It was obvious to him and apparently to Vaughn as well because he quickly moved forward to stop Brooke. Jayson was on his feet ready to intervene.

"Brooke, what's going on?"

"Nothing. Everything's fine, Vaughn."

"No it's not! We're friends, so why are you avoiding me? For the last couple of weeks, you barely even say hi before you run out of the room. What did I do?"

Jayson saw the snap in Brooke. He had been on the receiving end of her bad side before and he recognized it easily as she turned to face Vaughn. Her eyes narrowed as she closed the gap between them. Jayson quickly stood and took his spot next to Brooke his arm snaked around her waist to remind her that she wasn't alone and also ready to reign her in if she launched for anyone's jugular.

"You brought him here... into my life. I was fine not knowing but now..."

Her glare was cold and angry as she stared past Vaughn and looked at Max.

"My cousin?"

Brooke shook her head. "Your cousin... Grant Maxwell Tucker, III, son of Grant Maxwell Tucker, Jr and Ellis Tucker. Half Brother of Brooke Lynn Thomas, the illegitimate daughter that was raised by her single mother after her bastard father left her mother while she was still pregnant."

"Half-brother?"

Max's face paled, "You're a liar!"

"Watch yourself." Jayson's warning came with a low growl.

"The truth hurts." Brooke's eyes grew cold. "Call your daddy up and ask him if the name Evelyn Thomas rings a bell, he left long before I got my name."

"He wouldn't-"

"He did."

Chapter 27

Brooke

"So Jayson called me... do you want to talk about it?"

Val's face was serious as the two had a video chat session that morning. Her best friend knew that her ignored issues with the father she never knew ran deeper than Brooke had ever liked to admit. It was something that they rarely talked about but both of them knew that it was there, a tender soreness in her heart that seemed to grow over time rather than dissipate.

"I'm not sure. It's a lot, Val... like more than I ever expected. It's not like my sperm donor actually walked back into my life, it's his kid who kind of looks like me..."

"Your brother."

"*Half*-brother."

"But still your brother."

Brooke huffed. "And I still don't care."

"Okay hear me out. Maybe this is a blessing in disguise. Now you get the opportunity to talk to him-"

"I don't want to."

"Yeah you do. Tell him what you think about what he did to you and your mom. Ask him why. Tell him to kick rocks. Cuss him out if you want. It doesn't matter what you say but I'm your best friend and we both know that there's a whole lot that you deserve to say to him."

She had pushed Val's conversation to the back of her mind to focus on going over her notes that Friday afternoon. Now that March Madness was over, with Jayson and the rest of the Central Lions securing another championship win after yet another undefeated season, she could completely focus on the last half of the semester and her grades. Still she was feeling pretty wound up when Jayson let himself in the apartment with a bag of takeout from their favorite local place.

"Please tell me you have a bacon cheeseburger in that bag for me." She said in earnest tipping her head back to receive the kiss he pressed to her lips as he drew near.

"I do... with fries."

"I love you."

"Hold on to that thought for the next ninety years."

Jayson collapsed into the spot next to her. "Where's Trace?"

"She went to meet her study group for calculus. It's just me and you tonight."

"I love the sound of that!" Jayson grinned the dimpled smile that still gave her butterflies, mischief making his green eyes dance.

"Me, you... and all these notecards..."

"I know, I know." Jayson tossed his hat to the nearby loveseat. "Still it's nice. Just me and you studying, it's kind of romantic, you know back to how it all began with us right."

Brooke snapped her book shut. "And for that we're taking a fifteen-minute study break so I can kiss the crap out of you."

Before she could take advantage of the moment though, a knock came at the door. Brooke hustled to the door leaving a mumbling Jayson on the couch.

She opened the door to find an older gentleman, his suit was expensive just by the look of it.

"Can I, uh, can I help you?"

"You're Brooke Thomas…"

Brooke took a step back guarding herself. "Who are you?"

But she already knew the answer. It was a face she never expected to see in person.

"My name is Grant… Grant Tucker. I probably should have called first. I'm your father."

Brooke had been through a lot of emotions in her life, but the feelings that surged through her body in that moment were all foreign. Somehow taking in the cocoa brown skin and matching eyes that Grant had, the ones she saw a striking resemblance to in the mirror every day, the truth was obvious. The pain and resentment coursed through her blood and made her close her eyes to steady herself before she could find the words.

"I don't have a father."

"I know things didn't end well with Evelyn, but I am your Father. I knew it the moment I saw your face in that magazine article with your boyfriend and then seeing glimpses of you over the last two years, I'm sure of it."

Jayson had walked up behind her and put a protective arm around Brooke's waist tucking her into his side. "I'm not her boyfriend, I'm her fiancé."

"And like I said, I don't have a father. I have a sperm donor. You were gone before my mother even found out that I was a girl. Not a birthday card, or a dime was ever sent to me from any father. I didn't have a father show up to any of my award ceremonies or graduations. I didn't have a father by my hospital bed as I recovered from the worst… you weren't there. You were never there, so you can't be here now."

"Maybe it would have been that easy before Max knew… but he does know. He wants answers."

Brooke gave him a sardonic laugh. "Well anything for Max right? Since we know the truth isn't pretty, I'm curious to know what lie you're going to tell him."

"What I had with your mother… it wasn't ideal. My parents wouldn't have approved. I was set to become a great lawyer and politician."

"So you left her knocked up..."

"I gave her five hundred dollars."

"Ah yes the five-hundred-dollar payoff. Was she supposed to plant it and somehow make it grow into some magic money tree to raise me on? We both know what you wanted her to do with that money. You are a real Sir Lancelot. My mom took that five hundred dollars and started my college fund and you rode off and married the senator's daughter less than a year later and knocked her up. You think I don't know the truth?! I know everything." She held up her phone. "It's called Google."

Grant opened his mouth to speak but she didn't want to hear him... or anything. She still had things to say. Jayson's hand on waist bolstered her reminding her that she wasn't on her own. She was loved deeper than Grant could hurt her now.

"You stuck around that time why? Was his blood better than mine? What makes him worth sticking around for?"

"Look I really only came to ask you for... Discretion. I've had to explain things to my wife and my son but in the middle of the campaign this is something I wouldn't want the press getting a hold of in the negative light."

"The press." Jayson's words were short, the bite razor sharp.

"My image is important... the family man. I'd like to offer you two options. You can work with my team and we can come up with a way to soften the story... introduce you as a member of our family. You could bring your boyfriend to the interview, he's a familiar face and everybody already loves your story. Max is a big fan of yours Jayson. We could do a whole interview and photo shoot and really make this work for all of us."

"Fiancé. Not boyfriend."

"I'll tell you right now that's never going to happen."

"I see..."

Grant took a step back from the door way before reaching into his pocket and pulling out a checkbook. Brooke pulled her bottom lip between her teeth and bit into the soft flesh, the pain distracting her from the burning in her eyes and nostrils, the tears that were being held back ready to spring free.

"I wrote this out earlier but I hoped it wouldn't come to this. I'm prepared to financially compensate you... for your silence. You'll have to meet with my lawyers to sign some confidentiality agreements but I think you'd be pleased. It's a generous amount and I'm sure it would take care of all your expenses for a very long time."

"Well this has been informative. Mr. Tucker, this time I'm choosing to walk away from you. Please leave the property and kick rocks on your way out."

Brooke turned and walked away from him before she could hear anything else.

JAYSON

"I don't know what you expected coming at her with that approach. You owe people apologies that will never be enough for what you did. If you can't even begin to make things right, then walk away. Go back to your family and I'll take care of the treasures you treated like garbage. But hear me when I say this, I don't care who you are and how much money you have, if you hurt Brooke or Evelyn, I will do my best to return the favor."

Grant's jaw flexed several times before he spoke again. "Just tell her to give me a call when she wants to pick up the check."

"Yeah no, I won't do that. You really don't know the incredible daughter you could have had. Please see yourself off the property, Mr. Tucker."

Jayson closed the door swiftly and locked it behind him before heading off to find his Brooke.

"You okay in here babe?"

"My mom isn't answering her phone." Brooke paced the

room.

"She'll call back. Come here."

She silently moved into his embrace. He took hold of her shoulders. "What's going on in that beautiful head of yours?"

"He's not my father. I mean even if he is, he's not. I don't want him. I know that makes me sound like a selfish brat since you'd give anything to have your dad back..."

"Don't. You don't have to explain to me Brooke, I get it. My dad was a dad, yours hasn't been. They aren't the same situations. You have every right to be mad, to not want that in your life."

"Tucker! Brooke Lynn Tucker. That just sounds awful." Brooke covered her face with her hands. "He's not my father. I am not a Tucker."

He pulled her hands away from her face, his thumbs stroking the tears that fell. "I love you, Brooke Thomas."

"I love you too." Her voice was muffled "I don't need a father. I don't need a brother. I have my mom. I have your mom. I have four brothers already! Jayden, Jaylin, Jordan and Justin... Those are my real brothers. Brian too. Even Sean. Six brothers. I'm the *only,* only child that somehow ended up with six brothers! I don't want anymore. I don't need more if I have you."

He kissed her forehead gently. Her heart was raw emotion and he would do anything to soothe that ache. "You have me. Come lie down with me. Let me hold you."

That's just what he did. He held her. Gently soothing her with his touches and soft words until her soft sobs turned to even breathing and she fell asleep.

Together they slept.

When he opened his eyes the sun had long gone and he was in Brooke's bed alone. Her phone was on the bedside table but it lay there beeping with unread messages.

He left the room heading down the hallway to see if the

sounds he heard were coming from Brooke, but he only found Tracie cooking dinner in the kitchen.

"Hey you guys must have crashed hard; I was knocking to see if you were hungry..."

"Brooke's not out here?"

"No... I thought she was in there with you. I came home like an hour ago."

"She's gone but her phone is in the room on the charger." Jayson paced the length of the living room a few times and then he told Tracie all the details of their afternoon visitor.

"What a piece of- where do you think Brooke went?"

"I have no idea and it scares me."

"The sun is down... Jayson."

"I know."

Brooke

S he hadn't meant to take off without letting anyone know. She woke up in Jayson's arms and felt the panic growing in her chest. She needed to get out... away from everyone... just to get a grip on herself. She had never thought that her first meeting with her biological father would be quite like that. Emotions that she had no idea that she felt had bubbled forth and she didn't know how to deal.

Jayson had lovingly held her, he looked in her eyes, kissed her and told her that he loved her.

She was just finding it hard to remember why. *How could he love her when she didn't even know who she was?* Apparently she was half Thomas and half Tucker, and while she had always loved being Brooke Thomas, she hated everything that was associated with being a Tucker. *How could she have come from that horrid man who showed up at her door after missing everything in her life and gave her ultimatum between pimping her out in the press and paying her to keep her mouth shut?*

She had been Brooke, the quiet smart girl.

She had been Brooke, the artist.

She had been Brooke, girlfriend of Jayson Williams.

She'd been the girl who was attacked and almost raped.

She'd been the girl who killed someone.

And now she was the secret bastard child of the beloved politician.

How could Jayson want her still?

She pulled on her shorts and tank top and laced up her running sneakers for the first time in a year. She wasn't thinking when she left the apartment and put one foot on the pavement. No thoughts. No music. No talking. Just the steady thumping of her heartbeat in her ears setting the pace for her legs, reminding her that she was alive. This burn was both familiar and strange, the endorphins coursing through her blood cheering her on, saluting her power and strength. She ran fast and far, when her body tired she pushed it harder. The sweat and tears mixing and becoming one.

When she returned to her apartment her legs were shaking with exhaustion and she had barely turned the knob before the door flew open and Jayson's arms scooped her up.

"Baby."

That was all he said. But she heard his fear, relief, understanding and love.

"I'm sorry I worried you."

"I'm just glad you're alright, baby."

Later when she was fed and showered and in comfortable sweats with Jayson on the couch, she poured her heart to him hoping that he would understand her fears.

"I just don't know who I am anymore Jay... how can you want to marry me still?"

He pressed a kiss to her hands and looked straight into her eyes.

"*What's in a name? That which we call a rose / By any other name would smell as sweet.* You know who you are, there's just been a lot of distraction in the past year. You're Brooke Lynn Thomas... and in a few more weeks you'll be Brooke

Lynn Williams finally. You are the girl I fall in love with every day, the girl I've been in love with since I was a boy. Let me remind you how incredible you are. You have the biggest heart and you believe in true love. You're my very best friend. You are an amazing artist and you have a brilliant mind. You can walk around with rainbow paint freckles or charcoal smudges and you make them look beautiful.

You love to sing along with the radio and can rap with the best of them. You love Mexican food almost as much as you love Dominican food, and you believe pizza is a food group. Brooke, you are an amazing daughter, friend, and sister to the people that matter most to your world. You have the biggest heart and you are so selfless. You forget how strong you are but I don't. You inspire me every day to be stronger and worthy of being the one you chose. You're my Brookelynn... and you always will be."

"The things you do for my heart, Jay... I love you."

"The feeling is mutual. I want you to let me hold you while you rest. Tomorrow you're going to call out of work and you're going to let me drive you home so you can see your mom. She's expecting us around lunchtime."

"Jayson Williams, you are unbelievable. I can't wait to be your wife."

Chapter 28

Brooke

Brooke was officially done with sophomore year. Now she had nothing else to worry about besides packing up her apartment and traveling home to Paradise Cove to prepare for her wedding. *Her wedding.* She was dying to get to that day but more than ever she was determined to savor every moment that led up to it.

That excitement carried her throughout her shift at work and later that evening as she walked to her apartment with Tracie.

It carried her right up to the moment when she spotted Max waiting at her front door with a bouquet of flowers. Tulips. Her favorites.

"Brooke, I've come to apologize."

"It's not necessary."

"It is."

Tracie put a hand on her elbow. "Are you okay?"

Brooke nodded and watched as her friend left them in the hallway to speak privately.

"I'm sorry for the way I acted when you told me about Dad- Grant... I just, I didn't know."

"It doesn't surprise me, it's really not your fault. I was probably a bit rough in my delivery but my emotions were a bit fresh."

"Dad told me that you refused to sign the discretion agreement."

"I did."

"He also said that you didn't want to do an interview."

"I don't. Look, Max, I'm not interested in taking anything away from you or your parents. I didn't come looking for him, it just landed at my feet unexpectedly. I don't want the money and I don't need some press fluffed piece about finding my family... I already have a family. It's not the usual family but it's perfect and it's mine. I'm happy with my life exactly the way it is and I just want to move on and forget the rest of this episode."

Max shuffled his feet as he cleared his throat. "That's kind of why I'm here. I know you say you have your family and you don't want anything more. But you see I do. You said that you don't need a brother, but the thing is... I really want to get to know my sister because I'm pretty sure I need her in my life."

"Any broken bones?"

She'd spent the last three hours with Max sitting on the couch as they attempted to get to know each other. It was initially awkward trying to cram nearly two decades of likes, dislikes, and personal history into a rapid session but much to her surprise the awkwardness melted away and she was able to actually start looking at him as Max and not Grant's son.

Max shook his head. "None so far. But I've gotten some stitches after I fell out of tree house when I was eleven."

"I wondered about the scar."

"That bad?"

Brooke shook her head. "You can barely notice it. I'm an artist, it's my job to see the small things. It gives your shiny exterior some character."

He gave her a genuine half smile. "Okay my turn. Tacos or pizza?"

"That's an impossible choice."

"Okay fair enough. Maybe we can grab a slice sometime?"

"I'd like that."

JAYSON

That Friday he had packed up the rest of his dorm for the last time and loaded it in their Jeep.

"If you find anything I left behind, will you bring it to PC when you come in?"

Sean gave him a small salute. "Will do."

He gave his friend a bump of the fist but pulled him in for a hug. "It's been a great two years... I'm glad we got to room together."

"Me too. I gained more than a roommate, I got more family."

Jayson would be leaving in a few hours but his friends would be coming in over the next couple of days all excited to celebrate the big day. It was sobering to think that the next time he'd come back to this campus he would be a married man moving into his apartment with his wife. He drove the short distance to Brooke's apartment, parking in the front of her place and running up the stairs two at a time. When he reached her door he knocked twice but found it halfway open. He frowned at it. He couldn't help but to be protective of both of the girls and he had actually lectured them about keeping the apartment dead bolted when they were alone.

"Babe? It's me!" he called out as he stepped in.

"In the bedroom!"

He made his way through the maze of boxes until he got to her bedroom. She was taking the last of her books off her book shelf and looking at her in her deliciously short jean shorts and tank top stretching up on her tip toes, all he wanted was to grab her and love on her. Her shirt bunched up to expose her midriff and he was floored with how sexy that small piece of flesh was, and how sexy the butt right beneath it was. He gave it a loving squeeze.

She turned to face him. "Hey, handsome."

"Hey, beautiful. The door was open..."

"I know!" She bit her lip guiltily. "Don't be mad. We just turned in our keys to the landlord. Tracie just ran down to the corner to grab coffees and food for the train while we wait for the rest of the boxes to be picked up, I told her it would be fine."

He kissed her shoulder and then neck.

"I just don't want anything to happen to you girls. I worry."

"I know."

She gently gazed at him. Neither one of them needed to say anything more.

"Can you believe we're halfway done with school officially?!"

"I'm still kind of stuck on the fact that we'll be married in a week..."

She flushed. "It's surreal. Like all those things we talked about happening 'one day' are actually a few days away. I'm so happy."

She put the books in the box at her feet and moved into his arms. She fit against him so naturally and perfectly, he immediately felt a sense of contentment, or maybe it was completion. She hummed a happy melody. "No second thoughts?"

He looked down at her surprised. "Of course not baby! I am the happiest guy alive right now and the only way I could be any happier is if we were already married."

"I don't deserve a guy like you. You are so good to me."

"Brookelynn, you deserve the best. I will do everything in my power to give that to you. You have made the last few years of my life some of the best."

She lovingly smiled at him, then rubbed her fingertips over the tattoo on his wrist before sliding her fingers between his. "Forever."

He bent down and met her lips, kissing her longingly.

"Always."

Before he could kiss her the way he wanted to, they were interrupted by a knock at her door.

"Movers are here," Tracie called.

Jayson helped the girls separate what was going into which truck. Once they were done, he said his goodbyes to the girls. Jayson would be driving back their car back to Paradise Cove while Tracie and Brooke rode the train back to her mom's. Tracie would be staying at Brooke's house for the wedding. He waited until their taxi arrived to take them to the station, opening the door for her and kissing her one more time before they got back and the wedding madness ensued.

"I'll see you back in the Cove?"

"Absolutely. I'll text you when I get there." He gave her his dimpled smile and a not so subtle wink.

"Drive safe."

He made good time driving home, and his mother was on the porch before he even got out of the car.

"Oh, my baby is home!"

He rushed to her and lifted her off the ground in a hug. "And I'm starving!"

"I made all your favorites. Come in and eat."

"Oh, great. The guys should be coming in tomorrow morning. Are you sure it's fine if they crash here?"

Jayson held the door open for his mother as they reentered the house.

"Of course it is. I have lived with and fed five boys all these years, what's a few more?"

Jayson hoped his mother knew what she was getting herself into hosting his friends and their ravenous appetites. But for this evening, he was happy to have the house empty to spend some quality time with his mother. Brian had messaged him earlier to tell him he'd be arriving home later, and his brothers were scattered between their friends' homes, so tonight, he was having a dinner date with his mom.

She made him a plate as he washed his hands, then sat at the kitchen table.

"So, how were finals?"

"They went better than I expected. I got the final grades off my email yesterday, all A's."

She hugged him proudly. "You are amazing, son! I'm so proud of you, both you and Brooke."

"I'm not sure I ever got to tell you how glad I am you two get along so well. You both are the most important women in my life, and it means the world to me you love each other."

"I am so happy you found someone as wonderful as your Brooke. I couldn't have chosen a more perfect woman for you. She is your match... and you are hers. You have grown into such an amazing man, and I am honored to be your mother, Jayson."

They enjoyed their dinner, then Jayson got to work moving the boxes out of his car into the attic for storage. After he was done, he headed for a shower, then reclaimed his old bedroom so he could change and go to bed early. It would be a busy few days with all his friends in town and the scheduled activities from now until the wedding day, including his bachelor party.

Brookelynn: What are you wearing?

Jayson: Are you dirty texting me?

Brookelynn: Apparently doing a horrible job since you have to ask. I'm so excited I'm not going to be able to sleep.

Jayson: I know what you mean. Can't wait for all our friends get in tomorrow! If we can, we should get everyone down to the beach for a bonfire after dinner.

Brookelynn: I think that's a great idea. All our friends and family in one spot.

Brookelynn: Max is coming in tomorrow...

Jayson: You know I'm so proud of you for inviting him, for getting to know him. I know it's not the easiest thing.

Brookelynn: It hasn't been a long time, but future me would probably look back on the memory of our wedding and be happy he was there.

Brookelynn: He's not as cool as Justin ;) But he isn't so bad.

Jayson: Well, we all can't be Justin.

Brookelynn: I love you always, Jay. I'm so happy you're my Romeo.

Jayson: I'll see you tomorrow, Juliet.

Brooke

Brooke couldn't think of a better way to kick off her wedding week, than to have a girls' night in with her two best friends. Home was exactly what she needed, and it seemed as if Paradise Cove was working its magic on Tracie as well. Brooke had never seen her friend look as relaxed as she did sitting in Brooke's living room laughing as they set out the trays of food. The only thing that could make things any better was the much anticipated arrival of Valerie.

What she didn't expect was for her best friend to show up with her jet black hair natural and free of any bright and funky colors.

"Valerie! Your hair!"

"Please don't cry... my mother spent an hour fussing over it and kissing my head."

"You told me you were going to match the wedding colors!"

Val rolled her eyes, but her smile was too genuine. "I wouldn't ever take any shine away from my best friend, *the bride!* Now, let's get this party started."

Her mother teared up every time she looked at Brooke for longer than a moment, but she reassured her they were only happy tears. Brooke made everyone huddle up to take a group picture.

Girls' night in w/ my fave ladies @ValLEECali @TeeRacie and my mama. #weddingbellsareringing

"I am going to regret eating all this in the morning. I must have forgotten I do have to fit into my wedding dress in just days."

"You have nothing to worry about!" Val assured her.

Tracie nodded. "You're going to be stunning. But if it will make you feel better, I will wake up and run with you tomorrow to compensate."

"In that case, pass me another slice of pizza!" Brooke laughed. "I'm so glad you're both here. I didn't think I'd ever have a friend that would be like a sister to me, and, Val, you became that and so much more. Going to college, I was so sad because I knew I would never have a friendship like that anywhere else. Then I met you, Trace, and I was so blessed to find another sister there. You both mean the world to me. You've both helped me through a lot. Thanks for being my family. I love you both more than you'll ever know."

Tracie and Val both surrounded her with a big hug.

"Oh geez, I'll run with you tomorrow too, I guess," Val added with a grimace.

Evelyn teared up watching them.

"For a long time, it was just my Brooke and I. She never

got the opportunity to have siblings or a big family, and for a long while, a true friend. Thanks for loving my girl and taking care of her heart. Every mother wants their child to have friends like you two."

All three of them attacked Evelyn with hugs.

Chapter 29

JAYSON

The next few days flew by in a frenzy. Jayson had picked his friends up from the train station, and his mom's house was near bursting from all the testosterone. There had been countless spontaneous games of football in the living room, Madden tournaments on the PlayStation, and an ongoing basketball game of shirts versus skins in the driveway. It was the latter that was occurring when Brooke and her girlfriends arrived to drop off the boxes of centerpieces. He hadn't seen Brooke nearly enough the last few days.

She stood a few feet away in a tight white tube top baring her toned midriff, a beautiful, color-splashed maxi skirt low on the curve of her hips, and a simple yet perfect pair of sandals. The chestnut brown hair he loved to run his hands through hung about her face and shoulders freely. He froze in place at the sight of her.

"Daaaaang, Brooke!" Sean catcalled. His other friends joined in with wolf whistles.

"If you weren't marrying my best friend…" Brian teased.

"Hey! You better not finish that statement!" Jayson laughed once. He chucked the ball over to Jayden, then hustled over to his sexy wife-to-be.

"You look incredible, baby! You're really going to make the last couple days tough on me, huh?"

He wrapped her up in his arms, lifting her until only the tips of her toes touched the ground. She laughed and nibbled on her bottom lip, subsequently testing the limits of his self-control even further.

"I'm just glad you like what you see."

"I *love* what I see."

He kissed her before another moment passed, his hand pushing her lower back closer to his body. She cupped his face lovingly and kissed him back, giving him just enough motivation to grab a handful of her butt. She threw her head back in laughter as Val and Tracie exited the back door of the house.

"Hey, lover boy, sure could use some of that excess testosterone to help carry these boxes in!" Val called out.

"Best believe I'm counting down the minutes until I can finish this in private—finally," he whispered in her ear. "Let's go, boys. Duty calls."

Brooke

Brooke's knees went weak as she watched him walk down the driveway with his friends. Shirtless and sweaty, his natural sexiness was just amplified. It was a view she was never going to be tired of. Instinct had her licking her lips before her teeth found her bottom lip. She was going to be married to that man for the rest of her life. She rejoined her friends on the patio to watch them bring the boxes through. Grabbing her cell, she took a picture as he stood below her in the yard.

**Loving my view right now. Muscles
for days. Can't wait to be MRS.
@JayWilliams. I love this man!
#makingitofficial
#backwhereourstorybegan
#weddinginParadise**

"Good lord, it's like sexy exploded in this backyard!" Tracie eagerly whispered. Val nodded in agreement, and Brooke giggled.

"Lots of good looking boys here, that's for sure," Brooke said, still eyeing Jayson as he carried a box down the driveway.

"All this man meat... who's a single girl to do first?" Val shrugged with her mischievous grin.

"Sorry, what did you say? I got distracted counting six packs." Tracie grinned broadly.

"You both are trouble!" Brooke swatted her friends' butts playfully.

Tracie leaned over Brooke and gave Val an enthusiastic high five.

"Are you girls out here ogling?" Jisela chuckled as she stepped out on the patio.

"Oh yeah... ogling so hard," Tracie murmured dreamily.

Brooke and Val both erupted into giggles.

"I'm sorry, Mama J, your son is just too good looking. Sometimes I can't believe he's all mine. Yeah, I was ogling, I couldn't help myself." Brooke grinned.

She smiled. "Just like his dad..."

"Well, now we know why you have five boys!" Val teased.

Jisela laughed and shrugged playfully. "What can I say?"

Brooke laughed heartily as she embraced her future mother-in-law. "Gosh, I love you, woman!"

**Loving my view right now. Muscles
for days. Can't wait to be his MRS.
@JayWilliams. I love this man!
#makingitofficial
#backwhereourstorybegan
#weddinginParadise**

**@JayWilliams: @brookelynn
counting down the minutes... we
have some unfinished business...**

They all made it through the rehearsal, then congregated at Evelyn's house for a meal put together by their moms and Jayson's aunts. Brooke had changed into a cream crop top and a long cream lace skirt, her hair braided into a loose French braid. When she spotted his eyes on her, they shared a secret look, and Brooke hurried and rejoined him, sitting on his lap comfortably.

"You are the most beautiful woman in the world."

"No, I'm luckiest because I have a man like you who makes me feel like the most beautiful woman in the world."

He kissed her bare shoulder and wrapped her up in his arms. Tracie whipped out her phone and snapped a picture of them.

@TeeRacie:
Love is in the air. @brookelynn @JayWilliams are the best couple I know. So honored I can share in their big day! Love you guys (even though you're stealing my roomie @JayWilliams) #weddinginParadise

@Max.E.Million:
Sometimes things come along and teach you you were missing something all along. So happy to be celebrating my sister's special day
#weddinginParadise
#mysisterisbetterthanyours

@BMore:
When your two best friends are @brookelynn and @JayWilliams, it's really easy to believe in true love. Exactly 24 hours until they tie the knot and do the thang!
#weddinginParadise

@brookelynn:
Do the *thang*?! Really?! @BMore

@JayWilliams:
**23 hours and 56 minutes
@brookelynn #thethangwillbedone**

@ValLEECali:
**Please don't break my best friend!
#bowchickawowwow
#thedoingofthethang @brookelynn
@JayWilliams**

@brookelynn:
**@BMore @ValLEECali
@JayWilliams REALLY GUYS?!**

JAYSON

Their parents stepped up to gather everyone's attention.

"We just wanted to thank everyone for coming to support our kids as they make this incredible step in their lives. We know the parents usually do a big speech at the reception. But we both wanted to have a say tonight. First of all, I want to thank you, Jisela. You have done an amazing job as a mother, and it's evident in what an amazing man Jayson has become. You've become such a dear friend to me while we've both gone through trying times as single parents, and I'm so grateful for our relationship."

Evelyn and Jisela hugged before Evelyn continued. Brooke took a napkin and began blotting at her eyes, and Jayson stifled a smile.

"Jayson, I couldn't ask for a better son-in-law. You have shown my daughter so much love and respect, and it shows me the kind of man you are. You have earned my daughter's heart and her love, and you have earned mine. I will forever love you, not just as a son-in-law, but as a son. Tomorrow, I will officially give her away to you, with absolute trust you will take care of her forever. I love you, Jayson."

Jayson stood, gently taking Brooke's hand as they moved to their mothers. He let her hand go as he got to Evelyn and hugged her lovingly and kissed her cheek. "I love you too. "

"And to my Brooke, from the moment I found out I was pregnant with you, I knew I would love you with all the love I could ever manage to conjure up, but I couldn't have ever imagined how proud you would make me. From the day you were born, you were smart as ever, sweet as sugar, and more determined than I ever thought a person could be. I knew the world would have to get ready for you because you weren't ever going to change for it. I love you, princess. You have found your compliment in Jayson. You two have already weathered some storms, but have stayed together through the bumps and scary times. Even though there will undoubtedly be more to come, I want you to always remember the love you have for one another and the life you share. Remember nothing is stronger than that."

Brooke kissed her cheek, crying freely now. She hugged Evelyn fiercely. "I love you so much, Mom!"

Jisela wiped at her own eyes. "All of you are here because you are a part of these two young people's lives, because you love them. As a mother, you have a child, and from the moment you feel them growing inside you, all you can do is dream for them, pray they have a happy and safe life, and do your best to ensure that. I couldn't have asked for more happiness for my son than you have given him, Brooke. All of you know I lost my own love, Joshua, too soon..."

Jayson moved to take his mom's hand, her tears and words evoking his own tears.

"I had to watch my boys grieve while I struggled in my own grief. I watched you take on so much responsibility, Jayson, wanting to fill his void. But in the process, I watched you hurt so bad, you lost your smile. Then, one day, some years ago, you came bounding in the door with that smile I missed. That night, you told me about this new girl in your grade... this beautiful shy girl you were just crazy about, wanting my permission to date... and it only took you a few years to finally go on that date with her."

He smiled broadly as the room chuckled. Brooke let out a giggle mixed with her own teary emotions. Jisela extended her other hand to Brooke, who quickly wrapped her hand with hers.

"Little did I know, we would all fall crazy in love with her. I have watched this love story since before you even knew you were in love with each other, and it's a beautiful story thus far. You've proved young love can be strong love, and I am so proud of you both. I am honored to be your mother, Jayson, and, Brooke, it's such an honor to have you officially become a Williams."

She kissed Brooke on both cheeks.

"Evelyn and I have a gift we want to give you. We are giving it to you today since you'll need a little preparation."

Evelyn held out a plain, creamy white envelope. Brooke took it with uncertain hands.

"We decided since you've both worked so hard this year making this wedding come to fruition, you deserve a break... a real honeymoon."

Brooke looked up at Jayson in surprise. He squeezed her shoulders.

"After your reception, you'll have to get changed, get to the airport, and fly to Italy."

Brooke legitimately screamed in shock, while he replayed their words over and over again. They both enveloped their mothers in hugs, love, and gratitude.

After everything settled down, Jayson pulled Brooke outside on the back porch so they could speak privately.

"Babe, we got our dream honeymoon..." He kissed her lovingly.

"I know! It's unbelievable! I never imagined they were planning this behind our back!" Brooke gushed again.

"They are right, though. You've worked your butt off this past year planning and making everything for the wedding. Working extra jobs to compensate for things you couldn't make. Supporting me in basketball. Everything you do for me, I am going to make it up to you for the rest of your life."

"I did it for us, babe. We're a team."

She hugged him warmly, laying her head right over his heart. Surrounded by so much love, he couldn't help but think about his father again. He missed him every day, but this week, he missed him more than he had in a long time. He kissed the top of her head, and without him saying anything, she looked up at him, meeting his eyes.

"I wish he was here too."

Brooke and her friends stood before the large group of guys as they prepared to leave for their respective bachelorette and bachelor parties.

"Brian, I am holding you personally responsible for the events that come to pass tonight." She gave him a warning look.

Jayson smiled broadly. He had gotten that look plenty of times during his pursuit of Brooke. Brian tried his best attempt at looking innocent.

"Brooke! Come on, you know me!"

"Exactly! Why do I suspect tonight's events will revolve around a girl whose main skillset consists of spinning on a pole?"

"I would never!" he exclaimed in mock horror. Jayson couldn't hold it together anymore and bent over in body-racking laughs.

Brooke began laughing against her will, shaking her fist in his face.

"Mr. Moreau, you will have me to deal with."

Brian hugged her. "C'mon, Brooke, consider it a donation to a scholarship fund."

"Yeah, do it for the kids, B!" Sean cheered.

and she called him ROMEO

"You guys suck!"

Turning her attention to Jayson, she pouted a bit. They wouldn't see each other again until she was walking down the aisle.

"I will see you at the end of the aisle."

He kissed her softly. The next time he kissed her, she would be his wife.

"Absolutely."

Val cleared her throat. "I don't want to break up this loving moment, but we have to steal Brooke away... you know what they say, 'hoes before bros.'"

Brooke's hand covered her eyes. "Val! That's not how it goes!"

"Did you just call my wife a hoe?"

"Well, sweet virgin fiancée best friend didn't have the same ring! All right, dimples and soon-to-be Mrs. Dimples, kiss and let's get our party on!"

"You ladies be safe! Call us if you run into trouble please!" Jayson spoke to all of them, his friends nodding in agreement.

"Don't do anything I wouldn't do!" Brian added with a wink.

"It's like you don't even know me at all," Val sassed, giving him a pointed look.

"We will be safe, I promise. Have fun tonight." Brooke kissed him again, deeper and less restrained than she usually was in public, leaving him with a reminder. As if he could ever stop thinking about her...

@BMore:
@JayWilliams it's time for your
BACHELOR PARTY!!!
#bestmanduty #loveyoubrooke
#weddinginParadise

@VaughnCU: Tonight we party...
Tomorrow @JayWilliams becomes
Mr.@brookelynn #bachelorparty
#weddinginParadise

@RileyCoyote:
Mr. MVP is getting married!!
@JayWilliams is about to have his
last guys' night out as a single man
#drinksonme #weddinginParadise

Not much later, Jayson found himself sitting in a sports bar watching the basketball game with his friends, tables full of food and drinks, surrounded by waitresses in crop tops and short shorts. Jayson had shot Brian a look when the waitress first left the table. His best friend laughed and shrugged.

"Hey, they all have clothes on!"

Barely.

He kept his eye on his younger brother, Jayden, who was drooling over the flirty waitresses who kept commenting on how cute he was. Brian had told them all it was his bachelor party, and they were in fine flirty form. Jayson shook his head in laughter. None of them could compare to his girl on her worst day. Her last kiss still lingered on his lips. He pulled Brian over to him by the elbow.

"I need to call in a best man favor."

"Whatever it is, you got it."

"We need to make a stop later..."

Brooke

Brooke had just arrived from her night out of dancing with her friends. She turned the light on in her bedroom and threw her shoes into the near empty closet as Val and Tracie collapsed on her bed. Brooke released her hair from the bun she had pulled it into, letting it fall freely.

"That was an amazing night. Thanks, girls!"

"Absolutely! I haven't danced that much in ages."

"I know! I had a—" Val stopped mid-sentence.

"You had a what?" Tracie giggled.

"Shhh! Do you hear that? Like something hitting the

window or tapping on it?"

Brooke froze. She did hear it. Immediately, a grin spread across her face. She hurried to the window and pulled back the curtain. Sure enough, there he was, her Romeo. Laughing, she opened her window.

"Hey, Romeo, what are you doing in a tree? Do you want to break your neck and never play basketball again?" she said, instantly remembering the conversation that changed their relationship two years ago.

"I had to see my Juliet one more time before the big day."

She leaned out against the window sill. "That was an amazing night."

"The best night—the first time I got to hear you tell me you loved me," he corrected.

"I did. I still do. I always will."

Chapter 30

JAYSON

Jayson was anxious. He was ready to see his bride. He paced around the room so many times, Brian told him to sit down because he was making the rest of them dizzy. The rest of his brothers were dressed and playing cards. But he couldn't seem to relax. He wasn't nervous, he was ready. He wanted to marry his girl already.

"Have you seen the yard? Brooke did her thing!" Sean commented, walking into the room. It was true. The backyard he had known his whole life was a completely different place. There was a beautiful, large fabric tent up; its underside strung with hundreds of soft tree lights that would light up the yard once the sun went away. Every detail he had seen had his Brooke written all over it.

@JayWilliams:
Can't believe today is actually happening. I have dreamt of this day for so long. About six years ago, this girl walked into my class, and I knew she was the one for me. Today, it's going to be official. In just a little while longer, I get to marry my best friend, soulmate, and the love of my life. @brookelynn I'll be waiting for you at the end of the aisle...
#weddinginParadise

347

Brooke

Brooke sat as she watched her mom pin her veil into her swept up elegant bun. She marveled at her own reflection. The makeup, the veil... it all made her transform into the princesses she used to read about in her storybooks as a child. She exhaled, and it shuddered her body as she tried to keep her tears from spilling over her lids.

"You look beautiful, baby." Her mother lovingly squeezed her shoulders.

"Is this really happening, Mom?"

"It is. I'm so happy for you."

She stood and embraced her mom tightly as a knock came at the door. Justin stepped in.

"Justin! You look so handsome!" She beamed at him.

He smiled that dimpled smile she'd seen plenty of times in the face of his older brother. "Thanks. You look like a Disney movie!"

He blushed. She smiled even deeper and drew him to her in a hug.

"Thank you, little love."

"I have to give you this. It's from Jayson."

She took the box and the note. Opening the envelope, she slipped the small card out to read it.

It has always been you. Can't wait to see you soon. - J

Tears fell down her cheeks. He was amazing. Her heart fluttered as she opened the small box and found a gorgeous pair of blue sapphire earrings.

"Those are gorgeous!" Val gushed over her shoulder.

"I love them. I have to wear them right now."

"Well, now you have something new and blue, so that's perfect," Tracie pointed out.

"Justin, please tell Jayson I love them nearly as much I love him and I can't wait to see him."

She kissed his cheek as she slipped the sapphire studs in her ears.

> **@brookelynn:**
> **@JayWilliams... Baby, somehow you still knock me off my feet with your love even while keeping me grounded. I can't wait to be your wife for the rest of our lives. Today is our wedding day... today we show the world what we already know: we belong to each other.**
> **#heisMINE #IamHIS**
> **#weddinginParadise**

JAYSON

Jayson stood at the end of the aisle as the music began playing. Under the tent, all his family and friends, former teachers and coaches, as well as his Central University coaches joined them. They were all seated in a circle surrounding where he stood. Brooke had everything set up so she would walk down an aisle that ended in the middle of the tent. She wanted to say their vows surrounded by the love of those important people in their lives. He smiled down at where her hairband wrapped around his wrist, still laying across the tattoo she had drawn for him. His eyes anxiously focused on the aisle as their song began to play.

They had of course chosen *A Thousand Years*. It was their song, after all. He let out a nervous breath as their wedding party began walking in, his brothers taking their spots next to him. Brian squeezed his shoulder gently. He exhaled before fixing his eyes on the entrance of the tent. Then, she was there.

That woman—*his* woman—took his breath away. The dress was a stunning corset bodice that amplified her sexy curves and trim, tiny waist, then spilled out and down her legs like a waterfall of chiffon and silk. She was a fairytale come to life. He couldn't take his eyes off her. Even as they watered, he watched intently as she held her mother's hand and walked down the aisle toward him.

By the time she got to him, his hands were trembling with desire to just hold her. But he had some things to handle first, namely marrying her. They had both decided to write their own vows, and he spoke his own first. His breath came out shakily as she looked up at him with those chocolate brown eyes he loved so much. She gently squeezed his hand lovingly.

"Brooke, my sweet Brookelynn... once upon a time, you walked into the classroom I was in and took my breath away. I promised myself I was going to get you to go on a date with me and wouldn't give up. I went home and begged my mom for permission to date. It took me a whole week to convince her. You, on the other hand, took a bit longer. Three years and a lot of begging later, I finally got that date. You challenged me more than I ever knew how to deal with. You taught me about patience and perseverance. Brooke, you have been worth every second of that wait. You saw the potential in me before I ever saw it in myself. You motivated me to want to do better and be better. Behind every good grade and good game since was your encouragement and love. You saved me from my own grief, showing true happiness. I am forever grateful to you, and I'm forever honored to be your man, your husband. I told you long ago I would give you the world for every sacrifice you ever made to stand by my side. And I still promise you that happily ever after. I promise to love you forever, hold you through the bad days and laugh with you during the good ones. You are the love of my life. For me, it has always been you, and it always will be. I love you more than yesterday. I will love you more tomorrow. I will love you for always."

He slipped the cool ring over her slender finger, bringing her hand to his lips and kissing it gently.

Brooke

Brooke's heart thudded in her chest, and her tears fell freely as she began to speak.

"When I first saw you, I just knew you were a typical high school jock. I told myself you were no good and I would be a fool to think otherwise. Well, I was a fool. I was a fool for thinking you were anything typical. Jayson, you are the most extraordinary man I have ever known. I may have tutored you in English, but you're the one who taught me so much more. You taught me about life, family, and most importantly, love. You have loved me so consistently and so strongly for so long, I can't imagine my life without you, and I am so happy I never have to. I know so many people throughout the last few years have laughed our relationship off, ridiculed it because we were so young when we promised to spend our lives together... well, they don't have our kind of love yet. From the moment you first kissed me under that streetlamp, I knew I didn't want or need anyone else. I just wanted to be Brooke Williams, your wife. You have been my very best friend, my partner, my teacher, my encouragement, my Romeo, my hero... and today, you become my husband. I love you, I love you, I love you. I love you for all that you are, all that you have been, and all that you will be. I love you forever, and I will love you for always."

She slipped the ring over his finger and smiled up at him full of love. His own tears escaped, and she gently wiped them away with a gentle caress of his cheek. He turned into her touch, kissing her palm tenderly. She found it hard to focus on anything but his hands on hers and those green eyes full of so much emotion.

And then, they heard the words...

Jayson cupped her face and bent his head to meet her

mouth with his kiss. Their friends and family erupted into applause and cheers as she kissed him back.

"Ladies and gentlemen, for the first time, I'd like to present to you, Mr. and Mrs. Jayson Williams."

Epilogue

JAYSON & Brooke

"Do we really have to get out of bed?"

Jayson laughed as he pressed a kiss to her lips, then the bare skin of her neck. "We really do. But I'm flattered by your complaints."

"As I was yesterday when you complained about the same thing."

Together, they lay under the cool sheets in their hotel bed. Skin to skin. Lips grazing each other's as they spoke. They'd spent the first forty-eight hours of their honeymoon in the hotel room. They had tried to get out to experience the beautiful country, but their insatiable hunger for each other kept them from actually making it out of the room.

"We have to get out of bed. We haven't taken any pictures of this incredible place. Today, I'm going to take you out for a lovely breakfast, then we're going to Juliet's balcony. I have a letter I want to leave on the wall. Now, in order to do all that, I need my beautiful wife to wake up, grab a shower with me, then put on one of those dresses I spotted in the closet so I can show Italy how gorgeous she is."

"Mmmm..." She pressed her lips to his. "You had me at the invitation to shower."

"I can't believe we're actually here."

"It's a bit full circle, huh? If you hadn't needed my help with the play, we would have never had the opportunity to be Jayson and Brooke."

"I don't know about that. I'd like to think I would have manned up and said something before it was too late."

Brooke gave him a suspicious smile. "Maybe."

"Definitely."

His arms wrapped around her waist, and he kissed her shoulder. "I knew you were the one. I wouldn't have let myself lose you."

"I love you always, Jay."

"I'll love you forever, Brooke." Together, their hands snapped their lock closed, adding to the hundreds decorating the wall.

They took their pictures and ran their fingers along all the places they had talked about seeing one day enjoying the pure contentment of being in love.

"So, wife, I wanted to talk to you about something."

"Tell me what's on your mind, my love."

She pressed a kiss to his bare chest as they lay wrapped in each other's arms.

"I've decided after we graduate from Central, I'm done playing basketball. I don't want to go pro."

She sat up, letting the sheet drop from her grasp. "But your dream..."

"My dream is right here in this room with me, tempting me with a rather spectacular view."

She playfully scowled before covering herself up again.

"Aw! Don't do that. Those are some of my favorite things in the world to look at..." He hooked a finger in the top of the sheet and pulled her closer. "I'm not entering the draft. I'm not going pro. I don't want it."

"Well, what do you want?"

"I want you. I want to buy a house with my wife. I want to teach at the school where I fell in love with you, where I fell in love with books and reading. I want to go home every day after work and have dinner with my wife. When we start our family, I want to be there every day to help with everything. I want to tuck our kids in at night after bedtime stories. Then I want to go to bed with my wife and make love to her. I sacrificed so much time with you already for this sport, and the next two years will cost us more. After this, I'm done. I just want to live my dream of being Brooke's husband now. Is that okay with you, wife?"

Her tears fell in big fat drops down her cheeks. Nodding, she leaned forward and kissed him...

And she called him husband.

Acknowledgements

Wow. Well… first off, I want to say what a dream come true it is to be writing this passage.

Once upon a time, lost in a daydream, I scribbled out some words on a paper. I left it laying around thinking it was just a casual passage written on a spare piece of ordinary white paper. I never imagined it would be picked up by someone who would ask me what happened next…

That piece of paper held the first few lines of Jayson and Brooke's story.

For years, I lost myself in this world and fell in love with the characters in this story and the others still to come. But somehow, I always held back from putting my words out there. Until now…

I'd like to say thanks to my family. To my J — your support and motivation as I chased down this dream of mine has been nothing short of extraordinary. We continue to prove how strong young love can be.

To my three littles — even if you don't fully understand it now, I hope one day you'll realize the full significance this book has for me. Remember anything you can dream up is possible and I will always be your biggest fan. I love you beyond words…

To every single person who reads this story, I have to say THANK YOU. I've been a bookworm since I could read and because of that, I know there's so many things that go into choosing a book. I am touched something about Jayson and Brooke's story called out to you. I hope you found something you enjoyed and you'll stick around for all the stories to come. Did I say THANK YOU?!

Oh, and I'd like to acknowledge Justin Timberlake... just because I can. Hey, Justin!

About the Author

Santana Blair lives in Connecticut with her husband and three kids.

She enjoys long walks through bookstores and down stationery aisles. Her personal philosophy is rainy days are perfect for getting lost in a good book. She's a sucker for a good love story.

When she's not reading or writing, she enjoys music, movies, and relaxing with family.

Santana loves connecting with fellow readers via social media.

Website: www.santanablair.com/

Facebook: www.facebook.com/authorsantanablair

Twitter: www.twitter.com/santanawrites

Instagram: www.instagram.com/authorsantanablair

Goodreads: www.goodreads.com/SantanaBlair